Naomi of the Plains

Madelyn Guyette

TABLE OF CONTENTS

I

The Message

A horse whinnied close by and its shrill cry jolted Naomi awake. Although only noon, she'd fallen asleep in the parlor rocking chair, exhausted and all out-of-sorts from being awake most of the night.

"What's that? Jacob?" But as soon as she'd blurting this out in her initial state of confusion, she realized it couldn't have been Jacob Bowers. There was something about the horse …

"Your father's home, he's made it back!" her mother exclaimed from the cabin's back bedroom. "Oh, I knew he was all right. Well, what're you waiting for? Go on out and meet him at the barn, I'm sure he'll need help with the wagon."

"No, Ma, it can't be him, no one's in the barn yard, it's somebody out front."

"Not John? Are you sure? Jacob, then? Weren't you expecting him?"

"That was yesterday, he never came." *Could it be bad news about Pa?* she wondered, confusion giving way reasoning. *It must be. But why do I feel like this? Some danger is out there, I just know it.* With effort Naomi got to her feet and stood tense and motionless in the middle of the room, not knowing what to expect, only feeling a vague impression that whatever was out there was male,

NAOMI OF THE PLAINS

not female. Tempted to look out the front window, she was afraid it would give her away.

"Naomi!" her mother sounded more impatient. "What's happening?"

Then the nagging thought came, *What if it's important, though? Something about my father? An accident, maybe? Oh, if only Ma and I weren't alone here, and Ma so sick back there.*

"Naomi," her mother called out, "whatever's wrong with you? Can't you go see who it is?"

Yet Naomi could not seem to will her body into response. To make it worse, from just beyond the door came the sound of heavy footsteps on the front porch stairs, more crossing the porch, and finally stopping at the other side of the front door, only five feet away.

The first knock came, making her jump. More followed, each one louder and more aggressive, definitely not a visitor, hardly an ordinary messenger. The very sounds gave her an eerie sense of something unidentifiable, perhaps awe ... fear ...

"Naomi – for the last time, see who it is, won't you?" her voice rising in pitch. "Do I have to come out there myself?"

With effort, Naomi turned away from the door and tiptoed into her mother's bedroom. "No, don't get out of bed, Ma, and don't make a sound," she cautioned, sitting on the edge of the bed and raising her finger to her lips. "Don't let him know we're here."

"Why not? What's the matter? I don't understand why – " she broke off to suppress a cough, brought on by growing impatience.

"Hush! I don't know, it's some stranger."

" Sent from John, could it be? What else *could* it be?"

"Well, maybe so, yes a stranger, that seems the only logical answer. But there's something else, I feel it."

The knocks were repeated spaced out, three of them, louder than before.

"Here that? You know perfectly well, Naomi, any robber wouldn't knock, he'd just break in like that robber at the Nielson place last summer. He was after Lem's savings, which everybody knew Lem kept under his bed, not trusting the bank. A sorry thing because -- " another oncoming cough made her cover her mouth.

"Because, Ma, as you remember, a gang robbed the Prairie Lake later, one of the tellers was shot."

"You think whoever's out there has a gun?"

There was a deep growling, muttering sound from the other side of the door, and then another loud knock, full-fisted, insistent, conveying the person's conviction that someone *was* home and that the door *had* to be opened. Beyond that, came once again the shrill whinnying of a horse, as impatient as its rider.

"Best not to take any chances, Ma, best to pretend we're not home, we don't know who's out there or what he wants. Something tells me it's not good news, something seems threatening, especially to me. I felt it from the first."

At this, Naomi took her mother in her arms and held her close, her frail body seemed more than ever in need of protection. Both women sat there, gently rocking each other back and forth, waiting for they didn't know what, Naomi recognizing all too well how helpless they were.

"Bedroom window -- latched?" her mother whispered, sensing Naomi's apprehension.

Naomi's glance followed her mother's over to the small window on the opposite wall, its thin curtains stirring gently. It was open a crack at the bottom, but she dared not move to close it.

"What about the back door -- bolted?"

"Hush, Ma, you know it isn't usually locked. There's never been any trouble. You don't think he'll try it, do you?" Again she was torn between moving and giving herself away or securing it.

They waited together for several more long moments, with Naomi's eyes anxiously on the bedroom window or the floor beyond the bedroom door for any sign of a shadow passing across the parlor window. Her ears waited for the first sound of someone on the back stoop, then the jiggling of a door handle.

But now came different sounds from the front porch. "Listen!" Naomi whispered in her mother's ear, "I think he's going away." Her normal breathing began to return as heavy, shuffling footsteps unmistakably re-crossed the porch, followed by low muttering. "Yes, listen! He's leaving." There was the faint, receding sound of horses' hooves on the soft carpet of September leaves fallen on the lane.

"Gone, then?" her mother, still whispering, still trembling.

"I hope so, Ma, I'll look." Rushing to the parlor window, she cautiously drew aside an edge of the lace curtain. The lane was empty and she breathed a sigh of relief. Coming back to her mother's bedside, she adjusted the pillows and settled her back down under the quilt. "You rest a bit, now Ma."

"What was that all about, do you think?"

Naomi hesitated. "Perhaps ... perhaps someone had the wrong house," she said, trying to sound reassuring, but without conviction. It was someone – something meant for her. "Now just lie back and rest while I go heat up the soup I made for you this morning. Try to eat something, let's hope you're getting your appetite back."

"Did you use up the last of the parsnips?"

It seemed an absurdly normal kind of question after the past tense-filled moments, causing Naomi to smile faintly. "Yes, Ma."

"Good. I was afraid you might forget."

"I know, Ma. I'm doing my best." Naomi had heard herself say that often enough, however much she doubted it. Something always seemed beyond her reach. And now, with her mother so frail looking, it seemed almost like she, Naomi, was the mother, her mother the child. With that responsibility, she'd have to try even harder. And try harder still, in coming to some sort of agreement with Jacob.

"Can't deal with Jacob now, though, I don't even want to think about him," Naomi said softly to herself as her often-used method of confirming self-resolve. "Don't want to think about what's just happened, either, or the what if part – what if it'd really been a message from Pa? What if I needed to – what if I didn't --" She lifted one of the iron lids on the cookstove to drop in another piece of wood, then slid over the kettle to heat up. "No, no more what-ifs. I'll just have to put all that away in the think-about-it-later part of my brain. No, right now Ma has to be my main concern, my mother, Rebecca Beckman of Prairie Lake."

How many times had Naomi puzzled over the irony of names? How strange, she considered once again as she gave the soup another few stirs, that *she* was named Naomi, not her mother. Just as the biblical Naomi had followed Elimelech to the land of Moab, it was her mother who'd followed her father, John Beckman, from Pennsylvania to these Minnesota prairies to take up an 80- acre homestead. It was her mother, that once strong and tireless woman, who'd worked alongside her father out in the potato field, helped scythe the thirty acres of wheat in the south spread at harvest time, raked, lifted, stacked. *No*, she concluded her train of thought, *there is something wonderful about my mother's story and that other Naomi's story, but maybe it's too remote to relate to me.* Decisively putting an end to such speculation, she ladled up a small bowl of soup, placed it on a tray with a slice of buttered bread, and headed into the cabin's back bedroom.

"Tastes fine, my dear," her mother said, accepting the second spoonful, "although you forgot the nutmeg." Accepting another spoonful, "Oh, I'm afraid I -- "

"It's all right, Ma," and Naomi wiped away soup dribble down her mother's chin, then fed her another spoonful. *My own mother, Rebecca*, she thought, *that once strong and tireless woman reduced to this? Or to whatever the Lord might have in store for me before then?*

"I'd like to rest now, dear," her mother said weakly "Maybe you wouldn't mind getting that extra quilt out of the chest? As soon as the sun goes down, it'll get colder. Winter's not far off. And your father – out there somewhere -- "

She didn't finish. Naomi knew the winter would be hard, it always was. Snows so deep you could hardly get from house to barn … winds so strong they made their howling way through every crack between the boards, around window frames, under doors. No, she did not look forward to it. *Even more reason to worry about Pa*, she thought, *all those what ifs, Pa out there on all those endless plains to the west, trying to keep us alive through another winter with meat brought back, pelts to trade for whatever else we need … but what if … what if …*

Her mother was about to doze off. A good thing, Naomi considered, there might still be a chance of recovery, although Doctor Philips had seemed doubtful. She lifted the heavy lid of the chest and carefully shook out the folded quilt, smelling of cedar and camphor. It was her favorite quilt -- the Star of Bethlehem. "Remember making this, Ma?"

"Wasn't that the one with Mrs. Larson and – and maybe Lily Olson?"

"I think so, quite a few years ago, though. You were just teaching me how to quilt."

"Those blocks, so pretty. White calico stars on a dark blue background. Pity not all that blue material was the same shade, but, well, we used what we had. Now those there – " she broke off with a deep, rasping cough – "were from your blue wool dress, I remember. You were ten or so. Your Aunt Eleanor sent me that material from New York, so fine it was. And the red? Don't remember." Fingering the edge of the border, she added sleepily, "And that material – yes, I think from John's Sunday best trousers, dark blue they were, got too small around the waist, even after I let them out. Ah, so many blocks … all reminders of the Christmas story … a time of life … every one of them."

"Lie back now, Ma, and rest."

"Yes, I do feel tired," she said weakly, still clutching the edge of the quilt. "Do please, dear, light the oil lamp in the parlor window … dark before long … help your father find his way … his way … his way … " She fell back on the pillow and her eyes closed.

Naomi tip-toed out of the room. Putting the kettle on the range to heat up water for the day's dishes, she reflected again on her own and her mother's names. Naomi seemed more appropriate for her mother, an example she could hardly imitate. There was much in Rebecca Beckman's life that could serve as an example for anyone. Everywhere was the loving work of her mother's hands, on that quilt, in endless jars of beans, peaches, pickles, and jams at canning time. Only a few jars remained now, just as her mother's life seemed to be used up. A legacy of love, of work, of devotion, of faith, so many things to cherish.

And now these dishes, she thought, as she soaped them in the big enamel dishpan, then rinsed them in another pan with a boiling stream from the kettle before wiping each plate, each cup, each knife, fork and spoon with the flour-sack towel. *Is this truly what you'd call a labor of love? Was it contributing anything important to life? Could they be the same thing, the light of life --*

The oil lamp! She'd forgotten and now threw the towel down on the kitchen table and rushed to the parlor. Not much oil left, either, but surely Pa would be back before it ran out. She raised the glass chimney and turned up the wick. After lighting it with the long striking match, always kept in a small wooden tray beside the lamp base, she replaced and readjusted the chimney. Almost immediately the scent of kerosene oil and smoke began to fill the room. It wasn't unpleasant, she'd always considered, rather more of a comfortable smell, the smell of home, like cedar and camphor from the quilt trunk, like parsnip soup from the kitchen.

The door – the front door. In horror she realized the brass bolt hadn't been set. They'd never been concerned about security, locks were rarely set front and back unless they were going away for a day or two to the big market in Audubon. Nervously fumbling with the lock and checking the latch, Naomi felt shaken. *Whoever it was could so easily have come in either door or any of the windows, including the open one in Ma's bedroom. And to do what? What motive? Nothing of value – except maybe our lives …*

She sat down gratefully in the rocking chair by the large, field-stone fireplace. The chair had been her refuge so many times, her place of comfort, her place for thought, a place where she could raise her spirits. Should she build a fire in the fireplace – the work of her father's hands? He'd built it stone by stone while constructing the rest of the house, back when they'd first come through in the wagon train from Pennsylvania. It had always seemed the heart of the house, it's light and warmth bringing a sense of peace, security.

No, she thought, *that glow from the oil lamp is enough just now. Besides, there isn't much wood left, only old rolled-up newspapers passed on to me by Sam Hansen at the General Store in Prairie Lake. Wood – food -- time – all seem to be running out.* Perhaps that strange visitor earlier had unsettled her more than she realized.

Naomi's eyes fell on the old family Bible, lying on a shelf at the base of the lamp table. It lay open at the birth and death pages. *Naomi Judith Beckman, born Oak Grove Pennsylvania 7th June 1855.* She held it open in her hands, then laid it across her lap. *Judith, Judith – who was she?* She'd look it up sometime, it might make a difference, if names were really important, if they shaped character, hers in particular.

"I need help, Lord," she whispered, so as not to wake her mother. "Please protect us. And please help me decide what to do about Jacob, and give me the strength to do it." She thought a moment. "And the strength to help my mother, to follow her example. And – and -- " But enough asking for the time being, and she randomly turned over pages.

The gilt-edged pages now lying open before her were from the Book of Job. A strange feeling came over her, beginning with her head and passing all the way down through her body to her feet. Satan's words to God seemed to leap up, straight at her, off the page: *But stretch out your hand and strike everything he has, and he will surely curse you to your face …*

Was this happening to her? Was she being tested for something she'd done? Something she hadn't done? An instantaneous thought, connecting that stranger with Satan, or Jacob with Satan – Satan's agent, leading her into ways which were not right, punishing her for – for what?

Her thoughts, jumbled and confused, now raced ahead. *What have I done to deserve such trials?* She searched her brain, even that part where the locked-up things were. *There was that time in tenth grade when Jacob tried to kiss me up in the barn loft. I was rude and rejected him quite a few times. Oh, and yes, I was tempted by thoughts of love. Of marriage, a marriage bringing an easier life, the promise of wealth. New dresses, a horse and buggy of my own. Wealth, yes, wealth beyond measure from many acres of rich farm land owned by Jacob's family down near Fullerton. A big house with a curving porch around two storeys, lots of big windows, a new cookstove, children …*

Her eyes fell again on the pages open in her lap. *In all this, Job did not sin by charging God with wrongdoing …* Naomi sighed. It seems so hard to understand those words, Job's story, her own story. What did it mean?

"Yes, what does it mean?" she asked herself aloud. "My situation is so different from Job's. And to think of Jacob as Satan's agent? Impossible!" Through her imagination passed images of that tall, strong Jacob with his shock of straw-colored hair, the beginnings of a blonde beard, eyes purple-blue like the morning glories growing up the side of her house. The sensations of his first kiss, the promise of a secure life together …

With another sigh, deeper and more resigned, she laid the ribbon bookmark across that page, closed the book and set it back down under the lamp table.

Just as she rose to go back to the kitchen to see about something to eat, although she was scarcely hungry, again she heard the distinct whinny of a horse in the lane. *Jacob! He's come! Now what am I going to say to him about tomorrow? How will he take it?*

Another whinny, then heavy, shuffling footsteps across the porch. A tremor went through her and she glanced at the newly bolted door. It was not Jacob out there. It was the stranger come back.

"Ho, you in there!" A deep, husky, threatening kind of voice.

The silhouette of a tall figure filled the front window beside the door. He was looking in on her through the thin lace curtains.

A threatening knock, then another, then the door was being tried.

"Oh Lord," she prayed aloud, "please help me know what to do. Please protect me. *Oh Lord, the Lord is my shepherd* … " The rest wouldn't come.

In that instant she remembered what she'd just been reading about Job. *Satan … roaming through the earth and going back and forth in it* … Could it be he out there? What should she do? A heavy fist pounded against the door, the latch was tried again, his weight then thrown against the door. He was not giving up. She was going to have to meet whoever it was face to face.

"Naomi Beckman!" The voice was deep, almost a growl. "Naomi Beckman!"

My name! Satan knows people's names, he knew Job's name. "Who is it?" she called through the door, her voice unsteady. An unexpected need arose, irrationally it seemed, not for her father, but rather for Jacob to be there for protection.

"Naomi Beckman!" A shout this time, hollow-sounding, insistent.

" What do you want?" Her voice was so unsteady, that she wondered whether he could even hear it. "Who is it?" she managed to whisper, waiting, not knowing what to expect, yet afraid of an answer.

"Open!"

"What is it? Tell me what you want."

There was no answer, only the sound of the wind picking up outside and the brittle, rasping sound of leaves being driven into eddies around the corners of the house and the base of trees.

"I've got to face him," she said aloud in determined resolve. "I've simply got to find out what he wants of me." She placed her hand on the deadbolt, the latch would be next. "Wait!" she called out, "I'm coming."

There was some unidentifiable movement beyond the door that made her hesitate. After another moment of anxious waiting, another strange sound made her look down at her feet. A folded slip of paper was being pushed under the door, slowly, deliberately, until it stopped right up against the toe of her right shoe.

Cautiously Naomi took it by the edge, terrified that she might see the person's fingers reach under the crack in the door, in her imagination skeletal fingers grasping hers and refusing to let them go. But the paper slipped out easily and she picked it up, then brought it closer to the lamp. It seemed strange that it would look like the kind of paper her father used to make calculations regarding the number of bushes of potatoes the crop yielded and how much he could get for them from Mr. Hanson's store. Unfolding it carefully, her emotions mixed as she thought of the stranger and her father within the same set of images, and spread the small sheet out under the lamp.

Her first impression was that it was in her father's handwriting. Yet the more she looked at it, the less sure she became. It seemed different from his usual hand. A few letters were shaky or incomplete, and the words slanted upward across the page, not in the straight lines he usually made. She read the five words carefully, going back over them several times:

Come at once with wagon.

These were followed simply by a scrawled *"B. J. Fargo Sheriff" with no further explanation and no date.*

"What does it mean, come with a wagon?" she said through the closed door, assuming the stranger must still be standing outside, waiting for an answer. "And all the way to Fargo? That's – don't know how far – maybe at least two day's journey." There was no response. "Tell me, what's the wagon for? Why are my father's initials backwards? Why the Fargo office? Is my father in trouble. Why me? Is this some sort of a trick or a test? Who are you?" The words came to her, *"Satan, walking up and down on the earth … "*

Because he still gave no answer, there was nothing to do but confront him directly. She needed some answers. How could she be sure it was really from her father? How did this stranger find her? The thought crossed her mind that it might trick. Wasn't Satan supposed to be very clever?

"Wait!" she called, "wait!" Momentarily forgetting all about fear and caution, she slide back the brass bolt, pushed up the latch, and opened the door.

There was no sign of the stranger or his horse in the lessening light, no sound except a sharp whistling in the great burr oaks guarding the lane. He had disappeared as quickly and as silently as he had before.

"Oh, what am I to do? What am I supposed to do?" It came out almost as a wail.

Back inside, Naomi re-latched and bolted the door, sat down heavily, and absently rocked back and forth. She read the note again. There was something strange about it, something not quite right.

"Naomi – "

"Yes, Ma?" In all this, she'd entirely forgotten about her mother. Forcing herself to sound normal, she answered, " Do you need something? I've got tea coming, some toast. I'll bring you a tray."

"I heard voices again."

"You did?" Naomi wasn't sure how much to reveal. To tell her the truth about the mysterious stranger and his note would certainly distress her.

"A man's voice, didn't recognize it. Was he sent from your father? News?"

"A stranger came to the door, with a note."

"From your father? Was it about your father?"

What could she say? It could have been, she didn't know. Yet she also knew her mother, in her present condition, needed some assurance. "It must have been," was all she could honestly say.

Her mother's response was a combination of shock and joy. "Then John's all right, the Lord be praised. He's all right. Surely Frankson and his boy, too." Her excitement brought on a coughing spell, but once over, she asked, "Where is he, then?"

"Possibly in Fargo." This could be true as far as she knew. She needn't mention about the wagon. That could only mean there'd been an accident – or worse.

"In Fargo? All that way?" She sounded incredulous. "He was supposed to be up in northern Dakota territory."

"Yes, Ma, that's what the note said. I don't know how to explain it, either." *Those details – how to carry out the note's instructions?* she wondered. *It seems so impossible. A wagon, all the way to Fargo?. Yet what if it means saving my father's life? But then, what if it's all a hoax, something else, something …*

"Well, good news that he's alive."

"Yes, that's good news." It was a hollow conviction, however. She was at a loss to know what to think, what was expected of her, or whether she should take the note seriously.

Well, dear, I think I'd like more than just tea and toast this evening, perhaps more soup. You might want to add a sprig or two of thyme from the herb garden, not too late in the year yet." She patted the edge of the bed beside her. "Come, sit down here and eat your supper with me."

Later that evening, as they said their evening prayer together, Naomi silently added her own as she tucked the Star of Bethlehem quilt around her mother's body and watched her drift into a more restful sleep. As she mounted the narrow stairway up to her small bedroom in the loft, she prayed over and over again, *Oh Lord, grant me the wisdom to carry out this test. Show me the way and the power to fulfill your will …*

Morning light revealed that the Lord promised a clear and glorious day, and it seemed a hopeful sign. The limited view out the small, diamond-shaped window in the peak of the loft roof revealed a sapphire blue sky with no clouds. Just visible was a branch of flaming maple leaves, barely ruffled by a gentle breeze.

Naomi threw back the quilt and sprang to her feet. Her mother – she must go down and check on her. There'd been several coughing spasms during the night as usual, each time requiring Naomi to go downstairs, readjust the quilts, and settle her. And each time, remaining awake for a while at her mother's bedside, Naomi could not help but recall yesterday's unsettling events, events invading her dreams. What little sleep did manage to come was restless and troubled with dreams of dark figures, of a hooded, shadowed face peering in windows, of skeletal hands unlocking house doors.

Despite the promise of good weather, Naomi sighed, tucked her blue and white gingham shirtwaist into its matching skirt and hooked the waistband. Looking down, she realized there were a few beet stains near the hem from when she'd put up some pickled beets last Wednesday. She hadn't had time last week to do the washing, and she only had left her Sunday best frock, the green calico. Today she'd just have to go like this, stains and all, even if Jacob did show up like he'd said he might. Besides, with what she was going to tell him about the picnic, it didn't matter.

No, she thought, going down the steep stairway into the kitchen, *there's something much more important than beet stains – or how I look -- in the think-about-it-now. Pa's life may be at stake, that stranger at the door last night is another. Why did I let him go? I should have asked questions What about the Mr. Frankson and his son who'd gone with Pa for the hunt? It sounded as though something had happened to them. Why the wagon? Why Fargo, for that matter?* She couldn't dispel a sense of foreboding, a feeling of helplessness, and, worst of all, of apprehension about something unknown and undefinable.

Looking in the small mirror on the house wall up above the kitchen washstand while rebraiding the long, heavy lengths of her light brown hair and pinning the thick coils in a circle around her head, brought on different thoughts, thoughts of her mother, who should have been Naomi, the one who, like her mother, would have looked like an Israelite, with dark hair and eyes. *This* Naomi, the one who'd been born in Pennsylvania in the middle of the nineteenth century, was nothing like that, born with this color hair, gray-blue eyes, and -- a lack of courage.

Now, slipping on a long white apron over her dress, thankful that it covered up most of the beet juice stain, Naomi went into her mother's room. *Should I tell her what I really feel about that note? About that stranger?*

Thankfully, her mother was still asleep, making up for lost sleep during the night. In a way, Naomi envied her being able to do that. She'd lost sleep, too, but right now there were chores to do, the problem with her father to work out.

Back in the kitchen, Naomi filled the blue tin coffee pot from the pump at the sink, grateful, as she had been for the last two years, that her father had been able to connect a pipe to the well behind the house. They no longer had to carry in water for the cistern. She ground just enough coffee beans in the wooden mill for four cups and set the pot on the big iron cookstove after stirring up the live coals and adding a few of the last pieces of firewood.

As the coffee began to percolate, its fragrant odor filling the kitchen, Naomi sat at the pine table, her head in her hands. "Oh Lord Jesus," she prayed, "send me some sign, some answer. What shall I do? What is your will?"

A loud knock at the front door made her jump from the chair. *A sign?* she thought. *The Lord had sent a sign? Already? Was that possible?* But the next instant she sat down abruptly. *The stranger again. He's come back! A sign, not from the Lord but from Satan, walking up and down the earth.*

"Who's that?" her mother called weakly from the next room. "Is it more news of John?"

"I'll go see, Ma." How does one face Satan? What would he look like? Feeling weak in the knees, her breath almost failing her, Naomi edged carefully around the frame of the parlor window and looked out.

Jacob Bowers was tethering his horse, Prince, to the front porch post. Shock, then confusion, followed by relief swept over her like life-giving spring rain. Without hesitating she was standing in her open doorway. And there was Jacob, smiling and taking off that familiar-looking straw hat with the black ribbon.

"How do, Naomi. How's your ma this fine morning?"

"Much the same, I'm afraid."

"Sorry to hear that, mighty sorry. And say, I'm sorry about yesterday, Pa kept me busy." He stood with one foot resting on the bottom step, nervously, it seemed to Naomi, flapping his riding groves against the porch railing.

"I'd ask you in for a cup of tea, coffee, but my mother may be asleep and shouldn't be disturbed."

"That's all right, more private here outside on the porch anyway, that's why I didn't come round to the back door like I usually do. Besides, I can't stay long. Pa's expecting me back to haul firewood over to the south field."

"What for? Why firewood there? That doesn't make much sense."

"It's for the boiler on the threshing machine, you see. It'll take at least two wagon loads."

Wagon load … a thought suddenly came to her. *Could Jacob be the answer? Maybe it's too much to hope for.*

"Yes, it's sure going to be a big harvest this year, lucky for us, after last year's." Jacob shifted his position on the porch steps several times. It didn't seem a casual visit. "Say, Naomi, about that harvest picnic this afternoon, Prairie Lake Park."

"The annual picnic?" This was the question she'd been dreading. "Yes, what about it?"

"You coming? I came by this morning just to make sure."

"I'm afraid I can't, Jacob." There, it was out, but even as she said it, she regretted it. She'd been longing to go, and at that moment the temptation to accept almost overpowered her.

"Why not?" he looked surprised, disappointed, skeptical, all at the same time. "You said a couple weeks ago you'd like to go, that you looked forward to it. And I told you I'd come by yesterday just to let you know what time I'd be here today. Couldn't make it, so here am to tell you I'll be back this afternoon, around three o'clock or so. And now you're telling me you can't go?"

"That was before."

"Before what? What difference does it make?"

"Jacob Bowers – you know as well as I do. I can't go with you. Pa's gone." *How am I going to bring in that note?* she wondered. *I've got to work up to it.* "I only hope Pa's all right, I'm worried about him. Anyway, right now I can't leave my mother here alone, not while she's so helpless."

"Can't you get Mrs. Larson to come over? Just for the afternoon?"

"No."

"Why not?" He gave his gloves a strong, impatient flap.

"I've already asked her. She said she has to look after Willie. She also has to help Mr. Larson on the threshing rig. They have to get their wheat threshed next few days."

"Why the rush for the Larsons? My pa's on a schedule, too."

"It's the rental of the steam thresher, you already know that, Jacob. It comes to your pa next, I understand."

"That's right, that's why we're stacking wood. Say, you said Mrs. Larson's going to run the steam engine? Don't make me laugh. That's a man's job."

"Why?" His annoyance, his tone, disturbed her, even more so because of her present fragile emotions. She was determined to get back at him for that remark. "Why do you think it's a man's job?"

"Well, for one thing, I wouldn't expect a woman to know the first thing 'bout engines. Especially since I heard from Gabe Grant, down at the hardware store, that his is the first one of those new-fangled steam threshers in Becker County. Why, for that matter, hardly a man around knows how to run it yet."

"You might be surprised," Naomi replied, a smug edge to her voice. "Women can learn, can't they? They do a lot of things they couldn't do before the war. And we're in the year of our Lord eighteen-hundred-and seventy five. Lots of change, a new age as they say."

"I know what year it is," he said somewhat acidly, leaning against the porch railing.

"Glad to hear that." Was it her nerves, anxiety, making her turn this into an argument? At the same time, she knew she shouldn't be going in this direction, she shouldn't be alienating Jacob, not now. It seemed almost against her will.

"You don't think I've nothing to do? We've got our own harvest to finish, Pa's big farm down near Fullerton, a million other things."

"I know that, Jacob, but the obligations of your farm don't exactly apply to me."

"You think not? You think it doesn't concern you? You're pretty short-sighted, then."

"Well, what does that mean?" she blurted out, hoping to force him to explain and give some hint about her future. Almost immediately she realized this wouldn't do. She had to end things before they got out of hand, and while there was still a possibility of seeking his help. "I'm sorry, Jacob," looking back into the house, "I've got to go back in now, my mother needs me."

"No, wait a minute. There's a few more things I came to ask about. You said there's no sign of your pa yet? How long's it been since he and the Franksons left?"

"Over a month."

"That seems unusually long, that trip usually takes only three weeks or so. Anybody heard anything?"

"Well, not exactly," she answered lamely, hoping he wouldn't ask what that meant. Yet the thought came to her that this provided the perfect opportunity to tell Jacob about the note and introduce the problem of her getting to Fargo – and then ask him if – whether – perhaps --

But before she had time to organize what she intended to say, Jacob broke into her thoughts. "Yes, it's been a long time since they left, and I can tell you Mrs. Frankson's getting mighty anxious. You know she's got little Simon and Ben -- Mary, too." He suddenly looked embarrassed, as if he were well aware of Naomi's attitude toward Mary.

"I'm sure they all are worried, just like Ma," in a steady voice. She didn't want to reveal her own jealous feelings about Mary Frankson.

"Lots of prairie out there on those plains, a lot of trouble as well out there with the Shakota. Heard the men talking about that down at the livery stable."

Not only was this something Naomi didn't want to hear, but it was clear the right moment for bringing up the note about Fargo had passed. With a sigh of disappointment and frustration, she changed the subject. "I hope you understand why I can't go with you today. Now I'm really sorry, I'm sure my mother needs me inside."

"No, wait just another minute." He stepped up on the next porch step, insistent. "As for that picnic – well, look, it'd be only a few hours."

"Listen, Jacob. It'd take more time than that. The trip into town, providing you were willing to take me in your father's buggy – those five miles there and back. That'd be at least three hours. Then a couple of hours at the picnic, helping out at the church's food table. It'd be late tonight before I could get back. And my mother here alone." The image of that stranger crossed her mind, of doors and windows which could be opened.

Jacob stepped down off the porch steps and began kicking at pebbles lying at the bottom, his annoyance now peaked to anger. "I was counting on you bringing one of your peach cobblers. I also had something I wanted to ask you, something important."

"Something important?" Naomi dropped her head and wrapped her hands in her apron pockets. Hesitating, she added, "Well, I might have something to ask of you, too." Taking a deep breath, she blurted out, "You first -- why can't you ask me now?"

Jacob hesitated, obviously debating within himself. "Noo – oo," he said slowly. "Can't do that." He paused and shifted into a new thought. "Say, you sure you're willing to miss all that? Especially the – the – " He was searching for words in an effort to avoid any explanation. "Especially the – the – er -- baseball game between the Fullerton Blues and the Prairie Lake Lions?"

"It's not just a baseball game."

"What is it, then?"

"I'm not sure you'd understand, that you'd understand what I feel I have to do."

"Try me."

"I can't, I've already said what I wanted to say."

"But I'm not really understanding what you want to say."

"I don't know how – I can't – I don't know how to say it better."

"Well, if that's the way you want it, if that's the kind of sacrifice you have to make … "

He replaced his straw hat decisively and adjusted the black band to center its buckle directly above his forehead. With exaggerated deliberate movements he untethered his horse's reins from the porch railing and was poised to thrust his booted foot into Prince's stirrup.

"All right, one last time. Sure you won't change your mind? Everybody'll be there. And it's important to me for – well, I've got my reasons. I'll find someone to look after your mother and come back for you about two o'clock." He adjusted his hat further, tugging the side brims sharply downward.

"No. I can't. I'm sorry, Jacob." She was frustrated, confused, with all the wrong words coming out of her mouth, none of the right ones hiding deep within her heart. *Oh, how can I get them out?* she thought. *What if there's not another chance to ask him for help?*

"*Sorry* isn't enough, so I guess that's that." He swung himself up into the saddle and turned Prince's head toward the main road. In another moment Prince's four white legs were lost under the shadow of the two burr oaks marking the entrance to the Beckmans' lane. "Not enough," he repeated, calling back.

As she went back into the house and absently closed and locked the front door, Naomi felt drained. *Could I have handled it better?* she asked herself. *For that matter, surely he could have handled it better. What kind of sacrifice was he talking about? It's bad enough that Jacob steadfastly keeps to his own bad opinion about Christians and beliefs. What does he believe in, then? Only himself? How could I trust a man like that — or love him? That would require a real sacrifice on my part.*

"Oh Lord," she prayed softly, "have pity on me … "

2

A Proposal

Naomi's thoughts were in a turmoil, a thousand questions and no answers. They often began with why *did he* or *why didn't I --*

Her foremost question, however, was whether she should take the strange message as genuine, and if genuine, what she could do about it. *Don't know exactly how far it is*, she was thinking, *but it's way west, somewhere near Dakota territory. And leave Ma? Can't even leave her to go with Jacob to the Prairie Lake Picnic. And then there's the cow, the chickens, the wood box. One can ask only so much from neighbors, friends*. With a sigh, she walked distractedly into her mother's room.

"Was that Jacob?"

"Yes, Ma."

"What did he want?"

"Nothing, Ma. Just passing by."

"I see. Sorry I missed him. The boy's a bit too uppity for his own sake. Wealthy, his folks, may explain it … but on the whole a decent lad." She smiled faintly. "You could do worse."

"Yes, I suppose, Ma," was all Naomi was prepared to say. Besides, in her mother's condition, she couldn't afford to upset her by relating the details of Jacob's visit. "Could I bring you some breakfast?"

"No thank you, dear, didn't sleep well last night, I think I'll just rest a bit more. Maybe some tea later?"

"Let me know, then." For a moment Naomi suspended thoughts of Jacob to pour herself a cup of coffee out in the kitchen. Cradling the blue and white speckled tin cup in her hands at the kitchen table, the warmth of the cup was soothing, the fragrant steam somehow reassuring. How she wished she could prolong this moment and think only of such comforts.

"Oh Lord Jesus," she prayed, "send me some sign, some answer. What shall I do? What is your will?"

A gentle knock on the back door startled her and she jumped up from the table in panic. A sign again, Jacob sent as the sign! Surely the Lord had heard her, but surely he'd work in a different way and in his own time.

It was not Jacob. Mrs. Frankson stood in the doorway, the family wagon behind her in the barnyard. Her younger boys, Simon and Ben, along with her daughter, Mary, were bundled in the back with crocks and wooden boxes.

"Good morning, Naomi," she said. "Hmm, that coffee sure smells good, but no time to stop in. Heard from your father yet? No, I don't suppose so, haven't heard from Henry and Ted, either. I expect you're as worried about them as I am?"

"Of course, it's a great worry for all of us." Should Naomi mention the note? It was tempting, but something told her this wasn't the right time, at least not until she'd worked through the dilemma of its authenticity, its meaning, and its strange demands. "You're on your way to the picnic?"

"Yes, just came a bit out of our way to offer you a ride. As you can see, Mary and I have sure been busy. Couple of crocks full of lemonade, some apple strudel pies, and a couple loaves of bread for the church sale table."

It was a temptation, that offer. If it hadn't been for Mary, she might just have agreed to go, regardless of her mother. Surely she could have managed for the afternoon? And Mary would be there with Jacob. Mary Frankson had had her eye on Jacob Bowers for some time and didn't hesitate to let him – or Naomi -- know it. Their relationship, or possible relationship, made her uneasy. But no, despite the temptation, she couldn't do it, she couldn't allow herself to risk going with them to the picnic. And what would Jacob think, seeing her there after all? It would seem a betrayal, a betrayal for both of them.

"Thanks," Naomi finally brought herself to say, "but I'm afraid I just can't go this time. And I never did get around to making the peach cobbler. Ma, you know." Yet she knew it hadn't only been because of her mother. *That ominous stranger … the note … all the stress of uncertainty … and yes, fear …*

"Well, doesn't matter, we've got plenty, more coming from the Larsons and the Thoms, I expect. The Lord's bounty'll still be evident, although some folks for sure will miss your cobbler. And let's hope we make enough money for that new set of hymnals." She turned to go. "But come along, if you've changed your mind, you're more than welcome to ride into town with us right now."

"No, I'm sorry, I can't go. My mother, you see." But she knew this wasn't the whole reason.

"Becky still ailing?"

"Yes, I can't leave her. I'll miss the picnic, but I really can't go."

As Naomi glanced out to the waiting wagon, she saw Mary give a satisfied sort of smile. It wasn't hard to interpret that look.

Normally Naomi didn't feel overwhelmed by morning chores – milking Daisy the cow, feeding the chickens. But this morning, after that contentious conversation with Jacob and after watching the Franksons roll away to a pleasurable day in the park, a pleasurable day for Mary and Jacob, angry emotions were taking over. Although she tried to suppress them, she felt herself resenting constant attendance to her mother – changing her sheets, emptying the slop jar, and even preparing beef broth and an egg custard in order to tempt her to eat. By noon anger rose to a peak.

"Oh Lord," she said cried aloud, hoping he was listening, "why have you put me in these situations? What have I done to deserve them?"

Her only answer was her mother, asking for more broth.

"Yes, Ma, coming."

Later, seizing the opportunity of her mother's napping, Naomi fell into the rocking chair in the parlor, her only refuge. Although the kitchen was warmer because of the cookstove, Naomi needed the rocker's gentle and soothing motion. She glanced at the old family Bible on its shelf under the lamp table. The book of Job – perhaps –

Her eyes fell upon the page marked by the ribbon. *In all this Job did not charge God with wrong doing ...* Its message stunned her. It was clear. "Forgive me, Lord," she whispered, then repeated it louder. "Forgive me."

She read a few more pages, flipped to the Psalms, read several times Psalm 25, *show me your way, O Lord ...*

"Job – Job – Jacob – Jacob!" she cried. "Names almost the same. Why didn't I think of that? Is it possible Jacob was meant to be part of the solution? The sign?"

"Jacob -- solution to what, dear," her mother called from the next room.

"Nothing, Ma, just thinking aloud. Just rest, now."

"Weren't you and Jacob planning to go to the harvest picnic together?"

"No, Ma." She visualized Jacob enjoying himself with Mary, gorging himself on one of her apple strudels. "Our plans changed."

"Oh, that's too bad. I thought -- "

Naomi wasn't listening. The names were almost the same. What could this mean? Did she dare interpret that as the sign she'd hoped for, or would that be merely her own will? She paced up and down the small parlor, thinking. "Out for a little fresh air, Ma," she finally said, reaching for her shawl hanging by the door, although the truth was she didn't want her mother to ask any more questions.

Walking up and down the porch, then half-way up the lane and back, it suddenly came to her. She must reach Jacob somehow, apologize for her words, and tell him about the note. Then she must beg him to take her to Fargo.

"But how can I get to Prairie Lake?" she said aloud. "And once I find Jacob, what then? I only know there must be some connection – Jacob – Job -- "

Then the thought came, almost like a voice speaking from the oak trees, from the wind, from the falling leaves. *Job's neighbors. Her neighbors.*

Who were the closest? She reflected for a moment, sitting down on the porch steps. The closest neighbors were the Schmidts, about a half-mile down the road, in the opposite direction from town. She met them infrequently and didn't know too much about them. An older couple, without children, they'd always seemed a bit standoffish and distant. Would they be at the picnic as well? She had to risk finding them home.

She looked in on her mother. Still asleep, after that second cup of broth. She could step out for a few moments, at least. Naomi slipped off her apron, and, without bothering to change her dress, she tied her sunbonnet firmly under her chin, wrapped her knitted shawl around her shoulders, and headed down the road.

So thankful the weather's good, she thought. *Usually this road is a sea of mud riddled with deep wagon wheel ruts, now it's just packed dirt and loose gravel. Do you suppose the weather's a sign, too? A sign I'm making the right decision?* She quickened her steps, trying to keep to the road's grassy edge since it was easier on her shoes.

A gray-haired, bearded man answered the door. "Yes?" he said, opening it a crack and staring at her for a moment. "Oh, you that Beckman girl down the road?"

An unfortunate beginning. "I am, sir, and I've come to ask for help." She must come straight to the point, she hadn't much time, it was already past noon.

He looked nervous. "What kind of help?"

"I need to get into town."

"Why, that's a far piece down the road, over five miles."

"I know that, sir."

"What do you need to go into town for?"

"To see someone. It's urgent."

"Urgent, is it? How urgent?"

'My mother's ill." She couldn't very well explain about Jacob at this point, and she was losing patience with all this man's impertinent questions.

"Oh, you need a doctor, then?"

"Well, not exactly. I've already seen him."

"Why then – Look, I don't know what kind of help you need, but you're wasting my time." He started to close the door.

"No, you see, sir," Naomi thought she'd better take a different approach. She took a deep breath as she held firmly onto the outside handle of the door. "I need two things. First, I need to get into town to see someone, a person who's not a doctor, it's very urgent. Then, I need someone to stay with my mother while I'm gone."

"I see." The man stroked his beard for another long minute, "I see." He opened the door wider. "Best come in, then. I'll call the missus." He turned and called up the stairway, "Lottie! Can you come down?"

A slender, white-haired woman slowly descended the stairs, holding carefully to the railing. "Yes, Matthew? We've got company?"

Naomi explained the problem once again. "You're my closest neighbor. I didn't know where else to turn. My pa took our only horse, he's not back yet, may not be back from Dakota territory for a while yet."

"That so?" both Schmidts together.

"So I was wondering if I could borrow a horse from you? Or if – " she hesitated. This was going to be difficult to ask. "And also if Mrs. Schmidt would be willing to sit with my mother until I get back."

There was a long silence where the three stood awkwardly in the hallway. Finally, Lottie Schmidt said, "I dunno. My back's give out, I'm not much for – "

"Only for a short while," Naomi urged. "My mother's not much trouble, sleeps most of the time except for a coughing spell once in a while. And I'll set out her pills, the water jar – And there shouldn't be any lifting involved."

"Well, I dunno ...," Mr. Schmidt said doubtfully. "Couldn't let you borrow our horse, not a ridin' horse, you see, only good for a wagon." He paused, then seemed to work toward some decision. "But I could drive you into town, that I could." His wife looked surprised, started to say something but thought better of it. "Can't say as I'd object to looking in on that harvest picnic ... today, isn't it? Always good food, music, been a long time ... But you know, it's a long way, there and back, though. Take some time. Urgent you say?"

"Yes, sir, it is to me ... and to quite a few other folks as well." In fact, with that very phrase the enormity of the situation struck her for the first time. "And there's also my mother. You see, I really can't leave her – " Naomi began.

"Maybe I could give it a try," said Mrs. Schmidt hesitantly. "If, as you say, it's not too much trouble. Only met her a couple times, but she seemed nice, always ready to do somebody a good turn. Matthew, think you could drop me off on the way?"

"Reckon so," he answered. "But you'll have to give me ten minutes or so to hitch up old Bonnie. She's still out t'pasture."

"That's all right, Matthew," said Mrs. Schmidt. She turned to Naomi. "Just wait here – your name's Naomi? All right, then, you just wait here, sit in the parlor if you like, I'll go out to the kitchen and pack up a few things. As it happens I just put up some blackberry jelly, made some headcheese day before yesterday. Your ma'd like that?"

Naomi heaved a sigh of relief. The first obstacles, the first challenges – getting in touch with Jacob and finding someone to look after her mother -- these seemed overcome. To this she added a silent *thank you, Lord*, and, in fact, found herself repeated this all the way back along the road in the Schmidts' wagon.

"I'll just stay out here in the wagon," said Matthew Schmidt after they'd pulled into the barn yard behind the Beckman house. "You go on, take Lottie in to meet your mother. If sparks fly between 'em at first meeting, Lottie'd best come back out. We'll call the whole thing off."

But, to Naomi's intense relief, there were no sparks. "Nice to meet you again," her mother said to Mrs. Schmidt, gesturing toward the only chair in the bedroom, "won't you sit down? I'm afraid you find me in such a state."

"Not to worry," said Lottie. "We all have our ups and downs."

"It's so kind of you to stop by." Her mother seemed to be under the impression that this was a social visit.

"Mr. Schmidt's taking me into town for the harvest picnic in the park," Naomi explained. "And since Mrs. Schmidt didn't care to go," at least Naomi hoped this was true, "she thought you'd like some company." Surely she wasn't stretching the truth.

"Oh, how nice. You'll be seeing Jacob then? I'm so glad."

Naomi thought it best not to answer that question. Instead, she took Mrs. Schmidt out to the kitchen, showed her where the tea was, the cool box outside on the back stoop, and filled the water jar on her mother's bedside table.

"Best go now, I don't want to keep Mr. Schmidt waiting any longer," she said, giving her mother a kiss on her forehead, patting her arm. "I do hope everything will be all right. I'm so thankful you're here, Mrs. Schmidt."

"I can see we'll be fine," she answered, with an assurance Naomi recognized as genuine.

"Oh thank you, again, Lord," Naomi whispered to herself as she climbed up into Matthew Schmidt's wagon. "Thank you for showing me the way." She thought a moment, then added, "at least the first part of the first part of the way, this all seems too easy and it makes me nervous. Please, may your grace continue."

"What's that, miss?"

"Nothing, just talking to myself."

"That could be dangerous," he smiled. "I'm not much of a talker, not even to Lottie."

And to Naomi's relief, he didn't say much on the way to Prairie Lake, only an occasional command to the horse or a random observation about the condition of the road or the weather. Naomi was grateful for what seemed his deliberate avoidance of personal questions.

At the same time there was something attractive about the man, his fine features despite the dark beard mixed with gray, and the masculine strength this body seemed to suggest as he sat beside her on the driving bench, his leather jacket smelling of tobacco smoke like her father's. All these caused in her an uneasiness, and inexplicable feeling she knew she had to suppress. *Is it because this man reminds me of my her father?* Naomi thought. *Or is it somehow related to the fact that Jacob might actually have rejected me and I'm seeking some comfort in this man's male presence? Oh, how can I be thinking of such an unseemly attraction? It must surely be wrong, wrong, wrong to think such thoughts. I've got to think only about Jacob. I've got to work out what I'm going to say to him.*

Yet the closer to Matthew Schmidt's wagon brought her to town, the more her courage weakened. *Will Jacob still be angry about disappointing him? For that matter, what exactly am I going to ask him to do?* She hoped the Lord would help her form a plan in her so far blank mind, that the right words would find her tongue.

"You're not much for talking yourself, miss, are you? Hardly said a word since we left. Something big on your mind, some decisions? " His remark startled her, it was almost as if that moment he'd read her mind.

"Just lost in thought."

"Reckon so," he commented, glancing at her as he drove his wagon around the last bend in the road before it gently descended downhill toward the lake. "Hope you can sort it out quick, before we get there. Almost there, you see. Just listen to all that noise, music. Where's the music coming from, do you think?"

"I heard they were the Grace Notes Quartet from Fullerton."

"That so? The person you wanted to see – you're sure he'll be here? At least, I assume it's a him and not a her."

"I'm not sure of anything, Mr. Schmidt," she answered sharply, then immediately regretted it.

"Sorry, didn't mean to pry." He focused on finding a space at the park's hitching rail. "Ah, there's one, though it sure seems crowded. Reckon we're late coming. Whoa, Bonnie, old girl, this'll do fine."

There was no time for further conversation, to explain her errand, her thoughts, even if Naomi wanted to. Jumping down from the driving bench, she said, "I sure do thank you, sir. I shouldn't be too long. I've a fair idea where to find the person I'm looking for."

"That's all right. I've a mind to look around myself. As I said, haven't been to one of these harvest events for some time, but I do recall there's some good eats to be had, some good music to listen to. Come back here when you're done, or look for me if I'm not here and you're anxious to leave."

It was Jacob Naomi now had to look for. She began walking among the crowds, many families enjoying food on quilts or tablecloths spread out on the grass, others clustered around craft booths, and some sitting on benches around the bandstand.

Throughout the area were set up a large number of food tables. She looked for the table from Faith Church, where the Larsons and the Franksons, along with Mary, would be serving and selling items for the church benefit. That might be the most likely place to find Jacob, although she half-hoped he'd be somewhere else.

Sure enough, there he was, talking to Mary Frankson. They were sitting together on the grass a little distance away from the church's table. As soon as he saw Naomi, he said something to Mary, then stood up.

"Naomi! Thought you couldn't make it!"

"I changed my mind."

"You said you couldn't come, had to look after your mother."

"I found someone."

"How'd you do that? I thought you said – "

"Never mind. I haven't much time, I can't stay. I came to see you."

"To see me?" He looked embarrassed and glanced down at Mary.

"Jacob, I've something important to ask you. Could we talk?" looking pointedly at Mary. "In private?"

"Well, Naomi," Mary said curtly, "I don't know what it's all about, but maybe Jacob does." Obviously annoyed, she got up, brushed off her brown satin skirt with the pink roses, and picked up a large straw hat with pink ribbons, lying on the grass. "Now if you'll excuse me – " She walked stiffly toward the bandstand.

"Doesn't she look nice?" Jacob remarked, watching her leave.

"Always been a great dresser," Naomi observed, her discomfort rising. Her plain, blue and white checked gingham dress and sunbonnet couldn't even compare, especially with the beet stains around the hem of the skirt. But that wasn't her concern now. "You've been discussing things?" she asked Jacob for want of some better way to begin the conversation.

"Yes, things – and things. Harvest and such."

"Shall we sit down?" Naomi asked. "Or go somewhere more quiet? There's something I need to ask you."

"Here's all right, I don't mind," Jacob answered. He had a strange look on his face. "Were you fixin' to ask me 'bout my *important question?*" he asked, declining to sit and now leaning against a tree trunk.

"No. It wasn't that. Something more important."

"That was pretty important, to me at least," anger rising in his tone. "What, then? What do you want?"

"I need your help."

"My help? What kind of help? You know how busy I am, next few days."

There wasn't much time, Mr. Schmidt would be waiting. She grasped for the right words. What were they? *Lord, help me,* her mind repeated over and over again.

"What's happening, then? Don't know how you managed to come all this way into town, not after all you said about your mother. Now you've come all this way just to stand there tongue-tied?" He shifted his feet impatiently, ready to leave.

All in one breath, "I need you to drive me in a wagon to Fargo."

"What? What are you saying?" He backed away from the tree trunk.

"Take me to Fargo."

"Fargo! Why that's – that'—a far piece, that's at least fifty miles, maybe more."

"I know that."

"All the way to *Fargo*? In a *wagon*? Why? Have you gone completely crazy?"

How was she going to explain? But again, the words came. "There was a note from my father yesterday – at least I think it was from my father. He needs help – or at least I think he needs help. Or the sheriff needs my help. It's got to be right away, maybe. And with a wagon – at least I think the wagon's for him – or for Pa – or -- "

"What?" His mouth fell open. "Now I know you've gone crazy."

This was not going well. How could she explain what she didn't understand herself? Suddenly she had another thought. "And you know, it could involve Mary's father, too."

Jacob remained silent while bending down to examine a blade of grass here, a fallen leaf there. He looked off at the lake, calculated how far the branches were above him, stared at the band stand in the direction Mary Frankson had taken. Finally he said, "You know I can't do that."

"You can't do that? Not for me? Not – " No, she had to say it, "not even for Mary? Couldn't you borrow one of your father's wagons? He's got another one, two buggies as well. He's got your brothers, could find a few more hands for the threshing."

"Not that, exactly," he said evasively. After another pause, he added, "Question of time. We still got the sixty acres of wheat to harvest. Pa's counting on me."

Naomi felt a sinking sensation down from the top of her head to her spine. She'd counted on Jacob, was she not more important than his father? No other solution had come to mind, no other sign. She was glad she was sitting on the grass, for she knew her knees would not support her.

"But you said you had an important question to ask me today? Doesn't that mean something – that you care about me?"

"That may be as may be," he replied, again evasively. "You've no right to put those words in my mouth. Seems to me, it's my decision, ain't it? But your troubles – I don't know if – I – I can't – I've given you my reasons, that's all I can say."

"You don't need to say anymore." With that she stood up, turned away, and rushed headlong back to the park entrance and Matthew Schmidt's waiting wagon, where thankfully Matthew had just returned with something he'd bought at one of the tables. Seeing nothing, feeling nothing but an overwhelming blankness of spirit, she was scarcely aware of their turning into the main road and heading for home.

"Things not go right for you, miss?" Schmidt finally asked, breaking the silence after several miles. "Had a good time, myself. Ate too much, though, bought a pumpkin pie for Lottie, though it'll hardly compare with hers. Sorry about you, though. You look – well, you look disappointed, like."

"It didn't work out." What else could she say?

"Right sorry to hear that. Didn't mean to ask after your business."

Silence continued for another hour as the wagon rumbled along the east road. Finally, Schmidt exclaimed, "Look, isn't that your house up ahead ? Made pretty good time coming back, good time for old Bonnie. Must be she's anxious to get back home. Horses are like that, you know. Always sense just when they're heading there."

"Yes, good time -- home," she repeated vaguely, thinking of her father.

"Hope the missus and your Ma made out all right. Maybe a good thing for her – Lottie, she gets a bit lonely at times, with the children all grown – the ones left, anyways." There was a strange catch in his voice as he said that, and Naomi wondered what it meant, whether there might have been more to it. "Yes, rest all moved away," he continued, apparently trying to suppress some emotion. "Happens to families." He drew himself up, and flicked Bonnie's rump with the reins. "Well, here's your lane, all right."

"I'm so grateful to you," she said as they pulled into the barnyard.

"Nothing at all, glad to help."

"When Pa gets back from his hunting trip, I'm sure he'll share some of the game with you, maybe even smoke it for you, along with ours."

"We'd 'preciate that, miss, don't have a smoke house. When do you expect him back, then?"

"I wish I knew, sir," she answered, shaking her head. "I only wish I knew." *If, indeed, he makes it back – back home,* she thought to herself. *If he's still live, and I'm not too late.*

Disappointment that evening seemed to descend upon Naomi like an impenetrable, choking fog. Once her mother was settled for the night, seemingly brighter in spirit as a result of Lottie Schmidt's visit, Naomi sat rocking in the chair by the fireplace. She had neither the strength nor the force of will to light the oil lamp. There was only a candle left lit in its holder on the kitchen table.

I'm being asked to do something I don't understand, she thought. *I don't know where it's coming from or what it involves. I only know it requires a stronger faith than I' sure I have. Right now I don't think I even have enough strength of spirit to open this Bible beside me.*

What was she to do? Even a prayer to the Lord was difficult to shape. Jacob had disappointed her. The Lord had disappointed her. The signs she'd been give had proved false. How then, was she going to be able to recognize the right ones? She thought of Job, who could think of no reasons for his misfortunes. She thought of some of her own short failings, but her pride refused to consider them serious enough to count against her. There were many thoughts, a rapid string of them, all jumbled, confused. Too many to sort out.

At last the darkness, the stillness got the better of her, and she fell asleep sitting bolt upright in the rocking chair.

She awoke with a start at the sound of wagon wheels in the lane before the house. They came closer until they stopped beside the front porch. Her heart began racing fast, almost stifling her. The stranger had come on horseback, not in a wagon. The wagon could mean only one thing -- Jacob had come after all, and in his father's wagon to take her to Fargo.

Yet the footsteps now crossing the porch seemed to have a more halting gait, and once they stopped, the knocking at the door more tentative. It couldn't be Jacob, nor, thankfully the stranger either. This time, however, she didn't dare answer it until she knew for certain who it was. There was no light, except for a candle in the kitchen. Whoever it was would assume no one was home. She waited another minute, hoping beyond hope whoever it was would give up and go away.

Then, "Miss Beckman?" She recognized that voice, but couldn't quite place it. "Saw a light on in your kitchen, thought you might still be up. Sorry to disturb you so late." Silence for a moment, then again, "Miss Beckman?"

"Yes, what is it?"

"Well, miss, I've got something important to ask, but I can come back tomorrow." This sounded genuine enough. "Lottie and me, we've been talking, need to get something settled."

Lottie – Lottie Schmidt. Her neighbors, the man who'd driven her into town. "Mr. Schmidt?" she called through the door. "Just a moment, I'll let you in." She quickly lit the oil lamp on the table, unlatched and unbolted the door, opened it. Matthew Schmidt stood there, removing his hat and looking apologetic.

"Come in, please sit down. Here, won't you let me take your jacket?"

"No, thanks all the same. Can't stay but a minute. Lottie's expecting me back with an answer. Anxious, she is."

"An answer? There's something you want to ask *me*?" She was puzzled.

He cleared his throat as Naomi waited. She suspected he was going to ask a return favor and hoped it wouldn't be beyond her capabilities, her willingness.

He glanced over at the horsehair sofa. "Well, don't mind if I do sit. Been a bit of a long day, you know that yourself. You see, it's like this. My Lottie, well she got on so well with your ma this afternoon, that we was wondering – "

He paused, looked down at his feet resting gingerly on the braided rug. "Well, we was wondering if she could come over sometimes, maybe stay for a spell? Might be a bit of a help to you, too."

"Why, that would be – " A wave of thankfulness came over Naomi. "Of course, my mother and I would welcome her company, not to mention her help." *Someone to help stay with Ma,* she thought, elated, *so if I can just get Jacob to agree, even if after the harvest … probably wouldn't make a difference … could get there in time … "*

But Matthew Schmidt still hesitated, embarrassed. "Little more than that," he added. "You see, I've got to make a long trip on some business, question of a land title to clear up. It'll take me about two or three days there, then a day or so for my business, then another couple for return. Lottie's back – well not up to sitting in a wagon all that distance. Probably kill her, she says."

He smiled ruefully, hesitating. "I'd like to think she wouldn't be alone, could spend more time here. We've no stock to look after, only a few chickens for the eggs, you see. So that'd not be a problem, 'cause Jackie Olafson, neighbor boy on t'other side, he offered to look after 'em. His ma gets the eggs, you see."

He paused again and shrugged his shoulders as he looked at her, embarrassed. "It's a lot to ask, I know." Now looking only at the floor, he said, "If you could find it in your heart, miss – "

It seems what he was asking goes far beyond asking a favor of me, she thought. *It's more like me receiving one from him, from them.* "Of course, of course," she heard herself say, "that would be most welcome." To herself, she added, *Oh Lord, in your bounty --*

"Well, that's settled then. I'm grateful to you, and I know Lottie'll be relieved, me too. So I'll go ahead and get things ready. Moorhead's a far piece, two – three days, maybe, if the weather holds. Never can tell, this time of year. I need to get there soon's possible, 'fore the storms set in, settle my business."

"Moorhead, you said? Where abouts is that?"

"You don't know, miss? Why, I thought everybody knew Moorhead's on the Red River."

"But where's the Red River? I've heard of it, big floods there during snow melt."

"Up north, just west a bit. Across the river from Fargo."

"Oh!" cried Naomi, "oh!" leaning against the arm of the rocking chair for support, "*O Lord in your bounty …* "

3

Wagon to the Plains

Naomi sat beside the man named Matthew Schmidt as his wagon lumbered west down the main road toward Prairie Lake. Each long moment between Saturday night's decision to go and this Monday morning's actual departure had seemed endless, torn as it was by uncertainties, desires, and doubts.

"You seem full of thoughts this morning, miss," he said, with a sidelong glance.

"A lot of things that I'd like to push into the think-about-it-later part of my brain."

"Reckon so, reckon. Happens to all of us. Sometimes that's not possible, though. For one thing, I don't think the brain can be divided up like that. There's some things --" He broke off to give Bonnie a decisive flick of the reins.

"How do I know this journey to Fargo is the right thing?"

"Only you can decide that. Needn't worry about your mother, though. My Lottie's a good person, she'll do her best."

"I hope so. At least that's one thing."

"Something else?" Then, almost immediately, "Oh, I'm sorry. Don't mean to pry."

"That's all right," she answered, and lapsed into silence. *No, she thought, I can't talk about Jacob to this man. It really isn't any of his business.*

After they'd ridden in silence for almost an hour, Schmidt ventured, "you comfortable there, miss? Long journey ahead of us." He flicked the reins across Bonnie's rump, and the horse responded with a sudden jerk of the wagon, then slowed down to a walk again. "Bonnie ain't much for speed," he commented.

"Yes, thank you, sir." No, really, the truth was, she wasn't comfortable at all. It wasn't a question of her body against the hard wagon bench, the swaying and jolting of the wagon, or the road dust churned up from the wheels. There was so much more than her own bodily comfort to think about.

Now sitting there beside the man in this rumbling wagon heading for far-away Moorhead, the most reoccurring thoughts were about Jacob and she couldn't dispel them. "It's the Lord's test," she said.

"What's that, miss? You were saying something about a test?"

She felt the blood rush to her face, not aware she'd spoken aloud "Oh, it isn't important, just thinking out loud." She'd have to be more careful.

But my thoughts are important, she was thinking. *Jacob refused my appeal for help and I'm sure that was the Lord's test. Yes, a test of Jacob's feelings toward me and his character. Perhaps the Lord was revealing to me that I'd been misled in my feelings toward him. Oh, why am I so confused?*

Such confused thoughts were suddenly interrupted when Schmidt exclaimed. "There it is! Prairie Lake up ahead! Well, we've kept moving, that's for sure, Bonnie has gotten us this far, at least. Sure do hope she's up to the rest of the way. Say, I hope you don't mind, when we get into town, I need to stop off at Hanson's. Lottie packed a big food basket, all right, but she insisted I pick up a few more things."

"I'm afraid you've been more than generous, Mr. Schmidt. When she arrived with you this morning, she was carrying a big basket of jams, jellies, bacon, and what looked like potatoes. And then I helped you put a box of jars – looked like canned peaches and applesauce – down in the cellar."

"Well, old Lottie, she wanted to make sure she and your mother wouldn't starve to death."

Naomi shuddered at this remark, painfully aware of how close she and her mother were coming to that, and with her mother so ill, so fragile. That situation led her once more into questions about this venture. Was it a mistake to leave her? Was it going to be a choice between her mother's life and her father's? Without realizing it, her left hand had gone numb clutching the wire bench railing, the pressure of that hold unconsciously reflecting her fears and doubts.

"And my Lottie, of course," Matthew once again broke into her thoughts, "she's a great one for making sure everything's going to be all right."

Naomi couldn't help but smile at this. "I heard her, must have been two or three times, asking if you were sure the neighbor's boy, Jackie Olafson, would come around every day to look after your chickens."

"I hope he remembers, all right. Your cow and chickens as well. Don't think Lottie'd be up to that. And a good thing I took the time to split some logs for your woodpile."

"So grateful for that, too, sir."

"Your ma took your leaving right hard, though. Carrying on like she was never going to see you again, that there'd be some disaster along the way, that something dreadful had happed to your pa." He guided Bonnie into the bridge entrance. "Can't say as I blame her, though. Natural feelings, I reckon, that notion of losing family."

He looked more thoughtful for a moment, seemingly intent in getting Bonnie and the wagon across the bridge, which had several loose and missing boards. "But I'm sure she and my Lottie will manage all right. Lottie can have a bit of a temper now and then, especially when things don't go quite right."

"Oh? Like what?" Anything to take her mind off choices, doubts, or what might lie ahead.

"Well, like not having dishes put back in the sideboard just so when I'm doing the drying. Me bringing in mud from the barnyard. Her plum jam turning out too stiff. Things like that."

"But, sir, that seems perfectly normal to me. My mother's the same way, a stickler for details, at least when she was in good health, that's why she was such a good quilter."

Naomi couldn't help comparing the two women. It was clear they were both lonely, her mother anxious and keenly feeling the absence of her husband, Lottie Schmidt from something Naomi didn't know. There had seemed such a sad air about the woman, with her faded blonde hair, the sag in her shoulders, and the tightness of her lips. Naomi wonder whether it was all about some great loss, some great sorrow in the her life, some event she was trying to suppress. And Mr. Schmidt, as well. What could have happened?

"What was it – " she started to say, but suddenly realized it was none of her business, just as Jacob was none of Mr. Schmidt's.

"What's that?"

"Oh," she said, quickly diverting what she'd intended to as, " I was just going to say that possibly both of them need each other. Maybe it's the Lord's doing, bringing them together, don't you think?"

"Wouldn't know about that, miss," he commented cynically with a faint smile. "But didn't you think that they – Lottie and your mother, I mean -- seemed all right when we left?"

"That's what it looked like, at least. I made out a list of things your wife might need to know about, like where to find the coffee, or what to feed the cow, where the chicken feed was – in case that Olafson boy forgot, or my mother's pills. I'm sure things will be fine."

They were almost at the outskirts of Prairie Lake "Oh yes," Naomi continued, "it seems more than likely they'll manage. The last thing I heard coming from Ma's bedroom were things like *well who'd believe that …* or *did you hear about the new road to …* or *I always add a bit of allspice to my pickles …* . I even heard Ma laughing once. Hadn't heard her do that in a long time."

"That's good, then."

Making conversation with a man she hardly knew was awkward, and Naomi had overcrowding worries to think about, making it even more difficult. From time to time she ventured a few side-long glances down at his big, mud-spattered boots set firmly on the wagon floorboard, or at his brown twill work trousers, darned on the left knee. She could feel the coarse canvas of his jacket against her shawl, her arm, her dress, and the rough fabric of his work trousers against her thigh.

My thoughts seem so scattered, she was thinking, *I can't help but think about Jacob, about this man next to me. No denying his is a very real and male presence, a physical presence different from my father's. And yet somehow it reminds me of Jacob's, the times we've been together, the words spoken between us — maybe only just the good words, though.*

Then, suddenly, there it was! Naomi was jarred out of such reflections by a bright yellow object, stuck in the thorny branches of a buckthorn bush along the road, just as they approached the edge of town. Surely that was Jacob's old straw hat, unmistakably his from the black band around the crown. It seemed a striking coincidence, since she'd just been thinking about him. Perhaps it was a sign of some sort, something she shouldn't ignore.

"Stop, Mr. Schmidt," she called out before she could check herself, but instantly thought better of it. "Oh, never mind, it's nothing. Please keep going."

"Something you forgot? I'm willing to go back, that is, if it's that important."

"Thanks anyway. No, it's not important. Never mind." *Yet it was important, a reminder of Jacob,* she argued within herself, *a reminder of his passing along this road, a testament to his presence. I should have picked it up and kept it. And yet — and yet — why? I wish I understood Jacob better, myself better.*

They were now passing the Larson's house and barn. Just ahead was the last curve before coming out onto the Prairie Lake's Main Street. Schmidt slowed the wagon.

"It'll take me only a minute or two at Hanson's General Store. Sure hope he's open this early. Didn't think about that."

"Isn't that him out in front already?"

"Looks like it. Ho, there, Hanson," Schmidt called out, "see you're already rolling up your blinds. Looks like you're going to have a lot of bargains today, according to those sandwich boards you've set out."

"Morning to you, Matthew, can't start too early on a Monday morning with those little enticements, can we?" he laughed, as Schmidt drew the wagon up to the store's hitching rail

"I see young Joe Whitson's over there helping out at Grant's hardware, looking like he's going to sweep that boardwalk clear out into the street."

"Could use another boy myself, but they're all too busy with the harvest." He paused to readjust the angle of one of the advertising boards. "Say, how come you're out so early this morning yourself? And Miss Naomi? Pretty early for you, too. Come into town for a few staples? Heard from your pa yet?"

"No, not yet – not directly at least," Schmidt answered for her, to Naomi's relief. "And yes, we're needing a few things. Got a long journey ahead of us."

"Oh? That so? Where you heading, then?"

"Moorhead."

"That so? What's your business there? Far piece to go, I'd say."

"Your establishment open or not?" Schmidt asked impatiently. "No time this morning to stop and chew the fat." Then aside to Naomi, "The less he knows about my business – and yours – the better. It'd be all over town by noon, maybe even before. Now you just stay here in the wagon, I'll go in and pick up a few more things for the road. Lottie packed us a lot of food, all right, but beyond that -- not too sure how far it'll actually go. I'm also not too sure of what kind of inns or hostelries might be along the way, except for the one at Menasa, my cousin's place. Ain't seen him in a coon's age, though. Should reach there by tonight, all going well."

Or whatever else might be along the way, Naomi thought. Waiting there for him, the wagon moving back and forth slightly as Bonnie grew restless, Naomi struggled with a hundred images, a hundred anxieties. *Ma needs more than Lottie Schmidt's care … Pa somewhere in Fargo … some connection with the sheriff … the jail … an accident … Jacob's important question left unasked … Jacob and Mary … Mary in her brown satin skirt with the pink roses … Mary and Jacob … Jacob and Naomi … Jacob and Mary … Jacob and Job …*

A jolt startled her, a thud, as Schmidt dropped a box and gunnysack into the back of the wagon and climbed up beside her. "Guess we're off," he announced, with a "Hup! Hup!" to Bonnie and several encouraging flicks of the reins.

As they emerged from the western edge of town, Naomi turned to him. "Is the road this good all the way? What happens beyond here? I must confess, I've never come this far out this side of town."

"Dunno," he answered, shaking his head. "As for the road here, it's a government road, better described as an official trail. Let's hope it lasts most of the way. Soldiers generally keep it up, essential for troop movements, you see. There's still a need for them out beyond Ft. Kearney, all the way up north toward Ft. Buford. Ah yes – the army – " He broke off, lost in thought.

"Were you in the army?"

He didn't answer. She could feel his body beside her tense up, see his hands tightening on the reins.

"Oh, I'm sorry. I didn't mean to get personal."

"Long trip ahead of us," he muttered, "best not too. I'm helping you, you're helping me with Lottie. Best keep it to that."

He said nothing for the next quarter mile or so. Suddenly he squared up his shoulders as if resolved about something and scanned the horizon. "Road ought to be all right, unless it rains. Don't like the look of those clouds to the west, though. Unless that west wind veers more northerly, we may very well be heading into a storm." He gave a sharp flick of the reins. "Come on, then, Bonnie girl, move those four legs of yours, let's get a move on."

It seemed strange to Naomi, and the more she thought about it, the stranger it got. *Here I am, riding in a wagon beside a man I know little about, a man who talks easily about weather, roads, and troop movements, but yet refuses to talk about himself. He speaks well, as if he's had some learning. Yet when I look at the ruggedness of his face, the scars and calluses on his large, strong hands, I think he's been accustomed to hard work, even deprivation of some sort. There have been a few hints of something bad in his life, in Lottie's life, some disappointment, tragedy perhaps. Can I really trust him? Am I crazy to think so?*

The road west of Prairie Lake passed first through rolling hills, a challenge to Bonnie on the up grades, a challenge to Schmidt on the downs. More than once he had to manage the brake lever as the wagon gathered dangerous speed.

Naomi slid her black velvet reticule under her feet in order to hold onto the wagon bench with both hands, the thin wire rail with her left, the wooden edge of the bench with her right. "Will it be like this the rest of the way?" she asked anxiously.

"No, few more miles these hills, then flattens out. Real prairie up ahead, you'll see. Miles of plains, flatter'n a pancake." He paused to apply the brake lever again. "Then there's the river."

"The river?"

"Buffalo River. Not much of a one, but lots of rapids. You'll see when we get there. That'd be another mile or so, by my calculations."

This proved true. After a sharp descent to the riverbank, Schmidt braked the wagon to a stop. Ahead ran a rushing stream, broken above by rapids swirling and gurgling around scattered rocks, and down stream more of the same. Naomi froze at the sight, she could not explain why. The sight of water had always frightened her, deep pools, rushing waves filled her dreams. So illogical, because she'd never seen any large body of water, only local rivers and trickling streams. "Go back," she said, her voice scarcely more than a hoarse whisper. Then louder, "Go back!" This was a test she wasn't ready for.

"What? Go back?" he said in disbelief. "Can't go back now. What's the matter?"

"That water – "

"You afraid of that?"

"No – I mean yes!"

"It looks a little high, that's all. Nothing to be afraid of, we'll get across all right." He stroked his beard thoughtfully. "Don't know if we can manage a ford here, though. May have to go down stream a bit."

Naomi's heart sank. A delay – they couldn't afford one. How silly it was to think of turning back now, water or not. Resolved, she stood up in the wagon and looked ahead. She had no idea what she was looking for, something, another sign. Then she saw it. "Mr. Schmidt! See that?"

"See what? You see something I don't? "

"Out there – in the middle – something strange. Isn't the current moving differently?"

He stood up beside her, searching in the direction she pointed. "Maybe, could just be a big rock, a big hole. Current'll be stronger both sides." He offered a faint smile. "You'd better say one of those prayers of yours."

Naomi stared at him in surprise. "One of my prayers?"

" Hope you don't mind, Lottie told me some things your mother said about you." His smile grew broader, a cynical edge to his voice, "Well, miss, you'd better hope your God is listening and gets us safely across. Could lose the wagon, everything else."

In an instant, Naomi forgot about the waters churning downstream in front of them. *What does he mean by my God?* she asked herself. *Isn't he a Christian? Once I considered he'd been sent by the Lord to help me. Now I'm not sure. I feel so helpless, afraid even, which I haven't felt before.*

"Oh, Lord, why?" she cried.

"Why cross? Why cross this river, you mean?" mistaking her meaning. "Well, you know we've got to cross it, can't go back, lose half a day or so. And you'll agree this journey is urgent, wouldn't you?" He resumed his seat on the driving bench. "Look, miss, you just sit tight here in the wagon. Pull your feet up if you have to. Water may come up over the axles, hard telling how deep it is. There may be a few holes between here and there, take us down a bit. If not holes, then that's current itself surging a'round that rock."

Slowly he guided Bonnie to where the road leveled into the bank. There was a slight bump as the wheels rolled into the water. Immediately Naomi could feel Bonnie struggling against the current that rushed against the right side of the wagon.

"Hup! Bonnie, old girl," he called out again and again, "walk on, walk on."

They were only about three feet from where the river seemed to divide around the rock when Bonnie lost her footing and began to swim. With a frantic whinny, she fought the current as she slowly struggled to pull the wagon forward.

"Too deep here!" Schmidt cried. "Might have known. Couldn't see it from the bank."

Water now rushed across the wagon bed under Naomi's feet. In horror she looked down to see her shoes covered with water and her reticule swept up and swirling against the side boards, spinning around and around, in another moment about to be carried over them and swept out into the river. Her father's note, her money – In one swift movement she reached down and caught it, but lost her grip on the driving bench.

Schmidt grabbed her around the waist. "Hey there! Hold on to me. Let that thing go!"

But Naomi wasn't about to let the bag go and squeezed it between her knees. It was soaking wet. At least she still had it. Holding on to Mr. Schmidt's arm with one hand, the wire bench railing with the other, she felt the wagon slowly coming up out of the water. Bonnie had found her footing and they were now rolling through the shallower water toward the opposite bank.

Once over the bank and onto a continuation of the road, Schmidt drew the wagon to a halt. "Whoah, there, Bonnie old girl. Rest here a bit. You, too, miss." He looked down at her feet. "I see your feet got wet after all. Do you have another pair of shoes in that little wicker case of yours? Once leather gets wet, you know, it starts shrinking. Another hour or so, they'll be mighty uncomfortable."

He climbed out of the wagon and came around to her side. Reaching up, he said, "Wait, I'll help you down." After lifting her over the boards, he carried her over to the grassy clearing where Bonnie was now grazing between snorts and blowings from her muzzle. "Here you be, miss, safe and sound, only a little bit wet." He looked down again at her feet "Say why don't you take off them fancy button shoes, your stockings too. Leave 'em out in the sun to dry a bit, while we rest. Ain't nothing wrong with bare feet, is there? We all got 'em." He smiled in a strange way.

Naomi was shocked. "Take them off?" *He wants me to undress?* she asked herself. *No, however uncomfortable the soaked shoes felt, I can't do it, it's too improper.* She stretched out her legs so that the sun shone on them discretely. She wiggled her toes and flexed her feet in the hope that this would keep the leather from cracking and shrinking.

In her lap the black velvet reticule was beginning to soak through her skirt. Opening it, she counted out the five dollars in nickels, quarters, and two silver dollars. *Here's the note, only a bunch of wet lumps. Would rather have lost the money. The note my only link with Pa, something I can see.* With a resigned sigh, she threw the fragments into the stream and watched them float for a few seconds, then disappear into the foaming waters. *I must remember the note's exact words,* she thought, then another thought struck her. *The note's gone -- what if that's a sign, a sign this journey will come to nothing?*

"You all right there, miss? You're looking none too good, far as I'm concerned."

"That crossing was something I hadn't expected."

"Maybe more down the road, other delays. Hope not, for your sake, my sake, too."

"Let's both hope so. But to be honest, I confess I never imagined that this journey would be a smooth and easy run down a straight, well-traveled road. More like a test." She didn't dare mention her certainty about its connection with Job and Jacob.

Schmidt regarded her shrewdly, "Life is never like that, is it?" He sat down beside her for several moments, saying nothing, merely watching the rushing water. "Look off to the west," he finally said, pointing toward the horizon, "it's clouding up fast. Best to eat something now, let Bonnie rest, then move on as quickly as possible."

Getting up and going over to the wagon, he took out the food basket. "Got a little wet on the bottom, but Lottie's wrapped up bread and butter slices in oiled paper seem all right, and here's the smoked sausages from Hanson's. Couple apples."

Naomi didn't feel hungry. The enormity of this undertaking was beginning to make its presence keenly felt. She nibbled on a slice of bread and knelt down to cup her hands at the river-bank to scoop up water to drink. Almost as an afterthought, she whispered a short grace, "Oh Lord, bless this food, this life-giving water. Thank you also for saving me from its mighty power. And for the rest, let your will be done." She noticed the man smiling at her, his head cocked to one side.

After another ten minutes or so, he asked, "Ready to move on, then, miss?" He put the remaining food back in the basket. "You'll do this food this more justice later, I expect."

"It was welcome, and I feel much better, Mr. Schmidt." And that was the truth.

"That's good. And I've been wanting to say this for some time. If you're willing, you can call me by my Christian name, Matthew. Seems strange, being a Christian name, one of the apostles." He smiled faintly, keeping any more thoughts about that association to himself. "Yes, my name's Matthew, some call me Matt. No need to keep on being so formal like. We've a long way to go yet."

Should I grant him the same liberty? she wondered. As he lifted her up off the grass and set her down on the driving bench, she felt the man's strength, his closeness. The sensation was disturbing. *No*, she resolved, *I'm not ready to do that, I'll preserve my own name, Naomi. It's mine – not Rebecca, my mother's.* "Thank you sir," was all she could bring herself to say.

He stood beside her, as if hesitating. "Matthew's my name, you know."

"Thank you, sir – thank you – Matthew."

As the rolling hills settled into flat prairies, miles and miles of grasses waving like a gigantic yellow-green sea, the feeling of isolation and emptiness came over her. The fact that the sky was now completely clouded over with heavy, leaden-gray clouds added to her sense of unease. She knew the autumn rains were always heavy, unceasing downpours of icy-cold water. It looked as though they were about to begin.

"Where is there any shelter – sir?" She wasn't comfortable with his name yet. "I can't see anything like a building. There's hardly even a tree in sight, just empty prairie."

"Well, that's what's called the great plains, go all the way from Illinois to the Rockies, just empty territory for the most part, empty prairie."

Empty prairie, her thoughts ran. Her name, her self, her identity. Naomi of the plains. Naomi of the distant lands. Naomi without father, mother. Naomi in the land of Moab, among strangers. Her thoughts flowed as connections formed and reformed. The more she puzzled through them, the more the jolting of the wagon turned them into incoherent confusion.

Then it came. At first Naomi felt drizzle on her face and hands. In the distance she heard faint, rumbling booms. It seemed odd that the lightning flashes causing them were scarcely visible.

"Looks like we're in for it -- er, miss," Matthew said, giving an encouraging "hup hup" and repeated flicks of the reins to Bonnie.

"Where can we go, sir?" His name still came with difficulty.

He thought a moment. "Well, first thing, reach back behind you to that hinged wooden box. Lift up the lid and you'll find my oil slicker along with the few clothes and other supplies I've brought. We can pull that up over our heads and around us as far as it'll go."

"What about the food basket? The other things?"

"Dunno 'bout them. Maybe just have to let them get soaked." He gave a snorting kind of laugh. "Poor Lottie's bread and butter slices – them other things – she'd be mighty disappointed."

"Frankly, sir, I'm not concerned about what Lottie might think about soggy bread. Getting to Moorhead is more important. Then Moorhead to Fargo. Tomorrow – Tuesday -- there, has to be." Instantly she regretted the shape edge to her voice, brought on by frustration and discomfort. Whether he didn't hear or deliberately ignored it, she didn't know.

The rain came down harder in big, heavy drops, stinging like wasps. The man's oil slicker wasn't much help, because they were heading into the wind and the wind forced the rain directly into their faces and soaked their clothes.

Shivering, Naomi bitterly wondered whether this was at least the fifth of Job's trials. Surely the first was her mother's illness, the second her father's message, the third Jacob's refusal to help, and the fourth trusting in a man she didn't know. How many more were to come? She couldn't remember the total number. That passage from Job -- *Shall we accept good from God and not trouble?* She couldn't put aside the feeling she'd had for some time now, an intuitive feeling, an apprehensive feeling that one of those troubles to come, the biggest one, would relate to her father.

"Miss – I mean – " he paused, obviously uncertain about what to call her, "you keep a sharp look out, I've got to keep Bonnie out of the washouts along the road." It seemed as if they both were skirting around each other's identity.

Naomi peered through the driving rain, his hesitation regarding her name not escaping her notice. Everything was blurred, as if seen through a gray curtain. Squinting her eyes, shielding them from the rain pellets, she could just make out a gray shape in the distance.

"Over there!" She pointed excitedly ahead and slightly to the left. "Look, there's a building over in that direction, maybe a barn."

"What say? Can't hear you for the storm."

"I said a building – over there."

"Then there must be a lane leading off this road. Keep looking for an opening in the grass, for wheel ruts. Hup! Giddyup there! Hup!"

Another few yards and Naomi saw it faintly through the blurring rain, a large, square shape, surrounded by the dark triangular shape of pine trees, and off the main road to the left deep ruts made by wagon wheels. "Turn sharp left – the lane's not very big, hardly wide enough for the wagon."

"We'll have to risk it. How far now, what you saw?"

"Down at the end – I can see – " Her words were drowned out by a clap of thunder, sounding all round them and accompanied by blinding flashes of lightning. Naomi could not remember ever having been in such a storm. Thoughts of her father out in such a storm, somewhere in the Dakotas, or Fargo, cold, suffering, hurt, crowded into her mind in a series of painful images.

About fifty yards ahead the sagging big door of what was left of a half-ruined barn stood wide open. "Looks just like it's waiting for us!" Mr. Schmidt shouted. "Bad shape, but it'll have to do – some of the roof gone, looks like."

"Whoah, there, Bonnie," he called out as he eased the horse and wagon into the barn and over to the far end where the roof was still intact. "No choice, miss, no choice. We must stay here 'til it lets up."

"C – c- could you build a fire?" Her teeth were chattering and the soaking wet shawl of little use.

"Maybe." He got down from the wagon and began rummaging around in a box under the driving bench. "Always keep matches in a tin under here. Let's hope they're still dry." He broke into a laugh as he brought it out. "Look here – this old pill box of Lottie's – says *Baker's Liver Pills, for All That Ails You.* Now how about that? It's the cold and rain what ails us. Let's hope they can start a fire." It was the first time she'd heard the man really laugh, even if it did have a cynical sound to it. "Can you put on some dryer clothes?" he added.

Naomi was shocked. How and where? She walked around to the rear of the wagon and pulled out the small wicker case in which she'd packed her best dress, the green calico, a shift, and a spare pair of stockings. She'd debated about taking her black straw Sunday black straw bonnet with the silk lilies cascading over the brim, but at the last minute tucked it in. Under the present circumstances, it probably was an insane thing to do. Other things would have been more useful, like her wool cloak, another shawl. At least the dry stockings might help.

"I – I – I may have a few things," she stammered, hesitant, wondering how she would manage this in front of Matthew Schmidt.

As if in answer to this embarrassing question, looking out through a broken window at the rear of the barn, he exclaimed, "Look there! An old abandoned cabin just back of the barn! Still, it may be better than here. You wait here while I have a look, just to see whether anyone's around, or the place's been taken over by rodents and such."

This was her opportunity. Naomi took off her soaking wet sunbonnet and shawl and draped them over the sideboard of the wagon. She began unbuttoning the row of jet buttons down the sides of her shoes, but stopped with a noise behind her. The man was returning.

"Had a sudden thought," he said. "I'd better take my rifle, just in case. Good thing I thought to load it before we left." He reached into the box under the driving bench and took out what Naomi recognized as a Winchester, very similar to her father's, the one he always took hunting. "Be right back," he said, staring at her open wicker case for a moment, at her unbuttoned shoe, then disappeared around the corner of the barn.

He was gone for a good ten minutes, to Naomi's relief. With one eye on the barn entrance, she slipped off her cotton stockings and replaced them with the ones in her wicker case. They seemed damp, but she had no choice and it was the same for her shoes. They made for a slight improvement, yet still she shivered, unwilling to put her wet shawl back around her shoulders. *If only I'd brought another one,* she wondered, *or borrowed one of Ma's. Better still, my winter cloak. Hard to think of its ever being cold with the September weather so warm and balmy when we left. Come to think of it, it'd been hard to think ahead about anything, the necessity of the journey so sudden, the solution so unexpected.*

"Habitable, barely," she heard his voice before she saw him behind her. "The place isn't in good shape, full of dust, dried leaves through a broken window, maybe a squirrel's nest in one corner, but, still, better than this drafty barn."

He climbed up into the wagon and began pulling things out of the hinged wooden box behind the driving bench. "You're shivering, I see. Here's a wool jacket of mine, part of my best suit, brought it along, just in case. Warm, anyways, so slip it on -- that is, if you don't mind wearing it. I'll be all right in this oil slicker. Not so comfortable, of course, but keeps the warmth in, cold out."

Schmidt's suit jacket felt good when she slipped it on, although the earthy smell reminded her of home, her father's clothes, the odor of wool, of hair tonic, of the neats-foot oil her father used on tack leather. Masculine smells, comforting in their way.

"And if you'd be so kind as to carry Lottie's food basket, I'll bring in this quilt and the gunny sack and a couple other things. Looks like we'll be here for the night. That rain's not letting up, and it'll be dark early, too dangerous to try to follow the trail." He handed her the basket. "I'll unhitch old Bonnie, there's a bit of hay left in that stall over there." He unbuckled the traces and led her over to the dryer side of the barn.

"We must stay here for the night?" That sinking feeling descended all the way from her head down to her feet. Alone, with this man? Out in the wilderness? She expected this night's lodging at an inn somewhere, that's what she'd been told. "Couldn't we – " she began.

"But look at you, miss," he said, "cold and wet. Wouldn't be wise, wouldn't make sense in my opinion to go on. Besides,

I'm not at all sure where we are, how far Menasa is, my cousin's place. We'd most likely have pneumonia by morning. Leastways you would, I'm used to this. Come on now, no time for shilly-shallying. I discovered a fireplace in the cabin, or what's left of one, enough to build a fire to keep off the chill, even warm up a few of Sam Hanson's smoked sausages. I'd even venture to say you must be hungry by now, just pecking at your food earlier, like some bird or other."

Naomi couldn't help but feel he was making sense, practical, to the point, like Jacob. *Now if I were in this kind of a situation with Jacob,* she indulged her fantasies, *I'm sure he'd say the same thing. And what if we were all alone in this place, sitting cozy and warm before the fire, a storm raging outside. And Jacob would hold me in his arms, his voice imploring me, gentle, coaxing …*

"Here, miss," the man rudely interrupted Jacob's imploring, imagined words. "Take the basket and wrap this oil slicker around you. Quick, make a run for it, the cabin's only 'bout ten yards or so behind the barn. I'll be right behind you with this quilt and gunny sack, a couple other things."

His description of the cabin proved accurate enough. It must have been built twenty or so years before by the first wave of settlers in what was then called Minnesota territory. There were chinks between the square-hewn logs, the windows had originally been covered, not with glass, but with paper, long since torn off. A few still attached fragments fluttered from the frame in the wind and rain. The floor was still dirt, packed down in places with several layers of straw. The remains of a broken chair, a soggy mattress, several tin plates and cups, and pieces of wood were strewn around, left behind when the first settlers moved on. Naomi looked around in despair.

"Have to say, not what I'd imagined for the first night on the road," Schmidt seemed to echo her thoughts. "And then from there I'd expected we'd reach Moorhead easily the next day. As it is, looks like it'll be Wednesday." Giving her a searching look, he added, "You do understand, don't you, that we have no choice?"

Naomi shrugged her shoulders and sighed, "I guess so." But the night's accommodation was not her main worry. *I realize I'm in a questionable situation*, she reflected, *a challenging situation, a helpless situation. It all depends upon what this man intends to do. Upon what the Lord intends him to do – or upon my response.*

"There, that'll do it," he said, kneeling before the fireplace. "Difficult, but I finally got the fire going with the help of some damp matches, some damp straw, and some even damper branches. Some of that broken furniture next, as soon as the blaze catches well. Come over, warm yourself."

Naomi held her frozen hands over the welcome warmth, the golden light of the flames more welcome as darkness outside deepened. Already her wet clothes were steaming from the heat, although it would take a while longer for them to dry. She took out the pins from her coiled braided hair and shook it loose around her shoulders hoping it would dry more quickly. She was still hesitant to take off her shoes, glad that she'd at least changed into dry stockings in the barn.

"Your beautiful hair – it's – " he commented, starting to reach out to touch it, then thinking better of it. "Fire's doing well," he said abruptly, turning away. "I only hope I can keep it going."

His wool suit jacket felt good, the warmth from the fire now penetrating it and surrounding her body with sensuous comfort. She sat down on a pile of straw near the fireplace, tucking her legs under her.

Schmidt opened up the food basket and took out more bread and butter, slabs of spice cake, pickles in a small crock, and several apples. He laid them on the closed lid of the basket now serving as a table. "Take a look in that wrapped brown paper, miss, see if there are any of Hanson's sausages left. We'll have to drink rainwater, I guess. There's a couple of tin cups in the basket, cleaner, I reckon, than in that pile of junk in the corner. I'll just hold them out the window."

"Nothing wrong with drinking rain water. It's part of the Lord's bounty," Naomi remarked, remembering that moment of thankfulness on the river bank.

"I guess so," he mused, "not the time or place to talk about religion, though. Know what you're thinking, but I'm not one to share it."

Again, Naomi felt taken back. "Then do you mind if I keep to my own thoughts about that?"

"Long as you keep them to yourself. I've my own reasons. Some things happened – God let some things happen -- some things I don't want to talk about."

"What was it? Wouldn't it help to talk about it?"

"No. It's my business." He closed his lips tightly and frowned.

"Oh, I see." Naomi's earlier intuition about a great sorrow in his life, in Lottie's life, had been right. There seemed to be no more to say on the subject.

Instead, Naomi bowed her head. "Oh Lord Jesus," she prayed, "bless this food to our – *my* – use, and us – *me* – to your service. Keep us safe on this journey, keep Pa safe. Watch over us. In

Christ's name we pray, Amen." She'd laid particular emphasis on the *my* and the *me*, but she felt she should include them both as far as asking the Lord's protection for a safe journey was concerned.

"Think that'll work?" Again, there was a cynical tone to his voice.

"I trust in the Lord," she answered, as she took a first bite from one of the bread and butter slices. "And I think I'd like one of the sausages, please. And do you have a knife for the apple?" *I hadn't realized*, she thought, *how hungry I was. It's hard to think straight about anything else but food. I know I should worry about something else – Matthew, for one. But strength of the body now … and warmth …*

As soon as they'd finished their meager supper, he tossed the remains into the food basket. "I'll bank up the fire a bit more, though I don't think it'll last through the night. Best curl up in the hay over in that corner with the quilt and try to get some sleep. Long journey still ahead, maybe even into the day after tomorrow."

Best curl up in the hay -- Was he referring just to her or to both of them? Naomi warily watched him building up the fire with the remaining fragments of wood and branches lying around the cabin. She grew more and more anxious. *What are his intentions?* she wondered. *I know I won't be able to sleep worrying about that. No, I don't intend to sleep at all.*

"That fire'll last for a few hours, at least, but it won't keep you very warm," he said, eyeing her intently. "You've got that jacket of mine, at least."

Naomi's anxiety grew. "Yes, it will help." *What's he leading up to?* she wondered.

"Cold out there, still raining."

"Seems to be." Taking a deep breath and gesturing around the room, Naomi resolved to bring the situation to a head. "Where are you -- "

"Depends," he said. "Depends upon you."

Panic fell upon her, with the prickly sensation of fear. No, was it only fear? She'd never experienced such feelings before. It was something like -- like desire. Yes, desire, raw and simple, desire fed by the attractive male strength of the man, the sensuous smell of his jacket around he, a man neither her father nor Jacob.

"Where? That depends on you," he repeated.

"I – I don't think – " she began. *What do I want?* she wondered. *What kind of comfort, the kind I've never had before? A comfort greater than food or warmth.* Conflicting thoughts warred within her, confused, half-voiced desires and fears, becoming stronger.

"Well?"

A test. The realization came to her. *Job's trial.* Pulling the quilt more tightly around her body in a gesture of protection and defense, she stammered, "I-- I think you might be more comfortable in the wagon."

For a moment he made no answer. "If that's what you want, then," he finally responded, then with a shrug turned away to take up his rifle. He sounded disappointed, or rather, to Naomi, it seemed more like suppressed anger. "I'll be out there, miss," as he gestured toward the barn, "there's an extra quilt in the box. Won't be the first time -- " Still seeming hesitant to leave, he paused to kick a fallen ember back into the fireplace.

Naomi in one way was relieved, yet still felt emotionally confused. She had to say something to him, but wasn't sure what until her eyes fell upon the rifle. "No – yes -- would you – could you – "

"Yes?" With another unreadable look on his face.

"Would you leave me your rifle?" She hardly realized what she was asking, but something, some unknown fear from elsewhere had replaced the known fear of temptation.

"You know how to use it?"

"Yes—yes, I think so. It's a Winchester, like my father's. He taught me, said although I was a girl, someday it might be useful."

"Well, I'm hoping this isn't one of those times. Shout if you need me." He pulled open the sagging, rotting door, adding in a tone which might have been understood as vindictive, "Though I doubt I'll hear you through this rain." The door scraped shut behind him.

With the flickering light from the fire, the rhythmic sound of the rain on the cabin roof, and the enveloping warmth of the quilt tucked around her, and yes, even Matthew's wool jacket despite its suggestive associations, Naomi realized her resistance to sleep had evaporated. Her body felt heavy and her mind numbing into oblivion. "Oh gracious Lord Jesus, blessed Lord," she prayed, "thank you for -- " She fell into an exhausted and troubled sleep before she could finish what she was supposed to be thankful for.

It was much later that a sound became audible enough to penetrate through the deepness of that sleep. A soft, shuffling sound, like someone walking through fallen leaves, a twig snapping, something breathing.

Naomi sat bolt upright, dazed at first, then every nerve alerted. The fire had nearly died out, but there was enough radiant glow from the embers to outline the shape of the room, reveal the black hole of the window on the opposite wall. The cabin door, what was left of it, was shut, but the bolts were gone and the hinges broken. Now the sounds outside stopped at the door, started again, hesitated, stopped again.

Naomi made an unsuccessful effort to cry out, but her vocal chords were as if paralyzed. What was out there? Her thoughts ran to that stranger at the door of the cabin several days ago. *Twice, yes twice, he called my name … something about him … fear … apprehension. Satan could take any shape, he found me once, he could find me again.* She tried to gather her thoughts together, to work out what she should do. *Call out for the man? Would he hear me? Would he be angry and refuse? Or – or -- Lord, help me! Oh gracious Lord …*

The glow from the dying embers reflected on the barrel of the rife the man had left leaning against the fireplace. Naomi reached for it and felt for the cocking hammer. The shuffling sounds recommenced, this time coming closer to the window opening. With them came a low growl, like a deep voice down in the throat.

The sounds were unnerving, scarcely human, and she'd heard them before, that creature at her own door. With that came the more reasonable thoughts she'd prayed for. *It could not be Mr. Schmidt out there – that is, not if he really is who he says he is. He knows I have the rifle and can use it. It's not likely to be a person, either. Nothing would prevent persons from opening unlocked doors. No, it has to be a wild animal out there. An animal unable to enter closed doors, a big animal, an animal like a bear or a wolf looking for openings, for prey.* But then she had another thought, one that again brought on that prickly sensation of fear. *But Satan can take many forms, forms you don't suspect. Oh, what could it be out there?*

Naomi threw off the quilt in desperate resolution, stood up, and, bracing the rifle against her shoulder, cautiously approached the gaping hole of the window. Now the sounds were of shuffling, interspersed with heavy breathing, twigs snapping, then scratching along the logs of the cabin wall under the window.

Her hands trembling so much she had trouble drawing back the cocking hammer. Trying to steady her aim toward the lower part of the window, she fired. The kickback threw her to the ground. There was a crashing sound, a grunt-like wail, a series of indescribable cries, followed by loud snapping noises crashing through the brush that grew fainter and fainter, as she lay in a state of shock on the dirt floor of the cabin, unable to move. At last only the sound of wind and rain remained. She got shakily to her feet, still holding onto the rifle, unable to speak, hardly able to grasp the meaning of what had just happened.

4

Jacob's War

Jacob Bowers kicked at the pebbles under his feet in angry frustration. "Well, tell me what would *you* have done? he asked his friend, James Pratt, as they walked back toward the park hitching rail.

Saturday's harvest picnic at Prairie Lake park was over. The sun was already sinking behind strips of gold, purple, and pink clouds. Jacob wasn't paying attention to the sunset's glories, however.

"I can't get my mind off Mary Frankson and Naomi Beckman, especially those two awful conversations I had with Naomi, one this morning on her front porch, the other one here just now even worse."

"You're talking about Naomi's request?" James replied with a shrug. "Your commitment to her? How would I know? I do know you were interested in Mary Frankson, but you're also sweet on Naomi. In fact, last time I talked to you, you were really serious about Naomi. But then, it seems to me you've also been serious about Mary at various times. That could be a real dilemma, if you ask me, in fact, a big mess from divided commitments."

"The point is, James, how *much* commitment is enough?"

"To which one? Naomi or Mary?"

"To which one? That's the real basis of my problem." He kicked more vehemently at the pebbles, sending them flying in all directions. "But the real problem is, I let on to Naomi that I had something in mind."

"You mean marry you?"

"More or less."

"You can't just more or less marry a person."

"Didn't mean that."

"Well, then, when Naomi asked you to do something for her, and it sure sounded like a matter of life and death, why'd you refuse? And don't forget, Mary Frankson was involved, too. Her pa and her brother, Ted, are with Naomi's pa on that hunting trip, right?"

"Nobody knows that for sure what's happened, or even whether Frankson and his boy may be involved. That's just another part of the dilemma."

"I see."

"No, James, you don't see. Not the whole picture anyway. The truth is, Naomi wanted something impossible. She wanted me to drop everything and take her all the way to Fargo in Pa's wagon. It'd take two days there at least, day or two while she tracked down her pa, maybe the Franksons as well, then near two days back. Well nigh a week, and right in the middle of our harvesting."

"Bad timing, I admit."

"We've got to get the grain threshed and stored before the autumn rains start. You know how that is. We just couldn't afford to lose the whole crop. Not after last year, when we lost almost everything to drought. This year's crop, though, is one of the best, with those wheat stalks so heavy with grain they're almost lying down in the field. Everybody knows they're more than ready for threshing."

"Couldn't your pa have taken on a few more hands? I know I'd have been glad to help. My father'd give me time off from deliveries at the Mercantile."

"Thanks, I appreciate that, James, honest I do. But you've got to understand, there isn't enough time for all that. It's more complicated. We've got the rent of a new steam thresher right after Hank Larson, starting tomorrow and for only a day or so."

"Heard about those new fangled inventions, in fact caught a glimpse of it on its way down the road to Larsons'. How big a crew does that take?"

"Five or six, I reckon. Me and my brothers, Todd and Bill, Pa, Hank Larson himself – he'll be useful 'cause he already knows how to run that big rig, calls himself an *engineer*, and Tim Grant. His old man owns it, so Tim's keeping an eye on it. Naomi told me yesterday that Larson's wife was helping with the boiler. That's a laugh, isn't it? A *woman engineer*?"

James grinned. "Couldn't imagine my mother doing that."

"Mine? Well," he scratched his head, "maybe." After a brief pause, he added, "Naomi, maybe."

They'd reached the hitching post, where Jacob untied Prince's reins and James saw to his buggy. "Look, James, here's the long and short of my problem about that wild trip to Fargo. According to Tim, somebody over in Oak Grove wanted the threshing machine by Wednesday, latest. So we've got it only for a couple days – Sunday – that's already tomorrow – then Monday, and Tuesday."

"How about after that? You couldn't take Naomi to Fargo when you're done?"

"She claims she's in a big hurry, has to get there right away, like *now.*"

"I see," James said. "Does sound like you're in a bit of a bind as far as she's concerned. But still – "

"Oh, I know what you're going to say. I'll try to make it up to Naomi, somehow. Reckon she's not going anywhere soon, not on that crazy ride to Fargo, anyway."

"It may be too late for her to allow you to make it up." James stepped up into his buggy and turned the horse around toward the road. "I'm not much of a one to give advice about love, but I'd think about that if I were you. It depends on how much you think your relationship is worth."

"It's hard to weigh things like that. Especially because of the urgency of the harvest." He paused, then added, somewhat reluctantly, "And because of Mary."

As Jacob rode Prince alongside James' buggy out of the park and down toward the main road into the center of Prairie Lake, he said, "No, James, there's not much I can do 'bout it now. It *is* too late. I know Naomi's hurting, wouldn't be surprised if she refused to speak to me again. Guess that'd hurt me, too." He slowed the horse's gait, falling behind James' buggy. "Well, here's my road home, I'll talk to you later. The point is, there's nothing I can do about Naomi just now."

"Your loss, then," James said after a quick turn of his buggy onto the road. "And I don't think it's the end of the matter, either." A few yards down, he shouted back, "You may regret losing Naomi, though I can't say as I'd feel bad about that myself."

What did he mean by that? Jacob wondered. *A real slap in the face from somebody I considered a friend. I've always suspected James was sweet on Naomi, noticed that already back in high school.*

"Whoa, there, Prince. Know you're heading home, but take it easy." The horse had broken into a gallop. *Worse thing is*, his thoughts rambled on, *James and Naomi and Mary all go to the same church, that Faith Church on Third Street in Prairie Lake. Brings them together often enough. And I've got good reason for not accepting what Naomi seems to think so important, her darn religion. Never did much for my pa, won't do much for me.*

Riding through town and turning off at the corner by Grant's hardware on to the road to Fullerton, two miles due south, Jacob's thoughts mulled over what James had said. Was it too late to talk to Naomi?

"No," he reasoned out loud to reinforce his decision, "it's so late right now most everybody's packed up and left the picnic grounds. Naomi's surely gone to bed by now. And you know as well as I do, Prince, boy, it's not good to travel these roads in the dark. Especially not tonight with only that sliver of a moon, in and out of the clouds like that. You'd stumble, break a leg."

He paused. "Here, slow down a bit, will you? Know you're anxious to head for the barn, but just consider what'd mean for you to break a leg. Me too."

Jacob rode on another half-mile. "Besides, Prince, I don't know how Pa'd take it, me running out on him like that, just when everything's so critical. Besides, he needs our best wagon, the buckboard, for the grain." He flipped his reins impatiently, "Come on then, Prince, moon's out for now, you don't have be pick your way so much down this road. Let's get a move on."

Prince broke into a trot, but as soon as the moon once again disappeared behind a cloud, Jacob eased him back to a steady walk. Jacob let the reins relax in his hands while he tried to concentrate on the situation facing him.

"Never will get home at this rate," he mumbled. After another mile or two, lost in thought he burst out, "Say, Prince, what do you suppose Naomi thought of me this afternoon, eh? Sitting there on together on the grass, on Mary Frankson's nice soft buggy rug, all cozy like? Mary being so sweet and all that? Dressed so fine, too?"

He smiled to himself. "I'm sure I made Naomi jealous. Serve her right, putting me in such a bad spot. No point in trying to see her tomorrow, Sunday. She'll be in church like she always is, then there's always something going on there after church. At the church with James Pratt, no doubt. Besides, I've got to go over to the Larsons with my brothers to pick up the steam thresher. Hey! Whoah there!"

He pulled back on the reins as Prince suddenly reared from a rabbit running across the road. "Gotta be more careful there, boy." He settled back into the saddle, hardly noticing the road, the moon on the passing landscape, while he debated. "More careful – I should think about that, myself."

"Let's see, Monday. If I get time Monday, I run over to see her to try to put things right." He patted Prince's neck. "Think that'll do?"

Prince merely quickened his pace toward that comfortable waiting stall in the home barn.

Once at the barn, it was only after Jacob had unsaddled Prince, led him to the water trough, bedded him down with fresh hay and a bucket of oats, and headed across the barnyard over toward the house, only after he'd shifted his train of thoughts from Naomi's request, his time in the park with Mary Frankson, the food he'd eaten there, and James Pratt's words, that a thought he'd never before considered simply dropped, unbidden, into his brain.

He stopped dead in his tracks on the lowest step of the back stoop, his hand poised in mid-air for the knob on the door into the mud room as he tried to work it out. The light was on in the kitchen, shining out through the back window. Somebody was in there, walking back and forth, opening and closing cupboard doors.

He wasn't quite ready to go in and face whoever it was. *I hope it's not Pa*, he thought. *I'm not in the mood for any late night discussion with him about the threshing machine, or any other topic for that matter. Can't be one of my younger brothers, they'd be in bed by now. Most likely it's Ma, busy with something – she usually sets the bread to rise Saturday nights.*

Once again that earlier realization struck him, this time more logical, more reasoned out. *Take Naomi to Fargo? No, I could never have taken her, regardless of that business about threshing or pa's limited time with the steam thresher. Regardless of how much Pa needed me for the next week or so. Regardless of time, cost, effort, us and machines combined. No, it wouldn't be – wouldn't be --*

He searched for the right word. After a minute or two, he had it – *moral. Yes*, he considered, *it's a moral thing more than anything else. Taking Naomi to Fargo, just the two of us – no, it wouldn't be proper. Not married, we'd be alone together for nearly a week. What was Naomi thinking of, anyway? Surely she knew better, her and her fine morals, and yes, that moral there word I've been searching for most likely came from her. One of her ready words from that preacher of hers.*

He let go the knob of the mud room door and sat down heavily on the porch stoop, burying his head in his hands. It seemed he'd done the right thing in refusing. The justification was some consolation and lessened his feeling of guilt. Yet it also made matters more complicated. "What am I going to say to her now?" he wailed out loud. "Would she understand?"

"That you, son?" A beam of light fell across the porch as his mother opened the mud room screen door, squeaking on its hinges as it always did. "You're mighty late coming home." The light from the oil lamp in the kitchen framed her white hair in a circle of light. He could already detect, wafting through the doorway, that heady, yeasty smell of bread rising.

"Know that, Ma. Lot going on at the picnic. Lost track of time. Met a lot of friends, including James Pratt." He didn't feel he should mention Naomi Beckman, or Mary Frankson, either. "Haven't seen James for some time, not since he came back this summer on vacation from college."

"It's already past the opening of term, isn't it? So he's not going back to medical school in Minneapolis?"

"Taking a year off, he said. He's working at his father's store, the Mercantile, saving his money."

"I'm sure you enjoyed seeing him, maybe you can do a few things together, like when you were in school."

Jacob thought a moment before answering. "Reckon so," he said lamely, uneasy about where James' attentions were focused.

"Well, you'd best come in, your brothers are already in bed, although it wasn't easy to get them settled down. It'll be a big day tomorrow, with harvesting and all. You'll need your rest." She turned to go back inside. "Hungry? Need anything to eat? Some cornbread left over from supper, couple slices of ham."

"No thanks, Ma. Ate too much at the picnic as it was. Never saw so much food laid out all in one place before."

"Hmmff, too bad can't spread it around to them as needs it. That Koresky family down the road, for example – " The screen door snapped shut.

"I know, Ma. I'm not hungry, only a bit thirsty, but thanks all the same. Any of that cider left? Don't worry, I'll turn down the lamp wick in the kitchen on my way upstairs. You go on ahead."

Sleep did not come easily that night. After an hour of tossing and turning, he went through a cycle of mental reasoning.

Even if I were able to get away tomorrow long enough to go talk to Naomi, what would I say? I've refused her request for very real practical reasons. Couldn't get away for that long a time because of the harvest. My family's depending on me. Then – putting me down like that, refusing to go to the Prairie Lake picnic – I'd been counting on that. Feel real humiliated – no, betrayed more like it.

He turned over on his other side, readjusted the quilt, checked the alarm clock. *Then there's that other reason, the moral one. To have helped her might have harmed her. It would have meant putting her in a bad light, open to criticism from the town, from her friends, most likely, from her Pastor.*

Jacob felt tired when he woke up the next morning. It wasn't only his troubled thoughts about Naomi keeping his awake. Intermittent snores from his younger brother, Todd, in the opposite bunk contributed. And, in the back of his mind, there were nagging anxieties about running the threshing rig and whether he'd make a fool of himself because of his inexperience.

"Lookin' a bit peaked," his father remarked over breakfast, his mouth full of oatmeal. "Have a good time at the picnic yesterday? Somebody, pass me that pitcher." He proceeded to drown his bowl of cereal in rich cream, then sprinkled over it several pinches of salt from the salt cellar.

"Lot of folks there? Did you run into George McKnight? Heard he's been ailin'."

"No, Pa, didn't see him. Hope he's all right."

"While you was havin' fun, we was helpin' Pa," Todd announced in superior tone. "Me, and Bill, too." The point of Todd's remark was obvious and did nothing to help Jacob's sense of guilt over recent events.

"Yes, Pa," Jacob continued. "Lots of people, probably biggest crowd in years. No lack of food, as usual. Saw a lot of friends." He was not going to be specific.

"Fullerton Blues win the baseball game?"

"No, lost by two runs."

"Too bad. But those Fullerton boys, you know, lot's more to do 'round here just now than play baseball. Same goes for the ones in Prairie Lake."

"They don't play all the time, Pa," young Bill, ventured. "They'll do better when I get old enough to join the team." His brother Todd smirked.

"Well, right now's no time at all to play – or to smirk, either Todd Bowers. Come on, then, boys – Todd finish that slice of bacon – and you, Bill, no time for dawdlin'. We've go to get a move on." He pushed back his chair and took his denim work jacket down off the wall peg. "Martha, you fixin' to pack up our noon meal with couple jars water, or want us back here?"

"It's easier for you and the hands to come back, William. That way I can have a hot meal ready."

"Fried chicken? Biscuits 'n gravy?" Bill suggested.

"We'll see," she said, smiling.

"Apple pie?" Todd sounded hopeful.

"Maybe," she smiled more broadly. "Now Bill and Todd -- get your jackets, boots on. Pa needs you to help load up the wood." She began clearing off the table. "Jacob, you planning to ride Prince over to Larsons' to pick up that steam thing? No point in taking your brothers, they'd only be in the way."

"Yes, Ma."

"If you wouldn't mind, tell Elizabeth Larson I'd still like to have that recipe for her pumpkin bread, the one that just won first prize at the county fair." Setting down the dirty plates in the dry sink, she asked, "Say, I've been thinking. How'll you get that big rig out to the north forty? "

"Runs on a steam engine, Ma. Steam engines take the place of horses. The engine runs off steam power from the boiler. Wood feeds the boiler, the boiler produces steam, steam drives an engine, and the engine drives – "

"Never mind, never mind. Just go get the thing and get started with the threshing."

Hank Larson's farm was on the east outskirts of Prairie Lake, just off the same road leading farther east to the Beckman farm. Riding through town to reach it on that early Sunday morning, and with the annoying sound of that church bell in the distance to remind him, Jacob's thoughts were more on Naomi than on the steam thresher, even more so as he passed by Pratt's Mercantile at the corner of Main and Second.

"What do you think Naomi's doing now, Prince?" he asked. "Never mind, your horse sense not much help here."

For the next few minutes he visualized himself riding right on past the Larson's, riding down the next few miles to Naomi's house, coming right up to her front porch, tying Prince's reins to the porch post, and knocking right on her door. Her blue eyes would open wide in surprise when she saw him, her hand would fly right up to her mouth like she it always does when

83

she's excited. *Oh, Jacob!* she'd say. *You've come back!* Then he'd say, *I've come to apologize, to ask you the question I wanted to ask.*

But Jacob, deep down, wondered whether that generous gesture would really solve the problem. Where would he go from there?

Such thoughts were rudely interrupted by the sight of an enormous green and red machine blocking the road. The fact that it blocked the way to the road to the Beckmans' place seemed somehow significant.

"Hey, you, 'bout time you got here!" Hank Larson stood on top of the thing, waving a red bandanna. "We've got to move this threshing rig down the road and over to your place."

It was the first time Jacob had seen one of the new Case steam engines. It looked huge, its body a good four feet above the ground, supported by rear wheels bigger than his pa's whole wagon. A smokestack, looking like one he'd seen on the new railroad engines over near Audubon, where the new Northern Pacific line had just come through a couple of years ago, rose up another good four feet beyond that. Smoke was pouring out in black, explosive belches. The machine took up the whole road.

"How are we going to get it across the bridge?" Jacob asked in awe. "Will that old bridge hold up? Even under a loaded wagon it creaks and groans."

"Well, son, we'll just have to hope for the best, inch at a time. Be a disaster, all right, if it fell into the river." Hank Larson pointed to the boiler. "All ready got it fired up. Need you to stoke it, enough wood piled up behind the cab, I reckon, to get us to your forty acres. Just keep this here tractor moving, harder than anything to keep the thing moving once it stalls. Tim'll ride your horse and follow along behind, 'case we need help."

"What's that hitched up behind?" Jacob asked.

"That's the thresher part."

"The thresher part? But I thought – "

"You're new at this, I can tell." Hank shook his head. "Even Tim here seems to know more'n you do."

"There's a belt, see," Tim offered. "Connects with the engine once we get the rig in place. Then the engine keeps the belt moving, and the belt drives the machine that keeps the grain coming through and separating grain from chaff. Then a fan blows the chaff in one direction, and the grain goes up the chute and into the bags. Do you want it explained in simpler terms?"

"No need, thanks." Let them assume he knew more than he actually did. "We need to get started, then. Pa, along with Todd and Bill waiting for us – not that Bill's much help though, but he's useful enough for a twelve-year old. They're loading up the buckboard with wood for the boiler. We loaded up the shocks, more'n we expected, on the big wagon last Thursday and Friday. That wagon was so loaded, we had to borrow another one from Gabe Grant."

He climbed up into the cab. "You driving, Hank?" He hoped so. All those dials and gauges looked complicated, and there was a big wheel connected by a rod down to the front axle. It didn't look at all like how you steered a wagon or a buggy. A horse took care of that.

"Do my best," Hank answered, releasing the brake lever. The rig began to move slowly forward. "Have to be right careful, though. This engine's got a temper, she's a bit cranky at times. Too much pressure and she'd blow sky-high."

Jacob didn't like the sound of that. And he realized he had to hold tightly on to the frame as the whole thing shook and rattled while picking up speed. Each time Hank called out *"more wood,* " he had to let go in order to throw in another piece or two.

"Oh, hey! Lost my hat," he called out. With all the jolting and the effort of loading wood, he lost his straw hat, which blew off into a buck thorn bush alongside the road.

"Sure's heck can't stop now," Hank yelled back..

"No matter," Jacob shouted against the noise, "get it later." Yes, he'd come back on his way to see Naomi, as soon as he had the time. It was the first time he'd thought about her since first arriving at the Larsons' and confronting the steam thresher's challenge. There'd be time enough. First things first.

Hours later he was relieved to hear his mother ringing the dinner bell hung up in the windmill. He wiped the sweat off his face and neck with his shirttail, wishing he hadn't lost his hat on the road. "Whew," he remarked to Tim, "quite a job, even with that new-fangled machine."

"Sure is a big improvement," Tim said. "Back in the old days – scything through them stalks, then hitting them grain heads with a flail." He paused. "Say, just like in the Bible – Ruth and Boaz – remember Naomi's instructions about the threshing floor?"

"I can't say as I – " Although the name Naomi caught his attention, Jacob's ignorance about the Bible made him quickly changed the subject. "Seeing those shocks loaded into the bundle feeder – if that's what you call it, then carried along into that cylinder thing where the grain got separated from the stalks – that's really something." He had, in the course of the morning, picked up a few impressive technical terms.

"Reckon we got through nearly half of your pa's first wagon load this morning."

"Maybe all of it by the end of today," Jacob added hopefully. "Then only one more wagon load to go."

They reached the barnyard and proceeded to plunge their hands and arms into the cool water of the watering trough. "Best wash up out here," Jacob warned Tim. "And you, too Todd and Bill. Ma'll have a fit if we track all this dirt and dust into her kitchen."

"How many bags do you think we filled?" Todd rolled up the sleeves of his plaid flannel shirt, pushed a mass of blonde hair out of his eyes. "Never seen anything like it."

"I'd say at least ten," said William Bowers, coming up with Hank. "All that grain coming out, already separated from the blowers – sure made light work of it. And it looks like we'll have the best yield we've had in years."

"The Lord can be bountiful," Tim added.

"Well – "Jacob wasn't sure what to say. He never knew how to respond to those kinds of Christian remarks. "That may be as may be," he said lamely." Come inside, won't you, Tim? Ma's got that fried chicken and apple pie ready. I can smell it out here."

Although they finished threshing the first wagon-load of shocks by late afternoon, Jacob felt too exhausted to think about riding Prince over to the Beckmans' place to see Naomi. Besides, as sweaty and dirty as he was from all the soot and dust, he wouldn't have made a good impression.

Can't ask Ma right now to get out the tin wash tub and heat water for a bath out in the summer kitchen, he reasoned. *Missed Saturday's bath night yesterday because of the Prairie Lake harvest picnic. Maybe I should wait until tomorrow, Monday, when we're done and I can clean up first.*

Early the next morning, as the men assembled near the threshing rig preparing for the day's work, Hank came over to

Jacob, concern written on his face. "Say, Jacob, one of the valves came off boiler shaft just as we quit yesterday. Do you think you can ride real quick into town, Gabe's Hardware, and ask him if he's got a replacement?"

Saddling Prince, Jacob felt annoyed. *Sure hope we get done early enough so's I can get over to Naomi's,* he thought. *Not that it's going to be easy. In a way, not looking forward to it. Let's see, it'll take a couple of hours right now to ride into town, talk to Grant, and make it back here. That'll sure make it even later when we finish threshing. Of all the bad luck!*

Entering the southern outskirts of Prairie Lake, it occurred to Jacob that he had time to turn east down the road toward Larsons' and recover his straw hat, which he'd greatly missed the day before. Although it looked a bit like it was going to cloud up later, he needed it against the sun. The hat also provided some protection against the dust, which seemed to filter down through the air like fine snow and lodge in every particle of his clothing, every hair on his head.

And then, he was thinking, from Larsons' it was only another few miles to the Beckmans' place. *I'll have for a brief word with Naomi now, just before I pick up that darn valve, the men can wait. Have to be quick about it, though, have to find some excuse for them, but at least I can try to explain to Naomi why it didn't seem right for us to travel in my wagon together all the way to Fargo. I'll bring up the moral issue. She'd understand that one for sure.*

He was now about to pass the Larson's house on the left. Suddenly thinking better of it, he reined in Prince. "Whoah, boy, what am I thinking? No time to waste on that hat. No time for Naomi, either. No, right now the boiler valve's more important. The grain's waiting. The men are waiting. And will you look over to the west? Even the weather seemed to be waiting, with the clouds hanging there in the far distance. Come on boy, hup! Hup!"

Coming into Prairie Lake, Jacob sighed. It was one of those times when a person had to do two things at once, both equally important, both carrying serious consequences for failing to do them. To his relief, the front door of Grant's Hardware was open, although there seemed to be no one around. "Hey, there, Mr. Grant!" he shouted. "I've got some urgent business."

"Mornin', Jacob," Gabe Grant came out a moment later from the back storage room. "Surprised to see you here this early. Matter of fact, wouldn't be here yet myself if I didn't have some shipments coming in to stock, had to make room back there. Wagon load coming in from the rail station at Audubon, you see, may be here this afternoon." He removed his work gloves and stuck them into his apron pocket. "Well, now, what can I do you for?"

"Need a valve for that boiler of yours."

"Oh? Problems already? Those new machines tricky, all right. Never know what they're going to do next, mind of their own – just like horses. A valve, you said? What's it look like?"

Jacob reached in his front overalls pocket, then in his back pocket. "It was – well, I don't seem to have brought it with me. But I'm sure," he hastily added, "I'm sure I'd recognize one if I saw it." *What a stupid thing to do*, he thought. *Mind's been too much on Naomi.*

Gabe reached into a tall wooden cabinet and pulled out a small drawer. "Look through here," he said, setting out first one mechanical-looking piece after another. "I'd guess, from what I know about that machine, that it'd be this one? Or maybe this one?"

Jacob was at a loss. With every passing moment he felt a greater need to see Naomi. He wasn't exactly sure why. There were so many emotions going around in his head, his heart. To choose the wrong valve would prolong his frustration. "Could I take several, just in case?" he proposed.

Back on Prince, a packet of mechanical parts in his front overalls pocket, Jacob by now had succeeded in convincing himself to dismiss all thoughts of riding out the east road to see Naomi. *Not until later, not until today's work at least gets done. Late today, maybe, or tomorrow for sure, yes, after everything's done tomorrow and I can make myself more presentable.*

He was about to turn the corner and get back on the Fullerton road, when he saw Sam Hanson standing out on the boardwalk in front of his General Store, talking to two women about his sale advertising sandwich boards. He recognized one of them as Molly Cathcut, the school mistress he'd had back in high school. They nodded a brief greeting.

"Morning to you," Hanson called out. "Anything you need, Bowers lad?"

Jacob slowed Prince and nodded. "No, thank you, sir, not this morning. Came in for something for the steam thresher."

"Ah, a different matter from my wares, that is. How's that threshing coming along?"

"Going well, I think, soon's we get the engine going again. We'd hoped to get started earlier today."

"Everybody seems to be out early this morning, like Miss Molly, Miss Helen, here. Even saw Miss Naomi earlier today, just as I was opening up."

Jacob stopped his horse. "What did you say?"

"Said I saw Naomi Beckman today. Riding in Matthew Schmidt's wagon. All loaded up they were."

"Mr. Schmidt? That farmer, lives down the east road? All loaded up?"

"Yep, said they were heading on to Moorhead. Long trip ahead of them, I reckon. Course, it's none of my business."

Jacob sat on Prince, unable to move on. He simply stared at Sam Hanson in disbelief.

5

Disaster

"Where am I?" Naomi was still half in those dreams which troubled her throughout the night, the other half wrapped in a heavy, damp clamminess. Her senses disagreed with where she thought she ought to be.

Then she remembered. With that remembrance came a recollection of what woke her during the night. Terrifying sounds outside the cabin, first at the door, then the window. *I didn't know from what,* she tried to remember more clearly. *It seemed like that stranger at the door, my fear the same, growl the same. I didn't know whether I could reach the rifle, cock it, aim it, all in a split second and then fire through the open window.*

Turning over on her side brought a sharp stab of pain, reinforcing the realization that the rifle's kickback had indeed been real. Yet now came another realization, and the heaviness of cold, damp clothes urged her to get up from her bed of leaves on the cabin floor and do something about it. Throwing off the quilt, she realized she was still wearing Mr. Schmidt's wool suit jacket, still smelling of damp, soured wool. She unbuttoned it, slipped it off, and held it open before the nearly dead embers of the old fireplace, hoping it would dry out a little more.

But where is he? she wondered, *and what was he up to last night? Was he threatening me? Or making an offer? I'm not sure I know what he meant, I only know thoughts came to me unwelcome, unresisted, creeping in like a thief. It will be difficult to face him again, whatever I think of him – whatever he thinks of me.*

"Lord," she prayed, "grant me clarity of thought, lead me not into temptation, deliver me from evil, help me to – But, no, help me to what? Confront him directly? Wait? Go out to the barn and get my wicker case from the wagon, so I can change into something drier? No, it might wake him up if he's still out there. Then where would I be?"

Mr. Schmidt, however, already stood framed in the cabin's half-decayed doorway. "No time for prayers," he said gruffly. "Best get moving after a bite of breakfast and try to make up for lost time." Hiswhole manner seemed terse and uneasy.

"The weather?" A safe way to begin, it seemed to Naomi.

"Oh, better today than yesterday. Sun in and out of clouds, a slight wind from the west. What have we left to eat?"

Naomi took out the scant remains, some pickles, two apples, and one bread and butter slice. Spreading them out on the quilt, she offered, "This is all, and water."

"Not much to start the day on," he muttered as he bit into the apple, all the while avoiding looking at her. His eyes fell on the Winchester, lying on the dirt floor where Naomi had dropped it. Picking it up, he sniffed the barrel. "Been fired?"

"Yes."

"Why?"

"I thought I heard an animal out there, trying to get in."

He looked at her strangely. "I see. Get him?"

"No."

"Just as well." Seemingly short on words, he picked up his suit jacket. "Still damp, but never mind, I'll spread it out in the sun in the wagon bed. We need to get moving. If you'll bring out that empty food basket – for all the good it'll do, the quilt and that rifle … " He gave her a strange look. "Guess we'll be off."

Naomi gathered things together, listening to Matthew hitching up Bonnie and easing horse and wagon out of the barn. Although she, too, was eager to move on, the thought of spending another day alongside the man caused great uneasiness. *Something happened last night to change his manner toward me*, she reflected, *perhaps my manner toward him. Those strange feelings -- I know they aren't right. What's going to happen tonight – and tomorrow night – and the next? Fargo is still much ahead of us.*

But there was no more time for such anxieties. No sooner had Naomi climbed up the wheel spokes and into the wagon than Matthew savagely tugged hard at the reins. Bonnie lurched the wagon forward with such a violent jerk that Naomi fell heavily upon the driving bench even before she could grab hold of it.

They rushed headlong down the lane and swerved into the main road. "Bonnie's in good form this morning," he observed. "Good rest last night, even if it wasn't the same for everybody." A quick glance in her direction. "Hope the old girl holds up today. Still a long way to go."

They rode on in silence, the wagon lurching from the unevenness of the road and hitting occasional rocks or holes which he seemed not as careful to avoid the day before. He also seemed reluctant to talk, to Naomi's relief. She needed to think.

Finally he broke into her thoughts. "Come noon we should be about at Maplewood, if my calculations are right. Hard to tell, though, with all that rain it wasn't easy to know where we got to last night. Things look different today." He gave her a strange look.

"You said Maplewood? How big is it?"

"Small place, but there'll be a general store, maybe even an eating place."

"You've traveled much?" For whatever reason, he now seemed open to conversation.

"Yes, many roads before." He looked thoughtful for a moment. "Oh, I guess you mean this one? A few times. I've had business dealings in Moorhead off and on over the years. And, of course, my cousin's inn – you might call it a hostelry – in Menasa, just this side of Moorhead. That's were I figured we'd stay last night, as I mentioned earlier. But pity, we didn't get that far. Certainly would have been more comfortable than last night."

Naomi wasn't sure what he meant by that. "I must confess, it wasn't only the animal out there." Let him take that as he pleased. "I also had troubling dreams, maybe because I was so uncomfortable." And let him take that remark as he pleased, too.

"A person can't help that." He paused, reflecting, as if remembering something. "Being uncomfortable – mind or body – often brings troubled dreams."

"Do you believe in dreams?"

"Seems to me, dreams have a way of telling us things. Sometimes very private things, though I'm not sure what the difference is between a dream and a nightmare. My guess is dreams are a recollection of a bunch of memories, while nightmares tell us more about what we're afraid of, maybe what we need to sort out and come to terms with."

Astonished at this unexpected flow of words and opinions, Naomi merely answered, "That could very well be."

He looked thoughtfully out over the road ahead, as if deciding whether to expand on the topic. Finally he said, "Had quite a few myself, especially back at that time – over and over, I'd wake up in a cold sweat."

"What time was that?"

"Long time ago, miss, during the war. When – " He broke off. "Sorry, I can't talk about it." He hesitated. "Maybe I haven't gotten it sorted out yet."

What's brought on his strange, personal sort of mood this morning? Naomi thought. *It's as if suddenly hidden things, buried things in the mind, were coming to life. It could be that riding along, hour after hour, through vast, empty landscapes invites a person to think, to weigh thoughts, to work out problems. I know that's true for myself, whether good or bad. Maybe it would help if I drew him out more.*

"Sir," she began, "I don't wish to pry. But why are you so unwilling to talk about some things?"

He looked directly at her. "Aren't *you?*"

She was taken back and took a deep breath. "I had that coming and I apologize."

"No offence meant, I'm sure."

"I have – I have – " She hesitated. *Should I tell him about that think-about-it-later part in my head? This man's still a stranger, even stranger after last night. I've no real reason to try to understand him.* "Yes, you're right," she answered simply, "we all need that kind of self-protection sometimes." After another moment's thought, she added, "Maybe you could help me understand some hidden things. Maybe experience has granted you some kind of wisdom."

"Wouldn't know about that, miss."

Well, if you're willing to listen, I'll tell you about my dreams – or nightmares."

"All right," his voice conveying little enthusiasm.

"In one dream I was trying to find my way in a dark forest. Wet leaves kept brushing against me, branches were tearing at my clothes, trying to tear them off me. There was a faint light in the distance. I tried to reach it, but every time I thought it got closer, it went off in another direction. I kept falling down because my shoes were too big, they were someone else's shoes, but I had to put them on because I couldn't find my own."

"Hmm," he responded after he'd thought it over for several minutes, "sounds as though you were frightened of something, something you couldn't handle, something bigger than your-self." Smiling, he added, "Or maybe because your wet shoes were drying up and pinching your feet."

"I don't think it was the shoes." Was he joking or not? His earlier, more serious insight stunned her – of course, this journey to find her father had generated that nightmare. Simple enough.

Looking more thoughtful, he continued, "Or some decision you have to make about someone, a difficult decision you keep putting off – or can't make."

This sounded more complicated, perhaps even closer to the mark. She'd have to think about that, but sensed it could pos-sibly have something to do with the man himself.

"You said you had more than one last night? No wonder you didn't sleep well, shoes or whatever else." He smiled faintly with a slight turn of his head in her direction.

"It's still so vivid in my mind, it's actually painful to talk about it."

"Might help. Might help me understand you better." He paused, for a moment apparently concentrating on adjusting the slack in Bonnie's reins. "That is, if you'll allow me to. I've been thinking a lot about you, reckon you're a pretty deep young woman." He deliberately avoided looking at her. "Darn attractive, too." Staring hard at the road ahead, he added. "Any man might be tempted."

This disturbed her, no, alarmed her. What could she say? "I don't know about that."

"That other dream of yours?"

"All right, then. I was at the harvest picnic in Prairie Lake, you remember you were kind enough to offer me a ride there."

"Yes, and you said you had to see someone about something important."

"Well, in this dream I couldn't remember why I was there. Crowds of people were thronging around, talking, laughing. Some were laughing at me, at the way I was dressed. They kept pointing out the beet stains on my dress. Then I spotted someone I knew and wanted to speak to but he disappeared in the crowd. It was getting dark, people were packing up their baskets, gathering their children. The church's food table was still loaded with loaves of bread, apple pies, and pitchers of juice. No one had bought anything, so I decided to leave. Then the person I'd wanted to speak to came up to the table, kept insisting he wasn't going to buy anything, and turned away. I ran after him, but he got lost in the crowd. Suddenly I saw him going into the woods by the river. I ran after him."

"What happened next?"

"I -- I woke up." She wasn't willing to tell him more.

"Aren't you able to interpret that one yourself?"

"No, I was hoping you could."

"Seems rather obvious to me, but you know, I'm not one of those so-called mind doctors or what they call psychics."

"What, then? What was obvious?"

"Seems to me you were searching for someone you love, were in love with, but he rejected you."

Again, he seemed to have hit the mark. "What else do you think it meant?" Naomi asked, half afraid of his answer. Would he guess that the person she was looking for, the person whom she had in fact run after, was not Jacob? It was this man himself. It shamed her even to recall it.

He seemed to take some time in forming an answer. "More likely a nightmare, I'd say," he finally offered. Then, shaking his head, he added, "I don't think it's a good idea to go too deep into dreams. No, too painful, and worse, you might draw the wrong interpretation."

"But dreams can be important, they can carry meaning, give guidance. Why, in the Bible -- "

"As I said, miss," he answered curtly, cutting her off, " best not get into it."

Now, sitting on the wagon's driving bench beside him, more aware of the man's character, more sensitive to his moods and feelings, as he indeed must be of hers, the journey had taken on a slightly different nature. *I'm not as comfortable as I was when I left home*, she thought to herself. *Back then, at the start, I saw myself in my blue sunbonnet riding in a wagon beside a bearded, middle-aged man in a tan canvas jacket and a black felt hat, heading out on a two-day journey to Moorhead. But right now I see a slightly older woman riding along with a slightly younger man on a more complicated journey with a destination shrouded in mist.*

"Yes," she agreed after a minute or two of reflection, "best to think more about this journey itself, the road ahead of us, the miles before us to Fargo, the end of the journey … yes there is much think about now." After a pause, she said, "Yes, Matthew, much to think about."

He turned to her in surprise. "Ah, you know my name at last." Smiling, he looked ahead again, seemingly concentrating on the road. "Maybe that will make for better understanding between us – Naomi."

It seemed one of those special moments, a moment of recognition and acceptance. Naomi pointed to a long stand of golden poplars across a wide field lying to their right. "How awesome are those trees, shimmering in the Lord's glory," she said, ecstatic, "and look, that field's already had plowed the wheat stubble into the ground for next spring, the coming of new life."

Matthew looked over in that direction. "Bit early for that, I'd say. But here on the plains winter can come early, as I'm sure you know. Something about these plains that always makes one think in practical terms – to meet its challenges, you see."

With that he seemed to draw into himself, reluctant to engage in anymore talk. Naomi was relieved, feeling the same way. It could be that both had opened up their thoughts before quite ready to do so, and were uncomfortable about any further risk in revealing sensitive thoughts. Yet although she was reluctant to speak more about her dreams, she couldn't help thinking about them, especially the one in which the man she pursued was Matthew, not Jacob. *Has Lord spoken to me in some way?* she wondered. *I know the Bible is full of dreams, dreams of warning, dreams of wisdom. I need help in understanding the ones of last night. Oh Lord, please help me to a better understanding of myself, the directions I must take ... the directions Jacob must take – my father ...*

"Your father?" Matthew interrupted her thoughts. Had she said the last word aloud? "You've not said much about your father. And isn't he the reason for your journey?"

With a start, Naomi recognized this was true. She'd been so lost in herself, her own problems with Jacob, with Mary Frankson, with Matthew, that she'd given him little thought since starting yesterday morning. "Oh, Lord forgive me," she whispered softly, hoping Matthew would not hear and question her further.

Was God testing her? She could not help but allow her thoughts to run along this notion. But maybe he's also testing Jacob through Satan, even though Jacob's not a Christian. Job did not sin by charging God with wrongdoing. *Surely it's wrong of me to do so. In all of Job's troubles, he had to acknowledge God's power and wisdom. What was that passage from Corinthians? Something about the sufferings of Christ flowing into our lives and the fact that through Christ our comfort overflows ...*

"Comforting – " she said aloud.

"What's that? I asked you about your father. You find him comforting, is that it?"

Naomi smiled. "Yes," she said simply. She'd meant comfort of another kind, she doubted Matthew would understand.

"That note he sent you, asking you to bring a wagon to Fargo?"

"That was all it said. I don't know anymore."

"How'd you get it, then, who brought it?"

"A stranger came to the door."

"What kind of stranger? Didn't you ask him about it?"

"I was afraid, he seemed so – so threatening, just a dark, shadowy kind of figure beyond the window." She could not tell him she wondered if the messenger was Satan himself, *walking to and fro upon the earth* …

"Pity, pity. Not much to go on, I'd say. Reckon you'll have to ask some questions once you see the sheriff. Puzzling, though, that request for a wagon."

"Struck me, too. When my father and Henry Frankson went to Dakota Territory to hunt, Pa was riding his horse, Captain, and Mr. Frankson was driving our wagon with one of his horses. They needed the wagon for the game and pelts they planned to bring back. Why would they need a second one, unless they had more game than expected?"

"Possibly. Or maybe an accident – oh, sorry, didn't mean to alarm you."

"Pa's a good hunter, Mr. Frankson as well. They've gone hunting together in the fall for the last three or four years. They've never had a mishap, except the time they lost a box of cartridges in a river."

"Well, let's hope for the best." Trying to shift to a safer topic, he continued, "Say, now, your place – out there near mine west of Prairie Lake -- how'd he come to take it up? Know he's relied mostly on his potato crop these past few years."

"It was a government grant, a homestead grant. Compensation for re-enlisting after 1862. That was in the Second Minnesota Regiment."

"Ah, yes, that terrible war." He seemed lost in thought for several minutes. "Tragedy for so many families."

"You had a large family?"

He hesitated. "Yes, three boys, twin girls."

"Where are they now?"

He stared straight ahead. "All grown," he said at last. "Some, anyways."

Obviously there was more he didn't want her to know. "Oh, I'm sorry. We'll speak no more of it."

There was another long silence as they passed through a dense forest on each side of the road. Finally, "You thinking about a family, Naomi?

"Perhaps. At least I thought I was."

"Oh? What happened? That is, if I'm not being too personal."

"We had a – a misunderstanding. Jacob and I – that is – we both wanted something different."

"Jacob, eh. Not the Bowers family, over near Fullerton?"

"Yes." Now it was out.

"Was it important, what you wanted and couldn't have – or do?"

"Yes." She didn't want to add to that.

"I see." Suddenly reining Bonnie around a fallen branch across the road, he commented, "Looks like yesterday's storm did some damage. This tree's not the only one." He pointed off to the edge of a band of trees. "Quite a few down over there, tops gone from a bunch of others."

"So we missed the worst part?"

"Looks like it." Suddenly transferring the right rein to his left hand, he pointed ahead. "Look there, something coming toward us. Wagon of some sort. Seems strange we haven't met anyone yet on this road. Not much traveled today because of yesterday's storm, I guess. Between fallen trees, deep ruts and the mud, not easy to get to where a person has to go."

"Do you think it'll be like this the rest of the way?"

"Hard to tell, hard to tell. It can be perfectly dry less than a mile away from a big storm. Weather always freakish on these plains." He waved at the driver as the wagon passed by, both abreast too wide for the road, forcing Matthew to rein Bonnie almost into the ditch running alongside. "Road hog," he exclaimed.

"How much longer?"

"Dunno. Tell you this, though, I'll sure be glad when we get to Menasa. As for old Bonnie, she's already tiring and it's only about – " He slipped out a watch and chain from his overalls pocket. "Past noon. Don't see that town of Maplewood up ahead yet. Should have passed by there by now. Must not be as far along as I thought. So, we'll just stop here alongside the road for a rest, a bite to eat. What's left in that basket, anyways?"

Sitting in the shadow of the wagon while opening the crock of pickles and setting it on the basket lid, Naomi said, "I'm afraid that's all."

"No matter, we're sure to get to Menasa soon." He sat on the grass, his back against the wheel spokes, chewing on a stalk of wild wheat. "Concerned about you, though, you'll surely be hungry. Help yourself to the pickles. I'll manage."

Naomi reflected on how her impression of him had changed, not once but several times. His character seem to shift into different modes, at first seemingly kind and generous about the Forest Lake picnic and having his wife look after her mother. Then he seemed suddenly to change at the abandoned homestead into someone frightening, almost threatening. But then today he'd revealed something of himself in their discussion about dreams, a deeper something, something of herself as well. That was even more disturbing. And now he seemed genuinely concerned about her and her welfare. His concern – what was it, exactly? Not that of a father – perhaps of a lover? That was the thought that troubled her most. Satan … shifting images … Why had the Lord sent him to me? she asked herself. *O Lord, in your mercy …*

"Matthew," she said suddenly, almost before she knew what she intended to say, "what do you think about my name?" Satan had known Job's name. She would put *him* to the test.

He smiled and broke off another wheat stalk. "Always thought it suited you." He didn't explain why.

Wondering about his remark, yet unwilling to question him further, Naomi thought it best to follow his lead in getting ready to leave. As she replaced the now empty food basket in the back of the wagon, she saw a buggy approaching.

As it slowed, the driver asked, "You folks needin' help?"

"No, we're fine thanks," Matthew answered. "Just resting a spell, before we head on to Menasa. How far's that, do you know?"

"Oh, 'bout five just other side of Maplewood."

"How far's that, then?"

"Couple miles up ahead. Watch out, though. The road's washed out just a mile or so this side of Menasa. Take care – may have to go 'round through the fields."

"Thanks, neighbor," said Matthew. Then, to Naomi, "Best get moving, then, miss – I mean, Naomi. We're far enough be-hind as it is."

They did not stop in Maplewood, as Matthew originally planned. "Nothing here," he commented, "that general store looks closed up, smithy as well. Best go on and reach Menasa soon's we can, especially with the road washed out like the man said."

Yet the distance seemed longer than the man implied. With Bonnie slower and more erratic in her movements, and Matthew shorter in patience, there was still no sign of Menasa. It was also getting darker, the mid-September sunset, normally just after seven o'clock, seemed earlier because of a dense bank of clouds to the west.

Naomi knew Matthew was anxious. He hadn't said much in the past few hours, only wondering how Lottie was getting along with Naomi's mother, whether Naomi thought her mother's health would improve. She grew more tense with each passing mile, peering ahead intently for the first sign of the town. Her body protested sitting on the hard, wooden driving bench, her feet were pinched by her shrunken shoes. At least her dress, shawl, and sunbonnet had completely dried from the sun and the wind.

"How far now, do you think?" she ventured to ask, knowing full well Matthew wouldn't know either.

"Not far, not far," he tried to reassure her, although without conviction. "Don't know how much farther Bonnie can go right now. Let's hope we make it."

He flicked the reins, "Hup! Hup! Bonnie, old girl!" Glancing at Naomi apologetically, he added, "Best pray to that God of yours. Somebody needs to watch over us."

But Naomi had been saying prayers silently throughout the day, fragmentary of course, often interrupted by thoughts of Jacob or pieces of conversation with Matthew. Concerns about who Matthew truly was – a kind good man sent by the Lord to help her, or a man of different thoughts and a potential seducer – were perhaps the most frequent mental intruders.

Nevertheless, there was some comfort in those prayers, some comfort in the words of that psalm, which kept running through her head like the chorus of some hymn, *show me the way, Oh Lord … .Oh show me the way, Lord …*

It happened then, suddenly and without warning. Bonnie gave an agonized whinny of unexpected and brutal pain. The wagon tipped sharply to the right, throwing Naomi against Matthew's shoulder, then sharply to the left, heaving her out of the wagon.

"Matthew!" she cried. "What's happening – oh – I'm – " The force of her fall to the ground knocked the wind out of her lungs. For a moment she couldn't breathe, couldn't understand what had happened. She lay gasping in the tall grass alongside the road, a heavy weight pinning down her foot and something else pulling so hard against her shawl that it was choking her.

"Matthew?" she at last caught her breath. "Matthew! Where are you?"

There was no answer. The only sound was a strange, deep humming, which came from one of the wagon wheels, spinning into empty space. In the dim light she saw the wagon had overturned and that the edge of the driving bench, where she'd been sitting, pinned her foot to the ground.

"Matthew – help me!" Again, no answer. There was only silence, for the wheel had slowed, then stopped its spinning. No, there was another sound, a deep moaning some distance away. Desperately she wiggled her foot, sat up and tried to pull her leg free. At last, with a sharp twinge of pain, she succeeded. It was difficult to stand, she felt so shaken and light-headed and it felt as if a bone in her foot had been broken.

Holding on to the edge of the wagon for support, she moved toward the moaning sound. Suddenly there seemed to be no ground before her feet. A deep pit opened up, wide and dark. In the faint light still remaining, she saw Bonnie lying twisted at the bottom, still harnessed to the wagon tongue, which had broken off and gone into the pit with her. That she was gravely injured was clear. Matthew would have to use his rifle to put the poor beast out of misery.

"Matthew! Where are you?" she cried again. Still no answer.

She went back to the wagon and felt her way around the side where she'd fallen, then around the tailgate, then the opposite side. Still feeling her way she stumbled over something soft – Matthew's hat lying in the grass. Her next step came in contact with something more solid. It was Matthew's arm. Only his head, shoulders, and one arm were visible. His body lay under the wagon. His eyes were closed, he made no movement, no sound, and did not seem to be breathing.

She tried lifting the wagon off him, but it was impossible. To make it lighter, she lifted out the wooden box, her wicker case, the food basket. Still too heavy. She tried wedging the wagon's side up off his body with the food basket. It seemed to ease the pressure slightly. "Matthew?" Still he didn't respond.

Naomi knew then that she needed help. *How far to Menasa, now?* she thought. *The man in the buggy said the road was washed out just this side of town. Clearly we've come upon that washout suddenly and without warning.*

She walked out into the middle of the road. There was enough early evening light to see about a quarter of a mile in

NAOMI OF THE PLAINS

both directions, but there was no sign of the town. "If only someone would come along," she whispered. "Oh anyone, someone." She remained there for some time, until there was no longer light enough to see. People rarely traveled at night. She could hardly expect help now.

Naomi pulled her shawl out from under the wagon and wound it around her. Oblivious to the pain in her foot or the lightness in her head, she turned toward town. In front of her lay the gaping pit where the road had washed out. She somehow had to get past it, around it.

The man had said they might have to go around through the fields. A deep woods lay on her left, a field on her right. She stepped up over the bank lining the road and into a newly mown field. The stubble crunched under her feet, and several times she tripped and fell into a furrow. It finally occurred to her that, by walking in the furrow's depression, she'd get more quickly across the field. And in doing that, she'd most likely come to the house of the farmer who'd plowed it.

That furrow, however, led her not to a farm house but rather into a deep woods. By now a heavy, misty dampness was settling in. Surrounded by trees, by brush underfoot, and darkness, she rapidly lost all sense of direction.

"Oh Lord," she prayed, "show me the way. Let me find my way. I pray this in – " But before that final appeal and *Amen*, a gnarled, exposed root across her path caught her feet and she fell face down in a dew-laden bed of leaves, spiked with sharp ferns and broken twigs.

Her only thoughts were that she wasn't meant to get up. It was to be the end of things, her punishment, and so wrong to ask the Lord's help. She'd had guilty thoughts about Matthew.

No forgiveness toward Jacob. She was confused about God, about Satan. She would try, anyway. *O Lord, in your mercy ... I am in your hands ...* But the words seemed strangled, and she couldn't finish.

The cold dampness penetrated her cotton dress, her stockings, even the knitted shawl she'd wound tightly around her shoulders and waist. Then a thought struck her. *The shawl* -- her mother's knitting, each cross-over stitch made in love, the shawl a pattern of faith, each stitch a prayer.

It was some comfort, remembering that. Yet there was also anxiety, suddenly remembering her father's situation and his need for her. Was it really meant to be? Every moment's delay might have serious consequences. And Matthew – it was also true for him, lying there unconscious if not already dead under the wagon.

"And now," Naomi whispered to herself in the darkness, shivering from both cold and fear, "and now, the Lord must help me find a way. For whatever I've done wrong, I ask His forgiveness." She thought a moment more. "Oh Lord, I know that, I, too, must forgive. But, Oh Lord, I am not ready to do that yet for Jacob. Help me be ready."

Still lying on the bed of ferns, unable to move, she pulled her shawl more tightly around her, bringing it up over her head and wrapping her hands in its soft folds. Her mother's stitches, her mother's prayers. She needed them now. And yet there was a strange moment, an inexplicable moment of wordless desire for the comfort of someone else. And that someone was Jacob Bowers. *Perhaps*, she thought, *this might be the beginning of forgiveness.*

A small, sparkling light shone just above her head, unimaginable, wondrous. What light could there be, here in the midst of a dark forest? She reached up to touch it, to see if it were real. A drop of water, suspended at the tip of a fern leaf, broke into a myriad of droplets which ran down her finger tip and into the palm of her hand.

She sat up, aware of a change, a feeling she could now make the effort. Where had that light reflected in the drop of dew come from? She struggled to her feet by pulling herself by the low branches of a cedar tree. Now, looking between the two nearest tree trunks, she saw a distant light, the light which had been reflected in the drop of water, and it was now drawing her to it.

As she made her way with difficulty through the underbrush, the light took the form of yellowish light shining from an oil lamp, and it was framed within the four panes of a window. It could only mean that she had reached Menasa, or at least its outskirts.

As she struggled to reach that light, branches caught at her shawl and seemed to hold her back. Remembering the stitches, the prayers which formed them, she held it tight. She'd long since lost her sunbonnet. It didn't seem to matter.

Now came the smell of wood smoke, the sharp barking of a dog. She could see a second light, another window with a movement of people against it. Someone was playing a harmonium and people were singing with it.

"Help, oh help!" she screamed so loud it tore her throat. "Oh help!" she repeated, rushing toward that lighted window through what now appeared to be a clearing in the woods.

But in that rush, the weakness in her ankle from being pinned under the wagon caused her to pitch forward, and she fell onto a bed of pine needles. "Oh please help Matthew … " Then there came jumble of other words, voices she didn't recognize, smells unfamiliar, then darkness and silence for ages and ages.

"Take this," a voice said. "It'll help you feel better. You've been chilled to the bone. Got those wet clothes off you just in time."

A spoon with warm liquid was being held to her mouth. She opened her eyes, but the light made her close them in pain. The warm liquid was some sort of broth. It tasted good. She opened her mouth for another.

"That's right, dearie, keep it up."

Naomi opened her eyes more cautiously this time. She was lying in a big brass bed, in a room flooded with sunlight through a window framed by flowered curtains. Her body seemed to be floating, enveloped in something soft and warm, something ruffled around her neck and wrists. There was a woman sitting in a chair next to the bed, holding a bowl in her lap, a spoon in her hand. Her dark hair was tied back in a knot, her broad face rosy-cheeked. She seemed like Aunt Elizabeth, back in St. Paul – motherly, loud-voiced. No, she reasoned, this woman couldn't be her Aunt Elizabeth. She knew she was not in St. Paul.

"Try just one more, dearie," this woman coaxed.

Naomi did as she was told, feeling the soothing liquid ease down her throat, into her stomach. It made her realize she hadn't eaten since yesterday's lunch, the remainder of Lottie Schmidt's pickles from the crock.

Suddenly another realization came, the thought of Matthew lying injured under the wagon. "Matthew – must help Matthew!" she exclaimed and started to get out of bed.

"No, no, don't you fret none," the woman said, pushing her none too gently back against the pillows.

"But I've got to help him, he could be dead by now."

"Well, he ain't, if it's Matt Schmidt you mean."

Naomi looked at her in disbelief. She struggled to find the words. "Yes, the one under the wagon – on the road – the hole – Bonnie – "

"Miss, I don't know who this Bonnie is, didn't find no woman near that wrecked wagon, but I can tell you Matt Schmidt's here, room down the hall."

"Oh! I've got to go see him."

"No you don't, miss, not yet. Doc came early this mornin', taped up a couple broken ribs, said to let him sleep long as he could. You as well."

"How" – again the words wouldn't come.

"How'd he get here you're meanin' to ask? Well, I'll tell you. You a relative of his?"

"No, not exactly."

The woman raised her eyebrows. "Don't know what *not exactly* means, but I'll let that pass for the time being. We were all downstairs last night, celebratin' Mike Hauglund's birthday, Seventy-five if he's a day, one of the old-timers 'round here. Then the dogs started barkin' like crazy. Figured it was a bear out there, coyote maybe. Lot of them 'round here just now, lookin' to get fattened up for the winter. So my husband, Harry, he goes out with his rifle, Mike with him, carryin' a lantern. Hmmf, can't keep that old man back from wantin' any kind of excitement."

"But Matthew?" Would the woman never get to the point?

"So out they went, stumbled over you lyin' in the grass. What's a woman like that doin' comin' out of the woods like that, Mike seys. So Harry, my man, seys, must'a come from a wagon down the road. Maybe one of them prairie schooners with settlers goin' west. So after they carry you inside, they take a lantern and go on down the road a piece, found your wagon, found Matt, and between the two of 'em carried him back here usin' the tail gate of the wagon as a stretcher."

"Why – " Naomi wanted to know more, couldn't seem to find the words.

"Only Christian thing to do, I'd say."

Naomi took in her remark. "The good Samaritan – "

"Guess so, guess so. But you were sayin' somethin' 'bout another woman? A woman named Bonnie?"

"No, Bonnie was Matthew's horse. I remember seeing her down at the bottom of the ravine last night. Someone needs to put her out of her misery."

"You're right there, miss, I'll tell Harry. Say, what's your name, anyways? Matt hasn't been able to do much talkin'."

"Naomi."

"Ah, Naomi, Naomi of the Plains, then. That's what you just came out of." She broke into loud laughter. "Well, if that don't beat all!"

Naomi looked at her in surprise. The biblical story, that Naomi in the fields of Moab. How strange, how strange, yet how wonderful, that this woman had made that connection. She started to get out of bed. "We've got to leave."

"Where you goin' in such a hurry, then? No way Matt can travel yet."

"We've got to get to Menasa, find the owner of the inn there. I think his name's Harold Barnes."

The woman leaned back in her chair and gave out another hearty, raucous laugh. "That's somethin' ain't it?" She slapped her thigh and laughed again.

"You have, miss, you have. I'm Emma Barnes, his wife. Matt down there – he's my better half's cousin, you might say. Matt's wife, Lottie – well, she's Harry's cousin, their mothers' bein' sisters, you see."

She continued chuckling as she got up, straightened Naomi's pillow, put the bowl and spoon on a tray, and headed for the door. "Now you just rest a bit, get warmed up under them two quilts and a Hudson blanket. Later you can tell me why you're travelin' with Matt, and to where. And why you're in a hurry, and what we can do 'bout that." She paused, her hand on the door knob, "That is, Miss Naomi of the Plains, if there's anything we can *still* do 'bout it."

6

Temptations

In a guest room of the Menasa Inn on the outskirts of Menasa, Naomi lay comfortably in the brass bed, snuggled down under layers of quilts and blankets, enveloped within the softness of a ruffled, flannel nightgown, and with the warmth of chicken broth soothing an empty stomach. Late afternoon sun now mellowed the light from the window into pale gold. It was so tempting to forget everything except that precious comfort, within and without. Even that think-about-it-later part of her brain failed to tempt her. She did not want to lose the *now*.

No, Naomi Beckman, her brain kept insisting, warring against that comfortable feeling, *this isn't what it's supposed to be. Listen, you must bring your mind to think about something much more important than your bodily needs. Forget all this comfort. Your plans to reach your father – your efforts of carry out your father's appeal for help – No, think about them! Pa! Matthew! Jacob!*

"But I can't help but think about them," she argued aloud with her brain in protest.

"What's that miss?" The woman named Emma Barnes, the rosy-cheeked woman with the penetrating voice, was sitting in a chair beside the bed. "Think about what?"

"Oh, did I say something?"

"You did. Sounded real troubled, like."

"I guess I was thinking about a lot of things, Matthew especially."

"Called out another name, too, but never mind. I just now looked in on you again, to see how you were. But you just rest there, Miss Naomi of the Plains," commanded Emma as she got up, readjusted Naomi's top quilt, and started for the door. "Matt's all right, but them cracked ribs of his'll take some time to heal. The Lord in his wisdom brought him just to this place. But the Doc says he'll have to stay here for some time, 'til he's able to travel again." The door closed behind her.

While Naomi rejoiced that Matthew was all right, the cracked ribs sounded bad enough. Got to go see him, just down the hall. Not up to it yet, though, the bed was so comfortable and warm, after that terrible night. *Why has this happened?* she wondered. *Has the Lord sent it as another test, another challenge?*

Beginning to doze off from overpowering physical comfort, her mind was anything but comfortable. Whenever she felt slipping off to sleep, fragments of those nightmares in the ruined cabin came back, sometimes clearer, sometimes jumbled. So many challenges, it seemed. So many worries, first and foremost about her father, then secondly about Matthew.

What about Jacob, though? For the present, he'd somehow slipped down to the bottom of her list, although thoughts of him still persisted in various guises, chiefly in images of him at the harvest picnic in Prairie Lake, the last time she'd seen him.

Such thoughts coming in rapid succession were becoming hard to sustain. She felt herself slipping and sliding farther and farther away from resolving them. Sleep came, welcome and soon.

"Laid out your clothes on that chair," said a booming voice. "Had to loan you a few things of mine."

Naomi woke with a start in total confusion. "Clothes, what clothes? What time is it?"

"My Harry brought back everythin' in your wagon, includin' that little wicker case. Took your green calico dress out, that's on the chair. Had to wash out the one you were wearin', a real mess, stains and all, along with your stockin's, your shawl. They're down in the kitchen, dryin' on the rack. You've been asleep most of the day. Think you feel like gettin' up, get dressed?"

Naomi sat up and stretched her arms. She didn't really, but the woman's tone urged otherwise.

"Fine piece of knittin', that shawl of yours. Lot of love went into it, I can tell."

"Yes, my mother," she murmured. "A prayer shawl."

"Loaned you my Sunday best shawl, the one with the silk fringe for the time bein', but can't compare with yours. Well, I've got lot to do down in the kitchen yet before this evenin's meal. Birgitta's a great help, don't know what I'd do without her. Them Swedish girls – much in demand as domestic servants, 'cause they seem to know a lot 'bout runnin' a house. I heard they're put to hard work as just young girls.

"A Swedish girl, here?"

" Put an ad in the *Moorhead Examiner* for a *piga*, that means servant girl, you know, and would you believe it, right away got three or four replies. Birgitta – she seemed the best, willin' to work out here on the plains. For a spell, anyways. Soon's her contract's up, she'll be takin' off, I'm sure."

"Does she speak English?

"You might call it that," Emma answered with a broad grin.

"Does she ever seem homesick? How old is she? It must've been hard, leaving home like that, coming to a strange, new country." She couldn't help but be reminded of Naomi, the *other* Naomi, the mother of Ruth.

"A bit moody now and then, if that's what you mean. Her age? Ses twenty on her papers. Old enough to know her own mind, I reckon. But enough 'bout her. Now you go ahead and get dressed, come downstairs when you're ready." She paused at the door. "Say, you can help, if you're willin'. How 'bout bringin' Matt's tray up? Come down to the kitchen on the back stairs, just outside your door to the right."

It was good to change into fresh clothes, even though some of the things were borrowed and felt strange upon her skin. Coming down the narrow back stairway into the kitchen, Emma and a tall, slender, blonde girl were busily moving back and forth, slicing turnips, putting sticks of wood into the big iron range, laying out dishes, and checking something in a big pot on the range and another one in the oven. She was hesitant to interrupt them until Emma beckoned to come on into the room.

"This here's Birgitta," Emma boomed over the noise of the activity, "Birgitta Magnusson."

The woman nodded in her direction, dropped a slight curtsy with a "*God dag*," then continued slicing turnips on a big, wooden board. She glanced up at Naomi's clothes hanging overhead on the drying rack, apparently aware of Naomi's identity.

"Just gettin' Matt's tray ready. He's not into anythin' solid yet, but try to get this broth down his old gullet." She handed Naomi the tray, on which were placed two covered bowls, a small basket of bread slices, and a mug of tea along with a glass and pitcher of water. "He's in number six, end of the hall to the left. Careful goin' up them stairs, back stairs awful steep."

With some trepidation Naomi tapped gently on number six. What *condition is he in*? she wondered, *and how's he going to respond to me*? When there was no answer, she quietly opened the door.

"Naomi!" Matthew exclaimed weakly, trying to raise himself but then falling back on the pillows with a cry of pain. "Worried – 'bout – " He broke off. "Hard to talk." His pallor was in sharp contrast to his dark gray beard. "You do – talking," his words came in short gasps.

"Emma sent up some supper, some soup, slices of bread and butter. Feel like eating?"

"Maybe – take mug – right hand – left hand -- shoulder – painful." Slowly he sipped the broth as Naomi sat down in the room's only chair.

"Can't I help you with the rest?"

"No -- manage – move nightstand -- closer?" He took a few more sips, obviously suppressing pain down his left side. "Sorry 'bout – my fault – "

"No, Matthew, it wasn't your fault, nobody's fault. It was an accident, plain and simple." Still, she wished she could believe that in her heart of hearts. Surely tests send by the Lord were not accidental.

"What will you – "

"What'll I do now? I'm not sure. I know I can pray. Beyond that – "

"Hope somebody's -- listening."

"He usually is," she said with a faint smile. "Would you like anything else?"

"No –just heard -- Emma's --supper bell -- go down."

"Emma says you must finish what's on the tray. She's sure a formidable woman. I wouldn't argue with her if I were you."

He attempted a faint smile and a nod.

As Naomi descended the inn's main stairway which ran up through the center of the building, she noticed a large parlor to her left, with long windows facing the main road, and a small iron stove in the corner. Along the adjoining wall were two smaller windows through which a dense woods was visible. Between these windows stood a harmonium, no doubt the small organ she'd heard the night before, in a way drawing her toward it, like the light from the window reflected against the drop of dew, suspended just above her head. On the other side of the hall was a large dining room, also with large front windows. If it hadn't already been dusk, sunlight from the south would have filled the rooms.

The dining room had a pair of small, round tables close to the windows. At one were sitting two men in business suits. A long table, set for eight people, was against the back wall. While Naomi stood wondering about the eight places already laid out, Emma Barnes emerged from the kitchen, bringing with her the smell of grease, roast beef, and turnips.

"So, Matt up there in his room, takin' it all? He needs to heal, must eat to do that. Now you just come on in," glancing quickly at the two the corner, then toward the long table, "and sit here. Them Kellers'll be down directly Big family of seven, come all the way from Minneapolis. You didn't hear them arrive this afternoon? Made a terrific amount of racket, them children all over the place, stairs, up and down the halls. I had to quiet them down a bit, 'fraid they was goin' to disturb Matt. This is an inn, not a hospital, you know, but still -- "

"Guess I was asleep."

"That was good, you needed rest, some healin' to do as well. Got to get back out to the kitchen, pot roast's ready to take out of the oven. Don't trust Birgitta with the carving, though she's a marvel with any kind of root vegetable and all sorts of cakes."

What did she mean by *healing*? Naomi wondered, as she sat down at the empty table. But her thoughts went quickly to the men at the other table, who kept staring at her while making remarks to each other, the smoke from their cigars making her queasy. She was relieved when a burst of noise broke into the room from the Keller children, as they scrambled to take their places at the table.

"You're Miss Beckman, Mrs. Barnes said? How do, I'm George Keller, this my wife Lilian." He bowed slightly, as Mrs. Keller extended her hand. "We arrived this afternoon, been on the road now a good week from Minneapolis. Mighty glad to reach Menasa, especially before dark."

"And this inn, too," added Mrs. Keller. "Heard it's one of the best this side of the state." She grabbed the eldest boy by his shirt collar. "Now Carl, stop that! Sit down proper like. And you, too, Robbie and John. Sit down here." She pushed what looked like four-year-old twins into chairs beside Naomi. "I'm sorry – they've been on the road too long, getting more and more rambunctious."

"We'll be glad when we finally get to Moorhead and can settle down for a spell," said Mr. Keller, taking a little girl off the chair beside him and sitting her in his lap. "Here, come up with Papa, Lisa. That chair's too big for you."

"You're going to – " Naomi took a short breath, "going to Moorhead?"

"Yes, we've an aunt here in town to see first, then on to Moorhead to connect with some cousins. Haven't seen them in ages." Mrs. Keller sighed. "Seems families nowadays get so spread out and lose touch with each other."

At that moment Birgitta entered the dining room with a loaded tray of large dishes. With a smile and "*Varsågoda*," she set down a basket of bread, a bowl of mashed potatoes, a gravy boat, and a huge platter of pot roast, the meat oozing its own juices. Emma followed with another loaded tray of sliced carrots and turnips, swimming in melted butter, small bowls of mustard and horseradish, along with two pitchers of water and a ceramic pot of coffee. She distributed the items among both tables, then both women disappeared back into the kitchen with another waft of kitchen aromas.

Naomi had never been in an inn before, nor even an eating place. *It seems strange,* she though*t, that one could just sit there and have food placed before you, food that you hadn't prepared yourself. I'm not sure whether to start,* she wondered, *although just look at those Keller boys digging in. They didn't even say grace. I guess it's up to me, so I'll just go ahead and bow my head.* "Oh Lord, she said aloud, "I thank you for all your gracious bounty."

She noticed that Mrs. Keller paused in her eating and looked down at the table, listening.

"Where you heading?" Mr. Keller's mouth was full of mashed potatoes. At least this was what it sounded like.

"Fargo."

"Oh, that's just across the river from Moorhead," noted Mrs. Keller.

"Only a few miles, right Papa?" Carl seemed interested.

"You're traveling with someone?"

"A family friend." Naomi wasn't sure what else to say.

Mrs. Keller raised her eyebrows. "Oh?" She looked around the dining room. "One of those gentlemen over there? Wouldn't he like to join us? Or you join them?"

"No, but thank you. My friend's upstairs, laid up for the moment."

"I see. That's too bad. What's his name? What's he do for a living?"

"Does he have business in Moorhead?" Mr. Keller asked.

The conversation was getting awkward. "I believe so," she answered lamely.

"My cousins probably know him," suggested Mr. Keller.

This really was too much. Hastily swallowing a bite of roast beef and sampling the turnips, Naomi pushed back her chair. "If you'll excuse me – I really must go see to him."

"I'm sorry, a pity you can't stay. Heard Mrs. Barnes plans a sugar cream pie for dessert. That'll be – " He broke off to stop the twins from throwing pieces of bread at each other. "That'll be a real treat. And with some Swedish coffee, we're told."

She took refuge out in the kitchen with Emma and Birgitta. Harry Barnes was eating his dinner at the kitchen table. He nodded in her direction, his fork suspended. "Well, well, Miss Naomi. Glad to see you up and restored. I just came back downstairs from looking in on Matt. Still the worse for wear, I'm afraid."

"Thank you, Mr. Barnes. I haven't had a chance to express my gratitude for your help."

"Don't mention it, least we could do." And he recommenced his attack on the pot roast and mashed potatoes, drowning all with thick gravy. "Emma's cooking would restore anybody."

With gestures and a mixture of English and Swedish, Emma and Birgitta were cutting the pies and laying the pieces on dessert plates.

"Let's cut them all into eights," Emma decided, holding up eight fingers. Birgitta nodded and repeated the number in Swedish. "Let's hope there's enough to go around. Big eaters, those men in there."

Suddenly noticing Naomi, she said, knife poised in mid-air, "Ah, it's you Naomi. "Somethin' wrong? More food? We've still got leftovers, as you can see."

"No thanks. I wondered whether I should take up something more to Matthew." She didn't want to mention the other reason, that the company in the dining room, including the men's stares, had become unbearable.

"Well, he's sure to appreciate a piece of pie. Maybe coffee's not the best thing, though. You see, Birgitta here makes it pretty strong. Mixes an egg in with the grounds, pieces of the shell as well – the mess looks like mud, I'd say. Then she boils everythin' together, and somehow after that the grounds sink to the bottom, most of 'em, anyway. No, coffee's not good for Matt just now, I'd say. I'll heat up some milk and honey instead."

Matthew was nearly asleep when she entered his room with the tray. Her heart went out in pity for him, a man, so strong, assured, reduced to this. He'd left most of his earlier supper untouched, but she noticed he'd taken all the soup. "Emma sent you something else," she said, replacing the old tray with the new one. "This hot milk will help you sleep." She remembered how her mother had insisted on it every night, how her mother, that strong pioneer woman who toiled in the fields, had been reduced to hot milk at night, spoon fed.

Thinking about her mother added to her discomfort. *Ma's been left alone with a stranger – how're they managing?* she thought. *What if they discovered they couldn't get along, what if Lottie Schmidt just packed up and left? Surely the Pastor will look in on her, or Mrs. Frankson, or some of the others from the church. Isn't that what a community of faith is all about?*

"Worried – Naomi?" Matthew observed, picking away with his fork at the slice of sugar cream pie.

"A lot on my mind."

"Believe that – yes -- I'm -- cause – " Naomi smiled and patted his arm reassuringly. "No, Matthew, that's not true. You offered to help me when I most needed it, you and Lottie. I'll never stop being grateful. Now you drink that hot milk, finish up that pie. It sure looks good, but I didn't think I could manage it, not after Emma's dinner."

"Believe that – too. Emma's – good cook. Lottie – often jealous." He smiled faintly. "Lottie – miss her. Wonder – getting on -- your ma."

It seemed odd that Matthew had been thinking the same thoughts. "I'm sure they're doing well," though Naomi could only hope that was so. Smoothing out the bed clothes and adjusting his pillows, she said, "Now you get some rest."

As she closed his door quietly behind her and walked down the hall to her own room, her mind teemed with a jumble of contrary thoughts. While she for the moment was safe and well, while the Lord had blessed her in that respect, while Matthew had not been killed in the wagon accident, yet there were so many questions about what to do tomorrow, the next day, and the day after that. *How remarkable, that the Keller family just happened to be on their way to Moorhead,* she thought. *It might be a solution – that is, if they're willing to take me.*

The morning once again dawned bright and clear. Like so many mornings, Naomi often mused during her waking moments over the beauty of the Lord's world. Like that morning back at home, in her own cabin loft, the bright branch of maple leaves glistening in the window, when she formed the resolve to go rescue her father, if only she knew how and from what. Like that morning in the derelict cabin, when she'd been gifted a safe night in the wilderness. God's beauty was indeed everywhere, awesome, reassuring.

The text from Job came clearly to mind. *When God finally spoke to Job out of the storm, he spoke of His power, His might, His wisdom. Where was Job, the Lord asked, when the morning stars sang together? Or when dawn was given its place?*

A strange joy filled her heart, a feeling of reassurance. *This very dawn, I, Naomi Beckman, see the Lord's morning stars giving way to the golden light of dawn. Who am I, the daughter of John and Rebecca, to question that? Surely He will watch over me.*

Her first task this morning was to go see Matthew. Tiptoeing into his room, she found him still asleep, but his bedclothes were all twisted and half off the bed, one pillow had fallen on the floor, as if he'd had a troublesome night. She straightened things up as quietly as she could, thankful she hadn't waked him.

The inn was still quiet, clearly the Keller family hadn't come down yet for breakfast. She found Emma and Birgitta busy in the kitchen, Harry just finishing his breakfast of bacon, scrambled eggs, coffee, and apparently two plates of pork and beans with some left-over pot roast in gravy.

"Mornin', miss," he said. "Good rest through the night?"

"Yes, thank you. Matt's still asleep."

"Good, needs it," commented Emma. "Here, sit you down, you can start with some of Birgitta's coffee."

" That's sure to wake you up on all fours," Harry laughed. After finishing everything on his plate and reaching for another piece of bacon, he got up from the table. "Now if you women will excuse me, I've got a few chores needin' attention out in the barn."

After Harry, still nibbling on the bacon, went out through the mudroom and the door closed behind him, Naomi said, "Emma, if you've time, I need to talk to you."

"Of course." She motioned toward Birgitta. "Birgitta, go ahead, put some more bacon rashers in the frying pan, and the cinnamon buns are about ready to take out of the oven."

Birgitta looked at her puzzled. "*Ya?*" Emma's answer was to point to the bacon, the frying pan, the oven. "*Usch då,*" the girl nodded.

"She'll learn, I'm sure. A bright girl, or woman, I should say, a hard worker. I understand she's got a couple relatives some-where in America. I 'spect she'll want to be joinin' them, once her contract with me is up, can't remember exactly when that is, have to look it up, papers out there in Harry's little office, just off the hall." She shook her head. "But I'm getting' off the track. What is it you wanted to talk 'bout?"

Naomi smiled ruefully. "About much the same thing, about leaving. I need to get to Fargo as soon as possible. Did Matthew tell you why it's important for me?"

"Yes, he did. Seemed a bit fool-hardy, if'n you ask me, you're takin' off with him like that. Took a lot of trust, I'd say, a lot of trust in Matt. But, now you -- lookin' after family – that's im-portant. Can't help but thinkin' you're pretty courageous." She smiled. "You and Birgitta – some'at alike. And that other Naomi in the Bible – both some'at alike."

"Then you know that, because of this accident, his injuries, well – well, then I'll come right out with it." She took a deep breath. "How can I get to Fargo?"

Emma re-filled Naomi's coffee mug, poured one for herself, and sat down at the table. "Here, I'll join you. I've got a minute before people come down. Them Keller children – a handful. They'll probably want hotcakes and maple syrup for breakfast, probably won't eat half of 'em I fix. So now, you're sayin', how can you get to Fargo? That it?" She stirred sugar and cream into her coffee, the spoon clanking against the mug from side to side.

"The Kellers said they had family in Moorhead."

"Yes, that' right. Couple of cousins, I gather. Let's see, Moorhead's only 'bout ten or twelve miles farther on from here. Take 'em 'bout two, three hours."

"Do you think they'd take me?"

"Dunno 'bout that, Miss Naomi. They've got a big surrey, isinglass curtains all 'round for protection against the weather, be comfortable enough. Saw that big rig out back when Harry stabled the team. But you know, it's already a bit tight with them five children and all the luggage."

"Surely I could squeeze in, I'd be willing to hold one of the younger ones. And I've only got that little wicker case."

"That might work, might work." Emma thought a minute. "But say, there's those two gentlemen, them lawyers, comin' from some trial or other in St. Paul. They're goin' all the way through Moorhead to Fargo, leavin' right soon after breakfast, soon's they get packed and all. Asked for a box lunch for the road. It's a phaeton they're drivin'. And they're in a hurry."

"To Fargo? In a hurry?" It seemed too good to be true. Yet Naomi remembered seeing those men last night, the cigars, how they stared at her, seemed to watch her every movement from across the room. 'I'm not sure – I don't – "

As if reading her concern, Emma said, "Maybe you'd like to talk to them? They seem respectable enough." She glanced over at Birgitta. "Now, girl, no need to be listenin' in." Then aside to Naomi, "Really none of her business, though I doubt she understands a word."

She turned to Birgitta again. "Now Birgitta pay attention and look after those buns in the oven – do I smell somethin' burnin'?" She pointed to the kitchen range, held her nose.

"*Ach, ya!*" Birgitta hastily slid out the big metal tray of cinnamon buns.

"And now while they're warm, squeeze out that cloth bag of icing over them." She pointed in turn to the bag, the tray, the buns.

"*Ach, ya!*" Birgitta nodded and picked up the bag.

"Do you think – " Naomi began.

"Well, I think maybe you ought to talk to those gentlemen, at least. I'm sure they'd be all too willin' to take you. But yet – " Emma pushed back from the table and busied herself over by the kitchen counter under a big cupboard, pulling out big bowls, canisters. Turning around, she said to Naomi, "If you wouldn't mind waiting just a minute? I'll fix a tray for Matt's breakfast."

As Naomi headed back upstairs, carrying the tray, loaded with oatmeal, two rashers of bacon, and a pot of tea, she wondered what Emma's *but yet* meant. *She has a reservation about something*, Naomi said to herself, *and I can only guess what it is. It's those two men. I feel the same.*

She'd only gone up a few steps when she met one of them coming down.

He paused, nodded. "Morning, miss. A fine morning, don't you think?"

"Yes, sir, seems to be."

"Is that your breakfast? Wouldn't you care to join us? No need to eat alone. And my partner will be down in a few minutes." He was well dressed in a navy blue suit, with a ruffled shirt and a black ribbon tie at his throat. His dark brown hair was slicked back, emphasizing the size of his large moustache. He smelled of cigar smoke.

"Had my breakfast already, thank you. This is for someone else."

"Oh? Do let me help you, then."

She had no time to protest. He took the tray out of her hands and turned to go back up the stairs. "There's really no need, sir – " she began.

"It's a small thing, the gentlemanly thing to do," he answered smoothly. "Now where does this go?"

"Here, number six," she answered, knocking gently on Matthew's door.

"Come in," Matthew said, his voice still hesitant and weak. He looked surprised as they both entered.

"This gentleman offered to carry your tray up," she explained.

"All too happy to do so, sir," the man said. "I'm sorry to see you so laid up. An accident, I take it?"

"Yes," Naomi answered for Matt tersely. She resented the man's intrusion and felt he had no business knowing any more details. "You may put the tray down here on the nightstand, if you will."

""Happy to do so. Allow me to introduce myself. I'm Charles Billings, of the Fargo law firm, Billings and Fletcher."

"Heard -- of it," Matthew commented.

"And you, sir?"

"Schmidt."

" And who is this attractive young lady?"

"Miss -- Beckman." Matthew looked more and more uncomfortable.

"Well then, pleased to make your acquaintance, Mr. – er – Miss Beckman. Now I shall leave you to enjoy your breakfast, sir." He bowed slightly and headed for the door. "My partner, Mr. Randolph P. Fletcher and I, must make haste for Fargo. We're expected in court at two o'clock today. A criminal case of some importance, I might add." He turned toward the door. "So if you both will excuse me, I'll leave you to your breakfast, sir, and bid you, miss, a good day."

Watching him leave, Naomi hastily said to Matthew, "Now you know what Emma will say if you don't finish everything on that tray."

"Will try." Matthew raised his hand in a helpless gesture.

"I'm afraid I've got to get back downstairs, but I'll be up again soon."

Out in the hall, Charles Billings was just about to descend the main stairway. "Wait a moment, sir," something caused her to call out before she had time to reflect. "You said you were about to leave for Fargo?"

"Yes, shortly after breakfast, providing my partner doesn't delay us." He smiled and pointed to room number five, next to Matthew's. "Randolph likes his rest, he does. But you know, with our rig and a first-class pair of bays, we can fly like the wind. You came here by wagon? Ah, no comparison between a phaeton and a wagon regarding speed and ease of transport, I'd say." He eyed her closely. "You're planning to leave soon, Miss Beckman?"

"I'm not sure." He'd picked up her name, right off.

"I see." He stroked his moustache, smoothed down the curled ends, obviously considering something. "Is there a problem? Does it depend upon that injured gentleman? Could Mr. Fletcher and I be of any assistance? We'd be all too delighted to – "

He was offering her an opening. Here was her chance.

"I thank you sir," she heard herself say. "There may be something. I shall let you know." Why had she said that? Why hadn't she come out with her request right then? It was almost like the time she hadn't come right out asking Jacob to take her Fargo, and she'd lost the right opportunity, the right moment.

Back in her room, she knelt down beside the bed. "Oh Lord," she prayed, "if I ever needed your help before, I need it now. I know that I am unworthy. But *Oh Lord, in your wisdom, hear my prayer.*"

"Say," boomed Emma's voice as she stood in Naomi's doorway carrying a small tray, "Birgitta and I are really busy downstairs in the kitchen. "You'd do me a big favor if you'd take this hot milk in to Matt and check on whether he's finished his breakfast. It'll help him nap a bit, rest of the morning."

This time Matthew was actually looking better with more color in his face. He seemed to move more easily without twinges of pain. "Gentleman – you brought -- here," he smiled.

"I didn't bring him. He just came in on his own."

Sipping the mug of hot milk, to which Birgitta had apparently added cinnamon, Matthew looked thoughtful. "Heard -- that law firm," he said. "One --few good --in town." He took a few more sips. "Taken fancy – you?"

Naomi felt the heat rise to her cheeks. "Oh, I hope not. I didn't much like him, although he did offer to take me to Fargo. More or less."

Matthew set down the mug abruptly on the tray and raised his eyebrows. "That so?"

"But I was talking to Emma in the kitchen earlier this morning. She's sure the Kellers can take me to Moorhead, probably on to Fargo. They've got a big surrey, although the children might make the journey a little more challenging. They sure have plenty of energy."

"Perfect solution – but slower. At least – safe – no wash-outs – hope." He waved his hand toward the road, the gesture bringing about another spasm of pain. "Easier – my mind."

"Once I find my father, we'll come back through here. I'm sure you'll be ready to travel by then, don't you think? We can all go back to Prairie Lake together. We'll have a wagon, like my pa wanted."

He was silent for a moment. "No – " he finally said. "Business – must go Moorhead."

"But Matthew," Naomi protested, "you're in no condition to travel, not for some time at least."

"Business – urgent." He was growing more agitated. "I'll ask Harry – go with Harry – soon."

"But Matthew – "

"You go – Fargo, find father. Then go home together -- Prairie Lake."

"You mean you'll get Harry to take you to Moorhead, then you'll find a way to get back to Prairie Lake on your own?"

He nodded.

"I don't like that idea," Naomi said. "It's a long journey – and on your own?"

He nodded again. "Don't worry, I'll – I'll be -- able travel."

"Now listen, Matthew." Naomi pulled her chair up closer to the bed and took his hand in hers. "I only hope you're right. But just in case – here's what I'll do. Once I find my father and we're ready to return home, we'll come back through here. After all, it's the main road back. If by chance you're still here, then we'll see what can be done – about your Moorhead business and about going home."

Matthew regarded her thoughtfully for a moment, then shook his head. "What can be done … " He turned away, and Naomi knew she'd upset him.

"But right now, Matthew," she said as she pushed back the chair and headed for the door, "you must rest. Emma says so. And Naomi says so."

He gave a weak shrug of resignation.

Coming out into the hall, Naomi knew she urgently must pursue the problem of getting herself to Fargo. She'd speak to the Kellers. They were all now in the dining room, eating breakfast, with both Emma and Birgitta rushing back and forth, bringing out platters of fresh hot cakes and buns, taking back half-eaten remains.

"Well, good morning, Miss Beckman," said Mr. Keller. "Won't you join us?"

"No thank you, sir, I ate earlier in the kitchen."

"Then do sit down, at last have some coffee." Mrs. Keller waved to Birgitta to fill the ceramic pot on the table and bring an extra cup.

"You can have my cinnamon bun," said Robbie, one of the twins, extending it to her, white icing running down over his fingers.

"No, take mine!" insisted John, offering a half-eaten one.

"No, thank you, my dears. You eat them." As they eagerly carried out her instructions, Naomi wondered whether this was the right time to broach the subject of traveling with them to Moorhead. With all the noise, the coming and going, and the fact that the children were present, it was difficult to carry on a serious conversation. Nevertheless, time was passing and she couldn't wait for a better opportunity, like the last times.

"I hear you have family in Moorhead," she began.

"Yes, my cousins went out from Minneapolis three years ago. I'm anxious to see them and their children." Lillian Keller stopped to wipe off the baby's mouth and stop Carl from edging his glass of milk too close to the table edge.

All this time the lawyer named Billings seemed to be looking on with some amusement, occasionally saying something to each other. There was a sheaf of papers laid out on the table, which both of them from time to time were closely examining.

"How about you, miss? " Mrs. Keller was asking. "Where are you heading?"

"I'd intended to go to Fargo, but we had an accident on the road two days ago. Fortunately we were able to stay here."

"Oh, that's too bad," offered Mr. Keller. "When will you be moving on, then?"

"That's just the problem, sir. We can't."

"You can't?"

"No, you see, our wagon was totally smashed up, the horse killed. And now my friend is upstairs with several broken ribs, unable to travel."

"My, my." Mrs. Keller looked shocked. "We didn't know."

"So here is what I'd like to ask you, although I know it's unseemly of me to ask of strangers." As soon as she'd said that, she thought of the Schmidts and the fact she'd already asked help of strangers.

"But of course, whatever we can do – "

" If you are going on to Moorhead, as you said, would it be possible for me to travel with you? I need to get there as soon as possible to deal with a family crisis. I have a little money and could pay you something. I could also help look after the children."

"I see." Mr. Keller exchanged looks with his wife, and Carl stopped playing with his knife and fork to stare at her.

Should she explain anything more? she wondered. Or simply wait for their answer?

It was a minute or two before Mr. Keller responded. "Of course, if it's all right with Mrs. Keller, then I guess you are welcome to travel with us. I don't think space will be a big problem, do you, Lillian?" She nodded in agreement, although looking somewhat doubtful.

Naomi heaved a sigh of relief. "Thank you, I'd be so grateful."

At that moment the two lawyers finished their breakfast. Dropping their linen napkins on the table, they pushed away their chairs and recovered the sheaf of papers. As they passed by the family table, one of them, the one who'd introduced himself as Charles Billings, the one with the big moustache, nodded at Naomi. "Have a safe journey, then," he said, somewhat disappointedly.

She couldn't hear what else he was saying to her as he left the room because of noise from the children, arguing over the last cinnamon bun. It didn't seem to matter. She was relieved they were gone, that the temptation was gone to trust herself once again to strangers, this time strangers she had doubts about.

"As I was about to say, Miss Beckman, although you're welcome to travel with us, there's something you should know. " He coughed and exchanged looks with his wife.

"What's that?"

"It's like this." His words came in a rush. "We weren't planning to leave for at least four or five more days. That's how long we've booked our rooms here. We felt Lilian's aunt deserved more than a short visit."

Naomi felt her heart drop. "Four or five? Days?"

"That's right, I'm so sorry. But if you can wait that long – "

Her heart sank. *I can't wait that long*, she thought. *The trip here has already taken more days, so I should have been in Fargo two days ago. I should this very moment be standing in that sheriff's office asking about my father.*

"Is something wrong, Miss Beckman?," Lillian Keller asked in concern. "You've suddenly gone pale."

"It's quite all right," Naomi managed to choke out. "It's just that – well I thank you for your offer, but I'm afraid I must get there sooner. It's already been -- " she did a brief calculation when she'd first received the note, "already been almost a week since -- "

"Since what?"

"I mean, it's Thursday already, and I should have been in Fargo two days ago."

"That urgent, is it?" Mr. Keller asked.

"Yes, it is. I do appreciate your offer," she heard herself saying in an automatic tone of voice, "most generous." She rose from the table abruptly; unaware she'd knocked over Mrs. Keller's coffee cup. "I'll have to find another way."

Slowly she climbed the front stairs, feeling devastated and at an utter loss. Once in her room, she curled up in bed and pulled one of the quilts over her, trembling, not from cold, but rather from the sinking feeling that she was trapped. She tried not to think about Job. She dared not think about him and God's testing. She dared not think about those two lawyers, the one who'd seemed so accommodating, who'd offered to take her to Fargo, *faster than the wind.* The one who said they could be there today, by early afternoon. In a phaeton. A team of bays. She dared not – but now she *had* to think about Job.

Overwhelmed by a wave of frustration and disappointment, she must have fallen asleep briefly, for sounds coming from outside the window suddenly caused her to sit up in bed. *What time is it? How long have I slept?*

She went to the window to look down into the stable yard below to see what was happening. Harry Barnes was hitching a sleek-looking pair of bay horses to a black phaeton carriage. The isinglass windows on the leather curtains glinted in the late morning sunlight. Those lawyers about to leave -- it wasn't too late! She could still go with them, she'd be in Fargo in only a few hours!

Throwing her shawl around her shoulders, she rushed out of her room, down the hall, and down the stairs, two at a time. It was quicker to go through the kitchen.

"Why Naomi!" Emma looked at her in surprise as she stepped out of the way, potato peeler in hand. "What's the matter? Somethin' wrong with Matt? Shall I – "

"No, not Matthew. He's all right. Those men – those lawyers – have they left yet? I need to ask them to wait, to take – are they still -- "

Not waiting for Emma's answer, she rushed out the back door, through the mud room, kicking aside piles of boots, flinging out of the way hanging jackets, caps, and horse harnesses, and ran out into the stable yard. It was empty except for Harry, who stared at her as if she'd suddenly gone mad.

"They've left?" she shouted. "The men – for Fargo?"

"Just left. In a hurry, seems like. Why?"

Naomi felt her knees go weak. "Gone? Those men gone?" She sat down on the steps of the back porch, held her head in her hands, and forced back tears of frustration. "It doesn't matter now. It's too late, too late."

7

Jacob's Quest

I'm shocked, were Jacob's thoughts that Monday morning as he headed out of Prairie Lake. He slowed Prince to a leisurely gait so he could think better. *Shocked! That's what I am and I can't shake it off. What Sam Hanson was saying – about Naomi. She passed by his place early this morning in Matthew Schmidt's wagon. On their way to Moorhead, he said. Why Moorhead, not Fargo, like Naomi wanted?*

Jacob was scarcely conscious of arriving back at the farm, turning into the lane, riding Prince out through the furrows, or reining him in before the silent rig.

"Here's the part," he said dazedly to Hank Larson.

Hank turned it over in his hand. "Not the right one. You'll have to go back."

"What?" Perhaps he'd heard wrong. "What are you saying?"

"I said, Jacob, you'll have to go back. What's the matter, there? You look like you've seen a ghost."

What he'd heard from Sam Hanson amounted to the same thing. Jacob shook his head in an attempt to pull himself together.

"No, don't worry. No need. I've brought a couple more, 'cause I wasn't sure. The parts in Gabe Grant's hardware drawer all looked alike, so he said take a bunch of them." He reached down into his overalls pocket. "Here they are."

Hank looked them over and finally said, "This one might do, can't guarantee it." Walking over to the waiting machine, he yelled, "All right, men, let's get this here engine fired up and out to the field soon's I replace this thing." He took a wrench and started banging and scraping on the main boiler feed line, while Jacob's father, brothers, and Tim stood around, hands in pockets and their feet shifting impatiently.

"What's the matter, Jacob?" his father asked sarcastically. "Can't you make yourself useful here? Still half-asleep? We need more wood in the woodbox. And you, there, young Bill, go back to the house and ask your ma for a couple more water jars."

Then, surveying the wheat field stretching out before him, he remarked, calculating, "Should get maybe five or so of them acres done 'fore noon, what with this delay. Another ten maybe, if we're lucky, by supper time. Seems a lot to hope for, bein' done sometime tomorrow, Tuesday, so's them other folks can take that engine on."

He looked over at Hank, still working on the engine. "That is, if that thing goes like it should. No, I tell you, can't rely on somethin' like that, not like a horse. Take a horse, any day, over one of them fancy rigs."

'But Pa," Todd argued, "look, we done near twenty acres yesterday. Last year with old Blackie and Bob, how long'd it take us? Nearly a week, if I remember right."

Jacob scarcely heard what they were saying. At any other time he would have been interested in this argument and certainly come down on the side of his brother. Not right now. *Naomi Beckman – riding in Matthew Schmidt's wagon – all loaded up.* The words repeated themselves over and over in his head. *Heading for Moorhead – Moorhead. Matthew Schmidt – Schmidt – Schmidt –*

How'd she come to be with Matthew Schmidt? he wondered. *I scarcely know the man, he thought, met him only once or twice in Prairie Lake, at Hanson, maybe, or Grant's Hardware. Know he's a neighbor of the Beckmans, east of them, that's all. Why in the world would Naomi ask him to take her to Fargo? But Hanson had said Moorhead, not Fargo. How far's that from Fargo? Not sure. Only prairie out there, all the way through Dakota Territory, maybe doesn't end 'til it bangs up against those big mountains.*

Jacob studied the sky to the west, already beginning to cloud up. It wouldn't be long before the rains came, soaking the fields, the grain heads. If harvested then, they'd mold in the sacks or the bins, and they'd lose a whole year's income.

Jacob's father was shouting something. It was only after a minute or so that Jacob, so deep in shifting thoughts, actually understood the words. His father stood next to the thresher, also looking up at the sky. "Best hurry up there, boys," he shouted. "No time to lose, before that rain. See it comin', sure's you're born."

Jacob reluctantly dismissed those thoughts about Naomi, about Mary, about fathers – both of them. He knew instinctively that he was letting them go only temporarily. He knew they'd keep coming back, and back. He hurried over to the machine and climbed up into the cab behind Hank. "Think it'll go now?"

"Reckon so, only hope that new valve holds. Didn't fit quite right, but it'll have to do. Now get that fire goin', we've got to build up a good steam 'for we can move. You keep your eye on this gauge, I'll watch the other one. Awful lot of gadgets to watch. Your pa's remark about the old days with a team of horses pulling a thresher had some sense to it, I admit. The thing about this new fangled method is, though, you've got the wheat grains and the chaff separated right off."

He waved at Tim. "Checked that belt to the thresher? Don't want it to loosen up."

"It's all right, Hank, far's I can tell."

Jacob was kept too busy feeding the boiler fire during the next two hours to think much about Naomi's situation. A fragment of a thought here – *where's she now?* Or another there – *why didn't I?* Or another – *Matthew Schmidt?* fluttered through his mind from time to time. It was only when they'd stopped for noon dinner that he had time to sort a few of them out.

Taking off his gloves and laying them on the tractor fender, he joined the others heading for the house. *Got to sort things out,* he found himself deciding. *Mary Frankson's also involved. Her father and brother were with Naomi's father, leastways started out with them. Mary – always been attracted to her. Prettier than Naomi, maybe. But not as much – well, don't rightly know what you'd call it. And Naomi, with all her big ideas – laid an impossible thing on me. Mary wouldn't have done that, I reckon. And Mary's father and brother – shouldn't I have some responsibility toward them?*

Due to the urgency of getting through the threshing before the rain later that day, his mother's noon dinner was a hasty affair, despite the great quantity of food. She'd roasted one of the wild turkeys he and his brother, Todd, had shot down by the river bottom and added a generous amount of sage stuffing. The men passed platters around the big kitchen table, bowls of green beans, mashed potatoes, corn, baskets of butter rolls, dishes of plum jam. There was little time for talk.

"All right, men," his father announced just as they finished the last of the sweet potato pie, "back to work. Getting more clouded up every minute."

"We done so well this morning," Hank added, "that if'n we really put our backs to it, we might get finished by late this afternoon."

Once more out in the field, feeding the flames under the boiler, Jacob found himself inevitably, almost against his will, thinking of Naomi, of Mary, of that thing Naomi had asked, of the impossibility of it all. He could not get out of his mind the look on her face when he'd refused.

"Say there, Jacob! Pay attention, will you?" Hank's voice broke in. "Keep that wood feedin' in."

"Looks like we're almost done!" he heard his father shouting. "Come on then, step it up, only about another half-acre."

The desperate effort to thresh the last half-acre, to bag the grain coming out of the chute, to pile the bags onto the big, high-sided wagon, took Jacob's mind off his current concerns. He threw himself into the work, even, at the last moment, climbing down off the engine cab to help bag the grain.

"First spatters of rain!" Bill cried. "It's comin', Pa!" He climbed up on Blackie and urged the team forward. "Come on, then, you old nags, let's get this wagon movin'." Slowly the heavily laden wagon moved toward the open barn door. They'd barely reached it and driven the wagon inside before the first downpour hit.

"Great job, men," exclaimed Jacob's father, slapping Hank on the back. "Wouldn't have thought it possible." He laughed as he said, "Might just have to take back what I said about the old days. "So, Jacob, you helpin' Hank drive rig back to Gabe

Grant's hardware in the morning? He'll be pleased, he gets it back a day earlier as well as bein' paid the full price through Tuesday."

"Guess so, Pa." His mind was already forming a plan. While at Grants, he'd ask Mr. Hanson whether he knew anything more about Naomi's trip with Schmidt to Moorhead. Then he'd ride over to see her ma. She'd surely be able to tell him more.

Yet it disturbed him greatly, each time he thought of her in that wagon with Matthew Schmidt. *I know he's older — middle aged, maybe. But still, was it proper? That was my own thought, wouldn't have been right for me to take her, alone. Yes, I'm darn certain to have helped her would have harmed her, as I said before. And I guess that says something about love and respect — hadn't really worked that out before. Wouldn't put it past Naomi to claim it was only my own pride.*

Next morning in Prairie Lake he confronted Sam Hanson over the counter of his general store. There were several people already shopping, looking at canning jars, the latest delivery of newspapers, or discussing the cost of bags of flour. Jacob tried to keep his voice down low and leaned across the counter. "You said yesterday they were going to Moorhead?'

"Believe so. Least ways, they were heading down the main road east in that direction."

"How far do you reckon that is?"

"Almost fifty miles or so, I'm told, give or take a few."

"How long by wagon?"

"Maybe a good two days, maybe more. Depends on the weather. And judging by our weather yesterday, Monday's downpour hitting us late afternoon, they would have had the same but a couple hours earlier. Wind, bad weather generally comes from the west or southwest, you see, off the plains."

"Does that mean they might not have gotten far yesterday?"

Hanson smiled. "Come on, lad, you know you can't do more than twenty-five miles a day in a wagon when the weather's perfect. No telling how far they got, or where they are today. But say, why are you so interested in Matthew Schmidt and Naomi? You're suspecting something? Shame on you, Jacob. Why he's a respectable married man, must be near forty-five if he's a day." He paused and scratched his bald spot. "You can't possibly think there's something going on between them, can you?"

Jacob was growing more nervous. Several women earlier examining a set of pickling crocks had edged closer and were now looking at him, not the crocks.

"Course not," he snapped. Yet his thoughts were more than troubled. He really didn't know what to think, only that he had to get out of there. "Thanks anyway, Mr. Hanson," he said, as he almost ran to where Prince was tied up outside at Hanson's hitching rail.

"Let's go, boy!" He reined his horse to the right toward the east road. "We've got to make a call on Naomi's mother."

Passing the Larson house during the first mile out of town, he suddenly remembered losing his straw hat Sunday, when he'd come over to help Hank drive the threshing rig to his father's farm. "Watch for it, boy, it's blown into a bush somewhere 'long here. Rain prob'ly didn't do it much good." Then he saw it, fairly high up, caught in a supple buck thorn branch. He had to dismount and pull back bushes to reach it, their leaves still dripping from yesterday's storm.

"I was right," he said, tugging it on, "damp and all out of shape. Too bad I didn't have it yesterday, that sun was so hot. Anyway, it's better than nothing."

149

When he came down the lane to the Beckman house with its tidy front porch, behind it the solid oak door, he pictured once again standing there, talking to Naomi. *I was standing on those steps, she was leaning against the porch post, wearing her blue and white dress. Came to the park in it, even though she said she couldn't come, her ma doing so poorly, and her being so upset 'bout her pa. Perhaps those reasons were true, but what if only an excuse? Surely she knew the event was important for me. Maybe even suspected what I intended to ask. Hadn't I given it enough thought? Her enough hints?*

He hesitated before knocking. What was he going to say? What was Naomi's mother going to say? His emotions at a pitch, he banged on the door louder than he intended and it seemed a long wait before it opened. An older woman stood, there, her faded blonde hair streaked with gray, some apprehension in her expression. Jacob had never seen her before.

"Yes? What do you want?" Then, changing her tone to one sounding more hopeful, "Do you have a message from Naomi?"

"What's that ?" came a voice from inside, "something from Naomi?"

"No, Mrs. Beckman, I haven't, ma'am," he answered, "and it's Jacob Bowers from down near Fullerton."

"Oh, well then, come in, Jacob. It's all right, Lottie, let him in."

Rebecca Beckman was sitting in a rocking chair by the fireplace, a small fire throwing out some warmth against the chill of the day. She had a pair of knitting needles in her hands, a half-finished scarf spilled over lap. "Please, Jacob, sit down, won't you? This is Lottie Schmidt, Matthew Schmidt's wife."

Jacob nodded in her direction. "Ma'am." *Schmidt's wife?* he wondered. *What's she doing here?*

"Now tell me – us – Jacob, what news? You've just come from town? Has someone sent word? Have you heard from Naomi?"

"Or perhaps from my husband, Mr. Schmidt?"

Jacob twisted his straw hat around and around in his hands. He hadn't expected this complication. Sitting down awkwardly on the horsehair sofa, he could not remember a single word of his planned opening, despite the fact he'd rehearsed it over and over again during the five-mile ride.

He took a deep breath. "Well, ma'am, you see I only just learned yesterday morning – Monday, I mean -- that Naomi had left with Mr. Schmidt for Moorhead."

"She hadn't told you she was going?"

"No, ma'am. She did earlier ask me to take her, though."

"You refused, I understand?"

"Yes, ma'am. I couldn't very well do what she asked. My Pa and I had to get the threshing done."

"You explained that to her?"

"As well as I could."

"I see," said Rebecca. "The truth is, her decision to go with Mr. Schmidt came quite suddenly. I doubt if there'd been time – or even a way -- to tell you."

"Yes, quite suddenly, Mr. Bowers," Lottie Schmidt explained. "As it happened, my husband had some legal business to carry out in Moorhead. Something to do with our property, our wills. One doesn't live forever, you know."

She attempted a faint smile, even though her voice reflected concern. "So when he found out Naomi needed to go to Fargo with regard to Mr. Beckman's disappearance, and since Moorhead is just across the river, it somehow seemed providential."

"Providential? What's that?"

"It means something planned in advance."

"Can't see how that was possible." Jacob scratched his head.

"And Mrs. Schmidt, here, so kindly offered to stay with me, while I recover from this croup – or whatever it is. She's been a wonderful help, a pleasant companion."

Lottie Schmidt looked over at Naomi's mother. "It has worked out so well for both of us, hasn't it Becky? Truly providential."

"The Lord's doing, the Lord has been gracious," added Rebecca Beckman. "Say *Amen* to that."

Jacob still felt puzzled and confused. The situation was becoming even more difficult now that Naomi's mother brought God into it. He fished for words. "Mr. Schmidt – do you think he -- will he be able to – "

"Of course, you need have no fear of that. We packed up good supplies for the wagon, they also intended to stop at Hanson's. As for the length of the journey, Lottie tells me that they would have spent last night, Monday night, at the Menasa Inn. It's about half-way, you see, so that means they would be arriving in Moorhead late today."

"That's a regular inn – a respectable place?" It didn't sound right, Naomi and Mr. Schmidt spending the night together in some sort of hostelry along the road.

" The inn's run by Matthew's cousin, I believe, yes, quite a respectable lodging I hear." She paused in her knitting, "You're concerned about that?"

"I don't know, ma'am, hope so – respectable, I mean." He shook his head doubtfully, adding as an afterthought, "But what about when they're in Moorhead? How long there?"

"We're not sure," Lottie answered. "It all depends on that legal business. Matthew's intention was to take Naomi across the river to Fargo as soon as they arrived in Moorhead, and then directly to the sheriff's office. The note, as I understand, wasn't very helpful."

"Yes, Naomi had to take a great deal on faith." She slowly resumed her knitting, making each stitch a concentrated effort as if to dispel any anxieties of her own.

"You *will* let us know if you hear anything, Jacob?"

"Of course, Mrs. Schmidt, be assured of that. And now I thank you, ladies," he said, getting up to leave. "Right now there's not much any of us can do, I expect, except wait for news."

"Your harvest, Jacob – you did get your threshing done?" Lottie was preparing to show him out.

It seemed to him that Mrs. Schmidt's voice had a certain dryness, a kind of irony in it, as if she were holding that against him for refusing Naomi's request. "Yes ma'am. Couldn't have done it without that new steam thresher we rented."

"We are glad to hear it," commented Naomi's mother. Her tone, as well, seemed to convey more than her actual words. It was almost as if she were relieved that he'd refused Naomi and she'd gone with Matthew Schmidt instead. "Now please, give my respects to your father and mother. And tell them," she added with a smile, "they are always welcome at Faith."

As Jacob rode home, back through Prairie Lake and down the Fullerton road, he reviewed that conversation. *Two days to Moorhead? Not sure about distances, but that doesn't seem possible, especially because of that big rain storm yesterday. It's sure to have come from*

NAOMI OF THE PLAINS

that direction. Today already? That'd mean they were almost there. What are they doing now? Something deep down inside me makes me uneasy.

That evening, sitting around the supper table, Jacob argued with his father. "But Pa," he said, "I've got to go to Fargo."

"No, I need you here, son."

"But Pa, we've done with the harvest for this year, finished the last couple acres late yesterday. There's nothing to do that Todd, Bill can't help you with. Or there's the Grant boy, or young Tim Whitson for that matter."

"Your responsibility is here, Jacob."

"Now listen, Pa. I'm not a boy any more. I'm a grown man. I have a future before me. I'll have a family, responsibilities."

"You haven't got all those things yet."

"I'm worried about Naomi." He didn't want to add his concern for Mary and her father and brother.

"Ah, that's it, is it?"

"She went off on that hare-brained trip with Matthew Schmidt. She could be in real danger."

But Jacob," his mother interjected, "that was her decision."

"Not entirely her decision, Ma. She felt she had a responsibility. It was a big thing to do, a lot to take on. Maybe even a sacrifice." The real meaning was suddenly becoming clearer to him, his first insight into Naomi's motivation and perhaps, her real character. "If it really comes down to it, I feel partly responsible. No, maybe more than that."

His father stroked his stubby beard thoughtfully. "Never thought you'd come out with something like that. I'm impressed. But, son, what about concern for me?"

"Now William," Martha Bowers interceded, "it isn't the same. If you'd gone missing somewhere out there on those

154

dreadful plains, don't you think Jacob would go out after you? Don't you?"

William didn't say anything. After a minute or two fiddling with his empty coffee cup, a sugar spoon, and a loose button on his checked shirt, he got up from the table. "Take Prince," he said, a huskiness in his voice, "along with my pistol and cartridges, and make sure your mother packs you enough food for two or three days. We'll say our goodbyes at breakfast tomorrow morning. Now I advise all of you to go to bed and get a good rest. Much ahead of us. All of us."

During his restless sleep that night, Jacob's inner debates began again, impeded occasionally by Todd's snoring in the opposite bunk, Bill's insistence on a glass of water. *Am I doing the right thing*, he asked himself. *What good will it do to go out after her? She's likely already in Fargo, already meeting up with her pa, already heading home together with Schmidt and the Franksons in Schmidt's wagon. I'd be going all that way for nothing, probably wearing out Prince, he might have to be shot, I might lose my way, I might be robbed, or killed even.*

On the other hand, said that inner debating voice, *what if I could really do something? Naomi really in danger? Schmidt taking advantage of her? An accident, been robbed?*

Next morning he awoke with a heavy sense of foreboding. He couldn't explain it, other than it must be due to the fact that he was anxious about the long ride to Fargo and Naomi's safety. It seemed strange that each spike of anxiety seemed to sharpen and better identify the way he felt about her.

"Enough food in that one saddle bag to last you for a few days," his mother said, tight lipped, as he came down for breakfast. "The oilskin should keep it try, but probably only up to a point. Any heavy rain storm, make for some shelter. Somebody in town once mentioned a place called Maplewood, about three or four hours from here. If you run into bad weather, maybe you could put up there."

"Keep the cartridges dry, too, son," William added. "You can always shoot game for meat and you know how to spit it over a fire. And, by the way, there's a package of strikin' matches in the oil skin as well." He reached down into his overalls front pocket and pulled out a small leather pouch. "And by the way," he added, handing it to Jacob, "you'll need this. The ten dollars you've earned, well and good. But use the money – and the cartridges – sparingly."

"You goin' to shoot bears?" his little brother asked, wide-eyed. "Big, grizzly bears?"

"Don't be silly, Bill. Grizzly bears only live way out west. But," Todd continued, "There are plenty of wolves, coyotes, even round here. I saw wolf prints down near the river bottom the other day."

"That a fact, Bill? Say, you might be able to claim some of the wolf bounty money," Jacob suggested. "I hear the government's paying near twenty dollars apiece. You could buy yourself something at Hanson's, or save up for a horse of your own."

"Ha, that'd sure take a long time," Todd put in acidly. "He'd be an old man at that rate and too decrepit to ride a horse anymore."

"Now Todd – " cautioned his mother.

Bill looked excited. "That's a good idea about the wolf bounty, Jacob. Never thought of that." Bill poured more maple syrup on his flapjacks, then added, his mouth full, "You're sure about no grizzly bears, Jacob?"

"I'll go saddle up Prince for you," Todd offered. "Least I can do."

"You'll help Pa get the sacks to the grain exchange in Park Rapids?"

"Sure thing, Jacob." Todd got up to leave. "I'm sure Tim Grant'll be willin' to go. Likes the big town. Might just have a look around myself."

"We'll also be going with Hank Larson and Willie. They had a bumper crop, too," said his father. "Couple days – we should be back about the same time as you, if all goes well."

"Yes, if all goes well," Jacob repeated. He was half-afraid to sound confident, as if that somehow would bring bad luck. Naomi would put it differently, he knew. She'd say it was all in God's hands, it was all according to the Lord's will, not his. "Let's hope so," he was prompted to say. *Let's pray for it,* he knew Naomi would say.

It was still very early on a Wednesday morning when Jacob turned Prince's head left at the Prairie Lake intersection. Hanson's and Grant's were still closed and the streets deserted. *Thankful for that,* he was thinking. *For me to be seen going after Naomi, which is certainly what people would think, especially after I'm pretty sure people overheard me talking to Sam Hanson in his store yesterday, wouldn't be good. Talk in a small town gets around fast. For sure it'd affect my future, or worse still, Naomi's. Why's the situation getting more complicated like that?*

Jacob reconsidered that word, *complicated.* His life up until this point had always been reasonably free of complications, except when he had to made the decision whether follow his friend James and enroll in Hamlin College in Minneapolis. But actually there hadn't been much choice, with his father insisting he needed him on the farm.

Now this second complication, and Jacob began thinking about what all it involved. *Yes, it'll sure get more complicated once I get to Fargo*, he thought. *That is, if I get there at all. I refused to help Naomi, so she relied on a near stranger, not knowing whether she could trust him or not. That was like a slap in my face. Now what if she even refuses to see me?*

"Giddyup, there, Prince," he shouted to the horse, determined to divert his mind away from all this. "Giddyup!" he called out to the wind, to Naomi's God, to whomever might be listening. ""Yup, yup there! We've no time to lose!"

Jacob did not stop until he'd ridden for at least two hours. Even then, he wouldn't have stopped to rest had Prince not shown it would be madness to keep on at that pace. Foam dripped from the horse's muzzle and sweat ran in streams over his neck and flanks.

"All right, Prince boy," he said, pulling gently back on the reins. "Slow down, we'll walk a bit to get you cooled down, then the next time I see a bit of nice green grass, we'll stop. These hills have sure put you to the test." He hadn't expected the land to be so broken up, some of the hills quite steep and intercepted by ravines.

The sun was hot and seemed to draw out the brilliant colors of orange maples and golden poplars. Even Jacob, for all his haste and anxiety, felt buoyed up by the sheer beauty of it. Still holding Prince to a walk, he slipped off his jacket and wrapped it around the saddle horn. Drawing out a gourd flask which his mother had packed in a saddle bag, he poured the water into his mouth and let it dribble over his chin and neck.

"Ah, that's good," he said, "I was getting thirsty. That a river I see up ahead, Prince?" As if smelling water, Prince quickened his pace.

Everybody knew about the Buffalo River rapids. He hadn't expected them to look so wild, however. After the violent rains two days ago, the river formed a raging torrent between where Prince stood and the road took up again on the opposite bank. "Can't ford here, Prince. We'll have to follow along 'til we come to a better place."

It must have been close to an hour's picking their way carefully south along the bank before they came to a more level spot. There the foaming water slowed down to a series of swirls in between flint-like rocks and small pockets of spiky reeds.

"Watch out now, boy," he said, standing in the stirrups in order to get a better view of what lay ahead. Several times Prince slipped and almost lost his footing, nearly throwing Jacob out of the saddle.

Once on the opposite side, they had to make their way back up to the continuation of the road. "A couple hours lost already, Prince," Jacob complained. "Hadn't planned on that. Must be well past noon, by the look of the sun. But at least we've got the sun, although it's now to the point where it's right in my eyes." He pulled down his straw hat over his forehead. "That's better, though this old hat still somewhat the worse for wear. Hardly fits anymore."

When at last they regained the main road, Jacob let Prince graze in the grass, trailing his reins, while he sat down on a rock with one of the saddlebags. He took out the sandwiches his mother had packed and an apple. He felt something nudge his shoulder as he ate the first sandwich. "You want this apple, boy?"

He laughed to see Prince's deft response, closing his muzzle over the entire apple in one swift movement. It was a light moment and welcome, temporarily dispelling his foreboding thoughts about complications and set-backs.

After they left the river, the countryside began to flatten out into, first, rolling prairies, then extensive plains as far as the eye could see. There were only a sparse clusters of trees, mostly evergreens, but here and there flaming maples showed their determination to survive amongst seas of grass.

Far off to the left he saw what looked like a stand of cedars and the remains of an old barn, a log cabin falling into ruin behind it. "Settlers moved on, I expect, hoping to find better land to the west. Can't say as I blame'em," he added, looking around. "Good thing we don't have to spend the night over there in that run-down place."

"Say, Prince, we haven't come to Maplewood yet. It might be a good place to stop and ask about Naomi. Folks there sure to remember her and Mr. Schmidt passing through. Especially with so few folks traveling now the weather's been so bad. And Naomi, you'll agree, would be a hard person to forget, once you've seen her. Sure could use a good cup of coffee, myself, maybe pick up a bag of oats for you. Grass alone sure can't keep you going."

The first indication of Maplewood was a log cabin on its outskirts, surrounded by a barn and several outhouses. Next to it was a smithy, its broad door pulled shut and locked with a padlock. Across the street on his right was a larger building with the sign *Geske's Mercantile, Prop. P. Geske* over the door. Beyond that was an abandoned cabin, beyond that endless prairie.

Entering the store, Jacob saw only several wooden crates stacked against one wall, a table or two of kitchen and household wares, and a small, caged in cubicle with a window, obviously what passed for the local post office. The whole place looked as though it was either just setting up or about to move on.

"Hello?" he called out. "Anybody here?" After some delay, the curtains across a door in the rear parted and a woman emerged, dressed in man's overalls and a denim work apron with several bulging pockets filled with screw drivers and wrenches.

"Yes?" she asked, wiping greasy hands on the front of the overalls. "Goin' east or west?"

"West. How far from here to Fargo?"

"Don't know much 'bout miles. And that depends, don't it, on how fast you're goin'?"

"Can I get a cup of coffee?"

"That'll take a bit of time. Pot's gone cold back there. Been out back greasin' the wagon wheels."

"Well, could you warm me up a cup? Please?"

"I'll see. Can't promise it'll be drinkable." She wiped her hands on her overalls again and disappeared behind the curtain. Jacob heard rattling noises, mutterings.

He must have been sitting on one of the crates for about half an hour before the woman came out, a mug of coffee in one hand, a large pretzel in the other. "All I've got to offer," she said. "Last folks through ate up my corn pone. Ain't had time make up anythin' else. Maybe a can or two of beans 'round here, though. Real hungry?"

Ignoring her offer, Jacob's excitement grew. "The last folks through? Were they going west, in a wagon?"

"Yes," she said, "man and a woman."

"What did they look like? Were they in a large farm wagon?"

"Say, why you askin'? You from the sheriff or somethin'?"

161

"No," he answered. "No, they might have been – " He hesitated. "They might have been my folks, I'm trying to catch up with them."

"Then you've got a spot of catchin' up to do. They was here late yesterday. It's already late today, Wednesday. At least that's what my old snake oil advertisement calendar on the wall over there says."

Jacob's heart skipped a beat. "Late yesterday? Was it an older man, a pretty young woman with light brown hair, gray-blue eyes?"

"Couldn't take note of the hair, she was wearin' a sunbonnet."

"What color?"

"Don't recall."

"What about the man? "

"Big, tall, stocky like, beard."

He grew more excited. "Did you catch any names?"

She thought a moment. "Heard her call him Clyde."

The floorboards seemed to sink under Jacob's feet. Naomi and Mr. Schmidt apparently had not stopped here. That seemed strange because places along the road were scarce. Surely they'd needed to rest the horse and eat. Disappointed, he only said, "Well, I thank you ma'am, all the same. How much do I owe you for the coffee?"

"Well, nothin' if you'll do somethin' for me. Ain't as strong as I used to be, although able to do much of a man's work 'round here since my man, Mr. Geske, bless his soul, passed away. If you could just take down that box up there on top of that crate? Some parts for a sod plow, shipped all the way from St. Louis. Ordered it for Mr. Barnum, over at the Barnum place. Just set it down here, he'll be in for it directly."

After he'd performed this duty, Jacob hurriedly regained the road. What could have happened to Naomi and Schmidt? It gave him an uneasy feeling to think about the possibilities. "Couple more hours, boy," he said to Prince, stroking his broad neck. "That inn at Menasa – they'd have stopped there for sure. It would have been Monday night, the night before last. That's where we'll stop for the night, too."

He flicked the reins and dug in his heels. "Let's move, boy." Prince broke into a trot. "They must be in Moorhead by now. If Mr. Schmidt had to take care of some business, some legal business, they'll still be there. We'll have to ask around for a law office, but it's a small place and I'm sure we'll find the right one. If not, we'll go directly on to the sheriff's office in Fargo."

The thought of seeing Naomi started his heart racing as well as his imagination. "Just imagine this, Prince. Just picture our first meeting, her apologies, her joy at seeing me, then our return home together. But, you know, Prince, hadn't quite thought about the fact that Mary Frankson's father would be with us. I'd be reminded of Mary every foot of every mile."

His thoughts ran together, imagining this, imaging that. Suddenly he sat bolt upright in the saddle. "What kind of protection do you think that old Mr. Schmidt was able to give her? A lot of things could have happened along the way. Like – like – protection from himself, his urges?"

Prince, however, did not seem to be paying attention to Jacob's urgent questions. He slowed his gait and began to limp. "What's the matter, boy?" Jacob said, leaning across the saddle to look at the horse's legs. "Oh, no!" he exclaimed, pulling back on the reins and quickly dismounting. He lifted up Prince's right foreleg and examined the hoof.

"Thrown a shoe. Now isn't that the worst luck!" He knew that to force Prince to continue very far, even on the soft clay and gravel of the roadway, he might split his hoof and lame himself permanently.

"Well, Prince, boy, what should we do? I might try to get a ride from a passing stranger – no, wait, that woman back in Maplewood said not many were traveling this road, because of the recent storms. And she didn't know how far it was to Fargo. Should have tried to get a map, could have sent off to St. Paul. No time for that, though."

He thought a moment, looking down first one direction, then the other. Taking off his hat to scratch his head, then replacing it, he finally said, "No, Prince, here's what we'll do. Remember that place back there? I remember now seeing a smithy, closed up, but just maybe – " Remounting and turning Prince's head around toward the road east, "I've no choice, Prince, you've put me in a bad way."

After riding back down the road for about a quarter of an hour, he knocked on the closed door of a small barn-like building with the smell of horses about it and a horseshoe hanging above the door. There was no response. He walked around to the side, to the back. No one. He crossed the road over to Geske's Mercantile.

"What? You back already? First you're goin' west, now you're goin' east." The woman looked annoyed. "Hard to get any work done 'round here with all these interruptions by people not able to make up their minds."

"Where's the blacksmith?" Jacob asked.

"Oh, him? Not much business 'round here, as you can see. Well, you might try Barnum's place. He sometimes puts in a little work for him. Go left back down the road, take the first lane right. You'll see a fence, a big red barn."

Jacob had no sooner remounted when she came rushing out, a box in her hand. "Wait – mind takin' this to Barnum? He'll 'preciate it."

He found Barnum's place all right, but it looked deserted, too. "Prince, old boy," he said, "we sure are having a pack of troubles." He dismounted and looked in the barn, then walked over to the house, an expanded and reconverted settler's cabin. "Hello? Mr. Barnum?" he shouted as he knocked on the door.

After no one answered, he was just preparing to mount Prince when two men appeared around the corner of the barn. "What you want?" one of them said, none too friendly.

"Mr. Barnum?"

"Maybe."

"Mrs. Geske sent this package to you."

His manner changed immediately. "Well, I never – if she ain't now got delivery service." Both men laughed. "And who might you be?"

"I'm a man with a horse that needs a shoe."

"Oh, that so?" He turned to the other man. "Well, here's your smithy, all right. Jack and me, we were checkin' out my milk cow. She's by way of bein' poorly. And Jack, here, he's by way of bein' a stock doctor as well as a blacksmith."

Jack lifted up Prince's foreleg. "Hmmm, I see, I see," he said, "looks bad. He won't get far on that, mister. You go on, I'll get my horse, meet you back at the smithy."

As Jacob waited while the smith worked the bellows to fan up the fire, then began to pound an iron rod on the anvil, he grew more and more impatient. Of all the things to happen! It seemed he progressed only to regress, if that was the word. One step forward, two steps back.

"Already gettin' dark," mister," Jack announced as he nailed the finished shoe onto Prince's right hoof. "Plannin' on goin' on?"

"Yes, I must get to Fargo."

"Well, take my advice. Road's bad up ahead, big washout near Menasa. Wouldn't want to come on that in the dark, if I was you."

A helpless feeling came over Jacob. Another check, another obstacle, one step forward and two steps back.

"You're welcome to stay at my place. Got me a little place in back, an extra cot. Maybe I can persuade Hattie Geske to bring us over some supper. She owes you somethin' for deliverin' Barnum's package."

"Thanks," Jacob managed to say, fighting against his disappointment and frustration. "I guess I haven't much choice. I'd be beholding to you."

Leaving Prince in the work stall of the smithy, he followed Jack around back. Clenching his hands, he tried to focus on something more positive, more comforting. *For whatever it's worth,* he thought, *I must think of Naomi, of her confidence in her Lord's strength and wisdom, wisdom guiding ways to deal with bad situations, ways out of difficulties. How does a person pray? What do they say? How do you talk to God? Will he listen?*

But he did, however, remember a few words he'd overheard Naomi say. "Our Father … " he began under his breath," as he waited for Jack to unlock his sleeping quarters behind the smithy, "O God, who's up there somewhere, give us this day a good meal and shelter for the night and lead us not into a hole in the road but deliver us from evil. Amen."

8

Flight

Naomi's present dilemma struck her as cruel and unjustified. It was as if there'd been still another of Job's trials in the flight of the two lawyers without her.

After the Keller family announced over breakfast at Menasa Inn that it might be five days before they left Menasa, Naomi had considered those two men her only chance of getting to Fargo without further delay. Charles Billings implied they would help, and in fact he seemed eager to have her travel in their *faster than the wind* phaeton, as he described it. It could reach Fargo within two or three hours, he claimed, and before she knew it, she'd be at that sheriff's office. Now that chance was gone.

"Didn't they know you wanted to go with them?" Emma asked at the first opportunity. Aware of Naomi's distress, to divert her she'd sent her up to check on Matthew. Glancing at Matthew's breakfast tray Naomi had just brought back down to the kitchen, she said, "How is he? You can put that down here, thanks. Looks like he scarcely touched it."

"He seemed rather anxious," Naomi forced the words out. At the moment it was difficult to focus on Matthew's condition. Turning her thoughts to what was really on her mind, she said, "I thought --- no, I guess those lawyers didn't know. At first I didn't actually refuse their offer. Then I guess they thought I was going with the Kellers. It was – it was a sort of misunderstanding, you see, because those men had left the dining room before the Kellers announced they wouldn't be leaving leave Manesa for the next few days."

Why, oh why, she thought, *didn't I right then seek those men out and I tell them? Why did I just give up and hide in my room? I don't understand why …*

Emma pushed back a strand of black hair, escaped from the bun on the back of her head. As if reading Naomi's thoughts, she commented, "Well, too bad you didn't raise it with those lawyers just then. Still, though, who knows what – " she broke off. "But say, now that you're still here, could you give me a hand? I've got the rest of the dinner to prepare, them potatoes need peelin', the egg whites need to be folded into the *blanc mange* – Birgitta had a light hand for that, dunno 'bout you."

"Where's Birgitta? I thought she'd be here helping you."

"Not yet – that girl! Just after breakfast claimed she wasn't feeling well, homesick, maybe, needed some air, went back up to her room to get her shawl. Should be back by now, unless she got lost, 'though it's pretty hard to get lost in this town." Emma sighed, looking annoyed. "That girl knows full well there's a lot to do just now – Matt, them Kellers and all. First time's she's let me down."

"I'd be glad to start on the potatoes." It was good to have something to do, to take her mind off her disappointment. "Is this Birgitta's apron thrown over the chair?" When Emma nodded, Naomi slipped the long white apron over her green calico, the spare dress with the white lace collar she'd packed in her wicker case, and fastened the ties. The other one Emma had washed and Naomi repacked it in her wicker case. The dress now gave her a strange feeling, reminding her of home and all the times she'd worn it. *I wonder,* she thought, *how often Birgitta thought about her own home, so far away in Sweden?*

Emma handed Naomi an unpeeled potato and a paring knife. "Here, if you don't mind, when you're done with one, drop it into this basin of cold water with the ones I've already peeled. That way they won't turn brown. No, pity you missed that chance to get to Fargo. With those men, though, don't know 'bout that." Taking out a peeled potato from the basin, she turned her attention to slicing the potato on the cutting board.

"Though, *what?* You were going to say --?"

"Well, it's just -- here, you forgot to cut out the bad part of this one." She handed back the potato Naomi had just dropped into a basin of cold water.

"Oh, sorry about the bad spot. I wasn't paying attention. Why didn't I talk to them earlier? Well, I don't know. When the subject came up in my conversation with Mr. Billings – I don't know. It was tempting. Something held me back -- their looks, maybe, the cigar smoke, or maybe just the way they'd stared at me, the way Mr. Billings this morning insisted on taking Matthew's tray in to him. It made me uncomfortable, made me hesitate."

"Imagine Matt's eyes popped out, seein' Mr. Billings with you like that." She laughed. "But you know, thinkin' 'bout it, I'm glad things worked out as they did. Sometimes the Lord knows better than we do what's right, which way to turn. Those men, I ses to Harry when they first come in, somethin' 'bout them makes me uneasy like. Perfect gentlemen, but at the same time -- Reckon that's what I meant by the *though.*"

Emma began laying slices of potato into a deep stoneware bowl, interspersing them with lumps of cheese and milk from a pitcher on the table. "Hand me that salt shaker, will you? Pepper mill, too. Be interestin' to hear what Matt has to say 'bout all this. For all his faults, for all his feelin's about religion, he's got a good heart, that man. Him and Lottie – a good marriage, though not without its ups and downs, 'specially after what happened."

Naomi's interest quickened. "Can you tell me what did happen to Matthew? Every once in a while he says something, some hint about a tragedy in his life, a loss of some kind. I know it's none of my business, that's why I always hesitated to ask him."

"Most likely he wouldn't have told you, anyways. He and Lottie never were ones to talk about it. I must say, it sure didn't do them any good, harborin' it in their deepest heart of hearts all these years, grievin' without closing it off. I don't expect time has helped them get over it. A great pity, that is. No healin', no lessenin' of that sorrow, or guilt, for that matter."

"Can you tell what it was about?"

"This isn't the best time, there still a lot to do, dinner in less than an hour, but I'll try to give you the gist. You may know by now Matt wanted to join the army when the war between the states broke out. But they considered him over age and needed more on the home front. They lived in Indiana, then, down near Kentucky somewhere. He was a school master, fairly big school."

"You know, Emma, I sensed that about him."

"Well, before too long there was a battle goin' on just east of town. Matt gathered the children together – must've been twenty or so of 'em. He thought they'd be safer in the brick church across the road than in the school or bein' sent home, what with shellin', soldiers wanderin' all around shootin'. Anyways, most of their fathers were in the army, some already killed."

Emma stopped and glanced over at the kitchen range, where a large kettle of soup was beginning to boil. "Just a minute, I need to check on somethin'." She got up and slid it to one side. "Now then, where was I?"

"You were saying, Matt took the children into the church. What happened next?"

"Since I never got all the details out of either him or Lottie, I can't tell you exactly. What I do know is that, while they were all takin' cover in the cellar, a shell hit the church and the roof caught fire. Matt tried to get the children out, but a couple walls collapsed and they were trapped. He nearly killed himself, movin' big, heavy timbers, clawin' his way through bricks and stones, finally tryin' to pass the children out through a window, one by one. Before he got the last five out, though – two of them were his own young'uns, Michael and Joey, just little tykes – another wall caved in. Matt managed to carry two of 'em out through the flames, one of them bein' Joey. Others left inside burned to death and Joey died a couple hours later. Took Matt a long time to heal from his own burns. He never did heal, I expect, from somethin' worse."

Naomi had stopped peeling potatoes as Emma's account unfolded. The horror of it was overwhelming, something she could hardly have imagined. It brought sharply to mind the sight of his scarred hands holding Bonnie's reins, the times she'd sensed his sorrow but had no idea of the cause, the sense that he must be carrying some burden of guilt for something in his past.

For a moment or two she could not respond. Finally, she said, greatly moved, "You know, Emma, I think time has not yet healed him. It will take something -- someone -- far beyond that."

Emma looked at her intensely, as if understanding what she meant. "Those are good words," she said, slowly and carefully. "You've spoken wisely, and I thank you for it."

After a pause, slicing another potato or two and continuing to fill the dish until there was no more room except for several pats of butter on top, Emma's mood suddenly changed. "And, speaking of time -- " She glanced up at the round clock on the wall. "Look at the time, will you! Hope that old clock's right. Them weights need pulled up, the thing wound, should remind Harry. Now where's that Birgitta?"

"You said she seemed not well, disturbed about something. Any idea why?"

"Dunno, exactly. Couple days ago she received another letter from home, place called Borgholm. Leastways I think it was from home, don't know for sure. Soon's she opened it, she lifted up a stove lid and threw in the envelope. Can't think of where else she'd get mail from. Those letters always make her homesick, moody like."

"I felt drawn to her, somehow. She seems interesting, hard working. When you think about it, all of our families were immigrants at one time or another. It must be hard for her, out on the plains like this. Are there plains in Sweden?"

"Couldn't tell you anythin' 'bout Sweden for the life of me, only 'bout Wisconsin where I come from. Mostly hills and dells and cows." She picked up the crock of potatoes. "These'll do, looks like only the Kellers and us for the noon dinner." Slipping it into the lower oven, she remarked, "That ham's almost done, needs more bastin' with that honey and mustard sauce. Once everythin's ready, will you take up Matt's dinner tray? He's sure to be gettin' his appetite back. Doc Ferguson ses he'll look in on him early this afternoon. A dirty shame, that wagon crushing his ribs like that." She paused, looking thoughtful. "Nothin' like what happened before, though."

Wiping her hands on her apron, Emma headed for the back door. "Goin' to see whether Birgitta's comin'," she called back. "Where *is* that girl? Annoyin', her goin' off like that, just when I need her."

"Let me know what else I can do," said Naomi. "It's good to keep busy, that way I can use only the think-about-it-*now* part of my brain."

"What did you say?" Emma called back. She was out the back door before Naomi could answer.

She was glad when Matthew's tray was ready and seemed heavier than the earlier ones. It boded well for his recovery.

"Oh my!" he exclaimed, surveying the thick slice of ham, glistening with golden sauce and surrounded by cheesy potatoes, green beans glazed with butter and fresh dill, and a cut glass bowl of *blanc mange*. "Can't -- beat -- Emma's – " It was obvious he was still in pain..

"Don't talk, Matthew. Just try to eat something, that'll make Emma happy, me too." Naomi spread the linen napkin between the tray and his chin. "Can you reach the tray all right? Maybe I'd better cut up the ham."

"Emma – "

"Yes, it looks good, this inn offers a fine table. Now here's a fork, you just dig in. I'm afraid I can't stay, Emma needs help down in the kitchen."

"Swedish girl?"

"Birgitta? She seems a good, reliable worker and quick to learn according to Emma. For some reason, though, she seemed a bit upset this morning, so Emma sent her out for some fresh air. She hasn't come back yet, why I'm down in the kitchen helping out. That's good for me though. I need the distraction."

"Lawyer feller – "

"You mean Mr. Billings, the one that brought in your breakfast tray?" He nodded. "Left with his partner a while ago."

"Fargo?"

"Yes, that's where he said they had their law firm."

"Not – take you?"

Naomi wasn't sure what to tell him. "It didn't seem like the right thing to do," she explained hesitantly. Perhaps that was a partial truth. The whole truth might cause him some distress.

After taking a few bites of the ham, Matthew laid down his fork, a pained look on his face. "I -- bad situation."

"Not your fault, Matthew, I don't know how many times I have to tell you that. No, it was an accident, pure and simple. For whatever reason, it happened, and not your fault."

"Go."

"Go? But you can't go, you can't be moved yet. Not until your cracked ribs heal."

"No, not long -- I – "

"No," Naomi assured him, "not long, you'll be all right, you'll get to Moorhead soon."

Matthew shook his head.

"Of course," she went on, "just do what the doctor says."

He shook his head again and turned away from his dinner tray.

"Here, Matthew, you must eat more, your body needs it."

He looked at her strangely. "Body -- coat – suit coat," he tried to say, pointing to a honey-colored pine chest of drawers against the opposite wall. A small pile of clothes Harry had retrieved from the wagon lay folded on top. Naomi recognized among them Matthew's dress suit jacket, the one he'd put around her for warmth that night in the derelict homestead. "Coat – you wore -- "

"Yes, Matthew, back in that abandoned cabin, and I was so grateful for it."

"Coat – forgive – "

"I'm sorry, I don't understand what you're trying say, Matthew."

He tried to raise in bed himself but fell back against the pillows.

"Later," he said, "later at – at -- "

Naomi was still puzzled. Then she guessed what he was driving at. "But of course, Matthew, you'll be able to wear that later for your meeting with the lawyer in Fargo." She moved the tray closer to him.

He shook his head, pointed to the coat again, and decisively pushed the dinner away.

"Now really, Matthew, " Naomi said impatiently, "I must get back downstairs to help Emma. Let's hope Birgitta's back." She moved the tray on the nightstand closer, again handed him the fork, and readjusted the napkin under his chin. "Do, please, try to eat something, for Lottie's sake -- for my sake. Now I really must get back downstairs."

He nodded, seemingly resigned to something.

At that moment, Naomi could not help but regard him with pity, that strong, virile man, lying now pale and helpless. *My heart goes out to him*, she thought, *what has happened. All my feelings – changed from attraction and desire to something else. I only know I don't want to leave him. Yet I must – is this another one of Job's tests?*

As she caressed briefly his cheek in both pity and anguish, he caught her hand. "No wait – don't go."

"No, really, Matthew, Emma needs me."

"Wait – " he repeated, pointing again to the pile of things on top of the dresser. "Oil skin – packet – "

Naomi left his bedside and lifted the slim packet of papers off the dresser. It crackled slightly from the papers inside. "You want to look through these?" she asked.

"No," he answered. "You."

"Me? You want me to look through them? But really, Matthew, they're none of my business."

"No – take – " he made more of an effort to speak. "Take – urgent … name lawyer packet."

At first she didn't understand what he meant. Then it dawned on her that, given the delay because of his condition, he want- ed her to take care of his business in Moorhead. "Oh, I see Matthew," she said, however uncertain she was about how to do this, or even how she was ever going to get to Moorhead. "Of course, Matthew, don't worry, I'll take care of it." Slipping the packet under her arm, then replacing the fork in his hand, she said, "I'm sorry, now I really must get back down to the kitchen. But I'll be back up soon for that tray – and I expect to see all that food gone."

By the time Naomi got back to the kitchen after leaving his room and stopping by her own to toss the packet onto her bed, Emma seemed more than overwhelmed. "I can't imagine where that Birgitta's got to," Emma blurted out, "unless it was in them woods you got lost in the other night. She knows it's dinner time, them folks out in the dinin' room ready to be fed, surprised those children not bangin' their forks on the table already."

"Here, I'll take in that tray with the soup course. Places at the table set?"

"Birgitta did that after she'd cleared off the breakfast things. Thankful for that, at least."

The Kellers seemed surprised Naomi wasn't joining them but wearing an apron and in and out of the kitchen. "What's happened?" asked Lillian Keller.

"Want Naomi sit here," demanded Robbie, patting the chair beside him.

"No, I'm sorry," she said, "I can't. But I'll be seeing whether you eat up all those beans, young man." Then, to Mrs. Keller, "Mrs. Barnes needed some help, with Birgitta temporarily indisposed."

"That's a pity. Well, I hope she'll be all right soon. Perhaps it's fortunate for Mrs. Barnes that we've decided to leave."

"Decided to leave? Right now? For Moorhead?" She could not believe her ears.

"No, not for Moorhead," explained Mr. Keller. "My aunt here in town seems to have plenty of space. *No need paying good money for that inn*, she said this morning. We'd originally just stopped by for a brief visit, you see. Now at her place the children will have to sleep on quilts on the floor, but no matter. We can make it a sort of adventure for them."

"Adventure? With pirates?" Carl Keller looked up eagerly.

"I see." Naomi set down the heavy tray on the edge of the table. "So that means you're not going on to Fargo just yet, then?"

"No, maybe another four days or so. Depends on how long my aunt can take all this *adventure*." Mr. Keller smiled and looked pointedly at Carl and his brothers. "Do you think you can still wait that long, Miss Beckman? You're still welcome to travel with us."

"We can still squeeze you in," Mrs. Keller added encouragingly.

"Perhaps – perhaps," Naomi responded slowly. "It all depends." *I'm not sure what it depends upon,* she was thinking. *There seem to be no other options, unless through one of the Lord's miracles, like finding that Matthew was suddenly cured and able to drive a wagon to Fargo. Or that I found myself able to borrow or horse or wagon from the Barnes and making it there on my own. Yet Pa never taught me how to drive a wagon … and it's still a long way on my own. Could that be part of the miracle?*

But Dr. Ferguson, stopping by just after the noon dinner, could not vouch for a miracle from the Lord. Speaking quietly to Emma and Naomi in the front hall, he looked concerned. "The man must remain as immobile as possible, at least for the next week." Picking up his bag from the hall table, he added, "Keep a careful watch for any sign of fever."

Once the doctor's buggy rolled out of the stable yard, Naomi joined Emma back in the kitchen. "Fever, Emma? What do you think that means?" Emma merely shook her head.

"Any sign of Birgitta yet?"

"No," Emma, sighed, hands on hips, shaking her head again. "Now I'm really concerned. It's not like her at all. What could have happened?"

"She's never been this long away before?" Naomi asked.

"No, although I've never seen her like she was just after breakfast. Now that I think on it, the letter she got – stage coach dropped off the mail as they usually do Mondays and Fridays – she carried it around in her apron pocket since then, readin' it whenever she could, whenever she thought I weren't lookin', seemed upset every time. Say, you're wearin' her apron. Is that letter still in the pocket?"

As Naomi reached into the deep pocket, her finger tips touched a folded piece of paper. She drew it out and spread it open on the kitchen table. "There's just this letter, no envelope, so no postmark, just a date at the top. And it's all in what I guess is Swedish. Anyway, here it is:"

Lördag 13 september

Min älskade fästmö,

Nyheter från farbror Einar I S. Pol säger att du är rätt placerad. Jag vet inte hur länge

ditt kontrakt sträker sig, men jag ber dig att lämna värdshuset så snart som möjligt och

komma med mig.

Här är min plan. Gå till järnvägsstationen nästa torsdag. Jag ska träffa dig

där och vi kan ta fem och fyrtiofem-tåget till slutstationen kalama.

Om jag inte är där, eller om du missar tåget, har jag bokat ett rum på hotel under mitt

namn. Stanna där over natten och ta tåget på morgonen. Jag ser fram emot att vi åter

kan få vara tillsammans.

Din hängivna

E.

Might've known it'd be in Swedish," exclaimed Emma. "Can you make out anythin'?"

Naomi looked at it carefully, trying hard to make out a word here, a word there. "Looks like it's dated September 13th. Don't know the weekday, though."

"Who's it from?"

"Just signed E. There's another E, looks like Einar. Some words look like English -- maybe *kontrakt* for *contract?*"

"How about the names of places? That might give us a clue."

"No, not really." She re-read the letter. "Oh, wait, here's something that looks like *S. Pol* – maybe St. Paul."

"Why on earth there, I wonder. Such a long way east of here. Well, not much help, that letter. Just put it over on the sideboard, 'til she comes back. And all this work, them Kellers leavin'. Beds got to be changed, rooms cleaned, slop jars emptied. And now this pile of dishes from both breakfast and the noon dinner. Well, Naomi, let's get started."

Shortly afterward, while they were still drying and putting away the last of the pots and pans, Harry Barnes came into the kitchen from the barn. "Birgitta back yet?"

"No. Seen her anywhere around out there?"

'No, can't say as I have."

"Say," Emma suddenly asked, "she couldn't have left with those lawyers, could she?"

"No, they left alone in that phaeton, just the two of them."

"Then I'm even more worried. Think somethin' happened to her?"

"You checked her room up in the attic?" he asked.

"Hadn't thought of that. I'll do it now." Emma set down her dishtowel and headed for the stairs.

"So now, Miss Naomi, how's my cousin, Matt doin'?"

"Still confined to bed for the next week or so. The doctor seemed concerned, wouldn't say exactly why."

"Not to worry, he's right hardy for his age, and I'll be sorry to see him leave, once he's fit. Not to mention them Kellers.

I just got their surrey and team ready, it's waitin' in the yard, they're loadin' it up. So once they leave, this old place'll seem empty. Don't expect much in the way of travelers, what with winter comin', bad weather on the roads. Folks do well to stay home."

"What'll you do all that time?"

"Oh, we usually spend this time catchin' up, repairin' tack and so forth, Emma cannin' stuff, makin' preserves and such for the cellar. Do us for the winter, I 'spect. Bunch of ladies quiltin'."

Emma rushed back into the room, her usually rosy face drained of color. "She's gone! Bed made up nice and neat. Cupboard empty." Out of breath she added, "Found only this note." She handed it to Naomi. "Here, what does it say?"

Naomi looked at its words, scrawled on a sheet of paper, evidently torn out of Emma's household accounts book. She tried pronouncing them, *"Det var mitt eget beslut. Tak. Birgitta Magnusson."* I can't tell you," she said, "except that *Tak* must mean thanks, and then her name, *Birgitta Magnusson*. I wish I could understand the other words, but they're meaningless to me, just like the letter from whomever it was."

"She's run off, that's what it means!" Harry Barnes pushed back his chair so hard that it fell over backwards. "The girl's run off, 'fore her contract's up. She's out on the road somewhere, makin' her way – east or west -- the Lord knows where."

"Maybe east – St. Paul?" Emma looked more than upset – more, Naomi thought –like she'd lost somebody, somebody she really cared for, never mind losing just a hired *piga*. "Why would she do that? We certainly haven't mistreated her, not like some folks I've heard about takin' on foreign help. How far do you think she's got to by now?"

"When did you first miss her?" Harry asked.

"Just after she got through the breakfast dishes, 'bout nine or so."

"That's a good four hours."

Harry was pulling on his jacket. "I'm going after her," he said. "No telling what'll happen to her. Out alone on the road, like that."

"But which direction?"

"Don't know, Emma."

"That letter – " offered Naomi. "It mentioned both St. Paul – you can't possibly hope to follow her all the way there!"

He looked taken back. "Reckon not, if that's the way she went. No way I could manage that."

For an instant, Naomi closed her eyes and tried to imagine herself as a young Swedish immigrant, looking for somewhere to go, somewhere she knew about, somewhere where there was family. "You said she had a relative somewhere out west? Where was that?"

"She never said, exactly. Always seemed unwilling to talk about it."

Harry smacked his hand to his forehead. "Out west – could be anywhere, farther than St. Paul even." He thought a moment. "But say, come to think of it, if that's the case, it means she's got to go through Moorhead first, that's the only main road."

"What are you going to do?" Emma asked in concern. "A person can walk a quite a few miles in four hours, 'specially if they're determined. Evidently Birgitta was."

"I'll hitch up the wagon 'cause the buggy's got a cracked wheel. I'm sure I can catch up to her before she gets that far. Best hurry – back when I can."

Naomi stood leaning against the kitchen counter for support. Her legs felt weak, her head swam. "Wait – wait – " was all she could force out.

"Can't wait," answered Harry, sitting down to pull on his boots, "got to try to catch up with her before she gets into real trouble."

"Wait – for – me!" Naomi pounded her way dangerously up the steep back stairs. Frantically she tore off Birgitta's apron and pulled out her shawl and wicker case from the wardrobe, leaving the door wide open. Jamming in her other dress, the blue and white gingham Emma had washed along with her shift and other things, she fastened the catch. Starting out of the room, she suddenly remembered her black velvet reticule, containing all the money she had. Snatching it off the nightstand, she noticed Matthew's packet of papers lying on the bed and tucked it under one arm.

Passing by the open wardrobe door, she realized she'd forgotten her black straw bonnet with the silk lilac flowers and jammed it on her head. Her blue sunbonnet had been lost in the woods several nights ago. Once back out into the hall, she headed down the kitchen stairs two at a time.

Emma stared at her aghast, at the same time moving to block the back door. "You're not – You're not thinkin' of – "

"Yes I am," Naomi cried. "Don't you see – the chance I've been waiting for, the Lord-given chance. Sorry about Birgitta – but we'll catch up, she'll be all right, Harry – take -- to – Moorhead – Fargo – my father – "

"But Naomi – "

"Tell Matthew – " she was already in the mud room, pushing aside boots, flinging jackets out of the way. Tell him – not to worry – take care." The back door slammed behind her.

She reached Harry's wagon just as it turned the corner between the house and the barn. Grabbing on to the tailgate, she heaved herself over and fell into the wagon bed. "Going – with – you – " she gasped.

He turned around from the driving bench in surprise. "Whoa, there, whoa," he shouted to the team as he stopped the wagon and threw forward the brake lever. "What did you say, you're goin' with me?"

Naomi scrambled over the length of the wagon bed and climbed onto the bench beside him. "Yes, Harry. Let's get moving – we can't waste any more time."

"Now wait a minute there. Oh yes, we can. You're not goin' with me, not by a long shot. So get down outta this wagon, Miss Naomi. Hear me?"

"But don't you see, Harry," she insisted. "You may need help. Birgitta will need help."

"I'll manage that," his hand still on the brake lever.

"Look, here's all I have to say. You know how desperate I am to get to Fargo?"

"Heard that often enough, one way or t'other."

"Well, here's what I propose, I'll make a bargain with you." Her face flushed in desperation, her hand gripped Harry's jacket sleeve more tightly. "Listen! I'll go with you toward Moorhead until we find Birgitta. She could already have walked quite a few miles down the road, she could already be part-way there. It's only about ten or twelve miles from here, right?" He nodded. "If we do find her, then I'll come back to Menasa with you, and find some other way to go on."

"So what if not?"

"Then you take me on to Fargo and we look for her there."

He stared at her in astonishment. "That last thing – that's a tall order. Moorhead's a pretty big place. Fargo big, too."

"Please, Harry Barnes. I've got to reach my father."

He sat there for a full minute. "I dunno, I dunno. Emma, lot of work."

"She'll be all right, Kellers leaving, there's nobody staying at the inn just now. Business slacking off, you said so yourself. There's people around town could help, aren't there?"

"Reckon so," he answered slowly. "Got the church ladies."

"And you'd be back tomorrow early. Maybe even by this evening."

"Maybe. Depends."

"Well, then – "

He hesitated before he gradually, reluctantly and by slow degrees, pulled back on the brake lever. The wagon began to roll forward, even before he flicked the reins and the team responded.

The late September sun still beat down on the heavily rutted road, left more hazardous from the heavy rains of several days ago. Naomi sat on the edge of the driving bench, straining her eyes forward for any sign of Birgitta. She'd placed her black velvet reticule and Matthew's oil packet under her feet in the event of any sudden jolt, any further mishap, and tied the bonnet strings tightly under her chin.

Harry remained silent, concentrating on managing the team around the various holes, rocks, and fallen branches. Finally, he glanced at her with an accusatory look and muttered, "Lord help us."

Harry's accusatory look – I guess I deserve it, Naomi considered. *I think I know I'm asking too much. Outstripped the bounds, you might say. Same goes for agreeing to go with Matthew to Moorhead. Look where it got him. And I also think – but I'm not quite sure – I shouldn't have asked Jacob to take me to Fargo. Maybe he realized that. Maybe he was right to refuse.*

Harry lapsed into a steady silence. It seemed helpful in some ways. Naomi's mind wove in and out of fragmented prayers, bringing up thoughts of her father and the urgency of her journey … thoughts of Jacob … what he was doing. *Is it possible,* she asked herself, *he might try to come after me? No, not a chance. He made his situation, his feelings for me, perfectly clear.*

Harry's wagon was now well out of town. Before them the road stretched in a remarkably straight line ahead, toward where the sun was beginning to descend, and straight into a brisk wind off the plains. Naomi shivered and pulled her shawl more closely around her shoulders. Open plains stretched out on either side, creating an unnerving sense of vastness, of isolation. They had become so much a part of her, both physically and mentally. *Naomi of the Plains.*

Naomi's fragmented and confused thoughts turned from the landscape surrounding her to the Swedish girl, Birgitta, wandering in it and alone. Birgitta of the Plains. Had she left a sweetheart back in Sweden? Had she asked him to go with her to the land of Moab and he refused? Was she longing for him?

Her heart went out to the girl, stranded in a strange country, hardly knowing the language. Her attractiveness was also a liability. She was fair prey for any unscrupulous person to pick up. And Birgitta, Naomi was now convinced, had already been picked up along the road by the lawyers from Fargo. *Fair prey, easy prey. Like me, like me,* she concluded.

9

Questions and Answers

Watching anxiously both sides of the road and the plains beyond, Naomi and Harry Barnes looked for any sign of Birgitta Magnusson. "What was she wearing?" Harry asked, "do you know?"

"Impossible to tell," Naomi answered. "Emma said she'd taken what few clothes she had. She might have had time to change into something besides her working dress, the black and white striped one I've seen her in."

"Now if I were a woman – thankful I'm not," Harry observed, "and were headin' out some place special, I'd put on my best togs, my best hat."

"Did you ever see her in that? What were they like?"

"Not much of a man for women's finery. But I do recall seein' her once, comin' back from church, in a black dress, bit of white lace 'round the top. Big hat – real big, lots of stuff piled on top."

"That's some help, I suppose." She couldn't help but smile at Harry's remark. She, too, had snatched up her bonnet at the last moment, although it wasn't as grand as all that, simply an old-fashioned kind of black straw bonnet to which she'd added some small silk lilies, bought at Hanson's last Easter. *My old blue bonnet would have been more practical*, she considered, *too bad I lost it somewhere back there, probably in those woods.*

"Seems mighty strange, not any sign of her yet."

"Can't you make this team go any faster?"

"Goin' fast as it's safe, this here road bein' what it is. Would've been faster in the buggy, of course. Sorry I never got 'round to fixin' that wheel, but things got too busy."

"What time is it?"

Harry switched both reins over to his left hand, reached down into his pocket, and pulled out a chain with a large watch at the end. Opening the lid and putting it to his ear, he said, "It's runnin', anyways. Let's see, now, ses four o'clock, no, 'bout half-past."

"How far do you think we've come?"

"Hard tellin', exactly. Maybe six miles, little more. That's just over half way."

Naomi's heart sank. "that means at this rate, it'll be at least another hour, maybe two, before we reach Moorhead. Now if my guess about Birgitta's being picked up by those men in the phaeton is worth anything, she'll already be there. But where, do you think?"

"It sure is a guessin' game, for that matter. Can't very well drive up and down the streets in the dark." He thought a moment. "Reckon, though, by this time those lawyers would have taken her somewhere."

"Is there a hotel in Moorhead?"

"Couple of 'em, big one, the Walker House, on the main street."

"How about a boarding house?"

"A couple, I recollect."

"How about a railroad?"

"Yes, Northern Pacific comes through there, seen them buildin' a big trestle bridge. Train goes across to Fargo, couple miles beyond that. Still workin' on the line, braggin' 'bout trains goin' all the way to Seattle on the west coast." He slapped his knee, adding, "Now wouldn't *that* be somethin'?" He paused and added, "Say, now I think on it, there's also a hotel near the station, forget its name, not as grand as the Walker, though."

"How about Fargo? The train, hotels? Mr. Billings, the lawyer, said their office is in Fargo."

"Seems right. Not too familiar with that side of the river, though, only been there once."

"Do they live in town?"

"Wouldn't know that for sure. Lotsa folks live in one place, work in another. Gettin' back and forth, though, 'tween Moorhead and Fargo – not so easy with that ferry and all. That is, if those lawyers live in Moorhead. Could even be a town outside of Fargo, on 'tother side." He sighed, flicked the reins over the horses' rumps, and added, shaking his head, "You sure do ask a lot of questions, miss. Could tire a man out."

"Sorry, don't mean to." Naomi thought about Harry's last remark. *It's true, I've asked so many over this last week. Let's see, if today is Thursday, how many days since that conversation with Jacob on my front porch? Yes, seven days, and six days since the harvest picnic and when I asked Matthew to take me to Fargo. And since then I've asked the Kellers to take me, now Harry Barnes to take me. But of course, the biggest question is still unanswered – about my father. Is this all for nothing?*

Then, thinking aloud, "So many questions. Suppose he hadn't? Was all this for nothing?"

"What's that, miss? Who didn't do somethin' for nothin'?"

"Doesn't matter, Harry, just trying to answer some of my own questions."

"Hope all them answers are comin'," he said. "Big one right now is 'bout Birgitta. Whatever could have gotten into her? Plague take the woman." Interrupting his train of thought, he pointed over to the left, "See that big red barn over there? Boswell place? Means only two more miles. But as I was sayin', wouldn't trust those law folks, saw them gawkin' at her often enough. They might have something to do with her leavin'."

Uncomfortable, Naomi remembered all too well their stares at her. "That's what I'm thinking, too. If she intended to go to Moorhead, she certainly knew that's where those lawyers were heading. It's possible she asked them to take her to Moorhead – or wherever she wanted to go. Maybe they planned it together, and she got packed up right after breakfast sometime, never did do the dishes."

"Well, all I know is, she wasn't around after I hitched up them bays, feisty pair of critters I might add, weren't easy, went back into the barn to see if I'd left any tack layin' in the stalls. Took me a while, 'cause old Ginger, the cow, kicked over a milk bucket I forgot to take in to Emma. Got that cleaned up, checked the stalls them bays was in. Then, by the time I come out, them fellers was already headin' out the stable yard, faster'n a shot out of a cannon. Then I sees you comin' out of the back door like some kind of mad woman, wavin' your arms, shoutin'." He flicked the reins. "Nope, to answer your question, I didn't see Brigitta get into that phaeton."

They rode in silence for another half-mile or so until Harry pointed off to a wooden frame house on the right. "See that?

Belongs to a feller named Myers, owns the feed store in town. Done business with him often enough."

"Does that mean we're coming into Moorhead?" It was useful, she contemplated, having those landmarks to measure time and distance. She hadn't paid much attention traveling with Matthew.

"That's right, you'll see, just 'round the next bend. Road drops down from there all the way to the river, the town spread out mostly couple miles 'long the bank, Fargo on t'other side."

Harry's observations proved the case, for the wagon rolled along the road past a series of houses and other structures, built increasingly closer together. Several church spires rose up in the distance out of a spread-out pattern of roofs and smoking chimneys.

"Go slow now, Harry, keep an eye out for Birgitta."

"Got to keep my eye mostly on this here road," he muttered, somewhat annoyed. "Didn't 'spect so much comin' and goin', wagons, buggies, carts. Might just run over a dog or two. But I'll look on the right side when I can, you take the left."

They'd now entered Moorhead's Main Avenue, leading into the center of town. As they veered left, brick-fronted stores and occasional wooden structures lined both sides of the street. Noise erupted from a hostelry on one corner with sounds of laughter, a piano. People were coming in and out of a large hotel between a mercantile and a hardware store, obviously the Walker House. A restaurant seemed to be part of the building, with large glass windows fronting the street.

"Stop, Harry," Naomi said. "Can you tether the horse over there? I'll look in the restaurant."

"You want me to look in that there saloon? You think that girl's in there?"

"Unlikely, but the lawyers could be. And don't be tempted to stay in there long, hear? And while you're there, you might ask about them. They must be fairly well known around here."

About five minutes later, Naomi returned to the wagon and waited for Harry. When he arrived he smelled slightly of drink. "Find her?" she asked. "No sign of her in the restaurant, she said, "so I went to the hotel's front desk to make enquiries. No one had seen her, no one knew of her."

"Not a hide nor hair in that there hostelry, either. Did talk to a few fellers, though. Knew 'bout Billings and Fletcher, not regulars, mind you, but in there time to time. Nope, hadn't seen 'em today at all, but they thought they lived across the river in Fargo."

"How about that other hotel you mentioned, the one near the station?"

"I think it's next street up, another block and then down First Avenue North." After reining the horse in that direction, he said, "Yup, there it is, the Great Northern."

The station across from the Great Northern Hotel was full of activity. A train had just pulled in, its engine still emitting blasts of steam. Crowds of people carrying bags, packages, and valises were crowding along the platform and swarming out into waiting buggies and wagons along the street.

"No place to pull up," said Harry in frustration.

"Then you keep the wagon moving along slowly in front of the hotel, and I'll just run in and ask at the front desk."

She pushed open the swinging glass doors and rushed through the lobby to what she guessed was the front desk. "I'm looking for someone," she asked, out of breath.

The clerk, in a smart-looking uniform, trimmed with the initials *NP* on his breast pocket, looked up from a pile of keys he was sorting.

"A registered guest, madam?"

'I don't know whether she's registered or not."

"Well then, madam, how can I – "

"She may only have just arrived. She's a tall, very attractive blonde woman, wearing a large hat with flowers or ribbons or something piled on top of it."

He thought a moment, looking out over the lobby. "There are several ladies of that description here, madam. Do you see her?"

Naomi looked in the direction the clerk pointed. She was certain none of them was Birgitta. "Maybe she has already registered," she pleaded. "It's very important I find her. The name is Miss Birgitta Magnusson."

"Sorry, madam, our Register is kept confidential."

"But please, sir, it may be a matter of life or death." For all she knew, this was true.

The desk clerk hesitated, then reluctantly brought up the Register from behind the counter, turned it around, and opened it before her.

Naomi scanned first one page for the day, then the next. Several names caught her eye – *Mr. and Mrs. C. P. Olson and daughter, Mr. E. Pietersson, Mr. and Mrs. F. Kloke, Miss G. Johannson, Mr. and*

Mrs. L. Lundgren, Mr. and Mrs. C. Fryer. Mrs. B. Ericksson. But the names meant nothing. Yet what if Birgitta had registered under another name, and there was nothing to prevent her from doing so – or even registering with a man posing as her husband – one of the lawyers under an assumed name?

Disappointed, she rushed out, forgetting to thank the clerk, and caught up with Harry's wagon, already moving slowly past the Great Northern Hotel.

"Couldn't find a place to tie up," he said, "had to keep movin'. Well? Anythin'? Needn't ask, though, because I can see by the look on your face."

"What time is it?"

"You can't see that big clock in the steeple over there? If it's right, it's goin' on half-past five."

"We could take the ferry across to Fargo."

"What good would that do? Doubt them lawyers still in their office this late."

"Please, Harry. It's a chance we have to take. If they picked her up, they'll know where she is. You know, as well, that Fargo is also the key to finding my father."

"Dunno," he muttered. "Got to get back to Menasa. Emma'll be anxious."

"But Harry, it's already too late to go back, you can't travel that road at night, you said so yourself, or somebody said that."

"Dunno," he repeated. Taking off his straw hat, then scratching his head, and finally replacing the hat, he conceded, "I suppose we might as well get across to Fargo, spend the night there, though can't for the life of me think where, how much it'll cost. Then I'll head back to Menasa in the mornin'. And if'n you know what's good for you, miss, you'll head back with me, just like you said."

The brick road descending down to the docks along the Red River was steep. Several times Harry's team slipped where the bricks were wet, suddenly swerving the wagon and almost colliding with piles of bales, stacks of barrels, and empty wagons and handcarts all jammed together along each side. There was a lot of movement of people and horses, and cacophonous noises from every direction, particularly down closer to the docks, as well as the smells of tar, hemp, and horse manure.

Harry braked the wagon near the ferry dock, at the end of which was moored a large, flat-bottomed boat with rope handrails around the sides. A small, wooden hut, just large enough for the operator, sat on the deck at one end. The ferry looked nearly full, with several wagons, three or four buggies, at least a half-dozen horses, and a large number of people on foot all waiting for departure.

Naomi stood up in the wagon to read the sign over the entrance, giving times and fares. "Let's see now, *Departures 7, 12, 4, 6.* Then it lists all the fares. Looks like *Wagons, Loaded, 50¢.*" A bell on the boat's deck began to ring. "Oh, this must be the last crossing. We've just made it, Harry, and that's a good sign."

Yes, indeed, she thought, a sign … signs along the way … the first time something had worked out … the right timing had fallen into place. *Oh thank you, Lord, for showing me the way. Open the way ahead for me* … She reached down into her reticule for a fifty-cent piece.

The ferry was winched across the river by means of a cable, slack enough to lie on the riverbed once they'd passed. "Allows them big sternwheelers to pass over the cable, until they get a lift bridge built across," Harry explained. "They come down river all the way from Grand Forks, maybe farther north than that, Canada, maybe, to Ft. Abercrombie and beyond that. Wouldn't be surprised if they come into the Minnesota – that river'd take 'em all the way to the grand old Mississippi. Good way to travel, fast and easy." He smiled as he added, "Maybe not fast, but it'd sure would beat this rough wagon, these old nags."

Since Harry's wagon was the last to load, it was also the last to unload. Naomi felt keenly the delay as one by one people, wagons, buggies, and horses exited and crossed the ramp onto the dock. Time was passing, while the urgency of the task facing them increased.

"Crazy idea, if'n you ask me," Harry grumbled as they came off the ferry onto the dock. "How do you expect to find her here? Already nearly dark, them gas lights 'long the main street don't help much." He urged the team up from the wharf, past Second Street and onto Main Avenue.

As Naomi looked down its length, she saw it was lined with storefronts much like those in Moorhead. Most were dark and closed for the day. At the corner of Fourth and Main they passed a small hotel with a large sign in gilt letters against a green background, *The Lodge*. It seemed a much more modest establishment than the Walker House or the Great Northern in Moorhead, just the sort of inconspicuous place the lawyers might have taken Birgitta.

"Stop, Harry, let me look there." Rushing into the lobby, she saw two older men reading newspapers in one corner, a younger man in a dress suit behind the registration desk.

"I'm looking for someone,' she asked.

"Is he a registered guest, ma'am?"

"It's a lady, a lady with a large hat."

The clerk smiled. "Large hat, you said? Most ladies wear large hats these days, latest Paris fashion, you know. Our establishment prides itself on keeping up with such things. You'll notice our new portière at the entrance?"

Ignoring his remarks, Naomi raised her voice. "Her name is Birgitta Magnusson, would you please look in your register." The men in the corner looked up briefly from behind their newspapers.

Reluctantly, it seemed, the clerk glanced at his register. "No, ma'am, I can tell you there's been no guest of that name. In fact, the only guests so far today are a family with three children, those two railroad men over there, and an elderly couple."

"No luck?" Harry asked as Naomi climbed back up on the wagon.

"Afraid not," she said disappointedly. "But I'm thinking we should try the law office."

"What? Billings and Fletcher?"

"Yes, it must be near here. Don't you think it'd be located in the main part of town, most likely in one of these buildings? Do you think you could find out?"

Drawing the wagon up alongside a man pushing a handcart, Harry leaned down and asked, "Say, mister, do you live here?"

"Yup," he answered, looking up. "Sellin' tack, just picked up a shipment of leather over in Moorhead."

"Well, then, can you tell me where we can find the law office of Billings and Fletcher?"

"Couldn't tell you, don't have anythin' to do with the law, not if I can help it," he laughed, and moved ahead of the wagon to turn down a side street.

"We'll just start looking, Harry. It's got to be on this street, or another one leading off of it."

Slowly he drove the wagon down the length of Main Avenue, and, although there were clusters of pedestrians walking along the boardwalk, Birgitta did not appear to be among them.

"Look, Harry!" Naomi cried, pointing to an office up above a drug store on the corner, where a light shone through both windows. " Maybe that's it. Stop, I'll get out and read the sign on the door to the upstairs."

To her relief, the brass plaque beside the door read *Billings and Fletcher, Attorneys at Law*. "It's here, Harry, it's here. I'm going up." Opening the door she turned back. "No, you'd better come with me."

It seemed quiet as they mounted the stairs, with no sounds coming from the office. Naomi knocked on the door at the top of the stairs, holding her breath, hoping Birgitta was in there, hoping her suspicions were right, but also hoping Birgitta was safe.

After a long wait, the door was cautiously opened by an elderly woman in a long gray apron, a kerchief around her hair and a mop in her hand. "Well – what is it?" she said crossly. "If you're looking for them lawyers, they've gone. This office is closed, can't you read?"

Naomi looked at Harry. It was difficult to suppress her disappointment. What was she going to say now, what were they to do? Finally, she stammered, "No – I mean yes – I mean when did they leave?"

"Usual time, half-past five or so. Well, no, come to think of it, this wasn't what you'd call a usual day. They'd been gone more'n a week, you see, so I figured I'd come a little early so's they could tell me what they wanted done. They also owed me some past wages. They'd hardly come, looked through some papers, picked up another stack of 'em, before they said they was leaving early today because of some urgent business for a lady."

"A *lady*?" Harry and Naomi together.

"What did this lady look like?" Naomi asked, both excited and disappointed.

"Didn't see her."

"You didn't see her? She didn't come up to the office?"

"No, missus."

"It's already soundin' hopeless, Naomi," said Harry. "All this for nothin', absolutely nothin'. A wild goose chase, if you ask me. Come on, let's go. We've got to find a decent place to stay tonight."

But Naomi wasn't ready to give up. "You said they had some urgent business for a lady. Did they mention where she was, where they were going?"

"No, missus. They don't usually discuss their affairs with me. Wouldn't be proper, like, would it?" She shifted her mop to the other hand and started to close the door, then hesitated. "No, come to think of it. When I got here, must've been just after four, Mr. Billing's phaeton was tethered downstairs at the rail, like it usually is when he's here. I remember I couldn't help staring at it, though I know that ain't proper, either."

"Was there someone – "

"Yes, couldn't see her very well, 'cause of those isinglass curtains, you see. They was all closed up."

"Did you see anything at all of her?"

"Only her hat, big hat, with a bunch of red flowers on top, big black bow standing up high on top of them, almost reached the top of the phaeton. My, I said to myself, a hat like that'd sure be hard to manage in a high wind."

"That's hers!" Harry said emphatically.

"Do you know where Mr. Billings or Mr. Fletcher live?" Naomi asked. Harry glanced at her, his thoughts easy to read. *Are we going to go all over town now, tracking them down?*

"No, missus, I don't. They do all their work here in the office, come in most days. Or in court, some times out of town, like last week. All the way to St. Paul." She was becoming uncomfortable, shifting from one foot to another, the signal for them to leave.

"We thank you, ma'am," said Harry. "We'll be on our way, then."

They were half-way down the stairs when the woman called after them. "Do know, for a fact, Mr. Fletcher lives out of town somewhere. His uncle has a farm. Sometimes he brings in things for me, like tomatoes, corn. Much appreciated, I'm sure."

Naomi sighed. "That's still not much help," she commented to Harry, once they'd remounted the wagon. "Now we know, Harry, but we don't know enough. Where'd they take her? Where is she now, I wonder?"

"Could be anywhere. Out at that farm, even – wherever it is. It'd be like lookin' for a needle in a haystack. Especially at night. Let's go, then," he said, as flicked the reins, "we've got to find us some place for the night. Must be well after seven, already dark."

Naomi was becoming increasingly uncomfortable. *Here I am,* she thought, *once again having to spend the night alone with a relative stranger. I guess I never considered that, so anxious about getting to Fargo and chasing after Birgitta. I even forgot all about my father. Oh, Lord, forgive me … And yet, and yet, I feel such compassion for Birgitta, another woman, vulnerable, far from home, just like me. How can I get around this distraction, this conflict, this guilt?*

Riding beside Harry Barnes in his wagon through the darkened streets, lit only by the sickly greenish glow from an occasional gas light, she was finally forced to recognize what she'd done, what she'd committed herself to. It had started with accepting Matthew Schmidt's offer of a ride to Fargo. Prayer, which before had come so readily, came now so hesitantly and incoherent. "Heavenly Father – help – know – forgive – "

"What's that, miss?"

"Nothing, Harry." It was, in fact, very close to *nothing*. It was as if the Lord had broken her and reduced her to nothing. Naomi, not of the Plains, but rather *Naomi of the Nothing*.

They'd been going east back down to the river on one street, then west up the next street … and the next and the next. They were guided by infrequent gas lights or light from an oil lamp spilling out from some window. "Can't go on much longer," said Harry. "Team's tired long since, and it's getting colder. You've only got that shawl?"

Although glad for the shawl, her mother's prayer shawl, Naomi was shivering in her thin cotton dress. How foolish not packing warmer clothes. Foolish in another sense, dashing off today with Harry Barnes on what was turning out to be a wild goose chase. "I'll be all right," shivering as she said it, "long as we can find someplace for the night soon."

Another two streets, another three blocks, when they found it. Light came from a single upstairs window of a large stone house, its gingerbread eaves around an encircling porch a striking feature even in the semi-darkness. "Look, miss," Harry almost shouted. "That sign hanging on the picket fence – *Mrs. Ransom's Boarding House, Excellent Beds, Enquire Within.* Seems almost too good to be true."

"Do you think she'll have a room – rooms?"

"Dunno 'til we ask. You wait here." He handed her the reins.

Naomi watched anxiously as Harry opened the wicket gate, went up the walk, and crossed the broad porch to the front door. Raising the brass knocker, he struck it several times, the thudding sound reverberating into the quiet night. After what seemed a long wait, a wavering light from an oil lamp or a candle was visible through the oval glass window in the door. At the same time, several lights appeared faintly what must have been the parlor window and several windows upstairs.

I don't like this place, was Naomi's response. *Is it the isolation? There's only one other house on this street, way down at the far end, where the town's gaslights end. Total darkness beyond of the countryside. Yes, I think I can still hear the muffled sounds of Main Avenue, but way out there – only open plains, the yelp of coyotes feasting on their prey.* She shivered at the thought of helpless prey, of victims.

She glanced at the house again. Harry had finished talking to a woman holding an oil lamp, the light mostly blotted out, except for the window, when she shut the door.

Disappointment was on his face when he returned. "Won't take us, seemed mighty suspicious."

"What do we do now? There's that Lodge Hotel off Main Street, but I know I can't afford it. And Harry, I won't put you in a financial bind because of me. I've a little money left – almost five dollars, after I paid for the ferry. Let me try this place again."

Adjusting her best hat, making sure its veil was tied properly under her chin, Naomi climbed out of the wagon and rushed to the front door just as the light was disappearing behind its window. Frantically she banged the knocker.

"Yes?" The woman grudgingly opened the door several inches. "Told you we haven't any rooms. So I bid you and that man out there good night."

"Listen, ma'am," Naomi was tempted to put her foot in the door to keep it from closing. "It's not what you think," she said in a rush of words, "that gentleman has brought me here from Menasa to search for my father, we're looking for someone else who may be in serious trouble, can't return home now, there's no ferry, and Menasa is a good twelve miles on the other side."

The woman held the oil lamp closer to Naomi's face, and the draft from the door caused smoke to blacken one side of the chimney. She looked steadily at her for a few minutes, then opened the door another few inches. "What kind of trouble?"

"A young woman, on her own. Maybe with – " she started to say two lawyers named Billings and Fletcher, but decided against it.

"I suppose I could let you have a bed for the night. Be one dollar. But as for that man on the wagon – no." He'll have to find some other place. I keep a good, respectable house here."

Naomi gave Harry the message. He took it well, shrugging his shoulders, but betraying some disappointment and anxiety by twisting the ends of the reins around his fist. "Don't worry, the main thing is for you to have a place, to be safe." He glanced at the house. "At least I hope it's safe. You think you'll be all right?"

203

She nodded, not entirely convinced, but unwilling to worry the man. He waited in the wagon until she was inside and the door closed behind her. Hearing the team pull the wagon down the street, a sense of loss and isolation came over her. For the very first time since leaving Prairie Lake, for the very first time in her life, she was on her own.

Mrs. Ransom's house was big and drafty and smelled like cooked cabbage. It brought a queasy feeling to Naomi's stomach, and the woman's abrupt and almost hostile manner did not help. "Do you have many boarders?" she asked as the woman, carrying the oil lamp, led the way up a curving staircase.

"As many as I need," she answered evasively. "Last one just came in, late this afternoon."

Naomi's heart gave a leap. "Oh? Another woman?"

"Yes, of course, like I told you. Another young woman, like you, and you'll have the room next to hers." She stopped at the second door before the end of the hall. "This one's yours. I'll come in and light the lamp for you." Looking Naomi over, she remarked, "Just that one little case, I see?"

"I – I had to leave in a hurry. I didn't really expect – "

"Lots in life we don't expect," said Mrs. Ransom somewhat cryptically. "Could tell you a tale or two." She opened a small drawer in a cabinet beside the narrow, brass bed with its white coverlet and took out a box of matches. Lifting off the chimney on the oil lamp sitting on the cabinet, she turned up the wick, and applied the match. Naomi felt some relief as more light filled the room.

"Well, I'll leave you, commode's in the corner there, breakfast starts at seven, kitchen closed at eight. I'll take that dollar now, if you please."

Mrs. Ransom's reference to breakfast reminded Naomi that she hadn't eaten since breakfast. *Hunger's my least concern*, she was considering, *especially with that nauseating cabbage smell hanging so heavily here in the air. No, my main concern is more in the nature of Mrs. Ransom's life unexpectancies. What's going to happen? I'll see the sheriff tomorrow. What about Birgitta? A woman came in late this afternoon. What if --*

Naomi sat down on the edge of the hard, narrow bed, her head in her hands. *I've got to compose myself, I've got to keep hoping things will work out. For her – for me – for --*

Going over to the window, she idly looked out, not expecting to see anything except that Harry was gone and the street would be dark and empty. Empty, like her thoughts at the moment, like her will unable to think of God, of Job, of the tests.

As she watched, considering the emptiness of the street as a parallel to the loneliness in her heart, she thought she saw a figure walking down the far side. As the figure came under the circle of gas light, Naomi drew in a sharp breath. It was a tall figure, a woman wearing a dark dress and an elaborate hat.

She tried to open the window to shout something to attract her attention, but the window was stuck. Snatching up the oil lamp on the cabinet, Naomi rushed into the hall and down the stairs. The lamp's flame flickered and threatened to go out until Naomi put her hand partly over the top and set the lamp down on the hall table next to the door. She tried to open the door by the uncertain light, but the big brass key turned hard. Once the door was free, she stepped out onto the porch and peered down the length of the street, leaving the door open. It moved slightly back and forth on its hinges, threatening to close behind her, but at the moment she couldn't worry about that.

The woman she'd seen from her window was still walking in the opposite direction and about to come under another circle of light. Naomi rushed down the porch steps and out into the street, shouting, "Wait! Stop!" The woman turned slightly and looked back. "Birgitta!" Naomi cried and broke into a run.

But the woman, seeing someone running after her, only quickened her pace as she passed into, then through, the circle of greenish light, and finally into the shadows beyond. Just ahead was an alley to the left and then a cross street. Still pursuing her, Naomi stumbled and fell over a loose brick in the walk and by the time she'd picked herself up, the woman had disappeared. Looking down the dark alley, then the dimly lit cross street, Naomi could see no sign of her. There was no way of knowing which way she'd gone, nor whether the woman had indeed been Birgitta Magnusson.

Naomi was disappointed, more like frustrated, that she'd tried and quite likely failed in finding Birgitta. She was relieved, however, when she discovered that Mrs. Ransom's front door remained slightly ajar and the oil lamp she'd set on the hall table still have out an uncertain light. This place was a welcome shelter, at least, and Naomi prayed that the woman she'd followed down the street, whoever she was, would be as fortunate.

Relocking the door and returning to her room as quietly as possible, afraid of waking Mrs. Ransom, she sat down on the edge of the bed with a renewed feeling of lonely desolation. Even the bed, hard and full of lumps, seemed uninviting. *Excellent Beds*, indeed!

Somewhere from within the depths of the house a clock chimed nine. There were sounds from the room across the hall, someone moving around, opening drawers, closing them, and farther away down the hall someone coughing. Through the thin wall of the room next door came the sound of someone sobbing. Was it the woman who'd come in earlier that day? Had those lawyers brought Birgitta here? If so, her opinion of them began to improve. Perhaps they'd done the right thing after all.

Taking up once again the oil lamp, she knocked on the door. The sounds stopped. There was a long pause. The door opened partially to reveal a young woman, her eyes reddened, her long black hair loose around her shoulders, and both hands clutching together the edges of a gray, flannel dressing gown. It was not Birgitta.

"Please forgive me for disturbing you," Naomi whispered, shaken by this second disappointment. She had difficulty holding the lamp steady, and shadows staggered and fell along the long hallway. "I couldn't help but overhear your distress. I wondered whether there was anything I could do."

Dabbing at her eyes with a handkerchief, the woman looked embarrassed. "It is nothing. No, nothing. Can — not help. Thank."

She had an accent of some sort that Naomi couldn't identify. Perhaps this woman, like Birgitta, was a recent immigrant who'd suddenly realized the lonely consequences of such a journey. Perhaps she was feeling lost and longing for the comfort of family and home. What can *I do to comfort her? To offer her?* Naomi wondered, but then almost immediately realized there was nothing she could do or give.

"Well, then, good night," Naomi finally said lamely. "I hope things will be better for you." The woman nodded and quickly closed her door.

The consequences of her decision – Couldn't I apply those same words to myself, Naomi wondered. *Or to Harry's situation, now because of me out there on a cold night? Matthew's situation, lying seriously injured, depressed, in a bed not his own. My father's situation, lying somewhere … Jacob's situation – although I don't particularly care what that might be. There's a war going on in my heart between anger and forgiveness, as far as he's concerned.*

Naomi sat back down again on the edge of the hard, lumpy bed, trying desperately to position her body and mind within some more hopeful aspect of reality. *Tomorrow is tomorrow,* her thoughts ran on. *Maybe I'll find the right answers. Maybe, if I try hard enough, I can find the right words tonight for a prayer, one that could force my thoughts into the right direction, a direction where answers can be found.*

"Father – father – " she said, over and over again, at first uncertain whether they meant the Lord or her own father. "Oh help me, father in heaven, to shut out the sounds of trouble wandering around the rooms of this depressing house, the coughing, the restless footsteps, the sobbing of that woman next door. Help me not to yield to that emotion, my emotions …help me to find questions that *can* be answered … "

10

Jacob's Dilemma

Jacob woke up early. Nothing seemed right, from the bare rafters above his head to the hard, narrow bed. The rough, furry buffalo skin covering him – but only partially – stank indescribably. The snores coming from across the room were definitely not his brother's. Gradually he pieced together where he was, and why.

Let me think, now, Jack, the Maplewood ferrier, took me in last night, after he'd replaced Prince's shoe. I was desperate to go on, but he argued that the road ahead was too dangerous. And it was almost dark. Made sense. Then Hattie Geske, I think her name is, owns the Mercantile other side of the road – if you can call it that, brought over some supper for me and Jack. Wasn't too bad – fried mush, fried apple rings, fried bacon, fried potatoes and onions, and fried bread. Enough oil to run one of them threshing rigs. Jug of apple cider made up for some of it. My belly grumbled all night from the greasiness of it, still grumbling, feels like.

"Jack! I say Jack! You awake?" he called across the room.

"Uhh – what's the matter?" The smithy stirred in his cot, and, throwing back his blanket, sat bolt upright. "What's happenin'? Somethin' amiss?"

"Just my innards, but no matter, Jack. I've got to leave."

"In a hurry?"

"You already know that. Much beholding to you for the bed for the night, but I've got to move on."

"All right, all right. Let me get dressed, go over to Hattie's and ask her to bring over some breakfast. Otherwise your innards may be even worse off." A pause. "Although that's hopin' too much otherwise for Hattie's cookin'." The blanket fell to the rough wooden floor as Jack got to his feet, then he quickly pulled up his overalls over stockinged feet and a pair of red long johns. Stepping into his boots alongside the cot, he instructed, "You get dressed, back in a minute."

Jacob was in the smithy checking on Prince when Jack returned with Hattie. "Best come over to the Mercantile," she said. "Easier than transportin' food back and forth. Say, good lookin' horse there."

"Cost me a lot of lost time. Not too happy about that."

"Critters don't keep no 'count of time," was her pronouncement. "Wish that was true for me – and Jack here."

It seemed ages to Jacob before she came out of her kitchen with a pot of coffee to where he and Jack were sitting at a small table by the window. "Here you be, couple plates of ham and eggs, out of bread, some old hard tack better'n nothin', I expect."

After the first sip, Jacob decided it was no better than what she'd given him yesterday, but at least was hotter. He gingerly dug into the ham and eggs, bypassing the plate of hard tack. "Won't you join us?" It seemed the polite thing to do, as Hattie stood hovering over the coffee pot.

"Thanks, don't mind if I do." She brought over a stool from the counter. "Time, now, like I was sayin', you know Jack and me here, gettin' on. Place here more'n a challenge than it used to be. We're thinkin' 'bout goin' west, right Jack? More opportunities for folks out there, getting' off these darn prairies. Yup, lot more for folks like us." She checked on the contents of the pot. "More coffee?"

"No thanks," Jacob said. "You're thinking about that too, Jack?"

Going west – Jack's answer was lost as Jacob stopped listening, his mind occupied with his own thoughts. *Yes, what Jack's saying,* Jacob thought, *if it means more opportunities, more land, more future, then it sure is something to consider. But now, how about me and Naomi together? About her religion? A hard question. True, that God I prayed to granted me a safe haven for the night at least.*

"You'll be goin', now, mister?" Hattie asked, clearing away the empty plates.

Her words brought him back to the moment with a jolt. "Right away, ma'am, can't waste anymore time. I do thank you for the food, and for the night at your place, Jack. I'll just go back over, saddle up Prince."

"Wishin' you a good journey, then. Just watch out for that road washout this side of Menasa. Folks passin' this way say it'll swallow a horse and wagon right up."

"Thanks, Mrs. Geske, I'll be careful."

"Just Hattie will do fine. And if you come this way again – dependin', of course, on how far west you're plannin' to go and we ain't left yet, I'll have my coffee pot on the stove."

"Hope to, ma'am," he said, "sure do hope so." He didn't exactly mean the coffee.

As he saddled up Prince and prepared to back him out of Jack's work stall in the smithy, Jacob reached into his food saddle bag and handed Jack some bread and slices of ham. "Be pleased if you'd take this, Jack, for putting me up. How much for shoeing my horse?" He reached under the saddle for the money pouch he kept for security.

Jack looked embarrassed. "Nope, couldn't take somethin' from you," he answered. "Glad to have your company, for the short time it was. Get's lonely here, sometimes, 'cept for Barnum, and he gets right cantankerous at times. Same goes for old Hattie 'cross the way. You know, just maybe, Hattie and me, we'll get hitched and move on together. Homestead out west, some 'eres."

He glanced over at Prince. "Say, best let me check that hoof one more time. Hate for anythin' more happen to you on the road."

Within the next few moments Jacob was mounted on Prince and again riding west. Jack's words still resonated in his ears, *hate for anything more to happen to you on the road.* That couldn't have been closer to his own thoughts.

At least the weather was clear, and a hot sun soon persuaded him to take off his jacket and tie the sleeves around the saddle horn. Standing in his stirrups, he looked as far as he could down the road ahead. It seemed clear, although deeply rutted in places from heavy wagons passing through after the heavy rain of several days before. "Keep to the right," he said to Prince, guiding him with the rein. "A little grass along there, easier, we can make better time."

He urged the horse into a gallop for about a mile, then pulled back to a walk. "Rest a bit, boy, still got a long way to go. What'd that woman say back at Maplewood? Some twenty or so miles from there to Moorhead? Seems like we came about the same distance yesterday from Prairie Lake, so it looks like we'll make it there by late afternoon, that is, baring anymore mishaps. Say, it looks clear enough up ahead for a spell, hup – hup, giddyup!"

Prince responded, and they galloped until they reached a curve descending into a gully, where a shallow stream crossed the road. Jacob guided Prince around the loose rocks and snagged branches, then decided to dismount for a rest, both for himself and Prince.

Allowing the horse to graze leisurely on the grass beside him, Jacob sat down on a fallen log and took out the last food from his saddlebag. "Time for a second breakfast. No need to worry about running out of food," he said to Prince, "we'll be in Moorhead by supper. I sure am looking forward to a decent meal at some good eating place."

Biting into a thick slice of ham, however, he began to worry about something other than food. "Say, Prince, do you think we'll be able to find Naomi in a big town like that? Why didn't I ask Matthew Schmidt's wife about Schmidt's business there, somebody to contact? Only thing I know is, Naomi was supposed to go to the sheriff's office in Fargo, told that's just across the river, and that's where her father would be, Mary's father as well. I guess that's where I'll go, if I don't find her beforehand."

Staring unseeingly at the gurgling stream beside him, his mind began to dream up possibilities, that opening reaction of Naomi's when she saw him, how their conversation would go. *Why, Jacob, how did you get here? Followed me all this way after all?* Then he'd say, *I was afraid for you.* Then she'd say, *oh Jacob, how glad I am to see you, how wonderful and noble and brave of you to do all this for me!* Then he'd say, "Oh, Naomi, I want to – want to – but what, after all, *did* he want? He wasn't at all sure, and that was the truth of it.

Prince was wandering off toward better grass in a meadow against a slight hill with a crown of evergreen. No need to worry. He'd soon recover him and they'd be on their way.

Ah, now the journey back, Jacob began to contemplate pleasurably. *I'll ride alongside Naomi's wagon, we'll talk, eat together ... maybe I'll let her to ride Prince alongside, just for a change, while I drive the wagon ...*

Suddenly Jacob lost sight of Prince. He jumped to his feet, snatched up the saddlebag, and began running down the road. "Prince! Prince, here boy – Prince!"

Just ahead he saw him, nibbling at a patch of tall prairie grass, switching his tail, the reins trailing loose. "Prince!" Jacob shouted.

The horse raised his head, shook his mane, and moved nonchalantly to another patch. Jacob ran on another few yards, but Prince kept just ahead of him. "You ornery critter, come back here," he shouted. Again, Prince flicked his tail and moved on.

Jacob stopped in the middle of the road. "Too hot to chase after that horse, the sweat's pouring down my face. Prince! Whoa boy, whoa!" Taking off his straw hat, and beat it against his thigh.

Perhaps it was that gesture which spooked Prince. He pricked up his ears, shook his mane and broke into a gallop. Jacob stood there open-mouthed. "This is the last thing I expected, you fool animal," he shouted after Prince. "Of all the dumb things for that a horse to do, a horse I raised from a foal, trained, treated like a member of the family, just had shod. Prince – you ornery animal, stop! Stop!"

Jacob broke again into a run. He reasoned that as long as he could keep the horse in sight, he'd eventually catch up with him, depending upon who tired first. There was a turn in the road, which now entered a thick grove of oak trees. By the time Jacob came out the other side, there was no sign of Prince. He dropped his hat on the ground, sat down on a large rock, and buried his face in his hands. "Of all the bad luck, of all the rotten luck," he moaned. "Nothing for it but to keep walking."

Jacob had gone about a mile, the now near-empty saddle bag slung across his shoulder, when he saw a horse and wagon approaching. "Rotten luck again," he mumbled. "Going the wrong direction. Why couldn't they be going the other way and give me a ride?"

"Hey, there, mister," he called as the wagon neared, "seen a loose horse down the road?"

The man slowed but didn't stop. "Can't say as I have – run off did he?" He grinned broadly and added, "Long walk to Moorhead then."

"How far?"

"Maybe close to fourteen, fifteen miles." He flicked his whip. "Hup, hup, can't stay here all day, deliverin' the mail to Maplewood, got a few other stops as well."

Just after the wagon had gone on ahead and was now well past Jacob, the driver turned on the bench and shouted, "But Menasa's just ahead, couple miles."

Just maybe – maybe it wasn't too late to turn back and catch up with him, Jacob considered. *I'll ride with the man to Maplewood, borrow a horse from Jack, or Mr. Barnum. Then I'll ride like the wind to make up time, maybe even catch up with Prince. I'll sure give that critter a talking too once I find found him. Menasa – hmm, why does that name sounded familiar? Can't place it.*

Retracing his steps at a run, Jacob rushed back down the road toward the disappearing mail wagon. He came to the grove of oak trees and emerged out the other side. There was no sign of the wagon. A lane on either side led off into stands of oak and fir, and it was clearly impossible to tell which one the mail wagon had taken.

A feeling of intense anger came over Jacob as he stood in the middle of the road. He could not move, and his head throbbed from the quickened beats of his heart and the waves of heat surging through his body. He had never felt this way before and the violence of it alarmed him.

It was anger, yes, but it was also something else. A feeling that he had desperately tried to accomplish something, something worthy and honorable, but which had failed. Something – someone – had failed him. He looked up at the sky as he twisted his straw hat around and around in his hands."Yes, you up there! I failed to find the right words to your prayer. You never got it!"

To the west the clouds seemed layered in straight lines of gray and bluish green. This struck as Jacob as odd. He'd never seen clouds like that before, and guessed it meant another storm coming. The wind had picked up as well.

Tugging his straw hat down farther and slinging the near saddlebag once again over his shoulder, he headed into the wind and started walking. From time to time he ran until he was out of breath, then, gasping for air, slowed to a walk. "Menasa, Menasa. Why does that name keep running around in my head?" he blurted out.

There was still no sign of Prince. The sky was quickly darkening with spiraling clouds coming steadily toward him. The air was growing colder by the minute. He realized he'd taken off his jacket earlier, when the sun was hot, and tied it to the saddle horn. And the saddle horn was on Prince.

With the sun now so clouded over, it was difficult to know how late it was. He'd ridden for several hours, then walked for a few hours more. It must be well past noon, he calculated, probably one or two. *Wish I had a timepiece like Pa's. Hard to calculate time the old way, like from the position of the sun, the length of shadows, or even the distant church bell in Prairie Lake. With the wind just right, you could hear it plain as day a couple miles away.*

An unexpected space opening up in front of him caused him to slow down, then stop. He stood before a gaping hole in the road stretching all the way across it. Rocks and mud spilled down each side, and on one side was a deep ravine, still filled with several inches of water from the last rainstorm. Then he remembered – *Menasa*! The washed out road. Yet now he also remembered he'd heard that name before. From Schmidt's wife, something she'd said about a relative's inn.

"Could it be that Naomi was still -- " he wondered. But then immediately he answered himself, "No it's beyond hope, there's no way she could still be here. Her ma said she'd be already in Fargo, two days ago." It occurred to him that he might still meet her coming back, but he had mixed feelings about that. *Wouldn't mean as much*, he thought. *Not making it all the way to Fargo -- wouldn't have been able to prove myself as well to her.*

At the moment, however, he had a more immediate concern. He stood studying the hole and trying to figure out how to get around it. A farmer's field lay on his right, the water-filled ravine on the left. He climbed up the embankment to the field and started walking quickly across the furrows towards woods at the far end. Smoke rose up from a chimney beyond, although wind scattered the smoke this way and that, making it difficult to tell exactly where it was coming from.

Someone lives in that direction, he reasoned and quickened his pace. *That means shelter. It also means somebody might have seen Prince, or maybe even caught the critter, along with my jacket and my money.*

Through the thick stand of fir and other trees, he could see a large gray building, at least two storeys high, with what looked like a livery stable behind. Smoke was coming out of the kitchen spur chimney and another toward the front. "Maybe a hostelry of some sort," he muttered, then stopped dead in his tracks. "That inn! That's the one!"

Immediately, however, a troublesome thought intruded into this momentary relief. He had only a near empty food saddle bag, now useless. He had no money on him. It, along with his father's pistol and cartridges, was in a pouch under Prince's saddle, and his jacket was tied to the horn, and the horn was wherever Prince had run off to.

Coming through the last of the trees onto a grassy lawn, he saw a way to come around to the main road which the building faced. There was a large black and white sign on the road, but the letters were so faded he couldn't read them. Over the main entrance was a portico, and over that a board on which was painted in large black letters, *Menasa Inn. prop. H. Barnes.*

"Hello? Hello?" Jacob called as he opened the heavy front door. "Anyone here?" The place seemed unusually quiet for a public house. The faint odor of fish came from the direction of the kitchen, along with the rattle of dishes, pots and pans, and a woman's gusty voice singing snatches of a song. He stepped into the empty parlor, then across the hall to what appeared to be a dining room. The large table had been left hastily, littered as it was with dirty plates and a couple of tumblers half full of milk. A basket with the remains of several rolls tempted him, but he resisted the impulse.

After calling out several more times, Jacob decided that the only thing to do was head for the kitchen, the only sign of life. Tentatively opening the kitchen door, he was met with the strong lingering odors of food, steam from a kettle boiling on the large iron cookstove, and the sound of water being pumped from a hand pump attached to the sink. A dark-haired woman enveloped in a voluminous white apron was standing over the sink, her back to him.

"Hello?" he said.

Turning in a startled reflex, she dropped the dish she was holding onto the floor, and it shattered with a piercing crash. "Oh!" she cried. "Where'd you come from?"

"The woods. The road," Jacob answered.

"Didn't hear no buggy drive up."

"I wasn't driving one."

"Horse, neither."

"Wasn't riding."

"Well, if that don't beat all." She stood back, wiping her hands on her apron. "People comin' outa nowhere like that, no baggage, no nothin'. Becomin' a habit, seems to me. Had two of 'em last couple days."

"My apologies, ma'am, I didn't mean to startle you." He could hardly restrain himself from asking about the two people.

"What do you want, then? Got a room, if that's it." Clearly she was apprehensive and appeared to be reaching behind her back for a large butcher knife lying beside the sink.

"Came from Maplewood this morning, ma'am. My horse ran off 'bout half-way. Walked here the rest of the way." He looked longingly at the big tin coffee pot on the range. "Do you think – "

Without saying anything, Emma poured out a mug and set it down on the table. "Here, mister, sugar's in that basin, a bit of cream left in this pitcher from the noon dinner." She pulled out a chair, but kept the knife in her hand. "Set you down."

Eagerly Jacob sipped the coffee, a real treat compared to Hattie Geske's. The place seemed empty, the realization giving him a sinking feeling. Did he dare ask? Instead, he glanced up at the wall clock. "That clock right? It can't be five-o-clock already!"

"Keeps good time," she said, gradually edging toward the door out to the hall as if intending to escape. "You plannin' on leavin' or stayin'? Where you headin'?"

"All depends. Maybe Moorhead, then Fargo."

"I see. Well you won't make it 'fore dark, even if your horse turns up, if it's like you said."

"How far is it?"

"Near thirteen miles."

The man driving the mail wagon had already told him that. "Then I think I'll have to ask for a room." He didn't know how he was going to pay for it, unless she'd accept his offer of help somewhere – the dishes, chopping wood. Or if by some miracle Prince showed up with his money.

"I do happen to have some vacant rooms," she replied. "Everyone else left earlier today, 'cept for an older gentleman up in room six."

So that was his answer. A terrible disappointment, yet half expected. He'd already calculated that Naomi should have reached Fargo. "I see," he said lamely. "I guess I'll take a room then."

"You can come out to the front office and sign the register, when you've finished that coffee. It'll be two dollars for the room, that includes breakfast, but another fifty cents if you want supper tonight."

Jacob swallowed hard. He didn't feel he could explain his financial situation just yet. He'd made it to Menasa, all right, but he was as helpless as before, a real dilemma. He set down his coffee mug carefully beside the sink, and followed Emma out into the hall.

"I'm Mrs. Barnes, by the way, Emma Barnes. My husband, Harold Barnes, is out. He should be back any minute now."

As she glanced out one of the big front windows, Jacob could see she was nervous, even anxious about something. Coming back into the hall, she paused. "On second thought, sir, if you wouldn't mind, leavin' that register until later? You can take care of it when you're comin' down to supper. And I assume you'll want that?"

"Yes, ma'am," Jacob answered lamely.

"So, please, just make yourself at home in the parlor, I'll show you up to your room later, I've somethin' to do first."

I guess this should be a welcome reprieve, Jacob thought, relieved. *But sooner or later I know I'll have to confess I have no any money. Then she'll throw me back out on the road, or worse, have me arrested, that is, if this place has a sheriff.*

Emma headed back toward the kitchen. "I'll just run along back to the kitchen to fix the gentleman's tray. He likes a little tea and toast with his pills. And Mr. Schmidt needs to take them regular, doctor's orders."

Jacob stopped dead in his tracks mid-way to the parlor door. "What did you say?"

"I said I've got to fix up the gentleman's tray."

"The gentleman – his name?"

She looked surprised, then immediately suspicious. "Why do you want to know? Are you a law man? Look, sir, if you've a motive for coming here – if you're intendin' to – " She backed toward the front door.

"His name – I might know him."

She hesitated, then looked directly at him. "His name is Matt Schmidt, Matthew Schmidt. That is, if it's any of your business."

Jacob was speechless. Although he'd always thought of himself as being in control of any situation, and that included any with Naomi, he could not respond.

"What's the matter, sir? Are you ill?"

Jacob went into the parlor and sat down heavily in the wing chair nearest the door. Emma followed him in.

"I said, sir, are you ill? You look a little peaked."

Jacob felt his breathing failing him along with his voice. Taking a few deep breaths, clenching the arms of the chair for something to remind him of reality, he stammered, "I think – I do – yes, I do know him -- Prairie Lake -- " *That Matthew Schmidt should still be here – in this place,* he thought, *that means Naomi could be here.* "Naomi – Naomi Beckman – is she -- is she – "

"You know her, too? My, my, such a small world. Well, sir, she *was* here. Left with my husband Harry, just a few hours ago."

Jacob snapped back his head against the chair. "No! Left? With your husband? Just hours ago? No, no, that can't be, not possible!"

"It's true, they left in a hurry about the time of the noon dinner. You see, our helper – Birgitta – she just – " Emma broke off. "Never mind, there's no point in goin' into all that now. Anyway, Naomi went with Harry to try to find her."

"Where were they heading?"

"See here, sir. You're askin' an awful lot of questions. Why do you want to know? You got a good reason?"

Jacob hesitated. What should he say? Finally, he offered, "Naomi and I – well I – I mean she – "

Emma leaned back, her hands on her hips. "Well, if that don't beat all. Seems to me you need to do a lot more explainin', sir, but that can come later. To answer your question, they was headin' to Moorhead, 'cause that's likely that's where that girl Birgitta was headin'. If they – I mean Harry and Naomi -- found her along the way some'eres, then they'd all come back here. But, as you can see, they ain't come back yet."

"They're coming back here?" There was still hope.

Emma hesitated before she answered. "If they ain't back by this evenin', that means, sure's your born, they'll be stayin' the night in Moorhead." She shook her head. "So's you see, sir, it bein' already so late, that's the way it'll be."

She went out into the hall and toward the kitchen. "Now if you'll just wait here 'til I finish with Matt, I'll show you to your room. As for the two dollars – we'll talk 'bout that later. Supper'll be on the house. You *will* need to sign the register, though. What'd you say your name was?"

"Jacob Bowers, from near Fullerton."

"Seems like I heard that name before. Well, never mind, no matter."

Waiting in the green velvet wing chair in the parlor and watching the burning embers flake down into ashes on the earth of the fireplace, Jacob was having great difficulty sorting out his emotions. *On the one hand*, he said to himself, *I've found Naomi. Or that is, I now know where she was last. The problem is, I don't really know*

223

where she is now. Worst part of it is, she's most likely now in Moorhead, and now alone again with still another man, a relative stranger at that.

Jacob got to his feet and began pacing up and down the room, tracing the pattern in the flowered rug, pausing now and then to warm his hands before the fire. *How come that Schmidt is here? Why? Should have arrived in Fargo two days ago. What's going on?*

Jacob saw Emma Barnes pass the hall door, a tray in her hands, and start up the stairs. She must know what happened, Jacob thought. He'd ask her. Better still, he'd ask Matthew Schmidt. "Mrs. Barnes," he called after her. "I'd like to talk to Mr. Schmidt."

She turned on the stairway. "Not now I'm afraid. He needs his rest. Maybe after supper. I'll let you know. But meantime, follow me. I'll show you up to your room."

Room number three was at the end of the hall at the west end of the building. Balancing the tray in one hand, Emma opened the door." A bit small, this one, but you've got the sunset, always a bit of glory. And I believe, sir, you'll find the bed comfortable, some extra blankets in that chest at the foot. Key's in the door, most people don't bother to lock. No commode here, though, you'll have to use the common one in that closet down 'tother end, green door. Supper's in an hour, you'll hear the bell."

As she closed the door behind her, Jacob sat down on the edge of the bed. The moaning creak of the rope supports beneath him had a despairing sound. There was an overwhelming feeling about all this, yet to sort out.

Matthew Schmidt's here, just across the hall. Naomi was here, his thoughts raced on. *She'll return soon. Schmidt for some reason couldn't continue. Naomi stayed with him. Then for whatever reason she's just taken off with Harry Barnes. Some Swedish girl. Why not stay here with Schmidt? Why bother about that Swedish girl?*

He heard footsteps out in the hall, opposite his door. Mrs. Barnes' voice, no mistake, the woman fairly boomed.

"Now Matt, get that pill down your gullet, wash it down with some tea. And try to eat the toast, I slathered it with my apricot jam, and you know that always goes down real good. Be up here to check on you shortly, just before supper time." A door closed.

Schmidt across the hall, Jacob thought, *just behind that door. A strange feeling. I still resent the man, distrust him. Yes, I think I'm even afraid for Naomi's sake. What if something happened on that journey between Prairie Lake and Menasa? Between Schmidt and Naomi? What if -- ? No, I could never forgive her for that. And this journey would have been all for nothing.*

Jacob got to his feet with another moaning sound from the bed ropes. *No, too painful to think about. Even if the worst were true, could I face the man? Across the hall, only six feet away, maybe ten feet, away. Pa loaned me his revolver and cartridges. Didn't need them so far. But they're still in Prince's saddlebag. And where is that critter? Can a horse betray a man? Can a woman betray the man she loves – that is, if she truly loves him?* He fell back on the bed, muttering, searching for some coherence to all this.

Jacob must have dozed off out of sheer exhaustion of both body and brain. The sound of a bell downstairs shook his senses awake. "What – who -- ?" he cried as he sat up in bed. The bell again, persistent.

There was a wash basin with a pitcher of water on the washstand by the window. The water was cold when he splashed it on his face, but at least served to wake him up. Drying his face and hands on the towel hanging on the washstand's rack, he looked in the mirror above it, aghast at the wildness of his hair, the blond stubble of beard and moustache. *The last time I shaved was just before leaving home. No wonder Mrs. Barnes reached for a butcher knife. Razor and shaving cream, comb, in Prince's saddlebag, and as for Prince --*

"That horse's name ought to be changed, Jacob spit out disgustedly. "Certainly not a *prince,* as far as I'm concerned. More like a *deserter.*"

Feeling embarrassed about his looks, for the moment the more serious issue of Matthew Schmidt slipping back to second place, Jacob went down the main stairway to the dining room. It was empty. One place was set at a small round table in the corner by a window.

"Sit yourself down, Mr. Bowers," boomed Emma, placing a small soup tureen beside his bowl and plate. "When you're done, I'll bring in the fish and parsleyed potatoes, some green beans on the side. Will that be all right?"

"Sounds wonderful to me," Jacob answered, picking up his soupspoon. "Can't say as I've eaten well on this journey." He couldn't repress a smile, thinking of Hattie Geske's meal the night before, her breakfast this morning. At the same time, he glanced out the big window and noticed the failing light. Naomi hadn't returned. It would not be tonight.

Just as Emma turned to return to the kitchen, Jacob stopped her. "If you'll excuse me, ma'am, it seems a little lonely in here, so empty. Whatever you might think, wouldn't you care to join me?" What Jacob really wanted, however, was the chance to talk to her about Schmidt and Naomi.

Several minutes later Emma joined him, carrying in her supper on a tray, which she unloaded onto the table. "I don't usually eat with my guests," she said. "But in this case – " She slipped off her apron and sat down opposite to say a short grace. Unfolding her napkin, she looked at Jacob. "Now then. You're in love with Naomi, I take it."

Jacob was taken back. He thought he'd be the one to initiate the conversation. "Well I – that is – well the truth is, ma'am, I thought so once. Not sure now."

"What's changed your mind?"

"Things got complicated."

"Like what?"

"The whole business of her having to get to Fargo, to bring her pa home. And it wasn't only her pa. There was someone else's father involved."

"You're right about its bein' complicated. What happened, then? You refuse to do it?"

This really was becoming uncomfortable. Jacob put down his soupspoon.

"A ha," Emma boomed. "Hit the mark. Now listen, young man, whatever you did or didn't do, whatever she did or didn't do – that don't matter in the long run."

"What long run?" He could be direct as well.

"The long run of life. You'll learn that. I only hope when you do see her again that you'll talk about that, share your thoughts. That's the quickest way to get over whatever – that thing – that's between you." She ladled out some wild rice soup into her own bowl. "Now let's dig in, been an awful long day for both of us."

After supper, once Jacob returned to his room and found one of Harry's nightshirts laid out for him on the bed, he mulled over their conversation at supper. *No doubt her words conveyed a great deal of sense,* he thought.

His anxiety increased as he heard Emma coming out of Matthew Schmidt's room. "Hardly touched anythin', Matt," she said. "You look like you're beginnin' to waste away. Leastways, you're fever seems to be comin' down. Now you get a good rest, hear?" A door closed and Emma's footsteps receded down the hall toward what Jacob had earlier discovered were the kitchen stairs.

Now was his chance. The man wasn't asleep yet. Jacob's heart began to pound in his chest, and he felt heat rise in his face. *Surely this isn't the result of fear*, he thought. *What could the man possibly do to him? Maybe it wasn't so much what the man might do, it was what he might say. And what he might say could force me to react in a way I'd regret.*

He knocked softly on number six.

"Emma – I told you – not need – "

Jacob said, "It's not Emma. May I come in?"

When there was no answer, Jacob slowly opened the door. The room was in semi-darkness except for a small oil lamp on the bedside table, with a shade attached to the chimney in such a way that most of the light was directed up to the ceiling. It gave the room an eerie look and, combined with the heavy odor of menthol and something else Jacob couldn't identify, distinctly off-putting. A bearded man lay half propped up on pillows, his dark hair streaked with gray, his large hands resting on the top fold of the coverlet. The man looked greatly surprised as Jacob entered and uttered something between a moan and a gasp. He looked feeble and quite helpless.

Jacob began to feel his original fierce determination to get to the bottom of things with this man was waning fast. Matthew Schmidt was different from what he'd expected. He now seemed only a shadow of a man, and not at all capable of what Jacob had feared most

"Who – " the man tried to raise himself up.

"Don't be alarmed, sir. I just need to speak to you."

"Where – Naomi?"

"Indeed, Mr. Schmidt, that's what I'm asking myself as well. Where is she?"

"You – know my – name? Naomi -- not back – "

"No, she's not. Tomorrow, maybe."

"Who – you – " Matthew repeated.

"Jacob Bowers."

Matthew smiled faintly. "Ah, Jacob. Naomi – Jacob. Fullerton."

"That's right. So I've come in search of her, to protect her."

"Protect?" He looked surprised. "Against what?"

"Well, you see, I thought – "

"Protect – against me, you mean?" He gave a wry smile.

"Well, I -- " The man had guessed his meaning. Did that mean he was on the defensive, guilty himself?

"A knight in shining armor, you consider yourself?"

"Well, no, I -- " The man was being deliberately difficult, and Jacob felt his anger rising.

"Let me – tell you – Jacob Bowers." His breath came in gasps of pain as he turned in bed to face him. "You – might have had -- " A pause while he regained control. "Have had cause."

"What do you mean, sir?" His original suspicions were gaining ground.

"Just – that."

"I see," although he didn't really see. Not the whole picture, anyway.

Schmidt smiled again, faintly. "See here, though – you – she – Naomi – needs – " He broke off, waving his hand toward the door. "Go!"

Jacob thought a moment, a moment which suggested a way to redeem the situation. "Well, sir, I did think she might need some help, bringing her father back." That certainly wasn't what he'd intended to say to this man, although it *had* been one of his motives.

"Good," was all Matthew said, with a slight inclination of his head toward Jacob. "Good," he repeated. Then, closing his eyes, he turned his head away, waving again toward the door.

Jacob hesitated. Should he say more? Should he ask about what happened? With his thoughts more confused than ever, he was at a loss. Better ask Mrs. Barnes in the morning.

"Well, then sir, a good night to you then," was all he felt he should say as he shut the door of number six gently behind him.

Next morning, eating breakfast out in the kitchen, Jacob considered the three things on his mind. *I wonder, first of all when Naomi's arriving back. Next, I'd like to find out what happened to her and Schmidt. And last, I'm wondering how I'm going to pay for his room.*

"Mrs. Barnes," he began, after swallowing his second or third fork full of scrambled eggs, "what happened to Mr. Schmidt?"

"More coffee?" she filled his mug. "Late Tuesday, it was, nearly dark, he came upon that washout. You saw it?"

"Yes."

"His horse fell into it, broke off from the wagon. Then the wagon tipped over, crushed his ribs."

"Naomi – was she – "

"No, thank the Lord. She wasn't hurt, although some'at the worse for wear findin' her way here through them woods. Main concern right now is Matt. Doin' better, thank the Lord for that blessing as well. Time will tell." She sat down at the table with him to finish the breakfast she'd started earlier. "Say, how 'bout more bacon? Cinnamon bun?"

"No thanks, I certainly appreciate all this." Now was the time to bring up his third concern. "Afraid I haven't any money to pay for it – you see --"

"No money? But how – "

"It was in my money pouch, kept under the saddle. And now that ornery horse's taken off with it. But listen, Mrs. Barnes. I'd be much obliged if you'd let me work it off. I can chop wood, do most anything." He eyed the growing stack of dirty dishes by the sink nervously.

She thought a moment, sipping her coffee. "Say, there is somethin'. With Harry gone since yesterday, been worryin' 'bout the wood pile, also the the milkin', pitchin' hay from the loft, fillin' the feed bins – To make matters worse, we're expectin' more guests around noon, couple business men, as well as a travelin' man of the cloth – "

"I'd be glad to do that," Jacob said with relief. "Do you think I could borrow a jacket? A bit chilly this morning, and mine's – "

Emma burst into one of her hearty laughs. "You don't have to tell me."

Slipping on a red plaid wool jacket hanging on a peg in the mudroom, Jacob felt strange. *Jacket's way too big for me. That Harry must be pretty hefty. And that conversation with Schmidt last night left me a bit shook up ... Took on a bigger turn like I figured, like this big jacket ...*

Entering the stable, he was surprised by its size. But then, he reasoned, it was part of a hostelry, and guests would require accommodation for their horses, their vehicles. There were already two or three horses in there, a buggy with one wheel off, a dray wagon, one or two cows, and a bunch of chickens wandering in and out.

"The first thing," he said to himself, is to pitch down that hay." The loft was filled with the summer's sweet scented hay, still yellow-green, still resilient in its fibers. "That oughta be enough," he said, after five or six forkfuls. He climbed down the ladder and proceeded to pitch the hay into the individual stalls.

He heard a whinny which made his blood freeze and the pitchfork suspend in mid-air, its load of hay slowly filtering down stalk by stalk onto the barn floor. "No! It can't be!" he shouted, throwing down the pitchfork and walking quickly toward the back.

Prince stood there, still saddled, unconcernedly munching oats in an empty stall, his reins trailing on the barn floor. "Prince! How'd you get here, boy?" Prince pricked his ears, turned his big head slightly, gave what could have been a horse smile, and nonchalantly turned back to munching oats.

The only explanation, Jacob considered, w*as that Mr. Barnes must have left the door open, and Prince, recognizing a nice place when he saw one, offering all the comforts of his home barn, must have wandered in. There's no way of knowing when that was. That ornery critter might have been there all along!*

Jacob was overcome. Forgetting his earlier feelings of anger and resentment against Prince, even against Matthew Schmidt, Jacob put his arms around the horse's neck, buried his face in the thick mane, and wept. It was the first time he'd wept since he was a child.

Another hour went by, and Naomi and Harry Barnes had not returned. After a few brief words with Emma in the kitchen while laying two dollars on the table, Jacob drew on his jacket, retrieved from Prince's saddle.

"You're off then?" she asked. "You're not waiting for them to come back?"

"Can't risk that," he said, "I can't wait. It's possible she's not returning with your husband, but staying on in Fargo – for something connected with her father."

"Yes, that's likely. Matt'll be anxious about that, though."

As will I, Jacob thought, buttoning up the jacket.

"Of course, you realize, Mr. Bowers, you might just meet them on the way back if you leave now."

"Know that, ma'am, it's possible." Rushing out now through the mudroom toward the barn and Prince, he added under his breath, "Hope not, hope not."

11

In this Place

"Toast? Coffee?"

Naomi was disappointed. "Is that all you have? You don't include breakfast with the dollar I paid for the room?"

"Be another twenty-five cents," Mrs. Ransom snapped.

"I didn't bring my reticule downstairs with me," Naomi pointed out.

The woman eyed her shrewdly. "Leave the money on your way out, then. I'll bring some bacon and more toast directly, grape jelly on the side."

Naomi's thoughts poised briefly on the grape jelly, then went on to realize once again that she hadn't eaten anything since noon yesterday at the Menasa Inn. There'd been much of that on this journey, *depriving the body to feed the soul – was that it? What it means right now, however,* she thought, *is that I'm feeling a little light-headed. Not to mention having passed such an uncomfortable night. Empty stomach, food for the soul -- my head full of tests and trials – not only of my own, but also of others. Still, I shouldn't complain. The Lord has brought me safely here … Oh Lord, in your wisdom …*

"Here's your breakfast, then," a sharp edge to Mrs. Ransom's voice as she none too gently set down a cup of coffee and a plate with two pieces of bacon and one slice of toast. "Grape jelly out directly."

"Thank you," Naomi acknowledged, still disappointed at the plate's meagerness. Unfolding her napkin, she looked round the dining room. Only one other person was there, despite the many sounds of humanity all around her during the night. She was an older, gray-haired woman in the far corner, preoccupied with her own thoughts.

How unfortunate, Naomi considered, *not to see the foreign woman in the room next to mine. I'd so hoped she was Birgitta, as I'd hoped for that woman I'd run after down the street last night. Crazy thing to do, I admit.*

Hurriedly she finished the toast and bacon, the bacon rancid, the toast burnt, and the grape jelly never arriving. The coffee, as well, left much to be desired. She sighed in disappointment, remembering Emma's kitchen. Yet her first concern this morning had to be not food but rather finding the sheriff's office. She hoped Harry would come by soon to help her look for it.

I feel so sorry for Harry, she thought, *being turned away last night by Mrs. Ransom. Can't help but smile, though. Maybe he was luckier — excellent beds, indeed.*

As if in response to her thoughts, Mrs. Ransom suddenly appeared beside her. "Man for you." She pointed toward the hall, then disappeared in the direction of the kitchen.

"Mornin', miss," Harry said, meeting her in the hallway, looking somewhat uneasy while turning his hat around in his hands. "Hope it's not too early for you, but we got to get started. Everythin' all right here?"

"It provided shelter, at least, have to be grateful for that, given last night's circumstances. A sharp contrast to the Menasa Inn."

"Reckon so. We do try our best."

"Do you think Matthew will be all right?"

"Sure hope so. Nothin' we can do about it from here, 'cept trust Emma to look after him. I'm anxious to get back, as I'm sure you're well aware." He looked none too happy with her and with the whole the situation in which he'd unexpectantly found himself.

"Wait a moment, I'll just get my case, you go on out to the wagon." Naomi rushed up the stairs, down again, and laid a twenty-five-cent piece on the hall table. "Hope she's satisfied," she said in the direction of the kitchen.

As Naomi climbed up beside Harry, she recognized the enormity of what she'd asked Harry to do. In fact, there'd been something even greater in what she'd asked Jacob to do back at Prairie Lake's harvest picnic. All she could say to Harry right now, though, was, "I know you're anxious to get back, and I'm grateful for your help, more than I could ever repay, for your help with Matthew as well."

Disregarding her thanks, whether deliberately or not, he continued, "You know, as far as Matt's concerned, there's a possibility she'll get that old codger, Mike Hauglund, to come 'round, keep him company a bit. They'll have a lot in common." As he flicked the reins over the team's rumps, he said, "Well, miss, where to now? I'm all for headin' home, next ferry back to Moorhead in a half hour or so, we could just make it."

This took her by surprise. "Why Harry, you know I first need to find the sheriff."

"You're sure of that?"

"Of course, that's the whole point of coming here."

"How much time will it take?" He consulted his pocket watch.

She thought a moment. "If we talk to the sheriff, we might also find out more about Birgitta."

"Well -- maybe." After a wry smile, hiding something, "Reckon he'll know them lawyers, all right."

"Do you think we can locate the sheriff's office? Shouldn't be too difficult."

He smiled again. "No, reckon not too difficult. Slept there last night."

"*What?*"

"Said I slept there last night. It's on Second Street South, closer to the river. Couple more blocks."

"Harry! You *didn't* – you *weren't* – that saloon – "

"No, wasn't anythin' like that. After I left you at that boardin' house, I drove around back toward the center of town, wonderin' what to do, almost ready to curl up in the back of the wagon, 'cept them horses wouldn't been too happy 'bout that and it was gettin' mighty cold."

"Yes, you know I worried about you."

"Thought you might, you got a mind that kinda reaches out. Anyways, as I was sayin', so what do I see, turnin' a corner, but the sheriff's office, light in there, deputy asleep, feet up on the desk. He weren't too happy when I woke him up, but we got to talkin' and he finally said I could hunker down in one of them empty cells, put the team and wagon in their stable across the way. Not the most comfortable – the cell, I mean, couldn't vouch for the stable. You probably did much better last night – but leastways it was warm and dry. Ladies in the Eatery across the street always bring in the food. Breakfast this mornin' not bad at all – though couldn't compare with my Emma's, not in a thousand years. Long 'bout then the sheriff came in, talked to him, his name's Brian Jameson."

"You did?" Her excitement grew. "Talked to him about my father? *His name – B. J. -- my father's initials reversed – that explains the note.* Did the sheriff say anything about Birgitta?"

"Only about Birgitta. Your father's your affair and seems to me you'd best deal with it. Birgitta's really only mine."

Naomi didn't quite agree with him about Birgitta, but she asked nevertheless, "What did he say about her, then?"

"Said they'd ask around, keep an eye out for her. I had a pretty good description, you see."

"That depends on whether the lady in the phaeton outside the lawyers' office yesterday was Birgitta. But what about *them,* those lawyers?"

"Knew 'bout them, of course. Long term relationship, up and down one side of the law or 'tother. Sheriff some'at shy to talk 'bout them, couldn't figure that out." He slowed the team. "Whoa, there boys, whoa. But miss, you'll want to talk to the sheriff yourself. Said he'd be here most of the mornin'."

When he hesitated, she asked, "Aren't you coming in? I'd be grateful for your support."

"If you want, though far as I'm concerned, already took care of what I had to say about Birgitta and heard everythin' the sheriff had to say. I've got to get back, already missed the first ferry back to Moorhead."

"But I've still got that business of Matthew's to take care of." She'd almost forgotten. "I promised him. It was his main reason for leaving Prairie Lake."

"Important business?"

"Some legal matters, the papers are in that oil packet under this driving bench, forgot to take them in with me last night, good thing they're still here. I promised Matthew that I'd take them to his lawyer in Moorhead, he said his lawyer's name is among the papers."

Harry thought a minute, scratching his bald spot, replacing his straw hat. "Reckon that puts a different slant on things, good reason for my stayin' a mite longer. As it happens, I know two of them lawyers practicin' in Moorhead, other one by name only." He paused again.

"Look, here's what I'm thinkin'. I've a mind to take them papers and deal with it on my way back. After all, old Matt and me, well, we're kinfolk, you know." He reached under the bench, pulled out the packet, and unwrapped it. "Hmm, yup, Magers and Wilson. Done business with' em, had to borrow some money once to put on an addition back of the inn, kitchen never big enough for Emma seemed like. They helped me deal with the bank. T'weren't easy, didn't have much what they called collateral."

Rewrapping the papers in the oil skin, he became more serious. "Now listen, miss – I mean Naomi, 'cause I feel I can call you that, almost part of the family, now listen. You've got a much more serious thing to deal with. It'll depend, 'course, on what that sheriff in there has to say. I want to hear it, too, in case you need more help, in case there's nothin' for it but for both of us just to return to Menasa"

"Without -- " She couldn't finish. The thought of this being a dead end, returning without her father, was too much.

He looked uncomfortable. "You know what I mean. Now as for Matt's business – "

Trying to regain her composure, she said, "I feel responsible for Matthew's business. After all, he entrusted it to me, and it seemed rather urgent. But if you're willing to take care of that, Harry, I'd be most grateful. Now we'd best go inside. You might as well leave that packet in the wagon."

The sheriff's office, originally a wooden, one-storey building, had more recently been joined at the rear by a limestone extension housing the jail cells. Off to one side on First Avenue South was a livery stable, housing several horses and a wagon. Looking at the cell block, Naomi had a very uneasy feeling. Was it possible her father was a prisoner in there?

A man wearing a deputy's badge on his tan canvas jacket sat outside the office door, smoking a pipe. Seeing Naomi, he got to his feet and raised his dark felt hat. "Morning, ma'am, sir," he said. "Sheriff left a message for you, if you be Mr. Barnes, sir."

"I am," Harry assured him, then annoyed, "you mean he's not here?"

"Then I'm to tell you sheriff got called away this morning, just after he talked to you. Urgent business out Centralia way. Fellows got into an argument over a horse, one of them shot. The man not the horse. Sheriff says, if you don't mind, to wait."

"How long'll that be? I've got urgent business of my own."

"Can't say. Let's see, might take, say quarter of an hour ride down there, some time to look over the situation, ride back. You got the time, sir?"

Harry pulled out his pocket watch and flipped open the lid. "Ses eight, few minutes past."

"Thanks. Well, I reckon that means he should be back by nine, or thereabouts."

Harry looked at Naomi. "Of all the bad luck! Another hour lost."

Naomi felt this disappointment as well. "Can you tell me," she asked the deputy, "that is, do you know if my father's here?"

"Your father? You think your pa's here?"

"Yes, my father."

"What's his name?"

"John Beckman, from Prairie Lake."

"Hmm," said the deputy, rubbing his chin, "name don't sound familiar."

"But he must be here, you must know him, you must have seen him! He's a tall man, dark hair and eyes, a little bit of gray at the temples, a small beard, moustache – "

The deputy shook his head.

"He'd be wearing a black hat with a wide brim, a Hudson Bay jacket." She was growing desperate. "And with a man and his boy, named Frankson – and they – "

"Don't rightly know, miss. Sheriff'll know. You need to wait for him, sheriff's orders."

Naomi turned angrily to Harry. "They're hiding something, I know it."

"You're welcome to wait inside," the deputy offered.

"How long, then?" Harry insisted.

"Like I said, mister, 'bout half an hour, most likely more."

"Harry," Naomi insisted, "let's not waste this time, it's too valuable for both of us. Suppose we go over to the lawyers' office – " she glanced in a meaningful way at the deputy. "You know the one."

Harry scratched his head. "You think they might tell us -- "

"Can't be sure. In any case, I'm wondering if they could deal with Matthew's business in that packet. I know I have reservations about them, you know what we're suspecting. In any event, Charles Billings actually met Matthew the morning they left Menasa. And they know you and Emma, of course, as proprietors of the inn. Don't you think this might make them feel more responsible?"

"Dunno, dunno," Harry repeated. "Dunno 'bout that."

"If they can take care of whatever Matthew needs, then wouldn't that save you time? Otherwise, we'll just be sitting around waiting for that sheriff to get back."

This appeared to convince him. "We'll be back shortly," he said to the deputy as he helped Naomi back into the wagon.

Pulling up to the hitching rail on Main Avenue in front *of C. Billings and R.P. Fletcher, Attourneys at Law,* the first thing they noticed was a phaeton with a team of bays tethered beside them.

"They're here!" Harry exclaimed. "Dunno what we're goin' to say, goin' to ask, even. But I'll take in Matt's papers anyways."

Climbing the steep narrow staircase up to Billings and Fletcher's law office, Harry asked, "How do we bring it up? About Birgitta, I mean. Nothin' yet to accuse 'em of."

"You'd better do most of the talking, Harry," she cautioned. "I'm afraid I might start us off wrong."

"Why not with Matt's papers?" he whispered, knocking on the door with the frosted glass window and the lawyers' names imprinted in large black letters.

"Come in, unlocked," called a voice.

Charles Billings was standing at a tall wooden filing cabinet, looking through some files. He'd laid out several folders on the desk nearby. His partner, Randolph Fletcher, sat at a large oak desk in front of the windows. Both looked up in surprise as Harry and Naomi entered, with Fletcher suddenly pushing back his chair and getting to his feet. Billings slammed the filing cabinet drawer with a loud bang.

"Ah, Mr. Barnes and Miss – er – Miss Bolton?"

"Miss Beckman," Billings provided. "What a surprise to see you here in Fargo, what a most pleasant surprise. I did understand, however, back in Menasa, that you had some business here, is that not correct?"

"It is, sir." She didn't want to elaborate.

"How then may I – we – my partner, Mr. Fletcher, and I, be of service?"

Fletcher came around from behind his desk after first replacing his pen back in an elaborate silver caddy. "Do, please sit down, make yourselves comfortable." He gestured toward a row of four solid-looking oak chairs, upholstered in green brocade, arranged along the wall opposite the filing cabinet. "Ah, excuse me for a moment. I see the sun is in your eyes. Do allow me to adjust this window shade." He pulled down an oilcloth shade halfway, throwing the room into a soft greenish light.

It reminded Naomi of the gaslights on the streets the night before and of Birgitta and what they needed to ask. Nevertheless, she knew Harry had agreed to open the reasons for their visit, and she waited anxiously for him to begin, waited while both lawyers continued to make small talk – the weather, their trip from Menasa, the health of Mrs. Barnes, and, from Billings, the health of Matthew Schmidt. At the mention of Matthew's name, Naomi discreetly poked Harry in the ribs with her elbow, resting on the arm of the chair beside her.

He picked up his cue. "Well, now that you mention my cousin, Matt, sirs, that's why I'm here. He wanted me to take care of the business in this here packet." He pointed to the oil packet lying across his knees.

"What, sir, if I may ask, is the substance of that business?" Billings pulled out his desk chair and sat down, his desk being at right angles to Fletcher's.

"Dunno rightly. Naomi – Miss Beckman, that is – and I left in somethin' of a hurry, ain't had time to look through it."

"Perhaps you'd be so kind as to pass it over, sir?" Fletcher opened the packet and began looking through the sheaf of foolscap papers. Some were yellow, some with black print on white sheets, and a few were handwritten. There were also what seemed to be several half sheets of blue paper.

"Hmm," he said. "Look here, Charles, these pertain to property deeds, titles, these others to different matters. Suppose you look over the property business, that's your bailiwick."

Naomi and Harry sat in suspense while the lawyers examined the documents, sheet by sheet, fragment by fragment. Occasionally there were mumbled words like, *plat map … notary seal … land office … St. Cloud … deed … last will and testament …*

These last words alarmed Naomi. She recalled her last visit with Matthew. He'd seemed anxious about something. There'd been a kind of urgency in his gestures and his voice. He'd pointed to his good suit, folded on top of the dresser and kept mentioning the word *wait*. It didn't make sense, why hadn't she asked him to explain?

"There's a will?" she asked Fletcher.

"Yes, miss, a proposed Last Will and Testament. Two of them, in fact. One of them signed by Matthew Peter Schmidt, and the other by Charlotte Christina Hoffman Schmidt. But they are rough copies, with a noted request in what I assume is

Mr. Schmidt's hand, to have them drawn up formally and nota-rized." Naomi looked worriedly at Harry.

"How 'bout the contents?" Harry drew himself up, pointing to the papers.

"I'm afraid, sir, that is not possible under the circumstances. The information is confidential until the will is probated."

"That's correct, Mr. Barnes," Billings confirmed. "But as for these property deeds – parcel number forty-five east of Prairie Lake, and another referring to several parcels in the state of Indiana, these are what one would call in the public domain. It seems Mr. Schmidt, jointly with his wife, owned a large amount of property, both urban as well as rural."

"What about that property?" Harry asked.

"The instructions here are to verify this information by checking records held by state land offices, the one in St. Cloud, Minnesota, the other in Indiana. I'll have to confirm where ex-actly that is located." Billings coughed slightly. "It could be a long, drawn-out procedure, you understand. And costly."

Both men quickly scanned through several documents once again, taking notes and occasionally exchanging comments. Harry pulled out his watch. "It's gone on to almost nine. We'd best be going."

"But Harry – " she lowered her voice. How was she going to remind him?

"Well now, lady and gentleman," said Fletcher, "if that's all you require, we shall be all too happy to take care of these mat-ters. Mind you, they will take some time, as my colleague has said."

"How long?" Harry asked.

"I'd say about three, four weeks, wouldn't you, Charles?"

"At least. The work'll require some traveling on our part, some searching through records which might be hard to find, or incomplete. But rest assured, we shall do our best, as we always assure our clients."

Fletcher glanced furtively at Billings. "As for the bill – well, I see, looking at some of these papers, that Mr. Schmidt has provided his full address. We shall be sending him the statement, as well as copies of the documents."

"At the moment, however, sir, we require a retaining fee," Billings added.

"A retaining fee?" Harry blurted out. "What for? You ain't done nothin' yet."

"It is standard practice, I assure you," said Fletcher.

"How much, then?" Naomi asked, fingering her reticule.

"Three dollars. I shall be happy to provide you with a receipt."

Her heart sank. That would leave her only a few dollars. She looked appealingly at Harry.

"Didn't bring but a dollar with me," he said apologetically. "Sure didn't expect anythin' like what's happened these last two days." He reached in the back pocket of his overalls and drew out a wallet, and after looking carefully through it, handed her a well-worn dollar bill. "Say," he suddenly asked, "You fellers paid up at the inn?"

The lawyers exchanged looks. "Certain of that," Billings said. "Of course, as we usually do."

"Not too sure of that, Charles." He gave him a wink, a subtle gesture. "But suppose, Mr. Barnes, Miss Beckman, suppose we waive our fee for these transactions, considering that we expect to pass through Menasa again on future business. We shall look forward to your hospitality, Mrs. Barnes' excellent table."

Naomi gave a sigh of relief, but touched Harry's arm meaningfully. Not understanding her gesture, he replaced his wallet back in his pocket and stood up to leave. "So we'll be off, then, sirs. Short of time as it is."

"Wait, Harry!" It was now obviously up to Naomi to raise the question of Birgitta's disappearance. Taking a deep breath, she began, "Sirs, you may remember the Swedish girl at the inn? The domestic named Birgitta? Birgitta Magnusson?"

The men exchanged looks. Fletcher began leafing through Matthew's papers once again, taking up his pen as if to make additional notes. Billings coughed slightly, covering his mouth with a large initialed handkerchief. "You'll excuse me," he said, "I seem to have caught a slight chill."

"They're stalling, Harry," Naomi whispered, touching his arm.

"The girl," Harry repeated, realizing his cue to Naomi's relief. "She's disappeared, ran off."

"The day you left," Naomi added.

"Is that so? Do you have any idea why? Or where she might be?" Fletcher's manner was smooth, convincing.

"None," said Naomi. "We are very worried about her."

"Understandably, understandably so," said Billings. He made a move to usher them toward the door.

"And rest assured, if we receive any news of that lady, we shall most certainly do our best for her," Fletcher added, replacing his pen in the silver caddy and looking out the window.

The office door was hastily closed, the meeting terminated. Without saying anything, Naomi and Harry went down the steep stairway and out onto the street, where the team waited impatiently, having edged the wagon almost sideways against the hitching rail.

"What do you think, Harry?"

"Dunno what to think. Them fellers pretty smooth, all right."

"That's just the trouble. They were all too ready to end the conversation about Birgitta. You'd have expected them to ask more questions, wouldn't you? To make some suggestions about where she might be found?"

"You're right there," Harry replied. "And if you look up now, you'll see one of 'em watching us out the window."

Remounting the wagon, they headed for Second Street. "You know, I sure don't feel easy in my mind 'bout leavin' Matt's business with those two."

"Why? I don't think they can do much harm there."

"Reckon not," he said slowly, "hope not. Won't worry Matt with it, not just yet, anyways. I'm beginin' to wish I'd taken it to them lawyers I know 'bout in Moorhead, like Matt wanted."

On the short drive to the sheriff's office, Naomi's anxiety about her father increased. Her thoughts were hard to control. *I'm afraid of what this sheriff's going to tell me. I'd looked forward every moment of this long journey to the meeting with my father, I almost dread it. Everything points to something wrong. That deputy outside the office – unwilling to tell me anything. Surely he knows what's was going on? Is there some kind of a conspiracy going on here?*

As they entered, the sheriff stood up from behind his desk. "You've arrived, I see. My apologies for asking you to come back." His appearance was not at all what Naomi expected: a short, burly man in a leather jacket over a tan shirt, the lower part of his face was obscured by a large moustache, his eyes partially hidden by heavy, overhanging eyebrows. A cartridge belt with revolvers in both holsters was carelessly thrown on the desk. Her first impressions were decidedly off-putting.

As he came out from behind his desk, a decided limp rendering his walk awkward, he extended his hand. "Miss Beckman! I'm delighted you're here and mighty surprised, truth be said. I didn't expect it. A long journey for you to make, not many women, I'm thinking, would venture it. A real test of your grit, I might add."

Naomi looked surprised. That remark seemed so strangely relevant to the tests she was convinced the Lord had placed upon her, that it unnerved her.

His grip on her hand was so strong as to be painful. "We've been waiting for you since this morning, when I met Mr. Barnes. He told me a little about your journey, your circumstances. And about that – that other lady. I'm sorry to hear about Matthew Schmidt, however. Hopefully he's recovering well?"

"Appears to be, sheriff," Harry answered for her. "Leastways, last time I saw him."

"We both hope so," she added mechanically, still unnerved by the nature of the documents in Fletcher's hands this morning..

"Now then," said Jameson, "I know why you're here and I'm prepared to help as much as possible. But first, won't you sit down? Some coffee?" He turned toward a sliding door made of iron bars, leading into what looked like the jail section of the building. "Dirk – bring another chair, will you, and some of that stuff you call coffee?" He smiled, adding, "We kid Dirk, my chief deputy, all the time 'bout that, but the truth is, it's at least drinkable and we don't have much choice. He's a strange sort of critter, all right, sometimes hardly seems human."

Naomi sat down in the round-backed oak chair Jameson set for her, placing her reticule securely in her lap. All in one breath, she blurted out, "I need to know about my father, John Beckman, and where he is. I've come to bring him home."

"Ah yes, Miss Beckman, that is indeed the heart of the matter, but all in due time, all in due time. Right now, here's Dirk with a chair for Mr. Barnes, and his more or less drinkable coffee.

"Coffee, Sheriff, Miss Beckman," Dirk growled. "Waste of time, if you ask me." He set the mugs down on a corner of the sheriff's desk with a heavy thud, spilling a little on the sheriff's gun holster.

Naomi looked at Dirk with an uneasy feeling. There was something about him reminding her of that dark shadowy form she'd seen silhouetted against her parlor window, something about his deep, almost growl-like voice. "Oh," she exclaimed, "Aren't you the one who – "

He didn't answer but quickly looked away, whispered something to the sheriff, then quickly disappeared back toward the cells.

"Ah yes, John Beckman," Sheriff Jameson said coming back to the point. "That business regarding your father."

"Is he here? Please tell me, sheriff," she pleaded, "is he here in this place, in this jail? What is it all about? I need answers, and I need them now!"

"All right, to answer your question directly, no, Miss Beckman, he is not here."

However much she had expected such an answer, it came as a shock. Even Harry remained silent, leaving his coffee untouched, as did Naomi.

"No, he is not in this jail, never has been, that is, if that's what you were worried about."

"Where is he then?" Naomi realized she was holding onto her reticule so tightly that her hands were numb.

"He is at Ft. Abercrombie."

"Abercrombie!" Harry almost shouted. "Ft. Abercrombie – why that's way down river – or up river, that is."

"Indeed it is, Mr. Barnes. About thirty-five miles south."

"But why – how – is he well? What's happened? How – " Naomi's questions came in fragments, all at once. Her mind raced with possibilities, none of them making sense.

"Is he in trouble with the law?" Harry asked, his mind obviously still preoccupied with Billings and Fletcher.

"No, I'm happy to say, that is not the case." The sheriff paused, obviously working out how best to explain. "I know you are distressed, Miss Beckman, to learn he is not in Fargo as you expected. No doubt you have had a long and difficult journey all the way from – er – Prairie Lake, is it?"

"You can believe that about the difficulties, sir," commented Harry. "But look, can't we get on with this? Here's a woman who's been through a lot lately, long and anxious journey no exception. And I need to get back to my place of business in Menasa. So give us the facts, pure and simple. No more beatin' 'round the bush. The law ain't usually like that, I reckon, more direct, black and white, as you might say."

The sheriff smiled. "Quite right, well said. Here is what I must tell you." He leaned back his chair slightly, rocking it back and forth as he collected his thoughts together.

"I'll give you a brief summary, you'll be able to have the details later from – " he hesitated, " from someone, that is. About two weeks ago there was a skirmish between a couple of Shakota warriors and some settlers up in Argusville, some ten, twelve miles north. The warriors wanted to trade pelts for horses, the settlers needed their horses more than the pelts and refused. Shooting broke out, a couple of people were wounded on both sides, two men were killed."

"Pa – " Naomi drew a sharp breath.

"No, I'm happy to say – or rather, I should say relieved to say, he was only wounded."

"But sheriff," Harry interrupted, "what happened to Naomi's father? You said he got shot?"

"We'll never know by whom – possibly accidentally by one of the settlers."   "Wounded? How badly?" Naomi's distress was rising. "Where is he now? You said he wasn't here? You said he was down at Ft. Abercrombie? Mr. Frankson? Ted? Why send my father down there? Where are the Franksons?"

"Now please, miss, just calm down. I can understand, miss, why you have so many questions." Sheriff Jameson looked more serious as he finally pushed his holster belt aside from the spilled coffee and leaned across the desk. "You see, the bullet shattered part of the bone in his upper arm and infection set in. I have a copy of the surgeon's report on file here in my office, also a description of Mr. Frankson's condition, which I'll pass on to you."

"But why move him -- them? Harry asked. " Seems to me that'd be more dangerous."

"You must know that the Fort has an excellent military hospital, as do most of the larger forts in these territories. That's why he and Mr. Frankson were sent there, and Mr. Frankson quite naturally wanted to keep his young son with him. They were carefully moved from here by one of our Red River paddleboats. By the way, I understand from a telegram sent by the post commandant that Mr. Frankson is doing well."

"What about my father?"

Sheriff Jameson hesitated, fingering the cartridges in the belt on his desk. "Once he is out of danger, once there is no sign of gangrene, they assume he'll be able to return home. Of course, should the infection take a turn for the worse, should he be unable to – if by some unfortunate turn – "

Naomi understood the *if,* like a stab to the heart. The sheriff need not have completed his sentence. She had received an answer to the strange note, all right, but it was nevertheless still plagued with *ifs.* Much of the puzzle remained. "That message I received a week ago in Prairie Lake – it said to come to Fargo, to bring a wagon."

"Your father did not write that message."

"Not write it? Then why – "

"You noticed my deputy, Dirk, a few moments ago? The man who brought out the coffee, the chairs?"

"Yes," she said hesitantly. "He was the one?"

"Yes, he brought you that note. Being unable to write it at the time, your father dictated it to Dirk. Then Dirk rode all the way to Prairie Lake – a hard ride, two days there, two days back -- to deliver it, the postal service being what it is. Time -- the urgency -- was too important to risk sending it that way."

He glanced over at the door communicating with the jail block. "And, ahem, I must tell you, he was mighty annoyed when you refused to see him. Annoyed is probably not a strong enough word for it. He could have explained, could have told you about your father. As it was, he was given no indication of what your plans were, what we could expect here in Fargo." He paused. "Indeed, what response we could pass on to your anxious father."

Naomi was at a loss for an answer. "I'm sorry, I thought – he could have been -- " He could have been Satan, walking to and fro upon the earth, was what she'd thought.

"Well, whatever you thought, Miss Beckman, the results would probably have been the same. You see, your father, lying gravely ill in our local infirmary, wanted desperately to see you. At the time the prognosis was not good, and I'm sorry to say, that is still the case. Your father thought that the only thing to do was to send for you to come to Fargo to see him one last time. Should he recover, on the other hand, you could take him and the Franksons home. He'd lost his horse and wagon, his riding horse, and most of the game. He was sure that neither he nor the Franksons would be able to replace it with what few resources they had left."

"But I no longer have a wagon, sheriff, or a horse," Naomi shrugged her shoulders. "A neighbor kindly offered to bring me from Prairie Lake. It happened that he had business in Moorhead."

"Wagon got wrecked, had to put the critter down," Harry added, smoothing back his hair in a gesture intended to disguise his real feelings at the memory. "Dirty shame, that was. Left Matt – and Naomi here – stranded."

"But you see, Miss Beckman, the problem was, the note was sent off to you before he had to be moved down to Ft. Abercrombie. By then it was too late to inform you."

He glanced again at the cell-block door. "Certainly Dirk, even by my order, wasn't prepared to make that trip again. Besides, Miss Beckman, we couldn't know whether you'd already left or not. For all we knew, if you were already on your way, it would be too late. Your father might be – " He realized he needn't finish that sentence either.

The words struck Naomi forcibly. What had it all amounted to? Her father's trust in her, her own father's test of her, he and Jacob had laid it upon her, and she had taken it on. Could she think of them as the Lord's agents, as the Lord working through them? Her mind searched for Job's words, words that would help her understand. *Oh Lord – oh Lord – you were with me – you who made the rivers surge, the stars at night –* She knew she hadn't remembered them right. It didn't seem to matter.

"How, then – " she began. "Ft. Abercrombie? Thirty-five miles? South?" Although the text of Job's came to her, confused, perhaps, but nevertheless there, she could not think of the next step. *What will be demanded of me next,* she thought. *What way is open to me? Please, Lord, may it not be too late …*

12

River Currents

After her interview with Sheriff Jameson, Naomi stood waiting outside the office while Harry checked his team's harnesses and chatted with the sheriff's deputy. Naomi was only vaguely aware of what they were saying: *weather ... this time of year ... rained five inches ... river flooded last March ... wheat yield ... Shakota ... fort ...* They were merely words empty of meaning, confusy in sound. *I don't fully understand what the sheriff said about my father,* she thought. *My father gravely wounded – why, why? That's Harry over there, about to leave. I'll soon be helpless and alone. The Lord has broken me and left me reduced to nothingness ... Naomi of the Nothing... That seems the best name for me, the name the Lord has given me ... Naomi of the Nothing ... why? Why?*

Harry handed her the small wicker case containing the few clothes she'd hastily packed back at the Menasa Inn and repacked again at Mrs. Ransom's. She took it absently, and just as absently retied the ribbons of her black straw bonnet with the silk lilies. It seemed that being *Naomi of the Nothing* removed both body and brain, and that she was somehow floating around devoid of both.

"Well, now Miss Naomi," Harry said, unwinding the teams' reins from the sheriff's hitching rail, his last gesture before mounting the wagon, "sure do hate to leave you like this."

"It's – it's all right," she managed, but that was a lie. It was anything but all right.

"Got to get back to Menasa. Emma'll be right anxious, I 'spect. Been gone two whole days. Worried 'bout me, you, Birgitta."

"Imagine so."

"Wonderin' what happened to the girl."

"Likely."

"And now she's got all that work by herself, without Birgitta's help. Couple more guests expected – let's see, what day's today?"

"Saturday," offered the deputy, from his chair outside the office door. "Know that 'cause should of gotten the day off."

"Thanks. Yup, couple travelers due from the west yesterday, man of the cloth comin' from Iowa, forget who the other two guests are, may be due late today or tomorrow. And bein' the only inn for miles, you never know who'll drop in unexpected, like." He glanced at Naomi, as if reminded of her own *dropping in.*

"You're bein' awful quiet, miss. Know it weren't good news, all right. Hard to take in, your pa bein' shot up and sent down there and all."

"Yes," she managed to say, "a shock." *Shot up* – a horrible sound to it, why'd he say that?

"What're you plannin' to do?"

"Don't know." She shook her head.

"Well, I hope somethin'll come to you, you bein' the kind of woman so determined and all." He set his foot on a front wheel spoke. "I'll be off, then, but, like I said, hate to leave you here, stranded like this you might say. Sheriff'll most likely help." He gave a sardonic smile as he added, "Last resort, try them lawyers." Climbing up onto the driving bench and adjusting the reins, he asked, "Think you'll be comin' back through Menasa? Always welcome, you know. Best route back to Prairie Lake, anyways, and, like I said, not too many places to spend the night along the road."

Turning around on the driving bench as the horses pulled away and raising his hat, he called back, "Besides, you'll want to pick up Matt if he's well enough to travel – and if, of course, he hasn't already decided to come to Moorhead to check in with his lawyers himself."

As Harry's wagon turned the corner, a sudden weakness in Naomi's knees forced her to sit down abruptly on the steps. The sound of the wagon's iron-rimmed wheels against the brick pavement as they rolled away in the direction of the river ferry brought with it the shock-wave of reality.

"Say, miss, sheriff says – " the deputy seated behind her broke into her thoughts.

Still fighting against that confusion of emotions, trying to hold onto some reality at least, she turned absently toward the voice.

"Sheriff says, when that feller Barnes left, to come back inside. Got some talkin' to do, I reckon."

Slowly she raised the heavy weight of her body off the step, mechanically smoothed down her skirt, and picked up the wicker case and her reticule. She walked through the office door, unaware the deputy was holding it open for her.

"Sit down, please, Miss Beckman," Sheriff Jameson said, gesturing toward the chair beside his desk. Dirk or someone had apparently removed the extra one, where Harry had been sitting. The thought brought another acute reminder of his departure, her loss.

"Now we have some business to discuss." He looked at her intently. "Are you all right? Dirk – " he called toward the jail block. "Bring the lady a glass of water, will you?"

He waited until the water appeared, Dirk still avoiding any acknowledgement of Naomi's presence. "Yes, miss, some business, some plans, as I said."

"Plans?" She took a few sips, her hand shaking as she set the glass down

"Yes, plans for getting you down to Ft. Abercrombie."

Naomi stared at him. "Abercrombie?"

"That's what I said." He smiled faintly. "You don't think we'd leave you here? No, right from the start, we assured your father we'd look after you."

"After me?" Naomi still didn't seem to be able to follow him.

"Of course, miss. Now here's what I propose." He opened a desk drawer and drew out a printed sheet of paper and turned it upside down for her to read. "Here's a handbill for *The Morning Star*, a sternwheeler traveling up and down the Red. As you can see, there's a departure this morning from the wharf over near where the Moorhead ferry docks. I believe you came that way yesterday?"

"I guess so." It seemed more like several years, although she wasn't sure of anything anymore, let alone minutes, hours, days.

"So what time's it now?" He glanced up at the big wall clock. "Ah, yes, in just about half an hour. Takes about seven or eight hours, given the adverse current, avoiding snags. You should arrive just about dusk. I'll have my deputy send a telegram to the fort commandant. He'll arrange for someone to meet you when the boat docks."

Naomi looked at the handbill, with its attractive sketch of a large paddle boat, its decks lined with satisfied and waving people, smoke billowing from two enormous smoke stacks in front, and the river foaming up to an alarming height behind a large paddle wheel at the stern. At the bottom was a list of departure times and fares. "But sir," she began, "I don't have the – "

"The fare, you're trying to tell me? Well, don't worry about that. Before your father was sent down to Abercrombie, he left what little cash he had with me. It's over there in that safe, and he has the receipt for it. He said that, if and when you were to get here, to give it to you." He got up from behind the desk.

"Dirk – come out here again, will you?"

After several long minutes, Dirk came through the cell block door, looking annoyed. "Yes, sheriff?" he growled. He obviously considered Naomi had not only caused him great hardship and not a little frustration earlier, but was continuing to cause trouble.

"Open that safe, will you." Aside to Naomi he added, "Dirk here's the only one remembers the combination right."

After Dirk turned the dial back and forth several times, he opened the safe and took out a small manila envelope. Still never looking directly at Naomi, he handed it to the sheriff, then growled something under his breath as he shuffled back toward the cellblock.

The sheriff slit open the envelope and counted out ten, one-dollar bills on his desk. "All here, looks like. So it's yours now, Miss Beckman. More'n enough to pay that fare and then some. Now if you'll just sign this receipt?"

It took some effort to sign her name on the sheet of paper Sheriff Jameson slid in front of her, along with a pencil. It took some effort to make that connection between the letters of that name and herself. Laying down the pencil, she stammered, "But Ft. Abercrombie – but what then?"

"The commandant will also arrange that, never fear. Strange as it may seem, your father was considered to have participated in a kind of military action, helping to defend those settlers in Argusville. Don't rightly know all the ins and outs of military thinking, but not for me – or you – to question. Yes, the fort's a big place, with a barrack for visitors or often officers' families."

Still feeling dazed, still uncertain how all this was to come about, Naomi took the ten dollar bills, folded them into a wad, and thrust the wad deep inside her reticule. "My mother – word – "

"You're trying to say you need to get word home? Of course, I understand that. Meant to do that earlier, got caught up in things here. Wouldn't do to send Dirk again, though." He smiled ruefully in the direction of the jail block. "Maybe a telegram's possible, though I doubt it. Prairie Lake's not on a rail line yet. Don't worry, I'll figure something out."

"I hope – " Naomi started to say, then wasn't sure what she hoped. Events had happened too quickly, plans had unfolded with too much complexity. She sat there, silently, her mind blank except for words like *Job… Jacob .. Morning Star … the stars…singing of the morning stars… floods of water.* Although there seemed to be a linking thread, at the moment she could not find it.

"Are you hungry, Miss Beckman?" he asked.

"What did you say?"

"Would you care for something to eat?"

His question surprised her, not only because it came from the sheriff. It seemed so long since she'd thought about food. For a few moments this morning in Mrs. Ransom's dining room it had seemed important. Right now it was farthest from her thoughts. "I – I don't know," she stammered.

"Never mind, if you're willing, and we hurry, we'll stop by that Miss Jane's Eatery across the street, have her pack you a box lunch. Can't vouch for the food on that sternwheeler and you'll need something to sustain you. Then I'll walk you down to the wharf from there, only a couple blocks. No time to buy the ticket, you can do than onboard. Before I forget, though, there's a couple of documents, a letter, I'd like you to pass on to the commanding officer, Major Richards, once you get there."

He sighed as he opened the drawer of a small filing cabinet built into the desk. "All those legalities, you know. Hard to focus on the job, with all that paper work."

The sheriff drew out a manila folder, extracted several sheets, folded them, and slipped them into an envelope. "If you wouldn't mind putting these in your case, then handing them to the commandant after you arrive? He's meticulous about government legalities."

His last remarks evoked for Naomi thoughts of Birgitta Magnusson. *All those legalities ... those lawyers ... What connection was there? What did they know?*

During their walk down Second Street toward *The Morning Star*, with the sheriff beside her, limping from his peculiar walk, she couldn't dismiss the feeling that, although she'd worked through her first concern, her father's whereabouts, she was leaving another behind. This one was unsolved, the one concerning Birgitta. As she stepped onto the gangplank to board, she turned back toward the sheriff. Using her utmost efforts to speak against the overwhelming noise of the boat's whistle, the steam engine's eminent release of the huge paddle wheel, she shouted, "Something -- need -- ask you -- Birgitta Magnusson."

"Barnes explained," he shouted back. "Don't worry. Here, almost forgot your box lunch."

Noami tucked the box under her arm. "Those lawyers – Billings –" she was shouting louder now. "They know something – could tell – "

"All aboard – all aboard!" Naomi saw a deck hand was about to raise the gangplank and she hurried up the last few steps onto the deck.

"We'll do – best – question – " The sheriff's words were lost as the boat drew away   with the loud clashing of paddle blades against the resisting Red River current.

Standing at the rail, Naomi watched the dock and the figure of Sheriff Jameson standing there get smaller by slow degrees. *How small I feel myself now,* she thought. *I feel lost in a series of events in a landscape that seems to swallow me up. The only thing seeming real right now is the feel of my wicker case handle in my left hand, the strings of my reticule in my right, the bulky weight of a box lunch under my arm against my hip.*

"Ticket, miss?"

An officer in a dark blue uniform with a brimmed cap approached her. He waited expectantly, smiling politely.

"A ticket, you said? I – I don't have one."

He looked annoyed and his smile quickly faded. "You should have purchased one at the steamboat office."

"There wasn't time. The sheriff saw me aboard."

His manner changed again. "We weren't informed about any deportations. I'd better call the first mate."

"No wait," Naomi realized what she should have said. "I was told I could buy my ticket onboard. I have the money here."

"Two dollars, then, if you please."

She set the box and the wicker case down at her feet and reached into her reticule for two of the dollar bills the sheriff had given her.

"Thank you, madam," he said, handing her a slip of paper from a pouch he carried attached to his belt, then punched a hole in it, the shape of a star. "I'll wish you a pleasant trip, madam. For your comfort, refreshments are available in the lounge cabin behind you, or you may wish to take the air on the spacious upper deck." Punch in hand, he turned and began to work his way down groups of passengers along the deck.

Naomi only wanted a place to sit down. All this had left her drained, physically as well as mentally. Looking around she saw several long benches along the cabin wall. Through the windows the cabin looked to have several red velvet sofas, a crystal chandelier, and low tables scattered throughout. The grandeur intimidated her. The fresh air out on deck was far more inviting, although she needed a place to sit down, a quiet, secluded place in which to steady her emotions.

There appeared to be an open, circular deck up above, and on her left was a steep iron stairway leading up to it with a small enclosure at the top. A small bench in a corner on the upper deck just outside the stairwell enclosure seemed well protected from billowing funnel smoke, especially with the steady wind from the west. She sat down, setting the wicker case at her feet, Miss Jane's box lunch on the bench beside her, and adjusted her shawl. The wind threatened to loosen her straw bonnet, so she firmly retied it under her chin.

The riverbank was low, hardly rising above the level of the water, and overgrown with clumps of willows, reeds, and other brush. The view beyond the bank of the distant plains to the west, as the boat twisted around the many curves of the river, began to calm her, little by little. That space, that reassurance of the wonder of God's creation, was not something she'd expected. Yet it was something she knew the Lord had granted her. *Naomi of the Plains – Birgitta of the Plains --*

She woke to the sound of an insistent voice, unaware that she'd fallen asleep or for how long. Someone was bending over her.

"Refreshments, madam?" A woman in a uniform similar to the ticketing officer was holding a basket of bottled lemonade and small cakes iced in green and pink.

Naomi was tempted. She had money and could indulge herself. "Thank you, I think I'd like – " Suddenly, in that moment of temptation, a sense of practical reality came over her as she remembered the box lunch, that she'd had no desire to open, too overcome with emotion to think about eating. And she realized as well that she didn't know what might lie ahead of her, what expenses, what needs.

"No, thank you, I've change my mind."

"Disembarking at the next stop, then, madam?"

"The next stop? Ft. Ambercrombie?" In a panic she reached down for her case.

"No, madam, the next stop is Wolverton. Captain didn't think it worthwhile to pull in at Hickson, this trip. It's such a small place on the east bank, hardly ever has any passengers nor freight to speak of, mainly because the ferry across the river to Comstock has always been unreliable."

"Wolverton next, you said. How far? How long? Then the fort?"

"Wolverton? Hmm, about ten miles or so, the time depends. We seem to be making good headway against the current, so I'd say an hour-and-a-half, then I'd say the fort another two or three hours. Mind you, we only dock in Wolverton for about ten minutes. Even though it's at one of the main roads east, there's generally only a little freight and few passengers to take on."

Shifting her tray of refreshments to the other hip, she added, "well, then, madam, if you don't care for anything … " And she continued on down toward the stern, where small knots of people were gathered at the rails watching the passing scenery, chatting, and pointing out various landmarks.

Less than four hours to go. Her heart beat faster, and the palms of her hands felt moist. At the end of that time so much to face -- father's condition – decisions about returning to Prairie Lake --Henry Frankson and Ted – what about Matthew Schmidt?

Her brain teaming with such unanswered questions, Naomi got up from the bench against the cabin wall, retying the stubborn strings of her black straw bonnet against the wind, then placed the unopened box lunch and her wicker case on the bench so no one would sit there. Leaning against the railing, gazed fixedly down at the swirling current below, the mud-colored waters breaking and foaming against the side of the boat. They had an hypnotic effect, their turbulence somehow echoing her own emotions.

By sheer force of will she finally raised her eyes to the passing river bank, or the expanses of the land beyond, dotted occasionally with clusters of trees or small hillocks, and the sun's gilding of the clouds as it grew lower on the western horizon.

That sight seemed to give her strength and a strange feeling of peace.

. "Oh Lord," she whispered, "for yours is the glory — for yours is the greatness of this world — your graciousness — for these I give thanks."

At that moment, the throbbing of the sternwheeler slowed as its piercing whistle sounded up above her. There was a great rush of water around the stern as the engines reversed the paddle wheel, a shuddering, a slight rising and falling sensation.

"Wolverton! Wolverton!" came several shouts from the lower deck. There were movements around her, passengers heading for the stairs, and deck hands doing something with luggage and ropes.

Naomi looked about in surprise, not seeing any dock , merely several cottage strung out along the west bank. *It must mean Wolverton lies along the east bank,* she thought, *where there's a dock. No need to rush over to the other side and lose my place along this rail with its view of the plains. I've had enough of towns, buildings, people for a long while. Moorhead and Fargo, so confining, smoky, dirty, noisy. No — the peace out there — that's what I need right now. I lift mine eyes up unto the hills ... No, they aren't exactly hills, but they're bringing me closer to my father.* "Oh Lord," she whispered into the wind, let it be — let it be so — "

There were voices coming from the dock on the other side, an unwelcome intrusion into her thoughts. A deck hand ran past her, other sounds followed, a grating noise, a slight shudder of the boat. *What's happening?* she wondered, *some accident to the boat? Are we about to sink?* She turned to rescue her wicker case and box lunch, just as she heard more shouts, among them a distinctive voice. It was Jacob's!

"Jacob – is it possible?" she cried. She didn't know what to think, only that it seemed impossible. "What shall I do? Has he come to help me after all? What shall I do?"

Without realizing it, she sat back down heavily on the seat where she'd been sitting, still clutching her wicker case, her reticule, and the box lunch. It was difficult to think, to move, to react in any normal way. "Jacob – here" – the same words repeated, over and over again.

It seemed only a few seconds more before the engines recommenced their throbbing as the great paddle wheel began to turn and the boat slowly eased out into mid-stream. The shock of knowing Jacob was here on the *Morning Star*, made her short of breath, and she realized she needed air, the cool, fresh passage of air generated by the increasing speed of the steamer. She went to the railing and held to it tightly, watching the buildings along the west bank grow smaller, the landscape open out once again to distances far beyond. *Naomi of the plains … Yes, I, Naomi, here on these plains, will wait right here on this spot for Jacob to find me.*

"Pardon me, miss," said a man's voice behind her against the noise of the paddle wheel. " Have you seen a lady who -- "

It was Jacob! She was afraid to turn and actually see him, to confront him with whatever words might come to her. Her hands tightened on the deck railing, her mind racing as it searched for the right words. *Oh, Lord help me respond to him … not accuse him … welcome him into my heart …*

"Interesting view out there, isn't it?" he said.

"That depends." She had to give herself time.

"What did you say? It's rather noisy out here."

"I said, it all depends."

"Yes, it might. Say," he shouted against the paddle wheel, "perhaps you'd care to join me for some refreshments?"

"Can't hear you."

"Refreshments – we – "

"No, thank you, I'm expecting someone to join me." Naomi kept her eyes on the distant plains, the far distant plains, all her senses keenly aware of the next step. Loosening her grip on the railing, she turned to face him. "Oh, Jacob, how did you --"

It was not Jacob. A stranger stood there with his hat in his hand. She had never seen him before.

"Excuse me, ma'am," the man said, surprised. "Oh, I beg your pardon. You thought I was someone else? You expecting someone?"

Naomi could not answer. With a slight nod in his direction, she turned away and caught hold of the deck railing to steady herself. Tears of disappointment and humiliation came, obscuring the view, blotting out all else except her clenched hands and the strings of her reticule, dangling from her right wrist. She felt the pulsing of the steamer's engine beneath her feet, the acrid sting of smoke in her nostrils. Other than that, at that precise moment, she had no sense of where she was, nor even who she was.

She had no idea how long she'd stood there. After some time, the shivering of her body forced her aware of becoming chilled and she instinctively drew her shawl more closely around her. Slowly she came to the realization she must do something about not only her physical need for warmth, but also her brain's painful recognition that Jacob had not come after her, had not boarded the steamer at Wolverton, and that his had not been the voice she thought she'd heard.

But did I really expect him? she wondered. *Was it only a hope I never realized I had? Was that why I gave the voice I heard at the dock Jacob's voice? Oh Lord, clear my mind and heart ...*

Huddling up in the protected corner of the deck where she'd left her wicker case and box lunch, Naomi looked out at the passing landscape. The sun was rapidly descending in the west, descending into a hazy horizon over the plains that appeared to define their extent and limits. It was an odd impression, different from earlier images. *Naomi and Ruth, Ruth and Naomi, Naomi of the Plains,* she was thinking. *I've followed my father as Naomi followed her husband Elimelech. But it isn't the same thing. Jacob has not followed me. How could I even have expected that? It could not have been in the Lord's plan.*

"Miss! We'll be docking at Ft. Ambercrombie soon. Do you need a hand with your luggage?" A uniformed officer stood before her, looking down at her, the silver buttons of his uniform reflecting the setting sun.

"Docking soon? At the fort?" she asked numbly.

"Yes, see that block tower a mile or so up ahead, starboard bow? The *Morning Star's* already slowing, and you can expect to feel the paddle wheel reverse in just a few minutes."

It was true, her feet on the deck sensed the throbbing had become less, and looking up at the twin funnels, she could see smoke making only thin trails along the sky line.

"Do you need any help?" he repeated.

"No thank you," she answered, aware that she did need help but not the kind he was offering.

"Come down to the lower deck, then, miss," he said, "the gang plank'll be shoved out on the starboard side, but be careful, before disembarking wait for the deck hand to latch open the gate."

In an overwhelming wave of realization, she recognized that this was the end of her journey, the gate about to open to that end, the journey's sole purpose to be realized after all. She would put all thoughts of Jacob aside. He had not been a part of that purpose at all. She had found her father, he was alive, that was all that mattered. Her heart raced in anticipation of seeing him, although not without some anxiety. *I don't know what I'm going to find,* she thought. *I only know I must face it head on, and pray the Lord for strength to do so. Oh Lord, in your mercy ...*

And yet ... and yet. What about Job? she thought. *And Jacob? Could he have been part of the journey's purpose, after all?*

13

Revelations

The Morning Star had cut its engine and was now drifting from its own momentum toward the dock. Naomi had gone down to the gangway entrance, as instructed by the steamer's officer, and stood with a crowd of other passengers at the railing. Despite the people around her, however, she felt very alone. *I hope the sheriff did send that telegram about me to the fort's commandant,* she thought anxiously. *I hope they've sent someone to meet me, to tell me where to go. The place looks so enormous – and threatening.*

Just ahead all along the bank ran a long palisade of pointed logs with a blockade at each end. Their single narrow windows, flanked by heavy open shutters, faced the river. At the mid-way point of the palisade stood a wide gate, its double doors open to the river landing place.

"Will you look at that!" commented one of the passengers, pointing. "Built for defense, or military action, whichever the need might be. Can hardly believe it. That war between the states over for ten years now, but wars still going on out there on the plains, in fact all the way to the far west. Hard to imagine it's ever going to be settled."

"Sure looks like a busy place – a group of soldiers, other people waiting at the landing," said the man beside him. "Settlers, I expect, maybe some of the soldiers' families." He laughed as he added, "Sure can't tell whether they're coming or going."

"Going, mostly, I expect," said the other.

Following the crowd as they descended the gang plank, Naomi held tightly to her case and reticule, fearful in the rush they might be swept away. Finally, and with some effort because of the crowd, she reached the fort's main gate, only to be rudely stopped by one of the sentries.

"No entry, miss," he said curtly.

"But I have business here."

"What kind of business?"

"It's – it's personal."

He looked suspicious. "What do you mean, personal?"

Naomi didn't feel up to providing the full and complex explanation. "I was sent here by the Fargo sheriff." She hoped this would do suffice.

The man looked more suspicious. "The sheriff, eh? The Fargo sheriff?"

"You see, my father is here, he's – "

"Sheriff's name? Your father's name?"

"John Beckman, came here last week with another man." Her impatience was growing. To have come all this way – to be stopped at the gate?

"Do you have any authorization? Any papers?"

"No, I – " Naomi suddenly remembered the sheriff's envelope. "Yes, it's here." she opened the clasp on the wicker case and pulled it out.

"That won't be necessary, Miss Beckman," said a voice behind her. With a smart salute, the officer took the envelope, tucked it under his arm, and inclined his head slightly. "Lieutenant

Carlson, at your service, ma'am. Major Richardson sends his compliments and wishes you to accompany me to his headquarters. Follow me, if you please."

The lieutenant led her through the wide gate and out into an open compound. Although early evening light was failing fast, Naomi saw that Ft. Abercrombie was built as a large square around the compound, with several small log buildings along two sides. One of them was obviously a cookhouse, with smoke pouring out the stone chimney. Another looked like a barn, probably a stable for horses. Then there were several others, with no indication what they were used for.

"Major Richardson's expecting you," the lieutenant said. "Fortunately for your sake, *The Morning Star* wasn't delayed, as it often is – log jams, other obstructions, engine failure – going aground -- who knows what else. The Red's unreliable 'til it joins the Minnesota."

"My father," Naomi stopped and seized his uniform sleeve, "I must go to him first."

"All in good time, miss," he answered. "My orders are to report to the major."

Major Richardson's office seemed to be at the far end of the quadrangle, for there was a flagpole in front and a sentry guarding the door. "This way, then, if you please." Lieutenant Carlson stood aside, inclined his head briefly toward the door, allowing her to enter ahead of him.

The soldier at a small desk in the corner got to his feet and saluted. "Ah, Corporal Fournier," said the lieutenant, returning the salute. "Please inform the major that our guest has arrived."

Naomi felt her knees growing weaker by the minute as she waited, but there seemed to be no place to sit down. *What's he going to say?* she thought. *Does this delay mean something's more serious, that my father's worse?*

Within several moments the corporal returned from of the adjacent room. "The Major will see you now," he announced, holding open the door.

Major Richardson was seated behind a large desk, and made no effort to rise as they entered. He was dressed in full army uniform, his visored hat lying on a corner of the desk.

"Well, lieutenant," he said curtly, "here at last, Miss Beckman?" He looked keenly directly at her, regarding her thoughtfully for a moment. "I expect this cannot have been the easiest of journeys. No, nor will it be."

His blunt and very direct manner was unexpected. *Do they express sympathy or not?* she wondered. *He seems to imply that Pa's condition is worse, that the difficulties of the journey are far from over.*

"Won't you sit down, please." The major pointed to a chair symmetrically arranged precisely in front of his desk. "Now then, before we begin, Lieutenant Carlson, if you would be so good as to check the arrangements over in the visitors' barracks?" And contact the Frankson boy. Then I shall ask you to report back here. You will need to conduct our visitor to her quarters."

As the lieutenant saluted and left the room, Naomi could contain herself no longer and got to her feet in such haste that she knocked her chair over. "My father, sir, my father! I must see him. I've come all this way. I must go to him."

Major Richardson looked surprised. After some reflection, he folded his hands on the desk and leaned forward. "My dear Miss Beckman," he began, "you seem very blunt. So I, too, shall be blunt. I'm a military man, and, even though the military unit here is now only the Minnesota Volunteer Infantry, it still defines who we are and how we do things. Now please set down again and listen to me." He came out from behind his desk to right the chair she'd overturned, and she dutifully sank into it.

"To begin with, your father, John Beckman, was seriously wounded. The surgeons, both in Fargo and in our surgical ward, feared for his life. He is still in grave danger. It will be impossible for you to see him this evening. He knows you are expected, but the emotion caused by a visit may be detrimental."

But, sir, I've come all this way to see him," she wailed. "I was told by Sheriff Jameson that – "

"Whatever you were told," the major interrupted, "I must disregard for the moment in favor of Captain Clark's opinion. He is our chief surgeon and passed this information on to me this afternoon. His plan, for the sake of the patient, is to prepare him by degrees. He feels that you may be taken to see your father sometime in the morning, after a good night's rest and depending upon his condition at that time. The captain will send for you when that is possible, when the time is best for his patient."

Naomi sat silent for a few moments, the drumming of the major's fingers on his desk irritating. Finally, looking directly at the major, she said, "I understand, sir. If that must be so." Yet to herself she was thinking, another trial, another test of faith, still more to come. *Oh Lord, be with my father –give me strength --*

At that moment Lieutenant Carlson re-entered the commandant's office. "All ready, sir, and the cook has agreed to bring in a meal for the lady from the mess."

"Excellent, lieutenant, excellent. So now Miss Beckman, I must bid you a good evening, a good rest. My orderly – Corporal

Fournier — will come by your quarters shortly to see if there's anything else you require. He will also conduct you to the mess hall at seven o'clock sharp tomorrow morning for breakfast. Once you hear the company bugler sound reveille, you will have exactly fifteen minutes. Later we shall consult Captain Clark regarding your father's condition."

Walking back along the north side of the quadrangle as she walked beside Lieutenant Carlson toward a large, two-storied log building, he turned to her and said sympathetically, "I know you're disappointed, Miss Beckman, but perhaps it's best what the major said. Too much emotion — that could worsen your father's condition."

"It's hard to accept, sir, having come this far."

"How long have you been travelling, then?"

"Over a week, at least I think that's right. It's been difficult to keep track, so much has happened during that week." She paused, adding, "I really don't want to think about it."

"Oh?" he said, then obviously realized the conversation had taken too personal a turn. "I imagine so," he managed. They continued walking on the boardwalk around the quadrangle for a several more yards, Naomi grateful for his silence.

At last he said, "You know the Major asked me to find young Ted Frankson, I believe, and that's where we are now." They'd stopped at the entrance to a large log barracks.

"This is our visitors' quarters, not luxurious by any means, but as much as the army can offer." He smiled as he opened the door and motioned for Naomi to enter into a narrow hallway. "You'll see that this is the common entrance-way for both the men's and the ladies' quarters. Ted Frankson, if I can find him — he does tend to wander around the fort, will be up in the men's to the left. Your room will be up this stairway to the right, room number four I believe the Major assigned you. You'll notice that large room facing us, it's the shared common room. The mess orderly will be bringing a tray of food in there shortly. You may eat in there, although normally food is served only in the mess hall. But, given the lateness of the hour and the circumstances of your visit – "

"Thank you, sir, I understand," Naomi said without much enthusiasm. She'd left Miss Jane's box lunch on the steamer in the excitement of arriving, but, under the present circumstances, still felt little appetite.

"Now I'll leave you, Miss Beckman." With a hasty salute, the lieutenant turned on his heels and closed the heavy door behind him.

The cot in the small room upstairs was narrow, only a thin mattress on ropes strung across a low wooden frame. Yet to Naomi, suddenly overwhelmed with fatigue, it was welcome. She lay down without bothering to undress or even remove her shoes. She noticed a nightstand with a basin, a pitcher of water, and a tin cup. *I'll just take a brief rest*, she thought. *And after that I may take some water, I'm so thirsty. I may even go downstairs to see what food they've brought.* But sleep engulfed with a heavy restraint, even as she'd finished the first ten words of the prayer she was trying to shape.

The next morning Naomi awoke long before dawn. As she lay on the cot while the first cool gray light crept slowly through the small window looking out onto the quadrangle, she pulled up over her the coarse gray wool army blanket. She hadn't she'd realized slept without any protection against the night's chill, and she was shivering. The past hours seemed blank and dreamless.

The pinched blast of a bugle prompted her to throw back the blanket and swing her feet over the edge of the cot to the heavy plank floor. The bugle's call was shortly followed inside the barracks by distant voices, doors opening and shutting, and coming from outside in the quadrangle the confused sounds of much movement.

Crossing the floor to the small nightstand, she cupped the cold water to her face and licked the drops on her lips eagerly. The small mirror above the washstand was hardly adequate, but at least served to allow her to tidy her dress and refasten the pins holding her braided coils of hair in place. Someone passed her door, a woman's voice, those of children. Someone downstairs called her name. The major's orderly? Hastily throwing her shawl around her, she went down.

"Come," Corporal Fournier said in the hallway, "I'm to conduct you over to the mess for breakfast."

"There's no one else here?" Naomi asked, remembering the Lieutenant's promise to find Ted Frankson.

"I don't believe so," he answered, "at least I don't have those orders. You were expecting someone?"

"Yes, his name is Ted Frankson, a young lad, about fifteen I believe, here with his father, his father's in the infirmary."

"Well, miss, I can ask if – "

"Someone mention my name?" A tall, tow-haired boy came charging down the stairs as if out of nowhere.

"Ted – how good to see you," Naomi exclaimed, giving him a hug despite his shy resistance. "We have much to talk about."

"Come, miss, we must get to the mess hall before it's too late for breakfast," the corporal cautioned. With a slight frown, he added, "And I see you've left last night's meal untouched in the common room."

Breakfast in the mess hall was simple -- sausage, biscuits, and coffee. It was a long building, with trestle tables and wooden stools running down its length except for a partition across the far end, apparently reserved for officers. Naomi and Ted Frankson were sitting in another partitioned corner along with several families and three men in civilian clothes. Yet the room, the food, seemed of little consequence compared to the simple fact she'd been reunited with her father.

"Your pa sure stood up to them Shakota," Ted was saying between mouthfuls of sausage or pauses while pouring more honey onto still one more biscuit. "Came up to that town – forget its name, seems long time ago – real quiet like. Was gettin' dark, came out'a nowhere. My pa and Mr. Beckman was just startin' to negotiate a place to stay with one of them settlers. Just about got the man to agree to let us sleep in his barn. Already smelled snow in the air, 'though only September. That farmer seemed a bit worried about the fact we had a couple deer carcasses we wanted to smoke 'afore we headed for home, only way to keep the meat, you see. Already had a whole chest full of smoked trout, walleye, buffalo, not to mention a dozen or so pelts. Real nice fox, a couple buffalo, beaver." He held up his coffee mug as the orderly serving the tables passed by with a large black coffee pot.

"Sounds like you had a good hunt," Naomi remarked. "So you were just about to head home?"

"Oh, thanks," he mumbled while the orderly filled his mug. After several deep gulps of coffee, he went on, "Well, like I said, them Shakota – must'a been 'bout five or six – were interested in horses, made it known they had some pelts to trade. Now those three settlers with us weren't interested in their pelts, kept insisting they needed the horses." Several more gulps. "Same for us, you see."

"What happened next?" Naomi asked, her mouth full of buttered biscuit, having suddenly found herself hungry and putting away, not quite as much as Ted, but a respectable amount.

"Well, ma'am, to make this here long story short, an argument broke out. When them settlers – your pa and mine, too, kept insistin' they weren't going to make a deal, them Shakota got real angry. Couldn't hardly understand what they was a' sayin', that is, until them settlers pulled out a couple of guns and started shootin'." He paused to drain his coffee mug. "That when your pa, mine, got hit. To make matters worse, them Shakota took off with all the horses, your pa's wagon, all the meat. Left the pelts, though. Yours and theirs, too. Like they wanted to pay for everythin'."

"What happened to the pelts, then? All lost? That'd mean little to show for all that hunting, and no meat for the winter."

"I'm 'fraid so. But we was grateful we weren't shot dead. Couple settlers took your pa, me, my pa fast as they could down to a doctor in Fargo. He fixed 'em up pretty good – can't remember his name -- but there was somethin' wrong, so they sent us all down here to a couple army doctors – surgeons I guess they call 'em. Comin' down on that there sternwheeler was sure somethin'. Prob'ly could have ridden faster on the trail along the bank, but horses would have give out for sure, wagon rough enough to make a feller bleed to death."

Naomi shivered at the images his words conjured up. It was a relief to see Lieutenant Carlson approaching their table.

"Morning ma'am, I see you've had a chance to talk to Ted here." He placed a hand on Ted's shoulder, saying, "Just about convinced this young man to join the Minnesota Volunteers, right, Ted?" Ted stammered something and turned red in the face. "That is, he claims, if there's no real fighting going on, although truth be told, there is still."

"My father – what has the doctor said?"

"I'm to take you to Captain Clark now, Miss Beckman. You will want to talk to him first, he'll provide you with more details."

Naomi felt apprehensive as she followed Lieutenant Carlson out of the mess hall and around the corner of the quadrangle to a low, log building just to the left of the fort's main gate. It was the moment she'd been waiting for. It was the moment she dreaded.

In the surgery entranceway a soldier sat at a small writing desk with what looked like a ledger. "Miss Beckman to see the doctor, Private Sibley. He's expecting her."

"Very good, sir," he said, and, after entering something into the ledger, went into the next room.

As the door briefly opened, Naomi caught a glimpse of a row of cots, some separated by screens. The sounds from inside were unnerving and the strange odor wafting out made her catch her breath. A strong odor, indescribable and unfamiliar, it was totally repugnant.

"Are you all right, miss?" Lieutenant Carlson looked at her closely. "I can understand that, for a lady unaccustomed to such things, it must be hard to stomach."

At that moment the sergeant returned with the doctor, an older man, bald, clean- shaven, in shirtsleeves and dark blue suspenders rather than a uniform jacket, and wearing a long white apron tied around his waist with a cord, the apron showing a diagonal spatter of bloodstains. He brought with him a reinforcement of the ward's strong odor.

"Miss Beckman," he said, extending his hand, then thinking better of it, let it fall to his side. "I am Captain Clark, actually Doctor Clark, volunteered from my private practice in St. Paul which I took up again after the war. But the war left me a souvenir, you might say," pointing to his knee with a sardonic smile, "which eventually made it difficult. So here I am once again in service, as you might say. I'm happy to see you have arrived safely, and in time, too."

In time? His words confirmed her suspicions about the seriousness of her father's condition. From such thoughts, the sights, the sounds, and especially the odors, she felt queasy and light-headed, and the room began to swim in dizzying motions before her eyes.

Looking concerned, the lieutenant supported her by the elbow. "Perhaps it would be better, doctor, for the lady outside, some fresh air?"

"Ah yes," said Captain Clark, "forgive me, ma'am. I always forget how some — especially the weaker sex, if you'll forgive me, aren't used to these matters. Come then, there's a bench just outside the door, and the morning air is not yet too sharp."

Removing his bloodstained apron and slipping on his uniform jacket, which hung on a peg by the clerk's desk, Captain Clark ushered Naomi out to a wooden bench poised on the edge of the grassy expanse of the quadrangle. "Now, then, Miss Beckman, please sit down. And lieutenant, you may go. I'll see to her."

"Very good, doctor. I've some business to carry out for Major Richardson." With a smart salute, he walked down the path toward the commandant's office.

"Now then, as I was about to say. You will want to know about your father."

"When can I see him?"

"Ah yes, when can you see him. That is a good question."

"What is wrong?" she demanded. "Why are you keeping me from him?"

"Simply because, Miss Beckman, he is my patient, and I must look after his best interests."

"And what are they, if I may be so bold as to ask?"

"What are they?" He turned to her in surprise. "You seem a forthright sort of woman, so I suppose there is no point in beating about the bush. Here are the facts and my diagnosis. In medical terms, your father's left humoral bone was shattered by a bullet, the bone fragments lodged here and there in the upper arm and shoulder. These had to be extracted. There was considerable risk that surgical extraction might damage parts of the nerves and the muscles. That damage might result in paralysis."

"Paralysis, you said? What would that mean?"

"It would mean he'd lose the use of his left arm. There was also a strong possibility that he might suffer fatal blood loss as a result of the surgery. Could I have tended to him earlier, it would most certainly have lessened the risk. But as it was, and as I think Sheriff Jameson described to you, it was nearly five days before he arrived here in Ft. Abercrombie. That complicated matters considerably and brought about contamination through infection and a high fever, resulting in intermittent delirium." He glanced at her. "Are you following me?"

"I'm not sure."

"Well, perhaps it's not terribly important. I merely want to impress upon you the seriousness of his condition. To make matter even worse, and I hope I'm not distressing you too much, infection might still lead to gangrene, and gangrene to amputation."

"Amputation?"

He coughed slightly. "Severing the limb."

This last possibility struck her forcibly. "Severing pa's arm — why that would make him a cripple, make it impossible to farm, to hunt — "

"That could be the case. But come now, that has not yet happened."

The doctor's medical descriptions were indeed alarming, but Naomi understood well enough his message. "But right now — this morning? Am I able to see him?"

Dr. Clark hesitated. "There's a risk."

"What kind of a risk?"

"That any undue emotional stress might set him back."

"But he knows I am here, he must be eager to see me. Wouldn't that emotion be a good thing?"

"A risk, nonetheless." He thought a moment. "Yes, still a risk, but I think — yes, I think there is a chance it will do him good. But bear in mind that he must be kept quiet, and that his arm is still in a splint. It must be kept from any undue movement. Also remember that he is still in pain."

"Then surely it's all right for me to see him?" The thought of entering that ward made her stomach heave, but she was determined to endure it for her father's sake.

Captain Clark hesitated again, clearly of two minds. Finally he got to his feet and said, "All things considered, yes, perhaps it will do the patient good to see his daughter. If you will wait out here and give me a few moments, I shall prepare him."

These were perhaps the longest moments Naomi could ever remember. Sitting on the bench in the warmth of the morning sunshine as it turned heavy dew on the grass into delicate wisps of rising mist, she buried her face in her hands. "Oh beautiful and wonderful God," she murmured, "Gracious Savior, be with us now. Grant us the touch of your healing hands, let your holy spirit descend upon my father, grant me the courage … the strength to – "

At that moment the outside door of the surgical ward opened. "Don't keep him too long," he said. "I'm ordering Private Sibley here to keep an eye on him."

"Naomi!"

Her father was being wheeled out onto the path in a wheel chair. It was as if her heart stopped beating for a full ten seconds. She rushed over to him and knelt down beside him. "Pa – oh Pa," she cried over and over again. It seemed the only possible word.

John Beckman laid his right hand against her cheek and kissed her on the forehead. "Naomi, Naomi, my dear child," he said. "That you have come, that you are really here – tell me it isn't a dream, an illusion."

"No, Pa, 'though it seems like one. I never thought it possible. Well, I did occasionally, maybe not all the time. I can't even begin to tell you all that happened."

"Time for that," he said, "and there will be time. Already you've strengthened me just by your presence."

As Naomi looked at him, she realized how much he'd changed. There was more gray hair around his temples, his clean-shaven face revealed more obviously its thinness, his stark cheekbones, and his hollowed looking eye sockets. His hand shook as he touched her, and his voice had a weakness to it, slurring some words.

"I've come to take you home, Pa." Those words seemed to take on a meaning of tremendous proportions, words she had so often formed in her mind for when this very moment came, but words which now, once spoken, said much, much more.

At that moment the ward orderly walked over from where he'd been waiting a few yards down the path. "Sorry, miss, time to take Mr. Beckman back in, doctor's orders. We can't let him tire himself out, can we?"

Naomi put her arms around her father's neck, careful not to disturb the splint on his upper left arm. "Rest now, Pa. I'll come back later when they let me. Just remember, the sooner you're better, the sooner we can head for home."

As the orderly wheeled her father back inside, Naomi remembered she'd forgotten to ask about Henry Frankson. But then, his son Ted would soon be seeing him and relate that news. *So hard to understand all these strange feelings invading my brain,* she thought. *I never expected this. Never expected how shaken I'd feel from this meeting. Yet there's joy, yes, real joy. Joy surging through me, thankfulness to the Lord for it.*

The questions she hardly dared to shape she's have to force back into that think-about-it- later part of her brain, already nearly reaching capacity. Those questions about tomorrow … and the next day… and the next …

14

Unexpected Passages

Emotionally shaken by the meeting with her father, Naomi scarcely comprehended later conversations with Ted. She was vaguely aware only that over noon dinner in the mess hall there was talk of steam engines, wagons, cannons, horses, Ted's father. She did note, however, that according to Ted, his father was considered well enough to leave Ft. Abercrombie for home and could leave as early as the next morning. *If only, oh if only, that were true of my own father*, she thought. That phrase – *if only* – would be repeated again and again in her mind brain over the next many hours.

"I'm going over to the surgery again," she announced to Ted late that afternoon.

"Think they'll let you see your pa?" he asked. "The doctor says my pa'll be fine. I took him around the quad for a little walk just a little while ago. They'll let him out of the infirmary sometime tomorrow morning. Can't hardly believe it! We talked about plans for the trip home."

"I don't know yet about my father, Ted, but I'm going to try. I'm happy about your news, though."

Turning the first corner of the quadrangle, she stopped before the surgery door. The idea of entering was repellant, her senses well aware of what lay behind it. *I'm tempted to sit on the*

bench outside and wait – for what, I don't know. There was no point in
simply waiting, however. I've simply got to fact it, and go in there.

The orderly at the desk looked up in surprise from the ledger, his pen suspended in mid-air. "What are you – " he started
to say.

"I'm here to see my father, John Beckman." Her words came
in a rush.

"Mr. Beckman? But he's – "

"I want to see him. Surely that's possible? He seemed better
this morning, Dr. Clark said so."

"Well, I'll have to – "

"Then please do it!"

It wasn't long before the orderly returned. "Captain Clark
isn't in the ward at the moment. You'll have to wait outside."

"I insist upon seeing my father."

"I'm afraid I can't let you do that, miss. The ward's restricted."

"I don't care if it is or not." With that she walked past his
desk and pushed open the double doors leading into the ward.

Overwhelmed by the first impressions of odors, the smell
of death, the sounds of moaning, coughing, random words, she
hesitated, bracing herself against the door-jamb for support.
The ward was in semi-darkness, lit by two small upper windows
and a hanging oil lamp. Directly under the lamp was a long table
with leather straps attached to it, and over against the back wall
a row of white iron cots. Some appeared to be occupied, a few
empty.

"Miss, I said! You can't go in there." The orderly seized her
arm, none too gently.

Breaking away, she went over to the first cot, where a man
lay on his side, asleep. Then the next, and the next, which was

empty. A moan came from the next, and as she pulled back the sheet to see his face. The pale, bearded man gasped in surprise. He was not her father, nor Henry Frankson.

The orderly followed closely behind her, protesting vehemently and trying to draw her back outside the ward. "Miss – come away – you can't – "

"Naomi!" She heard her name called, weakly, from that last cot down the row.

Rushing between the beds, once catching her foot on something and nearly falling, she finally reached the last one. Kneeling down beside it, she laid her head on her father's chest. "Pa! I'm here," she murmured, so overcome no more words came.

"Naomi – Naomi -- you shouldn't be," he said.

"You've got to leave, miss," the orderly kept insisting.

"No, wait." Naomi's father raised his hand slightly. "Don't force her to leave –it will make my condition worse."

Private Sibley hesitated.

"Already feel much improved, can't deny that," he added, noting the effectiveness of this argument.

Private Sibley fell back a few paces, protesting under his breath.

"Is that you, Naomi?" Henry Frankson sat up in the next cot. "As I live and breathe, it's a treat to see you. Ted came in to see me 'bout noon today, told me how you got here and all."

"Hank's a lucky man," said Naomi's father. "Getting out of here later today – depending on Dr. Clark's decision, however. When'll you be heading home, then, Hank?"

'Hard to know, hard to know, John. Thought I'd like to wait for you." He turned over in his cot, facing the other side, as if hesitant to continue. Finally he said, "Some difficulty, though.

Even if we somehow get a wagon, it'd be hard for young Ted to manage all that way. I'm up to some of it, but -- "

John Beckman shook his head. "I understand what you're saying. I'd be nearly useless. But to wait for me to heal – well, let's face it. It'd be a long time – too long to wait. "

"Indeed it might be a long wait." Dr. Clark seemed to come out of nowhere and now stood at the foot of the last cot. "Strictly against the rules, Miss Beckman. I'm surprised at you, forcing your way in here."

"Buoyed up my spirits – no more pain," Naomi's father argued.

"Unlikely," responded Captain Clark cynically.

"I had to see him again," Naomi protested.

In a gentler voice, while helping her to her feet, the doctor said, "Best leave now, miss. I've some things to perform here you will not want to witness. Private Sibley, show the lady out, and then fetch my assistants, Corporals Jackson and Martin. They'll be over in their barracks. When you come back, please lay out my instruments."

"Are you – my arm?"

"No, Mr. Beckman," said Captain Clark, "be assured, sir, my surgery will not be for you, not today at least. But now let me have a look at that arm." He pulled back the sheet and looked at the cloth bindings around the splint. Then, looking back pointedly back at Naomi, he said, "Well, Miss Beckman – you *are* on your way out, I presume?"

"If I must, then." She embraced her father as well as she could, then turned away, keeping her head down to hide a welling-up of emotions. Private Sibley, looking relieved, eagerly held open the outer door and shut it behind her with a hollow slam once she'd stepped out into the fresh air and late afternoon sunshine of the quadrangle.

It felt good, after the fetid air of the ward. She began walking briskly around the quadrangle walkway, made up of split logs with the flat side up so as to form a level surface, somewhat springy to the step. To the west, rising up above the fort's palisade wall, she saw a distant, wooded hilltop. It wouldn't be long before the sun sank behind it. It felt good to walk, too, one step after another, one long, in-drawn breath after another of fresh, verdant smelling air. She pictured those winds, bending the grasses, scattering the dew over hundreds of miles of plains to the west. She felt somehow refreshed and restored. "Thank you for this, Oh Lord," she whispered.

And there was another prayer of thanks forming in her mind, that for her father. He'd seemed much better, those few minutes ago, his speech almost normal, although in the dim light of the ward it wasn't possible to get a good look at him. Still, a new spirit seemed to be there, in him as well as herself.

She quickened her step, occasionally passing a soldier or two, who looked at her curiously as they stepped aside to let her pass. She passed Major Richardson's headquarters, the flag on the flagpole flapping idly in the soft breeze.

Should I go in, she wondered? *But then, what should I say? No doubt he'll insist that I leave with the Franksons. He'll argue that it's awkward and inconvenient to keep me here on my own at the fort. Maybe I could argue that I'm not prepared to leave Pa here on his own. What if, I'll say to that Major, what if his condition becomes worse? What if —*

She quickened her pace on the springy walkway. *No, I'll insist, I am staying. No argument. And if there is, I'll contact those lawyers in Fargo — somehow. I'll get them to claim I have a legal right to stay here at my father's side. Otherwise, there will be* — but she was running out of *will be's.*

Unable to sleep that night, her mind in a turmoil from being confronted with more *what if*'s and searching for further *will be's,* she felt helpless. There was, in fact, little more she could do.

I so well know, she debated with herself, *how much I've already done, merely by reaching Ft. Abercrombie. And I know how much Matthew Schmidt served in all that. I'm grateful for the Barnes' care. Yet I also know I'm responsible for his accident. I'm hoping Harry's able to take care of his business with Billings and Fletcher, though I doubt their honesty. Surely they're responsible for Birgitta's disappearance. Maybe I'm responsible for that, too. What does all of this mean? My arrogant sense of being too sure of myself? My pride? And Jacob's pride, too?* All these self-reflections left her shaken and drained.

Breakfast with Ted Frankson next morning in the mess hall was somewhat reassuring. Drinking her second cup of coffee, she remarked, "Say Ted, you know the sheriff in Fargo was going to send word back home that I'd arrived safely and was on my way to Ft. Abercrombie. I hope he also put in some information about your father and mine. And now with this good news about your father and the possibility of your heading home soon, I'm sure the fort can send a telegram like that to your mother." *I'm not ready to let my mother know Pa's news yet, though,* she thought.

"A telegraph? What's that?"

Naomi shrugged, at a loss. "A letter that goes through the air. You'll have to get someone to explain all that, it's beyond me. I do know, though, that it has to go from one telegraph office to another one."

"Does Prairie Lake have one?"

"It'd probably need to be at a railroad station. Let's see, maybe Audubon, or Detroit Center. From there – dunno. They'd have to send a rider down to Prairie Lake with it. That might take a while."

"Hate to think what my poor ma's goin' through," said Ted. "Wonderin' if we'll ever come home. Been wonderin' that myself."

And so have I, Naomi thought. *After what Mr. Frankson said in the ward ... seems almost impossible with his condition and Pa's ... could take a long, long time. And what happens to us here?*

She decided not to pass on these concerns to Ted just yet, however. Instead, she said, " I agree. I know they've all been so anxious, my mother, your ma, Ted. All the way back to the time we first realized my father – and yours – were missing."

"She didn't want me to go huntin' in the first place," Ted commented. "Said for sure I'd get into trouble."

Naomi smiled. "And so you did, lad, so you did. Well, I'll meet you again here for the noon dinner. Right now I need to walk a little and clear my thoughts."

In contrast to the weather the day before, this morning was dull and cloudy, filled with that damp coldness announcing soon-to-come winter months. It seemed to match her mood of despair, especially the news Ted and his father were almost on their way home and she was not. She pulled her shawl around her shoulders, crossed it over, tucked the ends into her waistband, and started walking the circuit of the quadrangle. She reached the east wall and quickly passed the surgery, hardly bearing to look at it because they would not let her in to see her father this early. As she continued on down to the south perimeter, she soon found herself before the commandant's office. An honor guard was taking down the flag and they stopped to stare at her.

"It's 'bout to rain, miss," one soldier said with a kind of half salute, "best get inside."

She stopped in her tracks. *Best get inside --* Was it a sign of some sort? She had to work that one out. Did he mean the major's office? No, surely not, one didn't just burst in unsummoned. At least not as far as that commandant was concerned. *Anyway*, she reasoned to herself, *I'm not prepared to talk to him, not now, not later either. It appears to depend entirely upon Pa's condition and Captain Clark's medical opinion and the commandant's response to his opinion.* She paused in her walk, and shook her head. *Those two men are like – like --* She couldn't find the right simile. *They think they are the ones deciding events. I wonder if the Lord can reach them?*

Naomi continued walking, now along the west perimeter toward the visitors' barracks, where she hoped to retreat to her room to sort out her thoughts. Relieved that there was no one in the barrack's common room, although she could heard voices in different parts of the building, she slowly climbed the short flight of stairs and stretched out full length on her cot.

Yet it was difficult to shape her thoughts, even more difficult to shape her words. *It's as if I were drained of strength, of thought, of words, and had no will of my own. Let the Lord – let Clark and Richardson do as they will. And Jacob has failed me – any commitment to me dissolved like – like that mist in the air.* Jacob – Job – *that's how it was with Job, he had no will of his own. The Lord showed his strength against him. Oh Lord – your will be done.*

"Miss Beckman!"

Someone said her name. The Lord was answering her.

"A man to see you, Naomi Beckman. He's downstairs waiting, miss." Mrs.Petitjohn, the officer's wife in the next room, said through her door.

"A message about my father? Is he worse?" Her heart sank.

Anxiously smoothing back escaping wisps of hair and straightening her shawl as she thanked the woman and came down the stairs, she was surprised to see Lieutenant Carlson standing in the narrow hallway.

"Good morning, ma'am, I was hoping I'd find you in," he said, replacing his uniform cap. "I'm to take you to Major Richardson."

"What about?" Instantly she regretted what was most likely a breach in protocol.

Sure enough, looking at her with a slight frown, he answered curtly, "He will convey that to you himself."

Once out in the quadrangle, the light, drizzling rain had increased to a shower. Starting to pull her shawl up over her head, she said half to herself, "Should have worn my bonnet, more proper."

"Perhaps this will do instead, ma'am, here allow me." Lieutenant Carlson whipped off his uniform cape and held it over her head. "The least an officer and a gentleman can do," he said, although Naomi wasn't sure whether he was serious or not. Both gesture and remark seemed at odds with his usual curtness.

Naomi became aware that, holding his cape over her required him to put his arm around her shoulders, required them to walk closely together, required her to feel his body close to hers. She was also aware that he glanced down at her from time to time.

"You have everything you need here? Accommodations satisfactory?"

"Yes, thank you. Everyone has been most solicitous."

"I'm pleased to hear it." He paused. "You have friends to assist you in all this business about Mr. Beckman? A special friend?"

Shocked, Naomi looked up at him. Surely the lieutenant was not interested in her relationships, besides, they were hardly his business. "I – I don't know – perhaps not – " she stammered.

"I'm pleased to hear that," the lieutenant repeated. "I mean – well, I mean I'm *surprised* to hear that. Such an attractive young woman as you." It seemed his arm held her more closely under the protection of his military cape. A strange sensation seemed to invade her body. It was a good feeling, strong and comforting. "You will remain here at the fort long?" he continued.

"I don't know."

"Does it depend upon how soon your father is able to travel?"

"Yes."

"I see. Then let me assure you, Miss Beckman, I am always at your service. You may call upon me at any time. I promise to do whatever I can with whatever assistance I can offer. That could include working out a plan for getting your father safely home. I would like to have you consider me as a – as a – a friend."

Naomi was at a loss. On the one hand she felt helpless and vulnerable in what could be a developing situation. On the other, here was a potential solution to her most immediate problem. *And Lieutenant Carlson is a gentleman and genuinely solicitous of me,* she added as an afterthought.

Fortunately she was spared an immediate response to his offer by their timely arrival at the commandant's office. It became necessary for the lieutenant to replace his uniform cape and open the door for her.

The major's clerk, Corporal Fournier, rose from behind his writing desk as they entered the anteroom to the commandant's office. "The major's waiting for you," he said.

"I shall leave you here, then, ma'am." Lieutenant Carlson touched his cap slightly. "Look after this lady, corporal. I shall return in about half an hour to escort her back to her quarters. Perhaps then we might talk again, Miss Beckman? I should like that very much."

What's he getting at? was Naomi's first thought, feeling uneasy about this last encounter. *What's he going to talk about on the way back? And how will I deal with it if it's what I think he's leading up to?*

This time Major Richardson was standing to one side of his desk, reading a map tacked to the wall. At least Naomi assumed it was a map, with faint outlines covered with arrows and black dotted lines. "Good morning, Miss Beckman," he said, turning. "I trust you have been comfortable."

"Yes, major. Your hospitality here has been more than I expected."

"Ahem, well, we do our best." He seemed a little taken back. "You must understand that, as a military fort, we are not exactly in the hospitality business." Seating himself behind his desk, he gestured toward the chair. "Now then, I shall be brief. To come to the point at the right moment is always a good maneuver, wouldn't you say?"

Without waiting for an answer, he continued. "I believe Captain Clark has authorized Mr. Frankson's release from the surgical ward. And I believe he and his son are planning to leave as soon as arrangements can be made. You have been so informed?"

"Yes," Naomi answered, surprised at how stifled her own voice sounded. "My father -- " she began, the one question she needed to ask.

"I must tell you that I have also spoken to Captain Clark regarding your father. Your father's condition, as you know, is much more serious. He was in critical condition when he arrived here last week, and has been slow to improve. In fact, his life has been hanging off and on in balance."

"Yes, I know that, sir." Again, it seemed difficult to get the words out. *Sounds like bad news coming,* was her main thought. She gripped the arms of the chair for support. She tried desperately to focus on an old portrait of President Grant hanging on the wall by the map. Despite her father's improved condition yesterday, despite her hopes, it now sounded as though he'd taken a turn for the worse.

"I have sent for you to give you Captain Clark's report as of this morning." He paused and leaned across his desk. "I know this may shock you, but you seem to me a plucky enough young woman to handle it."

Naomi closed her eyes, held her breath, and waited, her grip on the chair arms desperately seeking support.

"In short, the surgeon, after examining your father late this morning, found him much improved and, for the moment at least, out of danger."

"What?" Naomi's head snapped back and her right hand went to her throat.

"Much improved, miraculously so, in fact. No sign of fever, only mild, intermittent pain, pulse more or less regular. You are relieved to hear this?"

"Yes – yes – I mean – I mean yes, of course. It does seem a miracle." *Thanks be to God,* she thought, *to God be –*

"So improved, as I said, that the doctor feels he may soon be released to return home." He paused, regarding her carefully to assess her reaction.

Naomi slowly rose. "Return – home – soon released – " her words came in fragments, hardly chosen as she would like to choose them. "When – how – "

"Please, sit down. I know this may be a shock. But a shock of most happy proportions, wouldn't you agree? Now here is what I propose." He reached across his desk for a note pad and pencil.

"I've made a few notes so that the organization of your departure may go smoothly. Tomorrow morning you, your father, and the Franksons, will be given passage up to Fargo on the sternwheeler, *Silver Falcon,* out of Wahpeton. Captain Clark will see to it that your father is made comfortable for the journey, and we are sending Corporal Martin along for assistance. This will be useful for us, since while in Fargo the corporal is to supervise receiving a shipment of supplies we expect to arrive by train from St. Paul."

"A sternwheeler?" Naomi asked, dazedly.

"Going down river, of course, as the Red flows, will be much faster, perhaps only four or five hours, a much better journey than the one you had on *The Morning Star,* am I correct? Leaving at seven tomorrow morning, you should arrive in Fargo in time for noon dinner. Once in Fargo, you will be out of our hands and into the sheriff's jurisdiction. I shall send his office a telegraph shortly with these details. "

"Quite frankly," he continued, now pacing back and forth in front of the wall map, " I would have preferred to combine your return with a platoon detachment I must send shortly to Ft. Alexandria by road. But the truth is, this would take you too far south, a bit out of your way. I'm sure you would not wish to wait another week?"

It took Naomi a moment to reply. So much to take in. So much to turn her thoughts in the opposite direction. So much to be grateful for. And yet, so much remaining to worry about. "No – not wait -- my father ready?"

"We cannot guarantee it, of course. So much we cannot be sure of. But doubtless his positive state of mind in response to your visit has been of great benefit."

With a motion of drawing this interview to an end, the major came toward her and took her hand. "I wish you and your father well, Miss Beckman. And may I say, please excuse my bluntness, if you were a man, Naomi Beckman, you would make a great soldier."

He opened the door. "Corporal! Escort the lady back to her quarters, if you please." He remained standing in the open doorway, watching her leave, until Corporal Fournier closed the outside door behind them.

The drizzling rain had stopped. "You may have a better day tomorrow, ma'am," the corporal commented as they walked back to the visitors' barracks.

"I hope so," Naomi answered, somewhat relieved that Lieutenant Carlson had not made it back to the Major's office in time to be her escort. That earlier walk had been disturbing through offering tempting moments of romantic fantasy and fragmented thoughts that contrasted his courtly manner with Jacob. Yes, an attraction she could not explain, not even to herself.

Finding Ted in the common room, chatting with several other guests around the iron stove in the center, she could hardly wait to tell him. "What do you think?" she cried. "We're going home, all of us!"

"All? You mean – "

"Yes, all. I just spoke with the major. Pa's improved so much." At once the realization of what she'd been told, the emotions and hopes so long repressed, burst out in a torrent of disconnected words. "Sternwheeler early tomorrow morning – named Silver something -- doctor's assistant coming along – sternwheeler – river to Fargo – sheriff – "

That evening, joined by Henry Frankson, their last supper in the Ft. Abercrombie mess room was a kind of celebration, lacking only the presence of Naomi's father. The mess orderly actually brought them a pitcher of apple cider, *with the major's compliments*, he explained.

"Sure will be glad to be home," Ted's father said, raising his glass. "Been so long since we left, so much water under the bridge, that I hardly remember it," he added smiling.

"Well, I remember every single detail 'bout home," Ted asserted, "especially that Joel Langtry who borrowed my baseball and lost it. I'll sure make him pay me back, soon's we get there."

Despite the lightheartedness of the mood, however, from the think-about-it-later part of Naomi's brain emerged a nagging thought, one already threatening to emerge several times over the past few hours, had threatened over the last few days, in fact. *What's going to happen in Fargo?* she thought. *We'll need things to get home – a wagon, horses, who knows what else? And then who's able to drive the wagon? Not my father, maybe Ted and his father only part of the time – if at all. Maybe me if I can learn quickly enough.* This uncertainty now replaced previous ones. *Oh Lord,* she prayed silently, watching and listening with half an ear Ted and his father's eager plans about the first things they were going to do, once home in Prairie Lake, *oh Lord, in your mercy, help us ... help me ... in this next test.*

There was a flurry of activity getting on board *The Silver Falcon* at seven o'clock next morning. The half-light of dawn was just beginning to dissolve into early morning sunlight, and a mist rose from the river. The major and several other officers, including Lieutenant Carlson and the doctor, came out to the landing place to see them off. The doctor's two assistants carried Naomi's father in a chair.

"I can walk, I'm all right," he kept insisting.

"Later, perhaps," said Captain Clark. "Conserve your strength for now – you'll be needing it later. By my reckoning, it'll be at least four days before you'll be sleeping in your own bed, so to speak. Corporal Martin will look after you as far as Fargo. After that – well, just don't try to do anything foolish, like drive the wagon. You've got a strong young man here to do that. Wouldn't be surprised if the lady could also manage." He smiled at Naomi in some meaningful way.

Handing her a small packet, he explained, "These are some dressings, his medications, a few notes."

"I'm so grateful, doctor. You will never know what a difference you've made in my life, our lives."

"I can guess," he answered. Then, looking off in the distance, "It wasn't only me, I don't think I need tell you that. There are things – there are powers – "

She understood. She'd always heard doctors and religion were rarely partners. Here, she hoped, was an exception.

Major Richardson came up, looking somewhat embarrassed, perhaps because of his remarks and unusual display of emotion during their previous meeting. "I wish you a safe journey, and that all will go as planned," he said more formally with a slight bow. "And if you ever -- " He looked as though he wanted to say more, hesitated, but instead stepped back to join the knot of soldiers remaining at the gate.

Naomi observed that he stopped to say something to Lieutenant Carlson, that they both looked decidedly in her direction. The lieutenant stood taller than the major, his appearance in uniform strikingly handsome. Perhaps she'd been too preoccupied before to notice it, or at least consciously to allow herself to notice it. As she watched, Lieutenant Carlson raised his hand to his cap, the expression on his face one of intensity, an expression she couldn't quite define, as if he did not want her to leave, as if he were contemplating a way to see her again. Such a possibility, and such unanswerable questions she instinctively knew would continue to haunt her.

"Come, Naomi, they're about to pull up the gangplank." Ted looked anxious. "Your pa and Mr. Frankson are already set up in the lounge, looking downright comfortable if you ask me. Looks too stuffy for me in there, though. I think I'll just explore around this steamer a bit, maybe the captain'll even let me steer."

Standing on the deck, Naomi watched the gangplank being drawn up and, at the same time, heard the deep whistle blasts of departure. The deck began to vibrate with the steadily increasing revolutions of the great stern wheel, drawing the steamer out into midstream. "I'm on my way, on my way … " she repeated to herself over and over again in that same rhythm. The crowd on the dock was thinning quickly, only the gate sentries and Lieutenant Carlson remained. Then, only the sentries.

Inside the lounge, her father and Henry Frankson were settled in one corner, John Beckman lying under a steamer rug and propped up on pillows on a red velvet divan, Henry Frankson in one of the overstuffed chairs opposite. On a low table between them was a water pitcher, a large silver coffee pot, several cups and saucers, and a basket of cinnamon rolls.

"Ah, there you are, Naomi, I was hoping you weren't left behind."

"No, Pa. Just taking one last look at the fort."

"A place of considerable importance in our lives, was it not?"

"Yes, Pa." Her father would understand some of that, perhaps. Surely not all. "Are you comfortable there?"

"I seem to be. That's Corporal Martin reading a newspaper over by the window. Nice chap, he does his best for Hank and me, most accommodating."

Have I really done my best? Naomi wondered. *What should I — could I have done differently? Or Jacob? Matthew Schmidt's injury, Birgitta's safety — am I responsible? And my hateful jealous thoughts about Mary Frankson …*

As if to make matters worse, Henry Frankson wanted to know more about his family back in Prairie Lake, especially his children, especially Mary. "My young'uns keeping out of trouble? Especially that Ben. Now that's a boy for you. And how's my Mary doing?" he asked. "Worried the most about her. Seemed in a strange kind of mood when I left those few weeks ago. Something's eating on her, I'm sure."

"They were all fine, sir," Naomi said with a catch in her voice. She knew exactly what was bothering Mary, and for a moment, felt a twinge of sympathy because Jacob was the problem, a problem for both of them.

When the *Silver Falcon* docked at Wolverton several hours later, hearing the officer calling out the name several times, Naomi recalled what painful emotions she'd experienced at Wolverton on the trip down from Fargo. She'd been standing on the deck on the other side from the dock, attracted by the view of the prairies off in the distance. Just after the passengers had boarded and steamer began pulling away from the dock, she thought she'd heard Jacob's voice calling her name. He'd come after all! In the next few moments, he'd be seeking her out on the deck, find her, and stand beside her. *"Oh Naomi,"* he'd say, taking her hand in his, *"please forgive me – how could you ever have doubted me?"*

But that had not happened, and Jacob now seemed irrelevant. She was the one bringing her father – and Mary Frankson's father and brother – home. *Was this God's plan all along?* she wondered. *Oh Lord, have I not passed this test, the last one?*

Looking now at her father, Naomi saw he was asleep. Ted and his father were over by the window, engaged in animated conversation with Private Martin. It did seem stuffy in there, as Ted observed earlier. She'd go out on deck and enjoy the fresh air.

Finding a protected corner bench on the upper deck, similar to one she'd enjoyed on *The Morning Star*, she curled up, content to reflect on the complex trains of thoughts which seemed to flow continuously through her mind. *Naomi of the Plains … Birgitta of the Plains … was Matthew Schmidt still in Menasa … Emma's ham and potatoes … Satan walking up and down upon the earth …*

"Hickson! Hickson next!"

Naomi's reverie slipped away, jarred suddenly into the reality of the moment. *I must have lost all track of time,* she thought. *How long have I been out here? The wind has picked up, almost lost my straw bonnet. We must be getting close to Fargo, I just wish I could remember how long it took between there and Fargo.*

"Hickson, ten minutes, miss!" an officer leaned over her, then headed toward the end of the portside deck and disappeared up the stern stairway. She heard him again on the lower deck.

In another five minutes the *Silver Falcon* began to veer toward the starboard shore, heading for a small settlement with a dock and several warehouses along the river bank. A small group were waiting to board, with a cluster of wagons and buggies nearby. Impatient at losing time through this insignificant stop, Naomi realized she was shivering and needed to go back inside and see if her father needed anything.

"No, can't say as I do, Naomi," he replied as she readjusted his steamer rug and filled his water glass. Putting down the newspaper, he remarked, "It was good to catch up on the news again, seems like ages since Hank and I left Prairie Lake."

"It does seem like that, doesn't it?" Naomi made herself in comfortable in the red velvet chair beside him.

"It'll be nothing short of a miracle, seeing it again," he added, shaking his head.

Naomi had her own thoughts about miracles, thoughts she was still trying to work out. At the moment, however, there was satisfaction in feeling the pulsating throbs of the paddle wheel increase as the steamer pulled away from Hickson dock and got underway toward Fargo, the final stop.

A cold blast of air came in as the deck door burst open and slammed back against the wall, causing the windows to rattle. The passenger seemed to tumble in with the force of it, and tried to regain his balance by catching hold of the back of a writing desk chair. Both came down together on the carpeted floor.

Before anyone rush to the man's assistance, however, he managed to pull himself up. "My, that's quite a wind out there, nearly blew me overboard, nearly lost my hat. Then, glancing around the room apologetically, he said, "Sorry, folks, about the --- " he looked shocked. "Is it – is it -- Naomi! You're here!"

Naomi stared at him, stunned. All the words she'd planned to say, should such a confrontation with Jacob ever occur, were forgotten.

It was John Beckman, however, who finally found a voice. "Why Jacob Bowers – whatever are you doing here? Naomi hadn't mentioned you, so I just assumed you weren't – " He motioned to another chair beside him, "here, join us, you seem winded. And Hank, you too, Ted, look, come over here and join us."

Avoiding looking at Naomi, Jacob sat down heavily on the other side. "Catch my breath in a minute, thought for sure I'd miss you this time."

"This time?" Ted asked, wide eyed. "You mean you been after us all this time?"

"More or less."

"Which was it, then, more – or less?" Naomi had found her voice and it was angry. "A little late, isn't it?"

"Now, Naomi, dear," her father interceded. "The lad's obviously been through a lot to get to where he's sitting now. Better let him explain."

"It'll take a lot of explaining, as far as I'm concerned," she retorted. But at the same time, conflicting thoughts plagued her. *Why am I angry? I should be glad to see him. He has after all come after me – isn't that what I wanted? What I'd asked the Lord for?*

"More coffee, madam, gentlemen?" A steward approached them with a tray of cups and saucers. "Or may I refresh yours?" He set down the tray and picked up the large silver pot and hovered over them.

When her father nodded and the steward filled his cup, then Henry Frankson's, Naomi considered that, although the coffee had seemed an unwelcome intrusion into an emotionally charged scene, it gave her a moment to regain control of her thoughts. Looking accusingly at Jacob, she blurted out, "You said you couldn't take me to Fargo, now here you are after I've already been and coming back. How do you explain that? There's no point to your journey now, no matter what you've been through."

"Now Naomi … " her father cautioned. "I'm sure the lad can explain."

"Can't explain everything, sir," Jacob said, sipping the coffee the waiter had just handed him. "Sure can't, not all those strange happenings."

"Try." Naomi's voice had an acid tone to it. It would take a great deal of explanation to change her bitterness toward him. Besides, her encounter with that attractive Lieutenant Carlson and his gentlemanly kindness toward her had somehow placed Jacob in an even more unfavorable light.

Jacob set down his cup and settled back in his chair. "Well, I'll be brief, only the main things." He thought for a few moments, twisting his straw hat with the black ribbon around in his hands.

"That hat – where --" Naomi exclaimed. The sight of it seemed to bring the reality of the moment back up to the surface, a present and surprising reality up against the more distant reality of home and Prairie Lake and the Jacob of that place.

"This old hat, you mean? Well, I found it on a buckthorn bush, when I was actually on my way to see you. Made my decision to get to Fargo two days after you left with Matthew Schmidt. Saw him in Menasa, but I'll tell you 'bout that later. Knew your father, Mary's father might be in trouble. Then there was – "

Taking a deep breath, Naomi ventured, "Did you make that decision for Mary's father, or for mine? Or out of sheer pride?"

He looked down at his feet, still twisting his hat around. "Can't rightly answer that just now."

"I see." Disappointed, it wasn't what she wanted to hear.

"Trip here wasn't easy, horse ran off, lost a shoe. Got to Menasa, must'a been only a few hours after you left with that proprietor for Moorhead. His wife told me she expected you both back that evening, something 'bout a Swedish girl. When you didn't return, not the next morning either – I took off soon's I could. Weird story 'bout Prince, but leave that 'til later. Anyway, I thought I might meet you with this Mr. Barnes on your way back. If not, then I'd keep on riding 'til I got to Moorhead."

"You expected to find me in Moorhead? How could you, it's a big town."

He hesitated, apparently embarrassed. "Didn't much matter, I hadn't really worked that out. But I did know you'd be looking for a sheriff in Fargo, across the river from Moorhead. And I knew once I found him, I'd find the Franksons – and you and your pa, of course."

So, that was it, thought Naomi. *Mary's father -- did that prompt his decision?*

"Anyway, like I was saying, I galloped poor Prince most of the way, got to Moorhead just about five or six. I thought I'd look around for Barnes' wagon, thought I'd see you in your blue bonnet – the one you always wear. Well, after that didn't work out, I decided to give up and go on over to Fargo."

"That was just about the time Harry and I left on the ferry for Fargo, we had to spend the night there."

Jacob's jaw dropped. "With that Barnes fellow – you spent the night with *him*?"

"Yes, and no." She'd explain later, after he'd done *his* explaining.

"Don't like the sound of that, Naomi. But, anyway, I went down to where they told me there was a ferry to Fargo. Of all the bad luck, the last one had just pulled out. So I spent a couple hours looking around town, like you said, a big place, and finally found a room for the night, pokey sort of hostelry. Couldn't afford more, even with my wages from Pa."

"So you were in Moorhead and Naomi was in Fargo on the same night?" Ted asked incredulously

"Seems like it," Jacob said, with a rueful smile. "Well, next morning slept late, pretty tired by that time, finally got the ferry across to Fargo come noon. Knew I should try to find the sheriff's office first. The town jammed with people, Saturday's a big market day, seemed like everybody I asked was some farmer from out of town, couldn't tell me. Hard to get through the streets, too, with all those wagons, cattle."

"Son, I can't believe you couldn't find the sheriff's office," Henry Frankson commented. "That's usually the best known place in town – except maybe the saloon."

"I did eventually find it, sir, not far from the river. I must have passed by close on the next street a couple of times. Anyway, it was probably about one o'clock or so that I got there." Eyeing Naomi, he said, "You weren't there, sheriff neither. Nobody seemed to know anything, or at least they weren't talking, especially a strange fellow there, named Dick or Dirk or something. Didn't seem willing to tell me anything, whether he'd seen you or not."

"I'd just left on the paddle steamer, the *Morning Star.*" *So Dirk was still full of resentment against me,* she concluded.

"Nobody told me about you being on that steamer. So what could I do but wait until the sheriff came back? I had no idea where you might be, although I was pretty sure you'd still be in Fargo. Where else would you be, trying to find your pa – and the Franksons? Didn't know what else to do, so I rode around town for a while, asking if anybody'd seen a man with a team and a wagon, with a woman wearing a blue bonnet."

"Wasn't wearing that."

"Oh," Jacob retorted, "how'd I know that? Might have made a difference. Well, whatever … Anyway, went back around five, found a deputy, not the other one, said you and the sheriff had left for he didn't know where, seems he's usually off duty by noon Saturdays. I was getting mighty frustrated, I can tell you."

"I imagine so," said Naomi's father, not unkindly.

"So it seemed a dead end. I was thinking about giving up and ride back to Menasa. At least, I didn't know what else to do, except wait there, figuring all of you might be returning home that way and it's the only good road to the east, as we all know."

"Did you? Wait in Fargo, I mean? That might have been the most sensible thing to do until you found out where I was."

"Well, in a way, that's what happened, can't explain why. It seemed like something was keeping me there. Nothing to it but spend another night there, this time a boarding house down near the river, by now my money going down fast. Little did I know the worst was still to come."

Becoming more agitated with the telling, Jacob got up and started pacing back and forth. "Next day was Sunday, town quiet enough, 'cept for them church bells." He looked accusingly at Naomi. "No sign of that darn sheriff, not even a deputy around. Guess that town doesn't expect any trouble over the weekends."

"That'd sure be the day," commented Henry Frankson cynically.

"You were still in Fargo on Sunday and Sunday night?" Naomi sounded incredulous.

"That's the way it worked out. So you can be sure, first thing Monday morning I got myself over to the sheriff's office, but he still wasn't there, deputy saying he'd been called out to a nearby farm over some shooting. Went back about noon and just happened to see him coming out of a place across the street called Miss Jane's or Joanne's or something like that. To make a long story short, he told me what had happened to you, said you'd taken the paddle steamer down to Ft. Abercrombie, but he didn't know when you'd be coming back."

"Nor did we," John Beckman put in.

"So here was my dilemma, and I'm sure – " looking pointedly at Naomi, "you will understand all about my many dilemmas. Should I wait in Fargo until you came back with your pa and the Franksons, or should I risk going down to the fort in the hope you'd still be there?"

"What'd you do next, then?" Ted asked excitedly, caught up in the drama of Jacob's story.

"Well, the sheriff told me that, if I wanted to get down to the fort and risk still finding you there, I could speed it up by trying to catch a paddle steamer headed down there – or up there, you know how that crazy Red River runs. I jumped at the chance, always interested in those steam engines, you see, after our threshing rig back home. I wanted to see how those big pistons or whatever they're called, really work." He paused for a moment of reflection. "You know, I just may want to go into the steam engine business myself, someday. Big future in them, I'm told. Just think -- " He broke off, lost in thought, as he continued his pacing back and forth in front of the group.

"The paddle steamer? Fort Abercrombie?" Ted prompted hopefully.

Catching himself, Jacob turned around and sat back down heavily in his chair. "Well, anyway, bad luck, as it turned out, the next steamer had just left, about noon. So I rushed back to the sheriff's office. 'Son,' he says to me, 'if you're really that desperate, you can ride down along the river, fast as that horse of yours can go, and make it to Comstock, 'bout ten miles or so south, Fargo side of the river.' Then he said I could take a ferry across the Red – providing a man named Bob Pritchard still ran it, to a place called Hickson, town on the east bank, first steamer stop. If I couldn't catch the steamer there, I could ride on another ten miles to Wolverton and catch the steamer there, that'd be about twenty miles this side of Ft. Abercrombie. Forget the name of that steamer – *Star* something, doesn't matter."

Naomi regarded Jacob strangely. "What day was that?" It seemed odd, indeed, that connection with Wolverton, where she'd imagined he'd boarded the *Morning Star* on the preceding Saturday.

"I'm not sure, because I began to lose all track of time. Monday, maybe, leastways that was the plan. As it turned out, when I got to Comstock that Bob feller was nowhere to be found and the ferry was moored over at Hickson on the other side of the river. Didn't know whether I'd have to make Prince swim across – sure looked risky – or ride down all the way to the fort along the west bank. Could've done it, but, you know, nigh onto thirty more miles – take me day and a half at least, and poor Prince had already just about had it."

He paused, smoothed back his hair, but after stroking the growing stubble of a beard and realizing what he must look like, seemed embarrassed. "So, the long and short of it was, I had to spend the night there in Comstock, no hostelry or anything, so I just curled up in my jacket and saddle blanket under some trees. Got mighty cold and hungry by morning, though, not to mention discouraged."

"What next?" Ted was still all ears.

"Well, I was thinking about what you might be thinking, Naomi – if you know what I mean, determined, and all. What were my choices? I could risk riding down along the west side of the river, all the way to the fort, even though it was a far distance and the trail looked pretty rough. Or I could wait for that Bob the ferryman. So I waited – and waited. Finally, way late in the afternoon there he comes along the pulley cable across the river. 'How about getting me across,' I said. 'I'm a man in a big hurry'. But he hemmed and he hawed, said I'd have to pay double, it being so late in the day."

"You got across to Hickson, then?" Naomi asked. "But Jacob, that would have been yesterday."

Jacob rubbed his hand over his stubble once again, clearly agitated. "Yes and no I got across, and yes, that was yesterday, and yes, at great expense – and with an awful sacrifice."

"What happened then? You swam Prince across the river and he drowned?" Ted asked, struck by the image of a horse drowning.

The look on Jacob's face was hard to interpret, a mixture of shock, anger, and frustration. "I got across, yes, but – "

Just then there was a blast from the steamer's whistle, and an officer poked his head into the lounge. "Fargo coming up, ten minutes, ladies and gentlemen. If you will please gather your belongings together and prepare to disembark from the lower deck, port side?"

Naomi got to her feet. "I'd like to go out on deck for a bit, before we dock," she said, "and get a little fresh air. You'll be all right, Pa? Here comes Corporal Martin to get you ready to leave the boat."

"I'll be fine, don't worry, dear, I'm in the corporal's capable hands. There's Hank and Ted as well – Jacob, too. I'll be glad for some fresh air myself when we dock. It's so stuffy in here I fell asleep a couple of times."

But to Naomi's surprise, Jacob said, "If you don't mind, sir, I'd like to join Naomi on deck."

"Of course, of course," with a wave of his hand and a faint smile. "You both have a lot to talk about."

Standing at the railing beside Jacob on the deck of the *Silver Falcon*, Naomi looked out over the plains to the west. Light streamed down through gaps in the clouds as they passed across the sun, illuminating patches of copper-gold brush, of bluish prairie grasses. As far as she could see, the plains stretched into faint distances beyond. She had reached this part of the plains, she had encompassed those between this river and those to the east. *I feel such a small creature*, she could not help but reflect, *such a small, minute creature in the Lord's vast creation. And yet – and yet – I know that even the sparrow –*

"Here we are, Naomi, heading home. Can you believe it?" Jacob asked, following her gaze to the west.

"There are so many things hard to believe."

"Seems like I'd never get here, wondering the whole time whether I was doing the right thing."

"What made you decide what the right thing was?" *He seems so nervous and agitated*, she thought, *not his usual decisive and logical self. I suspect he hasn't told me everything.*

"I – I don't know. Lot of things, maybe. I had too much on my mind."

"Whatever the reasons, Jacob, you've undertaken a long and difficult journey."

"Took me a while."

"Yes, but you *did* get here."

"Maybe I'm still trying to sort out the *why*. Things aren't as straightforward as I'd like, you know how I am."

"I'm not sure."

"Well, whatever you think of me … There are some things I have to – a few questions I need to – well, it's hard to explain. Your faith – well, that's one of the things. Then there's your father. Mary's father. I need to –" He turned his back to her and stood holding onto the railing a slight distance away.

Naomi wondered whether the Lord was testing him as well, setting up trials that he, too, must overcome. The realization of this possibility came as a shock. And with that shock came the words, *Oh Lord, help me to see, to understand – to forgive –*

"I'll try to understand, Jacob," she said at last, unsure about the forgiving part. They stood there apart for a few moments, each of them deep in private thoughts, puzzling questions, unshaped answers. "Perhaps it will take time, for both of us." *Right now*, she thought, *I can only put such questions into the think-about-it-later part of my brain.*

"We must be almost to Fargo. We're almost home," Jacob broke in, pointing ahead toward the bow. "See all that smoky haze? All those chimneys – can't miss a big town like that."

Just as he said that, the *Silver Falcon* began to slow down in a noiseless drift through the current. Within a few more minutes the steamer shuddered from a violent reversal of the paddle wheel, a foaming of water, a rocking motion as the boat slowed and, in another few moments, nudged against the dock. All around them came shouting of commands and throwing of ropes to be fastened around mooring posts. Corporal Martin and a deck hand had carried Naomi's father out of the lounge and were carefully managing the stairs down to the lower departure deck, with the Franksons close behind.

"Never thought it'd ever happen," Ted exclaimed. "Sure didn't. Say, Jacob, you going to go back up there to the bow, that other gangplank for the livestock, the buggies and stuff? Sure was surprised to see all that on a *boat*. I expect old Prince'll be glad to get off."

"No he won't," Jacob said slowly.

"He won't? He's not getting off? Then – "

"Not getting off. Never on."

"Jacob, why what happened?" Naomi asked. It hadn't occurred to her to ask about Prince.

"Never mind," he said tersely, looking upset. "Part of the story. I'll explain later."

Putting aside her questions, Naomi followed him and Ted down the narrow gangway. She had other concerns to deal with at the moment. Looking anxiously toward the wharf, she asked, "Is someone meeting us, Pa? I don't think the major said exactly."

"There must surely be," he replied, trying to conceal his own uncertainty, "but one's never sure about army protocol." He didn't explain.

As the group eventually made their way down the gangplank, Naomi recalled that feeling she had the morning Harry Barnes had left her at the sheriff's office, an uncertainty regarding the next step. Now with her father and the others – including Jacob – she seemed to have been thrust into even more responsibility.

"Ah ha! There you are." Naomi heard with great relief Sheriff Jameson's distinctive voice long before she spotted him pushing his way through the crowd. "Got two buggies waiting over there. Once I get you settled at the hotel, we'll talk about matters relating to your journey home, a few other issues as well." He waved the driver of the first buggy to move closer to where John Beckman waited on a bench with the Franksons, the doctor's assistant standing beside him.

"Your father seems a bit tired," Corporal Martin commented to Naomi, "but he's done well, so far. Once you get him settled, wherever you're being put up for the night, have a doctor come in to check his dressing and see he takes his pills. I have to leave you now, since I've got the major's business to attend to, so I'll bid you a safe journey home." He leaned over to shake hands with the men, touched his uniform cap to Naomi and Jacob, and strode up the street to the next intersection.

"Now then," the sheriff said, I've instructed the drivers to take you to the Lodge Hotel, a few blocks away on Fourth Street South. You'll be comfortable there, I hope."

Naomi drew in a sharp breath. That was the same hotel where she'd looked unsuccessfully for Birgitta.

"There are a number of matters we must discuss, financial and otherwise. Persons accounted for, legal matters, plans," the sheriff continued.

"Legal matters? Plans for what?"

"Plans? Have patience, Miss Beckman, such matters will be made known in due time, all in due time. This evening I plan to meet you at the Lodge for dinner, along with my one of my deputies. Their small dining room offers decent fare, I'm told. Yes, we'll discuss things then."

He said deputy? she was thinking. *Surely not Dirk – no, I could not bear to see that man again, whoever he is – whatever he is.*

"Yes, several, legal matters," Sheriff Jameson repeated. "But as I said – "

"Does it concern Birgitta Magnusson?" Naomi broke in. "Don't you remember? I was sure it had something to do with those lawyers."

He looked thoughtful for a moment, then drew himself up. "Ah yes," fingering his cartridge belt as if needing distraction from some challenging issue. "But all in good time, as I said."

The sheriff glanced over at the two waiting buggies drawn up nearby. "I see your family is anxious to depart and get settled in. It's been a long journey down river today already," and, eyeing Jacob pointedly, "especially, I suspect, for this young man. But come along now."

Limping slightly as they walked closer to the waiting buggy, he added, "Ah yes, so many things in life – so unexpected."

15

Lifemarks

What Sheriff Jameson had said about The Lodge hotel's dining room was true. That evening, after the plain fare of Ft. Abercrombie's mess hall, the pheasant with cream sauce, sugared squash, roast potatoes, gravy and more -- topped off with apple tart and whipped cream, proved sumptuous. It was a real feast, celebrating their first real meal together, their coming home.

"Won't you take some more tart, Mr. Beckman?" The sheriff had discarded his work clothes for a black dress suit, ruffled shirt, red brocade vest, and blue silk cravat, a dramatic trans-formation in Naomi's opinion, and totally un-sheriff-like. "Do take some of this whipped cream, sir. From your thin looks, you have a bit of catching up to do."

"Yes, indeed," John Beckman replied, "although food is hardly the most important part of it." Naomi knew exactly what he meant.

"May I ask after your health? It is improving? You've had some medical attention since your arrival?"

"Yes, sheriff, he has," Naomi answered. "Following Corporal Martin's instructions, I had the hotel clerk summon the nearest doctor to check my father's condition. He's tired from the jour-ney, but the incisions are healing well."

"If I may speak for myself, Sheriff," her father interjected while spooning on more whipped cream at the sheriff's suggestion, "the doctor pronounced my condition as stable as could be expected. He hoped the long wagon ride home would not cause undue harm."

"Ah yes, the return home. It's time to talk about that." Sheriff Jameson pulled out a silver watch from his vest pocket and flipped open the lid. "The hour's growing late, I fear, and you will no doubt wish to retire early."

"You mentioned financial matters, legal questions, plans?" Naomi was anxious to get to the bottom of things. Surely these were critical issues, although no one had yet raised them.

"Ah, anxious to get to the point, Miss Beckman, as I might expect." He pushed his chair back slightly from the table and cleared his throat. "Now Mr. Beckman, Mr. Frankson, you will recall you lost your wagon, your horses, and all your hunting gains during that night two weeks ago in your skirmish with the Shakota in Argusville?"

"That is correct, sheriff."

"How much worth do you estimate?"

"Everything? Well," Naomi's father thought a moment, "well, possibly around a hundred dollars. It would naturally depend upon how much we could expect in trade exchange for the pelts. The game, of course, we needed at home for the winter."

"Good. Now Sam, write that down, will you? About one hundred dollars." His deputy, not Dirk to Naomi's relief, sat beside him with pencil and pad.

"And your expenses since then as a result?"

John Beckman smiled and shook his head. "Nothing, isn't that right, Hank? The United States government, the army took it over. All that medical care, the transportation down to Ft. Abercrombie and back – my daughter's expenses, too. Wouldn't you think so, too, Hank, that we've all been well provided for?"

"That's right, John. Never expected it and can't stop being grateful, probably saved our lives when you come to think about it."

"Major Richardson told me we were owed something for assisting the settlers, opted temporarily into the military, so to speak," Naomi's father explained. "That's a little hard to believe. We did what any man would do, under the circumstances."

"All in all, however, it was an unfortunate incident, causing much in the way of pain and hardship. I would guess, too, it may be a while before you can get back into your normal labors around the farm."

Sheriff Jameson turned to his deputy. "So now, Sam, read off those figures on the other side of that page."

"I have $342.17."

"Explain where that comes from, Sam." He sat back with a satisfied look on his face.

"Comes from a collection taken up by bunch of settlers up in Argusville. Here's what they said. After them Shakota took off with everything, couple of men followed 'em and tracked 'em down soon's they made camp. Got back the horses and your pelts – as well as theirs. As for the game – well, they ate it. Not all at once, mind you. Shared it around, like."

"So," the sheriff continued Sam's account, "seeing as you saved Dan Johnson's life, his son and brother-in-law's, too, they thought it only right to pay you for the horses, which they were glad to keep, the loss of your wagon, which was too damaged to be repaired, and all those pelts, plus the game kept by the

Shakota, was worth $342.17. That is, give or take a nickel or two."

"Sheriff figured you could use the cash. Here it is." Sam drew out a leather pouch and dropped it on the table.

There was a gasp. "Really, sheriff – hardly necessary – all too generous – " protested John Beckman, accompanied by murmurings from Henry Frankson. Ted, however, looking more than interested, opened his mouth to say something, but after a pointed look from his father, changed his mind.

"Not at all, sir, not at all. Least we – they -- could do. Now here is what I suggest." He glanced briefly at his watch, replaced it.

"In the morning I'll send Sam over, say somewhere around nine o'clock. Not too early? Good. Then Mr. Frankson – I expect his son, too, with Mr. Bowers, should go down to the livery stable and fit yourselves up for the journey home. You'll need a bigger wagon, of course, and I'd suggest a buggy as well. It would be more comfortable for Mr. Beckman." He paused, looked again at his watch. "As for your stay here in this hotel – there should be enough in that pouch to cover it as well."

Naomi was speechless. Although there were many words waiting, they failed to materialize. Instead, she reached over and took her father's hand, her eyes stinging with threatening tears. "Pa, oh Pa – "

"Well, as I see," the sheriff pushed back his chair all the way and motioned to his deputy to do the same, "the hour's late. We'd best leave you to your rest."

"No, wait, sheriff!" Naomi had found her voice. "Birgitta Magnusson – you said you'd found out something."

"Well, I – " He hesitated, looking at Sam. "Why don't you go on out, Sam, bring our horses 'round from the Lodge's stable?"

As Sam left the hotel dining room, the sheriff said rather evasively, "I'm not sure what all I can tell you."

"Please, I was so much involved in her disappearance, maybe even partly responsible. I need to know. And the folks in Menasa will want to know, if you haven't already told them."

He looked somewhat nonplussed. "No, afraid I haven't done that yet. I'd have to send somebody, you see, don't know whom I could spare. You planning to go through there?"

"Yes, we need to pick up Matthew Schmidt. He should be well enough to travel by now. All that depends, of course, on whether he's still in Menasa."

"In Menasa? Where else would he be?" The sheriff sighed. "And how would you expect me to have known?"

"Harry might have taken him to Moorhead to take care of some legal things. Or, if he'd already done that, he be on his way home ahead of us. But if he *is* in Menasa and ready to go home to Prairie Lake, he could ride in the new buggy with Pa." She smiled at the picture of both men exchanging stories, talking about politics, their wives, their children. *No,* she instantly remembered, *not Matthew's children.* "But now, sir, what about Birgitta?"

With another resigned sigh, Sheriff Jameson leaned his chair back and crossed his arms. "All right, since you insist. Here's how it was. Got the story from Randy Fletcher last Saturday, day after you left, Miss Beckman. Went to his law office for questioning, as you suggested. He was in a great state I can tell you, office a shambles with papers scattered everywhere. Appears that Billings had just gone off with all the cash they had in their safe."

"He went off with Birgitta?"

No, miss, she'd already taken off."

"Already taken off? Without him? With somebody else?"

"Here's what Fletcher told me. While they were at the Menasa Inn, this Swedish girl gave them some sad story about having to meet her intended in Moorhead. She said her intended had a homestead out in the Dakotas, somewhere near Kalama. So Billings offered her a ride, claiming his phaeton could get her to Moorhead in time. But by the time they arrived, Billings had apparently persuaded her to forget about her intended and go off with him."

He gave a sly wink and smile in John Beckman's direction. "Always was known around here as a ladies' man. Well, then Billings, this Birgitta, and Fletcher crossed over to Fargo on the ferry, went by the law office to pick up something. At that point, the girl, playing up to Billings, persuaded him to book a room in a hotel for them. She suggested the Great Northern, near the station, claiming she wanted someplace special to spend the night with him. She suggested he register them under an assumed name. So the two of them took the ferry back to Moorhead to check in at the Great Northern."

"What time was that, do you know? I looked in that hotel just across from the railroad station. I might have seen them and not realized it." Naomi was distressed at the possibilities.

"Must've been 'round five or so. According to Fletcher, once they arrived in the lobby and Billings was about to register under a false name, she made some excuse – powder her nose or something, you know how women are." Another wink in John Beckman's direction.

Naomi bristled. "I doubt – "

The sheriff cut in. "So Billings waited and waited in the lobby until maybe about five or five-fifteen. Then it occurred to him that she might have gone directly into the dining room to wait for him there. So he looked, she wasn't there, so he decided to find a table and wait. She never came. According to Fetcher, he knew he'd been duped, got as mad as a wet hen.'"

"The hotel lobby – I was there just about that time, might have seen him! I looked around, asked, but had to rush off. Harry was waiting with the wagon in the street outside. He couldn't stop, he had to keep moving because there wasn't a place to tie the wagon."

"Did Billings ever find out what happened, sheriff?" Jacob asked.

"Well, Billings never said, had a lot of hurt pride, you see, but Fletcher put two and two together. He thinks Birgitta intended all along to give Billings the slip once she persuaded him to take her to the Great Northern Hotel."

"But why the Great Northern? Does anyone know where she is now?"

"Matter of fact, we do. I sent a telegram to the sheriff in Kalama. He made enquiries, got some answers. Seems that Birgitta's intended had already registered them at the hotel under Mr. and Mrs. -- his name is Erik Eriksson -- just so she'd have a place to stay if he couldn't make to Moorhead to catch that train. Once she discovered he wasn't coming – he'd missed the train from Kalama earlier, I reckon, she slipped out of the hotel and crossed over to the railroad station just in time to catch the five-forty-five west to Kalama in order to avoid Billings."

"I heard that train," cried Naomi, "so close I was, so close. That letter in Swedish I found in Birgitta's apron pocket – it makes sense now. I recognized the word *hotel* but the name *Kalama* didn't seem like a place, hadn't begun with a capital letter, you see. And that note Emma had later found in her room seemed to be making some apology, some excuse. We may never know all the details. Was there anything else you could learn about her, sheriff?"

"Yes, there was. It seems she and this Erikson were engaged to be married. The engagement had already taken place in Sweden. The plan was that he'd come over first, then later send for her once he got settled and had a little more money. Poor old Fletcher, though," shaking his head. "Still, I guess Fletcher must have had a good laugh over that woman's taking his partner for a ride through her clever little deception. Probably served Billings right."

"On the other hand, sheriff," Henry Frankson put in, "one can't help but feel sorry for Fletcher. He's the one who lost his business partner and most of his money. The reputation of the law firm will most certainly suffer."

"I'm only worried about Matthew Schmidt's legal business, the documents he left with them." Naomi couldn't feel much sympathy for Fletcher, certainly none for Billings.

"Not to worry about that," said the sheriff. "Fletcher assured me he'd take care of it and eventually send them back to the Schmidts in Prairie Lake."

Rising from the table, he said, "It's already long past time to leave. I expect Sam'll be outside the door with the horses. So we'll wish you folks a good night's rest, I'm sure it'll be welcome. Send word over to my office come morning should you need anything."

That night, sharing her father's room at The Lodge Hotel, Naomi's heart and mind were full. There was no question about pushing anything into the think-about-it-later part of her brain. All her thoughts were right there, right there in front. *Oh Lord, I thank you for your graciousness, for your healing, your bounty, for Birgitta's happiness. Oh Lord —*

It was a prayer she repeated again and again, until she felt sleep was falling heavily upon her consciousness. Her last thoughts turned, once again, to Naomi's story in the fields of Moab -- Birgitta Magnusson had followed the man she loved – her husband -- to foreign fields, risking all to work the fields with him.

Just before noon next day the Franksons with Jacob drove up before The Lodge Hotel. Hearing the commotion from where she and her father were sitting in the lobby, she rushed outside. Jacob was tying to the hitching rail a team of handsome sorrels pulling a large farm wagon. Ted and Henry Frankson were alongside in a phaeton hitched to a large bay.

"We did it!" Ted exclaimed with a satisfied grin.

"Pa drove a hard bargain at the livery stable, just look at these beauties!"

As they sat in the lobby, discussing the next step, John Beckman remarked, "How long will it take, do you think? When Hank and I took off on our hunting trip, we didn't come this way. No, we went a more northern trail up toward Grand Forks. We intended to come back through Moorhead, but," he glanced knowingly at Henry, "we got side-tracked, you might say."

"I can tell you about how long," Jacob offered. "From here to Menasa Inn, about twelve miles, maybe four hours, although with those great looking beasts out there, maybe less. Then from there – " he stopped. "Well, truth be told, I don't quite know. Got side-tracked myself."

"Four hours, you said? Is that right, Naomi?" Her father sounded excited. "What time is it now?"

Naomi looked at the large Seth Thomas clock hanging on the wall behind the clerk's desk. "Just past twelve."

He got to his feet, swayed a little, thought better of it, sat down again in the easy chair. "Why, we could make it, don't you think? To Menasa? By supper time?"

Naomi caught some of his excitement. The thought of starting home right away … there was, after all, nothing to keep them in Fargo. And the thought of seeing Matthew, of being able to bring him home as well … "Yes – I'm sure we could. I can get the kitchen to pack some provisions, we'll eat on the way. I know Emma Barnes can provide for the rest of the journey."

She threw her arms around her father's neck. "Pa – you're going home at last, and you're going to get well!"

"For sure, we're all happy 'bout that," Jacob commented. "As for me, there's something on my mind I've got to settle, and the sooner we get there the better."

Naomi looked at him closely. *He's holding back something. In fact, he's been rather cool and distant to me, ever since he appeared out of the blue at Hickson. Something's wrong.*

Within the next hour, Naomi was sitting beside Jacob on the driving bench of the wagon, with Henry Frankson stretched out on quilts in the back. Baskets of provisions, her wicker case, a box provided by Major Richardson containing her father's, Jacob's, and the Franksons' things was stowed alongside him.

"You think young Ted's all right back there with you father in the phaeton?" Jacob asked. "That boy sure does like to whip up them horses, right dangerous I think."

"He looks like he's doing all right, quite pleased with himself in fact. Next rest stop I guess you plan to change over? Ted'll drive this wagon, I'd like to be with Pa, you can come in the phaeton with us." *I'd actually prefer to be alone with pa, though,* she thought. *For whatever reason, Jacob's behavior troubles me more and more.*

"Not sure, we'll see," was all he said.

Out of distraction, she pointed to a house just off the road, "that's Mr. Myer's house."

"Do you know him?"

"Only that he's a friend of Harry Barnes. Along this road – any road, I guess, you need to know the landmarks."

Jacob chuckled. "Don't I know it! Remembering an old blacksmith shop once saved me from disaster."

"Oh? Tell me about it."

"Later, Naomi. There are a lot of things I'm not prepared to talk about yet – especially the landmarks."

"*Landmarks – lifemarks* – there ought to be a word like that." Her mind raced with possibilities.

"What would be the most important lifemark for you, Naomi?"

Surprised that he was drawing her out, she answered, "Maybe that straw hat you're wearing," she answered, "I found it once, nearly rescued it. Now it looks silly from getting all out of shape in the rain. It's so connected with you."

"Well, I'd say, as far as lifemarks go, maybe that black straw bonnet you're wearing, with those fake Easter lilies. It's already September, you know, and getting colder. Aside from that, though, I might have found you earlier if you hadn't been wearing it."

"But does that mean you were truly looking for me? For *me*, Naomi?" In her heart, however, she was convinced that had not found each other at all.

Not answering her, he said, "One of the things – " He broke off, fingered the reins for a while in his gloved hands. "There are a lot of things -- "

"Like what?" On an impulse, she added, "Like going to church?"

"Stop, Naomi. You know my feelings 'bout that -- church, and faith, and all that stuff."

"Yes, but I wish you'd tell me again. I want to hear your argument."

"Naomi, you always were one to be direct. Makes a man feel like he has to be real quick witted to keep up with you. Well, I've a hard time with that, with thinking the way you do, thinking about God and all that. I can't give you a clear argument. I've always had doubts, questions that couldn't be answered. You know I'm a practical man. Got to see it, touch it, to believe it's real."

"What about love? What if you know in your heart it's real? What if you can feel the Lord's presence? What if things happen, things that you pray for?"

"Like what? Do you mean the Lord's love? A person's love? Man's love for a woman? Or what? And praying for what? "

"Like finding my father, like healing for him."

"Did you ever pray for me?"

"Yes, often."

"Any results?" He smiled faintly.

"I'm still working on it."

"Well, let me know when you see some real results. I'd really like to --" Suddenly he stood up, jerking the reins to the left. "Hang on, Naomi – Mr. Frankson! Big hole in the road ahead." He guided the team sharply over to one side of the road, then glanced behind to see how Ted had managed the phaeton. "Whew, that was a close one," he said, "I should pay better attention to this road."

They rode on in silence for another quarter of an hour or so, Naomi lost in thought, unwilling to press Jacob further. *There must be some way*, she thought, *to help him pay better attention to my feelings, his feelings, and to help him see what he claims he can't see about faith. Oh Lord, please help me to find that way.*

It was already late in the afternoon when she spotted the first houses of Menasa, then the village store she'd passed with Harry, more houses, and just at the other edge of town the large gray frame building known as the Menasa Inn. "Drive around to the back, Jacob," she said, pointing to it, "there's a large barn and livery stable."

"I know all too well 'bout that barn," he commented dryly, "I'm thinking of Prince, thinking also of that woman Birgitta's ruse and how she turned up somewhere unexpected just like that horse. Yes, siree, that barn and I are old friends."

"Prince, now, you said you tell us what happened. Where is he?"

"Later, later," he answered, tight lipped. He turned the team sharply around the corner of the building and pulled them up before the barn door.

The wagon no sooner rolled to a stop, with the phaeton drawing up alongside, when the back door burst open. Emma erupted from the mudroom, waving a wooden spoon.

"Naomi! It's you!" she boomed. "Oh Naomi, so long without any word of you. And you, Mr. Bowers! You're with her. You found her!" She threw her arms around Naomi in a grasp so tight Naomi could hardly breathe, threw her arms around

Jacob, then stepped back and looked questionably at the phaeton. "Not them lawyers again?"

"I have my father with me," she said, "and the Franksons, too. Do you have rooms for us for the night? We must be on our way early morning."

"Of course, of course," Emma boomed. "Let me go get Harry, he's doin' books in the office. He'll take care of the horses. Come in, come in, and through the kitchen. It's family you are, for sure."

Jacob and Ted stayed behind to help Harry, who seemed equally surprised to see them, while Emma took Naomi, her father, and Hank through the kitchen and out into the hall. "Let me get the keys to your rooms. Only two other guests, so there's no problem about fittin' you in."

"Matthew – How is he? Still in number six? I'm so very anxious to see him."

Emma's manner immediately changed. She dropped the bunch of keys on the hall table with a loud jangle.

"I'm sure he's better, he was already on the mend when I left. Oh, I can hardly wait to see him." Naomi took the first two stairs.

"Naomi – stop! " Emma paused, nervously twisting her apron. "I'm afraid you can't see him."

"Why, has he already left? Did he go on to Moorhead? Or maybe he's headed back home with someone?"

"No, Naomi – I'm sorry to have to break the sad news to you. Matthew passed away in the evenin', two days after you left with Harry."

Naomi felt as if the hall were dissolving in mist, as if the floor were giving way under her feet. "But he was – he was – "

"Yes, he seemed to be recoverin'. But then fever set in, he had a hard time breathin'. Harry fetched the doctor, but Doc couldn't do much. All next day Matt struggled, like, then fell asleep 'bout midnight, never woke up."

"He died in his sleep?" The news made no sense.

Emma picked up the keys, obviously struggling to regain control of herself and the situation. "But here, I'm keepin' you folks from your rooms, sure you'll want to rest, freshin' up 'fore supper. Later, Naomi, I'll tell you somethin' 'bout Matt, somethin' will make you feel better."

Turning to Naomi's father, she asked, "And you, sir, think you can manage them stairs all right? Fine, hold to the banister, take one step at a time. So now just follow me up, then."

After Naomi had helped Emma with clearing up after supper, Emma claiming that she was thankful she now had some help during the day from a village girl named Anna Quast, she and Emma sat down in the kitchen over a cup of tea. Everyone else seemed settled down and the house was quiet except for the chiming clock in the hall.

"Now about Matt, like I said. His end was quiet, peaceful, you might say. Old Mike Hauglund came in evenin' just after you left. You remember him? Then next day happened to have a guest who was a travelin' preacher, name of Christiansen. Spent some time with Matt all that afternoon, evenin'. Don't know what they talked about, exactly, but accordin' to the reverend they prayed together, listened to him readin' somethin'. The reverend said Matt seemed to be coming to terms with things, kept talkin' 'bout at — can't think of the word, what was it? Oh yes, somethin' 'bout atonement. Seemed mighty concerned 'bout that dress suit jacket of his. Reminded him of somethin', a place, somethin' awful painful. End came, he seemed at peace, or so the preacher said."

"Where is he – "

"In the churchyard, that one among the fir trees down the road. Asked to be buried there, and in that best suit he had. Said somethin' 'bout the church forgiven and bein' forgiven. Might have somethin' to do with that tragedy I told you about, a shelled church cavin' in and killin' his children."

That night, in Naomi's old room at the Menasa Inn, she felt somewhat consoled by the thought that Matthew had, at the end, come to terms with something, as if he were sacrificing his old feelings in exchange for some inner peace. *I remember our last visit,* she thought, *when he had tried to talk to me about death and I didn't understand. I do now. He was already coming to terms with that path. Do you suppose I had anything to do with it? All that about the suit jacket, though. What could it mean? And that word Emma used – atonement. Doesn't that mean paying for something you've done?*

Suddenly, as if in a flash of brilliant light, the realization, the understanding came to her. *No, it wasn't only that guilt about the fire and losing his children. It was about me and that night in the abandoned homestead cabin. I was wearing that jacket. He asked to spend the night with me. He had something in mind, something he was having a hard time controlling. That's what it was. Atonement, forgiveness. That's what it was all about.*

Naomi sat on the edge of the brass bed, trembling from the shock of that insight. Her emotions ran from remorse to pity to guilt, guilt because she'd never had the chance to talk to him about the one issue which appeared to lie heaviest on his heart. Slipping off the bed, she knelt down beside it. "Oh Lord," she whispered, "forgive me as You have forgiven Matthew." She buried her face in her hands, unable to say more.

16

Sacrifices

"How far now, Jacob?" she asked the next morning as they were, at the first light of dawn, once again on their way. It was hard to leave the Menasa Inn, so meaningful had it become in her life, one of those significant *lifemarks*, even more so because of the revelation last night concerning Matthew. *In one way I caused his death,* she thought. *That heaviness of guilt will always be with me. One of the trials laid upon me. Yet, could it be that through our many talks along the way I might have guided him on a pathway toward finding the atonement he sought and the peace he deserved?*

"You asked, how far? I'm not sure," Jacob replied. "Even though I've been along this road, so have you, there were so many checks and delays that it's hard to know. I'd guess maybe Prairie Lake just before sundown?" He paused to check the reins, which had gotten tangled, then continued, "Say, I meant to tell you how sorry I am about Matthew Schmidt. Sad news, it'll be hard telling his wife. I met her, you know, just before I left."

"You did? Yes, Matthew's wife, Lottie … " Naomi hadn't yet thought that one out. "That'll be very hard, hard on my mother, too." She experienced another wave of guilt.

"I reckon Maplewood's not too far ahead. We'll make a rest stop there, water and feed the horses, and it's 'bout time we

339

check on your pa. Do you realize," he glanced at her, smiling, you've spent a lot more time riding here with me in the wagon than you have in the phaeton with him?"

"I guess not," she answered lamely, unwilling to confess she'd managed to arrange most of the exchanges. "Just seemed to work out that way."

"Looks like Maplewood coming up. Say, I wonder if old Hattie Geske still makes that awful coffee."

"Who?"

"And I need to tell that blacksmith 'bout Prince."

"Who? And what about Prince?"

"Never mind. I don't want to talk about it."

"Please, Jacob, it might do you good. And for that matter, an even bigger question, how you happened to board the *Silver Falcon* at Hickson, not on your way *down* to the fort, but coming *back up*?"

For a moment he concentrated on the road ahead. Then, with a sigh, he said, "Sure do miss old Prince, that's a fact. So here's how it was. I think I said I finally found that ferryman, Bob-Whatever. Must have been close to mid-afternoon three days ago. Well, after a lot of argument, hemming and hawing, that Bob agreed to take Prince and me across the river, but for one dollar, twice the usual price. Said it was because it was past the normal crossing times, and he'd have to make a return trip back to Comstock that evening in order to pick up some freight and passengers he'd already agreed take across next morning."

"That would have been, when?"

"Day before yesterday, I guess. It's still hard to attach a real time to things." Jacob paused, then continued even more reluctantly, "But well, that Bob wouldn't have made it, though."

"Oh? What happened?"

"So here's like it was. Prince and me, we go onto the ferry, tied up at Comstock's little rickety dock, Prince a little skittish and, as it turns out, for good reason. This Bob starts to winch us across by the cable, but 'bout halfway there's some sort of snag. The winch jams and he tries to clear it. Finally the cable snaps, the ferry starts drifting, banging up against rocks, twisting this way and that in the current. Prince is spooked and breaks free of the tethering rail across one end of the ferry. I try to catch hold of his reins to calm him down. Meantime, this Bob tries to maneuver the thing with a board he's using for an oar, no use. Prince by this time panics and jumps into the water, taking me with him. For a couple of minutes I'm able to hang on to Prince's saddle horn to keep afloat, or rather poor Prince trying to keep me afloat. That Bob tries to throw us a mooring rope, but the only way I can grab it is by letting go of Prince. So the horse is trying to swim against the current and I'm trying to reach him, trying to head him toward shore, but we're getting farther and farther apart. Finally I lose sight of him altogether, just as I'm snagged by some low-hanging trees on the east bank."

Suddenly Jacob pulled back on the team and guided the wagon over to one side of the road. "I'm sorry Naomi." Overcome, his shoulders heaving, he turned away and sat without speaking for several minutes, at one point waving the phaeton on ahead. Finally he said, "It's painful to relive it."

"I understand, Jacob," she said, resting her hand lightly on his arm. "Did Prince -- " she hardly knew how to word it.

"Gone," he answered, filling in her question. "By the time I got myself out of the river and up the bank, I could just see his head bobbing up and down, sometimes he'd scream the way horses do in pain. I tried running along the bank, but it was nearly dark. Finally, he was – he was gone. Drowned."

Squaring up his shoulders and flicking the team's reins, he set the wagon once more in motion. "So you see, after all my frustration about the way he ran off that time, all my anger at him, I cost him his life. I – I – you might say he sacrificed himself for me."

Giving him time to calm down, Naomi waited a few moments before she asked, "But then, after that?" She thought it best to guide him toward a new line of thought.

"Well, then I met this Bob, scrambling along the same bank, looking the worst for wear, carrying on 'bout losing his ferry, no concern at all 'bout me losing my horse. 'We've been swept back toward Fargo, away from Hickson', he said, 'I reckon it's a half-mile ahead, but nothing to do but make for Hickson, not another town for miles.' So we finally staggered into town, dripping wet and shivering like the dickens. 'Know a friend here,' he offered, 'put us up for the night, maybe some grub.' That old Bob owed me that, at least. Truth is, I'd just lost everything – " He paused, a catch in his voice. "Not only Prince – I was soaking wet, all my extra clothes, even my money, were tied onto Prince's saddle."

Shaking his head, he muttered, "But you know, strange thing, that wasn't the first time I'd lost everything. It was like the time I first got to the Menasa Inn."

"Like the first time?"

"Never mind, that's another long story. So there I was with that Bob, left with nothing but the soaked clothes on my back, this hat, which for some reason I can't explain, floated along with me and got snagged on that tree limb." Smiling faintly, he added, "Sure must've been a sight yesterday when I burst into the steamer lounge like that?"

Naomi shook her head. "I didn't really notice your clothes. I was too shocked just to see you, since I'd no idea you'd left Prairie Lake."

"No idea how I was going to pay my steamer fare – just hoped back in Fargo that sherriff would straighten it out. Appears he did. Then at the hotel I borrowed a couple of things and a razor from Hank Frankson and a razor, trying to make myself look fairly decent. Feels strange though, wearing somebody else's clothes. Wondering who I really am just now."

"Perhaps you're not the only one," Naomi commented.

He threw a glance her way but continued, "Well, as for that Bob feller, back there at Hickson, when I tried to argue the accident with the ferry was his fault and I needed some recompense for what I'd lost, he downright refused and threatened to call in a sheriff."

"So you were left with nothing?" A fleeting thought of Job – he, too, was stripped of everything, perhaps, too, wondering who he was.

What could I do, what *should* I do? Two big questions plagued me: were you and the Franksons still at Ft. Abercrombie and would I have time to get there by steamer before you left? If you were already on your way – and you very well could have been, should I return to Fargo by steamer as soon as I could and wait for you there? Either way I knew I'd have to convince some steamer captain to let me pay for the ticket at the destination, hoping somebody would come to my rescue."

"So you decided to return to Fargo and wait for me there?"Naomi could not help but smile at the apparent irony of it. "Was I supposed to rescue you there? Like I was supposed to rescue my father?"

"I really didn't have much choice, Naomi." By the droop of his shoulders and the way he tightened the teams' reins, she knew his confession embarrassed and humiliated him.

"If it's any consolation, Jacob, it's possible the sheriff took care of it, though we may hear something from him about it later." *Events have happened so oddly*, she thought in wonderment, moved by Jacob's sacrifice however motivated, whether for her or someone else. *I feel compassion for Jacob, a strange, new feeling for him. Oh Lord, in your mercy …*

Riding along in silence for another mile or so, she realized this was probably the right moment to raise an issue regarding Jacob which she'd had for some time, perhaps during the last few years. Although that particular issue disturbed her greatly, she'd hesitated to have it out with him. Now, with his surprising new interest in steam engines, she'd come up with a way.

Scarcely daring to look directly at him, she began, "You know, Jacob, I had a thought about something which might surprise you."

"What was that? Your thoughts usually amaze me, more like it."

Letting that pass, she said, "I was thinking about steam engines."

"What? You?" He laughed, gave a forceful slap of the reins across the horses' rumps. "What'd I just say about amazing?"

"What makes them go?"

"The horses or the engines? Why, steam? The engines, I mean."

"Can you see that steam? Feel it?"

"Sometimes, could sure burn you."

"But can you see the force that goes from the steam to whatever turns the wheels or whatever it turns?" She sensed she was getting in deeper than she could handle and silently hoped something would come up to end that particular topic -- at least until she could work it out better. She knew where this topic should eventually lead; she just didn't know how to get there.

He remained silent for several moments. "Have to think about that, though I can't imagine why you brought it up."

Suddenly he flicked the reins against the teams' rumps, and the wagon jolted ahead. "Whup! Hup! Come on you nags, see there, Maplewood just ahead." Within minutes, he'd no sooner braked the wagon to a halt in front of Geske's Mercantile, when he exclaimed, "Oh, no! They've already done what they planned to do. Look there, see, the store windows are boarded up, and the smithy doors across the street are padlocked with a chain across."

"What do you mean, planned?"

"It's just that they'd about decided to sell out and move out west. Guess I'll never know whether they actually got hitched, though. I'm sure sorry to miss them, they were sure helpful to me before – specially with Prince, probably saved his life." He paused, then added, "At least that time."

"It's good to stop anyway," Naomi offered. "We can sit down on those benches in front of the store and eat Emma's provisions."

"Can't spend long here, though," Jacob cautioned. "We've still got a long ways to go before we reach Prairie Lake – and we'll have to get there before dark. After we eat, I'll get Ted to drive the wagon, and I'll take over the phaeton with you and your pa. Then after another couple of hours, we'll switch back."

Another two hours, and Naomi had just switched over from the phaeton with Jacob driving, to the wagon where Jacob replaced Ted. It had been a useful phase of the journey, providing a much needed opportunity for herself, her father, and Jacob to talk. She was sorry, however, she that there hadn't been an opportunity to return to the steam engine topic.

After another half hour it was clear that it would be a race against time to reach home before the sun set. "How far is it now, Jacob?" Naomi asked, her anxiety growing, due both to her desire to reach home and her frustration at not being yet able to come to terms with Jacob. Once they were both home, they would each fall into an established pattern of non-communication, and from there into an evermore distant relationship, and from there none at all.

"There's no exact way of knowing," he answered. "Although I do remember crossing that stream back there when I came. It looks a little less high than it did then, good thing for us forded it easily this time." He took off his straw hat and scratched his head. "Now let me see, it was about a couple of hours after I left."

"So that must mean – what?"

"Maybe an hour or so left." He whipped the team into a fast trot, causing the wagon to jolt dangerously over rocky stretches and its wheels to get caught in an occasional hole.

After much discomfort throughout her entire body, Naomi finally said, "I know we're all anxious to get home, Jacob, but going so fast is dangerous and we may lose the wagon. I'm especially worried about Ted back there in the phaeton with Pa. He's reckless enough. Can't we slow down a little? And there's poor Mr. Frankson here in the back of the wagon, being jolted to death."

"Well, if you say so." He slowed the team, and Ted drew the phaeton up alongside.

"Switching over?" Ted asked.

"Say, listen, Ted, it looks like we're only a couple of mile or so from Prairie Lake and that turn off to the Fullerton Road. Would you mind staying in the phaeton with Naomi's pa and letting me go the rest of the way in the wagon?"

"Sure thing, Jacob. Me and Mr. Beckman was just havin' a fine conversations, anyways. Talkin' 'bout huntin' game and all."

"All right, thanks." He turned on the driving bench to Naomi as he snapped the reins. "Hup, hup, giddyup there, you nags! Well, Naomi, we're almost there. There where we should be, need to be."

Again, one of Jacob's cryptic remarks, she thought. "What does that mean?"

"Been thinking 'bout you," glancing sideways at her, then quickly turning away. Been thinking 'bout a lot of things. Been thinking 'bout steam engines."

Naomi instantly raised her head. Exhausted from the strain of the week past and now from the long day's ride, despite her growing anxiety she'd been nodding off. In that moment of confusion, she simply stared at him. "*Steam engines*? Why, steam engines? Are you and your pa planning to buy one?"

"Well, maybe. No, I'm thinking more 'bout the force that drives it, the force within the steam. Something you said. You can see the steam, all right. But you can't see the force that drives the machinery. No, you can't see it. You just know it's there." He paused, thought a moment. "Maybe trust there, too. Just can't see it."

"Jacob, are you referring to what I said earlier? Just before we got to Maplewood?"

"Maybe."

"What does *maybe* mean? Did you understand what I was trying to get at?"

"Maybe. Maybe it has to do with faith." He cleared his throat, shifted a little on the driving bench. "Maybe faith's a force you can't see in itself, only what it does. *Maybe* you just have to trust it will do that."

He's got it, Naomi thought excitedly. *Yes, the meaning has gotten through to him. Oh Lord, thank you …*

"But now, you're expecting me to say something more? I'm not sure I can say more, not just now, anyway." He seemed to draw himself in, his body tensed up in some sort of resolve to keep to itself.

After several minutes of weighted silence, Naomi, in exasperation, reached over and firmly took his arm. "If you've nothing to say to me, Jacob Bowers, then I've something to say to you. And it's not about trust. Or steam engines. Or about *maybes*." She glanced back to see whether Henry Frankson was listening. He appeared to be curled up asleep under some quilts in the wagon bed.

She had to have it out. "I love you Jacob, have ever since that tow-headed brat named Jacob Bowers first pulled my braids in school. And I want to marry you, it seems have always wanted that. And although I thought you'd changed your mind, you did come, risked so much, and supported us all through these last few days. Yet I still don't know whether it was for me or Mary Frankson's father."

He looked shocked. "You always *what?*"

"Never mind." She drew a deep breath. "Now here is what I'm going to say, and you'd better listen. I'm not going to have it out with you again. You will have to choose between Mary Frankson and me. Once and for all." Another deep breath. "Now I've said it."

He looked away, inadvertently slowing the wagon, distracted by the impact of her words. Clearly he hadn't expected her sudden declaration and was struggling for an answer.

Absently fingering the reins in his gloved hands, he finally said hesitantly, "But, but Naomi – you see, I wanted to risk everything for you. It was for *you*, I know that now." He paused. "Of course, maybe Mary's father was part of that. At least at the beginning."

"You could have told me that."

"I just – well, I'm not as good with words as you. Besides, I couldn't then, I had a few things of my own to sort out."

"I have, too, Jacob – that sorting out part. It will always trouble me that you can't accept my faith, but I'm willing to accept that out of love for you. You may call that a sacrifice -- maybe that's what it is. A sacrifice like – like your horse, Prince."

"Wouldn't exactly compare you to a horse," he laughed. Suddenly he stopped the wagon, with shouts from Ted behind him that he'd almost run into him with the phaeton.

"Watch out," Ted cried, "want to bang up this here fine horse? This expensive rig?"

"Go on, Ted, take Mr. Beckman home. We'll meet you there. But don't blurt out anything about Matthew Schmidt, not just yet. We'll try to do it more gentle, like."

With a wave from Naomi's father, the phaeton pulled ahead and continued at a dangerous gallop down the road. "Idiot boy," Jacob mumbled under his breath.

Turning around to Henry Frankson, he said, "Say, Mr. Frankson – "

"Eh? What is it?" Frankson threw off the quilts and sat up. "What's the matter? We're there? Say, is that my Ted taking off in the phaeton like that? Oh, that all? Can't stop that boy, not so close to home."

"No, I wasn't going to try, but I need to ask you to do something."

"What's that?"

"Maybe you could get down and check on the wheel spokes? A few of 'em seem loose. We may need to have 'em looked at later at Grant's Hardware. Don't want a wheel to fall off, not so close to home, as you said."

Frankson nodded and climbed down, somewhat reluctantly, to inspect the rear wheels.

"Listen, Naomi," Jacob said in a low voice of rushed words, "now that we're alone, you've got to listen to what I need to say, what I want to say. Maybe you'll fill in for me if the words aren't right." He let the reins drop to the wagon floor and turned to her. "You're were talking about sacrifices?"

"Yes," she said slowly, puzzled.

"Well, I have to tell you, I did pray on the way to Fargo, have prayed a lot since. I struggled to find the words, wasn't easy. And then I started thinking about steam engines, that force. What you said made a bundle of sense to me. Can't see it, but it's there all right. I guess you'd say that about the Lord?"

"Yes," she answered, surprised, "I suppose so."

"Then I reckon that, for me to accept your faith, which I'm about to do, that's not making a sacrifice but receiving a gift. That sound right?"

She was amazed and pleased he put it that way. It *did* sound right.

"Would you have a sacrifice to make – for *me*? He glanced at her, questioningly.

She took a deep breath. She needed to respond in the right way. "A sacrifice for you?" Another deep breath. "No sacrifice, Jacob Bowers. Only the gift of becoming your wife."

Grinning broadly, Jacob took up the reins. "All right, then, Mr. Frankson," he called back, "we're off." After a slight shake of the wagon and some muttering from Frankson as he climbed back in over the tailgate, Jacob released the brake and snapped the reins sharply cross the team's rumps. "'Hup, hup, walk on you beautiful sorrel beasts, no time to lose. That's our Prairie Lake just 'round the next bend."

"Yes, Jacob Bowers -- a gift," Naomi repeated simply as the wagon lurched forward so forcibly that she had to grab hold of the bench railing. *Oh Lord*, she thought, looking into the distance, scarcely aware of anything except Jacob sitting beside her and words shaping themselves in familiar phrases: "*O Lord, I praise Your name, for now my ears have heard You, but now my eyes have seen You.*

Made in the USA
Charleston, SC
25 June 2014